The New Adventures of Tom Sawyer and Huck Finn

Lisa Mannetti

Adult Edition

Praise for Lisa Mannetti's
Tom & Huck

"With charming Twain-like wit and style, Lisa Mannetti brings to life an engaging tale that will capture readers' imaginations and take them on the magical ride of their lives. Who wouldn't love feline familiars such as Huck and Tom? I can't recommend this book enough!"

–Elizabeth Massie, Bram Stoker-winning author
of *Sineater, Playback,* and *Homegrown*

"There's no way to really explain how incredibly charming this book is, or how wonderfully funny, or the delightful wealth of Twainian scholarship involved. Or even just how much fun it is to read! It's not really like anything else out there. You'll just have to experience it for yourself."

–Robert Dunbar, author of *Martyrs & Monsters*
and *Willy*

"Take one part Mark Twain's Huckleberry Finn and one part Bell Book and Candle. Add an ounce of Blithe Spirit and a pinch of Bewitched. Stir briskly with a rolled up copy of Cat Fancy magazine and you'll come close to concocting a potion worth of Lisa Mannetti's The New Adventures of Tom Sawyer and Huck Finn."

–Hal Bodner, author of *Bite Club* and
The Trouble with Hairy

"Lisa doesn't merely throw some witches and werewolves into some of Twain's old lore. She crafts her own story by absconding with two literary icons and dropping them quite unceremoniously in her world. And the way she does it is both mischievous and charming."

–Gef Fox, reviewer for *Wag the Fox*

"Mannetti weaves a beautiful, heartwarming, and humorous fantasy with the delectable Tom and Huck, but resurrects them with the love and care only a true fan and scholar of Twain could."

–Meli Hooker, reviewer for *Dreadful Tales*

The New Adventures of
Tom Sawyer
and
Huck Finn

Lisa Mannetti

Smart Rhino Publications
www.smartrhino.com

Smart Rhino Publications Adult Edition

The New Adventures of Tom Sawyer and Huck Finn.
Copyright © 2014 by Lisa Mannetti. All rights reserved.

Cover illustration Copyright © 2014 by Glenn Chadbourne. All rights reserved.

ISBN-13: 978-0-9896679-0-6
ISBN-10: 0989667901

*For Barbara McGill—who intuited my path when we were both nineteen
and helped me find my power as a writer;*

and

*For the real-life twin cats, Tom Sawyer and Huck Finn—
two lovable rascals so aptly named,
they inspired an entire website
and this book.*

Introduction by

Jonathan Maberry

In our American literary landscape there are few characters more emblematic of 'teenagers' than Mark Twain's legendary Huckleberry Finn and Tom Sawyer.

Huck Finn is the most famous of the two, and *The Adventures of Huckleberry Finn* has been required reading in schools for over a century. It is also a book that has hovered in the center of a massive controversy stretching back generations. The novel introduces a poor kid from the Deep South who runs away from a violent drunk of a father and who takes up with a man named Jim who is an escaped slave. The iconoclastic elements of the novel are many—it deconstructs the role of children in a family, it discusses child abuse, it explores racism and fairness, and it depicts a friendship that crosses racial lines.

On the other hand it is frequently vilified for the use of the dreaded 'n' word even though that word was contextually (if not morally) appropriate at the time. Some educators (and let me pause here to vomit) have suggested replacing or removing the word because they claim it promotes racism. That would only be true if, while teaching the book, teachers didn't use it as an opportunity to discuss the horrors of slavery, the terrible conditions blacks were forced to endure before and even *after* the end of slavery, the struggle for equality, the whole civil rights thing, and the fact that even now, nearly one hundred and thirty years *after* the Civil War, there is still destructive racism in our culture. If a book like *The Adventures of Huckleberry Finn* rubs a sore spot or raises an embarrassing question—then, hey, the author is continuing to do his job. He's making people think.

1

So, yeah, Huck Finn? We like Huck and we're glad his story is still being told.

Ditto for Tom Sawyer. And, okay, Tom isn't at the center of a social firestorm. Tom became iconic in another way: he is the embodiment of American ingenuity, resourcefulness and courage. He's small-town American values and proof that 'country don't mean dumb', that simplicity of lifestyle isn't part and parcel with dull wits. For those and other reasons, *The Adventures of Tom Sawyer* has become a beloved classic, a book every teen should read. And maybe every adult, too, because it's nice to touch base with those things about being a kid that made us happy to be alive.

Huck and Tom were never real boys, of course, but we can accept them as real because of the way author Mark Twain conjured them. You see, fictional characters are seldom woven from pure imagination. More often than not, and certainly with some of the most memorable characters, there is a thread of the real world sewn through the fabric of these characters.

Huck is, in a way, a character reborn. Or, perhaps, remade. Mark Twain based Huck on his childhood friend, Tom Blankenship. The author had no interest in writing a straight biography of Blankenship, so—as writers are wont to do—he took the most interesting elements of the true story, added them to a bit of this and that, and spun a tale that was pure magic. And he wove into that some elements of other real people. This created a magic tapestry from which a realistic and believable boy emerges. Even if we're from other parts of the country that are radically different—big cities, the southwestern deserts, snowbound ski towns, or New Jersey beach communities—we can relate to Huck. We *get* him.

Tom Sawyer is a more autobiographical character, drawing on the author's own experiences growing up along the Mississippi River. Bits of Twain, bits of his friends, slices of life as he experienced contributed to the construction of that character. And, again, we recognize Tom. We know someone like him—that clever kid who figures things out, the one who's on the cool side of geeky, the book nerd who doesn't mind getting dirty climbing a tree or exploring a cave. We like to think there's a little of Tom in us, and often we're right.

Huck is also brilliant in his way. He's a problem-solver, too. And he's braver. They're the Holmes and Watson of barefoot southern boys, and Twain put them together in a number of thrilling adventures that got them lost in caves, traveling around the world, and solving murders.

So ... Huck Finn and Tom Sawyer? If either of them said, "Hey, c'mon, let me show you something fun!" We'd put on our adventure sneakers and go running after them.

For a century and a quarter writers have taken them and remade them into thousands of different forms. So many of the 'buddy picture' movies have a Huck and Tom vibe.

Now that brings us to THIS book.

Lisa Mannetti has brought Huck and Tom into modern times.

Kind of ...

This is a very twisted tale of these two heroes, and part of the twist is that two heroes have tails.

They are, you see, cats.

I'll give you a minute on that.

Yes.

These new adventures take the essential qualities of Huck and Tom, spice them up with a nice dose of magic, and present us with a pair of house cats whose souls are those of Huck Finn and Tom Sawyer.

And—here's the craziest part—it *works*.

They are reincarnated as familiars of a modern day witch. The novel is equal parts Mark Twain's quaint and homespun humor and Mannetti's sharp-as-a-razor modern day wit.

What we have here is an adventure into the funhouse of intelligent imagination. The qualities that made Huck and Tom so endearing and so important to us are all there: wits, resourcefulness, decency, a thirst for adventure and some good old fashion laziness (most of the best heroes enjoy a good nap, let's face it!). At the same time each character has a new feline aspect skillfully stitched into their personalities, and that brings with it some playfulness, some predatory ruthlessness, and some very dangerous curiosity. The mix is a delight to read.

Having read far too many pastiches and reworkings of Huckleberry Finn and Tom Sawyer, I was apprehensive about a cat-themed novel featuring two of my favorite characters. That apprehension melted away within the first few pages and I never got another twitch of it.

3

So, pour yourself a saucer of milk, curl up in a warm patch of sunlight, nibble a few catnip-flavored treats, and drift down the lazy river of imagination with the 'boys'. They're the same Huck and Tom we all know and love ... only furrier.

—Jonathan Maberry, *NY Times* bestselling author of
Dust & Decay and *Flesh & Bone*

PART 1: THE FORMATIVE YEARS

Explanatory

Huck always said it was a powerful lot of trouble to write a book, and if he'd a known it ahead of time, he wouldn't a gone through with it. That's his version of the truth, anyhow. And it's a lot more work than anyone bargains for when they sit down to write—but you add writin along with me and Huck comin back as twin brothers and the feline familiars of a twenty-first century witch—and you got even more trouble. A whole cauldron-full more. Anyhow, this time I guess it's me that has got to tell our story.

CHAPTER ONE

OUR FIRST FAMILY—COCONUT AND CREAM PUFF—
THE OLD RELIABLE BACKFIRES

Me and Huck were born seven years ago up there in Dutchess County, New York—a redneck, backwater area if ever there was one. And we got adopted bang right out the chute—so to speak—by a lady named Ellie who positively swooned over our white fur and bright blue eyes. Trouble was, she was havin a baby in a couple of months, so even though me and Huck were makin ourselves right at home and generally bringin our sterlin personalities to the fore, she warn't happy with us. We *tried*, I tell you. She actually called us Cream Puff and Coconut— and if havin those wimpy cutie pie names warn't proof of how much we put up with, I don't know what is.

Anyway, I guess she couldn't wait for her baby, so she adopted us in the meanwhile. At first she picked us up about a zillion times a day, and she was always croonin and kissin us. "Ooooooh Cream Puff ... precious Coconut!"

Do *not* even ask me to remember which of us was Cream Puff and which was Coconut; we both ran when we heard the food box rattle, and Huck's take was that long as we were warm and gettin fed, it didn't matter what she called us because humans don't have no sense anyhow.

5

'Course, we didn't know she was actually havin a baby—we were pretty much babies ourselves. We come back knowin a lot and rememberin a lot, but boys ain't always interested in ladies' doins, and cats, well, cats natur'lly have more important things to worry about. So, take it all around, we just thought she was growin real fast—and that was a sign of good things to come for us.

"Look at that paunch," Huck said. "Give me high fives!" We slapped paws. And Hucky butted my head with his.

"Ya can't beat it—she naps all the time and she's eatin like her hair's on fire. No special diets for us," I said.

"We can eat till we're round as marshmallows—"

"Sssh—"

"What ya shushin me for?"

"Don't give her any ideas—Cream Puff is bad enough."

"Yeah, the way she's eatin she's liable to change Coconut just cause it doesn't remind her enough about junk food ... or reminds her too much of starvin like in that *Robinson Crusoe*."

"Am I Cream Puff?"

"Who cares—she can't tell us apart most of the time, nuther."

That's how it was. Plenty of food, kissin and pettin and playin— with me and Huck doin our part to keep everything just as cheerful as a bowl of warm milk.

* * *

The first inklin of trouble we had was when Ellie set up this little room next to ours—I mean hers. It was painted the most god-awful shade of lavender. That was the downside. On the upside, there was a cozy sort of bed with bars and it was stuck right in a huge flag of sunshine that came waving in every single afternoon.

You could jump inside it like anything because there was a white wooden bench right next to it that Ellie called "the baby's toy chest." We didn't care what she called it; it was a gateway into a magical kingdom. One jump and even tiny critters like us could plummet straight into the best nappin spot in the house. Inside that crib, or whatever you may call it, there was soft sheets and fuzzy yellow blankets and about a hundred stuffed animals—everything from tiny bears to big buffaloes to long-furred monkeys and dogs—which we could lay all over and play hide 'n seek behind. And along with a very big oversized bear, there was even a lion and a tiger. Oh my ... it was prime. And after we finished nappin, we could climb on that towerin pile of toys and amuse ourselves for several seconds with this sort of dangly thing that hung down and begged to be swatted. Take it all around, the room and everything in it, was fine.

But more of the downside came when Ellie took to keepin the door closed and hissed at and shooed us every time we tried to sneak in. Which, bein the adventurous types, we did often.

One warmish afternoon, not too long after me and Huck came to live there, Ellie fell sound asleep in her bedroom. The shades were down. Up on the ceiling, a fan made slow lazy circles. Ellie didn't know it, but she was doing her best imitation of Huck's Pap layin up in a hogshead and sleepin off a two-day toot with White Lightnin Moonshine—she was flopped onto one side, her hand danglin over the edge clutchin the tip edge of a paperback, and she was snorin loud enough to deafen old people and scare small children. There bein no old persons or small persons around, she was just rattlin china figurines on her dresser and makin the dust devils kick up under the bed.

It only stands to reason me and Huck would want to nap too— seein her so decadently and deliciously asleep. And what's more, we'd naturally want a bit of quiet.

It warn't anything for me to stretch myself up like a sort of elongated backward comma and give the spare-room doorknob a shake or two. Or sixteen. Huck, he started off on this foray as our look out, but cheap doors can be hard to open.

"C'mon over here and when I twist, you push," I told him.

"I'm supposed to whistle up sharp or meow twice if Ellie comes," he said.

"She's down for the count," I told him. "Help me get in that room before we go deaf like them other white cats we was born with."

A stretch, a turn and Huck's bulk thrustin against the flimsy wood—he was heavier than I was then—and we were in like anything. And five minutes later we were snuggled up together in the middle of that crib and we were purrin in each others' ears. Heaven.

"—You! Coconut! Cream Puff!"

She lighted on me first and hauled me out by my collar, but in her fury, Ellie herself couldn't even remember which cat I was.

"Get out! How dare you! All over baby's things!"

She gave me a pretty good wind up and fling, and I landed just outside the doorway in the hall.

Huck was next, but she just gave him a toss—like the way a girl who's too young to do better throws a basketball up at her big brother's hoop. He landed splat next to me, and Ellie didn't know whether to descend on us further or get to shakin the fur out of the bedclothes and toys. Of which there was considerable, since me an' Huck went into the crib every time we could.

In fact, if old Ellie had wanted to take up knittin as a hobby—instead of those plastic sun catchers she was always making and melting down in the oven and which stunk to high heaven—she could've knitted baby a carload of cat fur blankets—an' done her Christian duty by donating the leftovers.

"I never!" She was screeching, and I was starting to get worried she was going to report us to the man who came home with the newspaper and ate dinner there every night and actually slept on her bed and had the nerve to insist me an' Huck were not allowed up on it—and I was watchin to see if she was goin to make a beeline for the telephone, cause she was stampin around a hell of a lot.

"Make a distraction," I hissed at Huck. Chances were always good she could never remember where she left the phone anyhow—and if we could get her on another path, she'd probably even forget to go to the wall unit part in the kitchen and press that button that made the phone shriek like a body having hot coals pressed to its flesh and gave me and Huck the fan-tods topped up with sinus concussion; it was like having your ear slapped with a baseball bat. We called it "The Terror."

"Distraction," Huck whispered back.

He did the best he could—he did what he was good at. He began to gawp and make that jaw-poppin yarky sort of sound, and sure enough an excellent-sized hair ball come up and splatted on the floor, followed by a goodish amount of watery drool. "Good work," I told him.

But Ellie. Oh my, she liked to have died. You'd have thought it was acid and gonna eat right through her floorboards.

First a long wailin gasp came out of her mouth. "Fuhhhhhhhhh! No, no, no!" She was screamin at the top of her voice. "You! Cat! No! Stop. *No*, not there, not there! Not there, you dumb beast!"

Her feet flew across the room, and she snatched Huck up and hove him into the bathroom where he skidded right across the tile floor then fetched up against the tub and got so scared he puked again.

Ellie was dancin around and she didn't know whether to kill him or me or both of us, or wipe up Huck's mess. I had never known the Old Reliable hairball trick to fail. Usually if one of us just made the upchuck noise, Ellie scooped us up or patted us and fretted over how we were feeling. But the closer it got to the blessed event, the more she lost patience with us.

We scattered fast—headin for the basement. The washin machine and dryer were down there, and a body could take some comfort in the warm dark and the narrow little spaces between them and the walls. Upstairs we could hear Ellie mutterin curses and stomping around to fetch cleanin aids—paper towels and Murphy's Oil Soap—as we knew from past yarkin episodes.

"Laying right in baby's crib," I heard her crump. "Like a coupla Arabian princes in a harem. Fur everywhere, and now I've got to wash every bit of the sheets and blankets and they were new. *New!*"

Huck put his ears down and tried to squeeze behind the dryer before the washin machine got to clumpin and gurglin with baby's layette.

I thought when the man who read the newspaper every night came home, we were probably in for it. He was no creampuff; that's for sure.

CHAPTER TWO

HERE'S BABY–BIG MAMA–
DARK OMENS

Well, just as you might expect, the next big hullabaloo between us and Ellie come right after her baby was born. She was a pretty little thing—all pink and white and blue-eyed that Ellie named Theandromula.

"It's a hideous name," Huck complained. "I'm goin to call her Thea, cause cain't no one say that other Theatrical Mule thing—not even the tall guy hangin around here come supper-time every night."

"Are you kiddin? That child is lucky she ain't callin it Good N' Plenty or Godiva Truffle or anything else you can stuff in your mouth." I warn't so fond of Thea myself—not after all the rigmarole I put up with from Becky Thatcher—but Huck took a shine to 'er.

For one thing, Huck said she smelled good. "Like a buttermilk biscuit," was how he put it. For another, she was always wailin and mewlin. Huck was a natur'lly vocal cat, and he liked that about baby Thea, too. Huck's whinin drove the man who brought home the newspaper into hissy fits, but Huck really liked that he and Thea had the cryin thing in common.

11

"Cain't that child quit bawlin for two seconds?" I'd say when it started singin "Ave Maria."

"Jist talkin, Tom," Huck would say. "She's just lettin on she wants changin or something to eat."

"Well why can't she do it in a way a body can understand, 'stead of lettin on like she's havin Chinese chopsticks run under her fingernails?" She was worse than The Terror—almost—and I reckoned the govm'nt might want her as a secret torture device. I thought about sellin to her to the CIA lots of times.

"Hush, baby ... Sshh," he'd say at her sweetly, and then he'd go fetch Ellie and thump his tail at her to go get Thea.

Ellie's heart was in the right place—I guess. But she warn't the sharpest cheese in any dairy bin. 'Course she was payin a lot more attention to Thea than to either me or Huck, but every time Huck thumped at her to let 'er know something was up with Baby, she thought he was clamorin for attention.

"Go 'long," she'd shout, "I've got to tend to Thea." And Huck would trot off toward the hall with a touch of sadness in his step. He was only tryin to help.

Same as when he got into the crib of a night with Thea. He wanted to sniff her good smell a little and snuggle—he was always a prime snuggler. But knowin Huck, I knew he mostly wanted to bring that bit of extra comfort and furry warmth to Baby T.

Ellie, of course, didn't see it that way—not by a long shot.

* * *

Ellie had her superstitions—same as Jim, which from time to time, me and Huck recollected about. If she was laying the table and a fork skittered out of her hands and hit the floor she'd say, "Company's coming." We didn't think much of that one—Ellie had a slew of friends who was always droppin by—not to mention a mother and a sister who was both fat and interferin. Huck believed they was so interferin they seemed even fatter. "Them two," he'd sigh at me, "weigh enough to set off Richter scales clear up to Vermont."

Anyway, Ellie still held with that old ritual over salt. Except instead of tossin it over her shoulder, she made a little cross with her thumb and forefinger and whispered at it. She got a lot of her signs for what was comin down the pike from the newspaper and from the ugly plastic box she called a computer, and that she got so excited over, but which tasted just terrible. And if she didn't look over her horrorscope in the paper or online, then her sister, Debbie, would phone her up to give her the hot flash: "Taurus," she'd bray so loud me and Huck could hear her right over the phone. "Finish old business. New enterprises can come later. The vessel must be empty before it can be refilled."

"What news," Huck would hiss at me. "Call that a sign! It's like sayin have lunch before you eat dinner."

"Digest dinner before you embark on snackin," I said back, and we both laughed.

Meantime, Ellie would be suckin on her lower lip and rollin her eyes heavenward the way she did when she was on the phone and ponderin the disembodied voice from the other end of the line. "Yes, I see that, Deb," she'd palaver and start in on how she oughta finish up the counted cross-stitch of Bless This Mortgaged Home before she took up the one with the teddy bear for Baby's room and the itsy bitsy pillow hangin from the doorknob that said, "Ssh ..."

"Sh—shucks!" I said. "Finish up the Oreos before you start in on the Fig Newtons."

"Throw out the plastic sun-catcher kits, Ellie, before you start the cross-stitch—or you might accidentally burn the house down and kill us all." Huck winked at me.

Anyhow, mostly that was Ellie's kind of signs about luck and what to do. Her mother, as we heard more than once, came from the old school though. Mama had a heap more signs in her vernacular, so to speak. P'tickly on the subject of cats.

"Black cats hold the shadow of the devil," she said one afternoon about a month before Baby Thea hove in. She was sittin at the dining room table over a regular trough of food that would embarrass an entire baseball team to sit down in front of.

"Black cats are sneaky," Mama went on. I reckoned she woulda glared at me and Huck right then, but her attention was focused on her fourth ear of buttered corn.

"Oh, Mama," Ellie put in.

"They used to say being around *any* cat was unlucky for a pregnant woman," she said. "And wasn't that the truth of it when they discovered that the litter box is just full of toxic plasmatics. It's death to change a litter box."

"Toxoplasmosis."

"Poison is poison," she said. "The old-timers didn't always have a name for things, Miss, but they *knew*." She bit into her corn and sent juice spraying for emphasis. "And Cat Scratch Fever," she said, layin down the corn and wipin her hands. Ellie didn't answer but only watched her mother fasten on the white servin platter of steaks and spear her third slab of red meat.

"One tiny little scratch," she said, indicatin her forearm with her dinner fork. "And how long will it take for that poison to seep into a tiny baby's tender skin? Huh? How long do you think?"

"Longer than it takes for Mama to polish off a two-pound T-bone," Huck whispered at me and winked again.

"You ought to have them two declawed," she said and pointed at me. There was a kind of window box in the dining room with a little built-in seat and a flowered cushion. It was prime for nappin, peerin out the window and eavesdroppin—which is what we was really doin right then, since there was nothing in Ellie's side yard at the moment but an old frumpy-lookin tennis ball settin stock-still.

"But if I have them declawed, I can't let them out," Ellie said.

Out. Out sounded interestin ... Huck had been mighty fond of sleepin outdoors and had found houses positively crampin in the past. I reckoned it sounded great on a balmy sunny day—but what about winter? I already knew I wasn't going to like going barefooted in the snow. Inside was dry. Outside there was rain—

Huck thumped his tail to make me listen up again.

"Well, mark my words," Mama said. "They'll be in the crib and sucking up the baby's breath in two months' time."

Ellie didn't let on we'd already been in the crib; she didn't say a word. She just drummed her bare feet against the floor.

"We got our own breath," I said to Huck.

But just then, through the window, I saw a little milk snake creepin along on the flagstone patio ... it stopped dead in front of where we was sittin. And accordin to our lights, that was the worst kind of bad luck. Jim would've said so; that's for sure.

"Cats don't suck a child's breath," the man who read the newspaper and ate dinner said. "It's called SIDS"

"Crib death is crib death," Mama said, swallowin mightily to get her point in. "And smothering is smothering."

"But—"

"You listen up, Ellie." She paused. "Your own sister found the cat right on top of her baby's chest licking milk from Tod's lips."

Ellie gave a little gasp at that. Whether she'd forgotten or didn't know, I never found out. Because when she gave the gasp, her hand flew up, and she knocked over her glass. It was empty, but it cracked when it struck the table.

"We're in for it," Huck said, jumpin down from the window seat. He was headin toward the hallway, and I followed.

* * *

You'd think that with all that talk and the signs and all, that woulda kept Huck out of the crib. But that's just how bad luck works if you ask me. Even if you know you should be lightin out for new territory, it's like the bad luck draws at you, and you can't help it. Bad luck is a black hole that gets a hold of you and won't let go, suckin you straight down into its maw.

CHAPTER THREE

DISCOVERY–ORPHANS–
THE VET'S RESCUE

Huck was just a naturally sweet-natured cat. You mayn't believe it, but it was so. He just doted on Baby Thea.

"She's like the prettiest piece of candy in an Easter basket," he'd say, fetchin up a sigh while he crouched in the hallway and mooned over her.

"Don't—"

"Let's us go sniff at her a little."

He wouldn't wait for my answer, but in a bound or two, he'd be in the crib. I tried to tell him he was leavin signs of his visits—and naturally puky as he was, he still tried lickin up whatever fur clung to the teddy bears and blankets. It made him sicker, but he was bound to Baby Thea by a stronger force.

"Who *wouldn't* love that baby?" he'd say right before he hid himself in the room when Ellie went in to sing Thea a lullaby and say g'night.

"Any number of people," I'd say, wishin I had the ear mites I was born with back again so my hearin was out of whack.

Doesn't take a genius to figure that it was only a matter of time before Ellie caught him smack-dab in the crib one night. The baby waked up and started cryin. Ellie had the monitor on in her room, and before Huck could spring up and away, Ellie was in the room and shriekin.

She'd felt safe with that closed door, and she didn't know Huck was up to my old trick of sneakin in and out of places of a night. Shoot, Thea's room was only half lit, and it was just pie hidin in the shadows.

Meanwhile, Ellie hauled Huck out of the crib. This time though, she warn't worried about gettin him out as much as she was frettin over Baby. She left him flat and scooped up the child.

It might a actually ended right there, but Mama was overnightin. She warn't going to let it go. Mouths to feed—any mouths to feed— were anathema to big Mama. And as far as she was concerned, we were not only a drain on the food budget, we were useless to boot.

"What happened, what happened?" she said, crash-thuddin into the room as big as a walkin gantry and usin up all the available oxygen. She 'most gave me night terrors just listenin to her from out in the hall.

"Cream Puff—I mean *Coconut* was right in the crib with Thea."

You can guess the rest.

* * *

The next mornin, before the sun was really up, me and Huck was unceremoniously thrown in a cardboard box that had a couple of small holes cut in the sides and the top securely taped. I thought I heard Ellie give a little cry, but that could have been Huck mewlin alongside of me.

It was dark as the lowest rung of hell inside the box—which the man who hid behind the newspaper, that is, Thea's father—put in the backseat of his car. The engine hummed, and we was off to the unknown.

* * *

Huck never did get over it. To this day, put him on a broomstick or flyin carpet, and he'll shriek with glee. Get him near a car, and it's pure panic. We was abandoned—like Moses in the Bulrushers—which as you already know is a story Huck never had any stock in whatsoever.

Turns out Thea's father dumped me and Huck on the doorstep of a vet'nary clinic before openin time. Maybe *Snow White* inspired him. Anyhow, Huck was already traumatized enough, so I never did tell him that Big Mama wanted Thea's pap to just open the box (or maybe leave it shut) and drop us in the woods. Or near a housin development. Or behind the Salvation Army. Or *anywhere* we could not find our way back to Baby Thea. That woman had no more heart than a stone head on Easter Island. But maybe *he* figured once Ellie calmed down she'd get to feeling guilty and want to know we hadn't been left to starve. Or freeze. We was still practically babies ourselves.

So, toward the end of September, we were in the cold and dark on a set of stone stairs, huddled against one another and cryin.

The technician who unlocked in the mornin for Dr. Peter Bennett found us.

She got that box top off in a hurry, you bet. "Oh, you darlings!"

The rest of the hands-on staff—and the office help—was already startin to meander in.

"White cats, blue eyes!"

"They're twins!"

It didn't take us but the merest fraction of an hour to win over the whole roomful of 'em.

"They're about four months," the vet said, holdin Huck in his arms and pushing back a lip to look at his teeth. Peter Bennett didn't smell good—he'd been around too many other animals—includin dogs, and I don't like dog smell a bit. But he scooped me up when he was done with Huck, and I licked his arm and looked right in his blue eyes. He grinned and gave me a tickle behind my ear. I purred. He was the first man I ever liked.

CHAPTER FOUR

ADOPTED FOR GOOD—OUR NEW HOME—
FAMILIARS TO A WITCH

'Course we couldn't a known it, but Lady B—who is the woman
we finally come to live with—had a hankerin for the vet. And purely by
accident (though she held there warn't no accidents), she ran into him a
couple of nights later at a bar clear over to Millerton. She'd actually
gone there to have dinner with a couple of her pals, and when it
appeared a band was going to play, why, she stayed on to listen. And it
warn't no time at all before she had a suspicion and looked up, and in
the crowd, which had swelled prodigiously, there was Peter Bennett
standin in the crush tryin to buy himself a drink.

She nudged her way over.

"Peter!"

"Barbara!"

"What are you doing here?"

"Trying to get a drink," he laughed. Oh many's the time Lady told
us how even the very first time she laid eyes on him she liked to have
swooned. She was a good lookin woman herself, and she warn't
without experience, and me and Huck figured she could get just about
any man she wanted, but she said when she brought her cat, Tennessee

21

Williams—which she had before she got us—for a routine visit and got a look at Peter, a shudder ran right through her. "Never happened before or since, boys," she told us.

"I'll buy *you* a drink," she told Peter.

And Peter, she reckoned, never knew how she did it—he was six feet tall, and *he* couldn't get the bartender's attention—but ten seconds later she was puttin in their orders, smackin a ten on the bar and leadin him to her table.

Tennessee had died about two months before. Lady B had owned him since she was in her twenties—and while twelve was pretty old for a cat, it warn't *that* old. She missed him somethin awful.

Peter told about us and how we'd been left on the doorstep and had been breakin hearts for three days around his office.

"Twins, you say," Lady said—she was no slouch of a purrer herself.

"Yes. I'd rather not see them separated," Peter put in. "They seem unusually devoted to one another, but if someone doesn't take them both soon, I'll have to let one or the other go—lots of people want one, but ..."

"Sold," Lady said.

Peter laughed and put his hand over hers.

And you can say she said yes because she was so taken with Peter and she wanted to get on his right side, but me and Huck know better. Lady just cast her mind around and found us and she knew. Knew all about us, it seems.

"I'm going to call them Huck Finn and Tom Sawyer." Yup, she knew.

She was as good as her word. She come to the clinic the next morning, took one look at us, paid for our shots and such, and adopted us on the spot.

We warn't orphans no more.

And neither was Lady B.

* * *

Lady B's house was a stunner. It was prime all around—just like her. To start with, it was a great big place up in Rhinebeck, New

York—which is where the quality hang out when they come to Dutchess County.

The house was white with black shutters and stood on a little knoll that was set back from the road a piece. It was built more than a hundred years ago, and Lady always said Mark Twain himself would have visited there—if he'd known the Roosevelts were going to be living practically right down the street in another fifty years or so.

People were always after her to turn it into a Bed & Breakfast kind of inn, and she could have made heaps of money doin it, but she said she liked her privacy in the mornin and didn't want to get up at the crack of dawn to make coffee and serve up Eggs Benedict Arnold to a bunch of strangers. Also, like she said, people who stayed at them places stole everything that warn't red-hot, nailed down, or alarmed to shriek like a fire engine. The more you charged, the more folks figured they had a right to steal. That was the quality for you. So take it all around, she figured she'd leave innkeepin alone.

She made us at home, I'll say that. The first week, so's we'd get accustomed nice and easy, she made us a big fluffy beanbag bed in the corner of her own bedroom. She kept the door shut so we wouldn't feel too anxious about the size of the space, and she came to see us continually. Huck'd laze up and stretch tall right against her leg like she was a scratchin post when she came in, and that always made her laugh.

She knew which of us was which right from the get go—and never made a mistake, not once. People thought we were identical, but we warn't, and Lady knew it. I was smoother and Huck's fur was more rumpled—just as you'd expect. Huck had a little nearly invisible scuff mark on the fur across his nose, and Lady said it was just like Huck Finn—the boy's—freckles. Not only that, I was more of the ringleader between us. And Lady, she knew it. So the namin was not only just right on account of our looks—but our personalities, too. But mostly I think Lady B got it right because she really did love us—loved both of us just about to death. We three, we were just suited, you might say.

Lady B—she doted on doin for us. At night she picked us up and put us right on her high four-poster bed—and all three of us snuggled up tight.

And the food was just as nice as could be—none of your supermarket bargain brands. She bought us the best and kept those dishes filled. We even had a little plug-in water fountain that burbled and made sighin sounds and spurted a steady stream into a basin.

"We couldn't a done better if we landed inside the Pearly Gates," Huck said straight off.

"Been there, done that," I said, grinnin.

"Have you now?" Lady asked, scratchin the top of my head slowly.

"She understands us, Huck," I said.

"Certainly, I do," Lady said.

Huck and I was turnin our heads back and forth and looking at each other with unfeigned amazement.

"What, can *humans* understand *cats?*" Huck said. He brought up the time he tried to explain all about language and Frenchmen to Jim when they was on the raft.

"Not all humans. Just some."

"Which ones?"

"Well, mostly they're like me. Witches—"

That was all Huck had to hear.

"Witches! No, no'm I do not want *one* single thing to do with witches. Tom, hain't we been terrorized by witches more times than a body would believe—"

"I'm not that kind of witch," she said, liftin up the goose-down coverlet on her bed, which Huck had dived straight under after his last remark. "Huck," she called. "C'mon, Tom's not afraid—"

"Because Tom Sawyer never had the *sense* to be afraid—don't tell me, I'll tell you. When he gets his mind around a thing, he just ignores whatever goes against it."

"Huck—"

"Hain't I seen it a hundred—no, a *thousand* times! He'll tell you a Sunday School primer class on a picnic is a load of Arabs. And a cartful of turnips is jooles and diamonds. Nope, you can't tell me anythin I don't know 'bout Tom—"

"*Real* enchantment," I said.

"He's already got that schemin light in his eyes," Huck said. "Next he'll be talkin all around about how *gaudy* it is, and what *style* there is—"

"Oh Huck, it'll be truly adventuresome—"

"And I know what comes next," he interrupted. "All 'bout how won't the boys be pea green with envy when they find out Huck and

24

Tom is familiars with real witches. But there *ain't* no Joe Harper nor no Ben Rogers to lord it over now. There's just us—a century and longer come back as cats in a big house—"

"Familiars," Lady B put in, "certain familiars can become human again—"

That was all I had to hear. I had the grandest vision of robbin and ransomin folks and being as piratical as the dirtiest pirate that ever lived. And no one could ever catch me, because the minute they came lookin for me, why all they'd find was a white cat.

I was in it for the glory from that second on.

CHAPTER FIVE

WITCHCRAFT 101–LILY BLUM–
OUR FIRST SPELL

"When does we get to be Tom and Huck again?" I said. I was all afire to be a regular boy. We'd been at her house for about two weeks, and it was getting on for the end of Sepember. I figured since we already missed the start of school, and we was goin to be cats a lot of the time, she warn't about to make us go listen to a lot of truck and nonsense about photosynthesis, the use of the gerund and the Gettysburg Address.

"Well, there's a lot to it ... it's not something you can do straight off. Come with me."

We trotted close at her heels and into a room next to hers on the second floor. She kept this room as a kind of library-office thing. It had big, white-curtained windows and tons of books and a big old-fashioned desk. And a stuffed chair that looked just prime for napping. She called it a "chase lounger," and it had flowery down-filled pillows and a soft cashmere throw for winter that was just the pearly blue gray color of the river at twilight—and which you could see straight out of the winder from up there.

"This is going to be our schoolroom," she began.

"No'm, no ma'am, I hain't stayin for school," Huck started to head for the doorway. "I didn't hold with it much before, but if there's any benefit to bein a cat, why, lettin readin and writin and folderol with mathematics *alone*, is it—"

"Now Huck—"

"And if I have to shin out from school and start havin a conscience and feelin guilty when I'm a cat what don't generly never have to attend no school—"

"But it's not—"

"It ain't that kind of school, Huck," I said.

"Well, I guess *you* know all about it, Tom Sawyer—since you studied up on pirates and highwaymen and every other kind of flimflammin gaudiness."

"Shh now," Lady said. "See this," and she pointed to another long table shoved against one wall. A person comin into the room would probably think it was just a place where a body could spread out a whole slew a books at once or maybe do some writing—it was three times as big as the desk. And all it held, at the moment, was a big fat biblish-looking book with leather covers—'most as big as a dictionary—and a candle and a jar with some pens. There was a long narrow rectangle of a mirror hung horizontal over it and against the cream of the walls.

"This is my altar," said Lady B. "And while some people are going to call me Ms. Barbara DeSimone, and others will call me B.D. for my initials, when I'm in here, I'm the Lady B—which is short for Lady Bastet. Every witch has got a witchy name, and mine is Lady Bastet."

"Seems to me you'd pick a better name than basta'd which is a swear word, less a course you didn't get no choice. A body might get saddled with all kinds of ugly and troublesome things. I just knew this witch thing was gonna—"

"Bastet," she repeated. "It's from the Egyptian—she was the goddess of cats."

"See there Huck, now that's more like. We was *worshipped* in ancient Egypt."

"Well we warn't worshipped none in St. Petersburg, Missouri—and plenty of times, you know your own self, Tom Sawyer, you was powerful attracted to *dead* cats." He gave off a little Hucky-mewlymoan, which was his trademark cry.

"'Ts, all right, Huck," she said, givin him a good long pet between his ears and strokin down his back. "You'll see." Her voice *was* always silk—whether she was in her witchy mood or not—and he calmed right down, and Lady, she began to larn us.

"Cats are naturally psychic," she said. "It's just that most people don't know it."

"Or don't want to."

"That's right, Tom. It all depends on how open a person—or a witch—is."

It was then I noticed how fancy-carved the table she kept for an altar was. It was all heads with great, starin eyes and fabulous claws and such. And the jar she used to hold the pens warn't no way ordinary. From one angle, it was a white skull—and that was a little bit scary, like witchcraft itself, you might say. But if you turned your head or cast your eyes just that fraction, why you could see how beautiful it was, and it was the head of a Botticelli girl with the most gorgeous face and long sumptuous hair.

Lady, she talked on about how the outward things *was* mostly things, and it was what was in your heart and mind and soul that gave things the power. And she stroked us, and I seen her lookin at me, and right then, me and Huck knowed it was all goin to be all right.

* * *

Well, that very week, we got our first taste of things that warn't to our liking so much at Lady B's. It warn't nothin to do with her or the house. No. Lady B had barrels of friends—some of whom was in the witchy way, and some of whom was not—but this one particular friend was just a twin you might say to Big Mama, which was the nail in our cross over to Ellie's. This'n was little, but she was mighty. And since she only lived a block or two away, she could take a notion whenever she wanted just to drop on in. She was like mail—she showed up every day and ninety percent of her was junk which warn't worth totin into the house. But you needed a monstrous big container to hold all of the trash that made up Lily Blum. Monstrous big.

"I'd just love to see the boys," she said in a voice that was about as sweet as the brayin of a jackass. "Last time I was here, B, they were too new to the place and up in your bedroom and asleep, you said."

We were downstairs in the dinin room, right around the corner that made up the doorway to the kitchen, which was where Lily had plunked herself. She used the back door a lot—like she was family—or thought she was. I peeked around the edge and saw a woman around fifty years old wearin leather sandals and a long white dress, which she called a "kurda" and probably thought looked all foreign and exotic, but put me in mind of a shroud you'd wear if you was going to a Halloween party dressed as a day-old corpse. Lily Blum was sort of a fallen woman, I reckon, who had rovin' eyes. She was a divorcee, and the thing she wanted everybody to know right off the bat was her name was pronounced Blum to rhyme with plum, and *not* Bloom to rhyme with plume—because she couldn't bear bein one of those folks who was so unfortunate as to have a cutesy name—like Cedar Rapids or Sugar Cane or Penny Ante—what marked them forever as not even being in the shade of a real, regular artiste like herself. Her witchy name was Luna Raven; she thought that was noble artistic.

"They're a little shy," Lady B said. She was about to push a plate of cookies toward Lily, but it warn't necessary. Lily's hand found the dish same as a dowsin rod jerks right around, twitches and falls *bang!* when it hits near hidden water.

"Going to take some mighty big paws to fill Tennessee's, I guess. Guess that's why you needed *two* cats this time!"

"Emmm," was all Lady replied. The clock in the hall struck 9 p.m.

"Say, B, I was wondering if my coven could meet here at the next full moon—my place is so small and you've got all this lovely room."

Well there was two statements sandwiched into that one. First of all, she said "my coven," in a voice like Father Damien out on Molokai sayin "we lepers" once he caught that dratted pox. Lily sounded intimate and chock full of humility—but that was just to smudge over any rough spots. You know what I mean—she was really lettin on *which* trees made shingles and *who* was boss of the sawmill.

But secondly, though it was true her house warn't much bigger than a wigwam, she was always after Lady B to give up bein what witches call a "solitary" and join up for a coven. *Her* coven in p'tickler.

We knew Lady's take on covens by that time, you bet.

"Make a diversion, Huck," I said.

He made a beeline for the kitchen, and I went after him. This warn't goin to be no yarkin episode. Huck had learnt a spell or two, and he meant to try 'em.

* * *

"Oh, I spy," Lily gushed the minute Huck rushed in, and she was about to scoop him up when he darted past her chair. By then I'd honed in on Lady's mind—and I knew Huck had, too. He opened and squinched his eyes shut three times, gave a soft hiss and muttered his spell. And before Lily could make her grab, she was stopped as solid as Medina cement. I'd said the words right along with Huck, and it went down easy and smooth as swallowin Turkish delight to turn her into a statue—however briefly.

"Thanks, boys," Lady said. "Give us all a chance to hear our own thoughts for a minute or two."

Lily was sittin frozen—one hand stretched out and her fingers splayed. Her mouth was a perfect O, and even her eyebrows was canted up into black arches and 'most right at the top of her hairline.

Huck jumped up on the table and inspected her teeth at close range and sat watchin the saliva sort of slow drip down—like regular stalactites.

"Guess the spell won't last long," I sighed.

"No," Lady B said, "but she won't remember it either, and in the meantime we can take a little stroll around the yard—get some *fresh* air."

Well, I was agreed to that.

"She's awful yellow," Huck said, looking at Lily. He put his paw out and gave a little swipe at a big hunk of turquoise she had hangin around her neck. It swung like a pendulum across the flat of her chest. "Why's she so yellow?"

But Lady wouldn't answer—not just then. She strolled out the back door and me and Huck tagged right after her across the lawn and under a big silvery three-quarter moon.

CHAPTER SIX

THE LADY'S TREE HOUSE—FREEING LILY

There was a little wooden bridge in her yard—like the kind you see in a Japanese garden. That night its boards seemed to have a glow in 'em.

"Like foxfire," Huck said.

I nodded, for we'd used its phosphorescence to light our work the time we was freein Jim when he was already free, but the gleam was brighter than foxfire. "But you know, Huck—really, it's like the moon got caught here in the wood."

"Not everybody can see this bridge," Lady B said. "Nor what lies beyond." She paused, her long skirt shimmerin in amongst the light and shadows. "Can you boys? Can you see it?"

Through what looked like mist, I saw the enormous girth of a tree risin straight up. It went so high you couldn't see the top.

"They's a tree," Huck said. "A reglar mountain of a tree."

"It's magic inside," she said. "And nothing in the wide world can hurt us in there. Nor make us sick, nor get older nor ever die. And no one else can ever enter it—it's magic, and it's only for the three of us."

And before my astonished eyes—on my soul—Lady B disappeared inside the skin of that tree like you'd melt through fog to a

33

place where nobody could see you. And me and Huck went through it right after her.

* * *

"It don't make sense," Huck said. It was like we was inside the tree, the pale bark all around us, but we could see outside and through it at the same time.

"Magic doesn't make sense—not in the way of logic, Huck," Lady says.

You could see up to the sky and the stars and the moon peekin through the canopy of leaves; you could look out and see the lamp in Lady B's special room shinin. But inside, it was also like whitewashed walls and just the coziest most wonderful house you ever saw. With everything just bully—books and carpets and big sofas to curl up in. There was a potted palm and a fireplace with blue and white Dutch tiles linin it. There was a kitchen with shinin copper pots, and it smelled like somebody'd been bakin apple pies. There was a big, standin harp in another corner made by the angle of the stairs, and I could just look right through the joists and see upstairs was a big tidy bed and lots more books and things. And all of it was just as neat and pretty as new pins.

"I conjured it, boys," Lady B said. "So it's a little bit of Pooh's Corner and Christopher Robin and a little bit of Mole's End—because I loved those books when I was a girl. But it's also the place I come in my mind now that I'm grown up. So at times we'll find the pyramids of Egypt, or a white beach that slants down to the sea, or a garden in Paris—or a place that's never yet been built." She sat on one of the divans, and me and Huck jumped alongside her, and her strokin us and talkin some more. "But we'll always be together in here, and we'll have fine times—just the three of us—taking in the whole of the wide world and all it's ever been and will be."

"Take it all around, the whole planet is your raft and your river," Huck said.

And the minute he said it, I knew Lady had just reached inside those books Mr. Twain wrote and reached inside those times he described, and that was how me and Huck had come to be here by her side. And I didn't never want to leave. Preachers may think they have the inside track on what heaven is and what it ain't, but Lady B—she'd done the thing up and served it on a china plate.

* * *

None of us wanted to go back to the house, but we'd left Lily Blum settin out and droolin like a Roman fountain, and by now, Lady figured, there'd be puddles a plenty on the floor. Not to mention her kurda dress was most likely soakin wet.

So we left the Tree House and went trottin back to the regular house and set about to unfreeze Lily.

"Just as I suspicioned," I said, while Lady B got a mop and started swabbin under Lily's chair.

"I'll give it one more lick and one more promise, and then we'll turn her loose, boys." She finished up, then put the mop back in a closet.

"Ready?"

We all three stared at her, fixin our eyes like steel bore bits on Lily's stiffness. Her hand still hung in the air as if she was a soverign dippin her fingers while she waited for a kneelin duke to kiss her ring.

"She looks better that way," I said, "when she's stock-still."

"Her mouth's drippin again," Hucky sighed. "If we don't do her now, Lady'll have to re-towel the floor."

"Right."

"Okay. Ready ... Set ... Go!" Lady said.

There was a sound like peelin an ice cube tray what has stuck to a pound of hamburger inside the freezer—*Prrrrrrrrupppppppppppppp!* And a second later, Lily's mouth shut on itself, she blinked twice and she was back.

"Next week? The full moon," she raved at Lady. "Ooooh Huckleberry Finn," she sang. "And Tom Sawyer!"

"You was right. I liked her better as a popsicle," Hucky said, buttin my head with his.

Me and Huck ran before she could get halfway out of her chair and light on either one of us.

35

CHAPTER SEVEN

RITUAL PREPARATION–PETER'S CELEBRITY RIVAL

Well, it came out by and by the reason Lily Blum was so yellow was because she'd taken to smearin herself with a salve that was a mixture of things—including saffron—so she could learn to fly, what witches call "transport."

"Better she should transport herself by orgasm," Lady B told us a coupla days before the full of the moon while we were up in her altar room gettin ready for the ritual ahead. She was determined to stay a solitary—she was skippin Lily's shindig—and whenever she planned a night for the three of us, she always got the room ready in plenty of time. She dusted everything and washed the windows and curtains and made it all just as spruce as can be. She was neatenin up the desk, and the image on her computer screen showed the moon nearly round and white against a dark sky.

"Orgasm. Is that the same as orgies?" Huck asked.

I knew he was thinkin of those times I'd told him and the boys in our gang back in St. Petersburg how if we was going to be robbers and highwaymen, we had to have 'em—cause all the toniest gangs had tons of orgies.

"It's something like," Lady said, softly—but I seen half a smile creep around her lips.

Well, I warn't a boy yet—so holdin a book posed its difficulties, but I was nigh on to a six-month cat—which meant I'd had a few transports of my own. Huck, he was smaller than me then, so it didn't take him that way—not yet. But two nights before I felt a strange stirrin in my nethers, and then my tail got to waggin, my hips shook like a hula girl's, and inside of a twitch, I was a boardwalk automaton and got so excited I backed up against an open weave laundry basket that had Lady's underwear in it, and out come a whoop and a squirt.

It was only a dollop of wet—so I didn't think Lady would know I'd been sportin in her lingerie. But all the same, I felt my whiskers flutter while we were talkin–same as if I'd been back in St. Petersburg, and my face went red.

"On the night of our ritual we're going to call up Peter Bennett," Lady said.

"Cain't we just use the phone?"

Huck was enchanted with modern technology and as far as he was concerned, it was a kind of witchery all on its own.

"We could. But we want definite results," Lady said.

"Why won't we get 'em with the phone?" Huck persisted.

"'Cause men like to feel when they want a woman, it was all their own idea."

I suddenly remembered how Becky Thatcher had made me burn with jealousy whilst she looked over a pitcher book with that sissy boy, Alfred Temple, and before I could stop myself, I blurted out, "The surest way to get him is to make him think he cain't have you cause you're already taken with somebody else—"

Lady fixed her eye on me. "Tom?"

"You know, if you were moonin over some other man, why Peter'd get reeled in faster than you could say 'Victoria's Secret.'" She looked at me again, and I blushed wonderin if she'd caught on that I'd sniffed over her laundry basket. About ninety percent of Lady's panties came from that free, fancy catalogue—which I judged was savin American men thousands on buying dirty magazines. The other ten percent—well, let it go for now.

"It's true," she agreed. "But it's not so easy to find a willing Alfred Temple."

"Ain't they no male witches?" Huck said.

She nodded. "I believe there's even one or two in Lily's little group."

"Less us conjure one of them first, then call up Peter," Huck said. He'd jumped on the desk now, and he was more or less on eye level with Lady.

"Yes, but what would we do with him afterwards? Men you don't really want are troublesome—and hard to get rid of."

I had a sudden brainstorm. "You leave that part to me and Huck. If we cain't fetch Peter *and* get rid of his rival—we'll, we'll ..."—but I couldn't think of no punishment or comeuppance to raise our stakes.

"We'll take baths!" Huck jumped in with.

Lady, she just laughed.

"Okay, boys, it's on you."

* * *

The Tree House was the peacefullest place to think a thing through, so that was where me and Huck headed.

It was a little chilly, so the minute we got inside, Huck winked at the fireplace and a nice warmin glow come up. We sat ourselves down straight in front of it on this furry, long-haired rug Lady called a Flokati and was as warm as toast. It was 'most the same color as we were and you could hardly tell where the rug ended and Huck began.

"What's your idea?" I said to Huck.

"Send one of them nonnamous letters—like we did that time 'bout Jim—and get this Peter all riled up and a b'ilin to come over here and scoop up Lady B. It worked noble good before."

"Yais, but this time we hain't got anything to get old Peter steamed up over. What we gonna say? Come and woo Lady B 'less you want to lose her to another man? Since he ain't involved yet, he won't pay it no mind. 'Sides, it'll make her look silly."

"Well, what's your idea?"

"She's goin to conjure him up and chances are he'll sleepwalk right over. Well, if there's another man here, why, when he sees them together, he'll start pinin—"

"Where we gonna git him from?"

"We're goin to make him—"

39

"Make him what?"

"Make him—like Brer Rabbit and the Tar Baby—and bring him to life."

"Tom Sawyer, you have lost your mind if you think you're gonna fool a vet-a-nary *doctor* with a tar baby—"

"You'll see Huck, you'll see."

* * *

I don't say it warn't a heap of work to contrive the man. Neither me nor Huck could hold a needle properly and he was downright lumpy in places. But we done it. We made us a regular effigy and we stuffed 'im up good with our fur leavins. I let on like it was done to increase the power of the spell—but it was a sight easier collectin our own fur than if we had to go hunt all around Rhinebeck for straw— and newspapers get heavy fast when you gotta carry 'em.

"He needs a face," Huck said.

He was just a sort of pillowhead, you might say at that point, with the open end of the case tied low down to show where his neck oughta be. But he wasn't all that different from the scarecrows what used to be back in Missouri—and he had on a blue chambray shirt, jeans and boots. We used gloves for the hands and tied them on, too.

"The piller case makes him look like a executioner with a hood," Huck said.

"Well, we cain't use scissors, no how, so we'll tuck it in and call it his ascot."

"What's ascot?"

"It's a tie rich men wear to horse races."

"That'll fetch 'im," Huck agreed. "But he still needs a face—and a good one. Peter's no slouch in the looks department."

We couldn't use scissors—but we could press buttons and run a computer and a printer.

"Huck, there's 'bout a million faces inside that computer box. And all we have to do is pick one."

"How we gonna do it—"

"Celebrity websites," I said.

Course I didn't know that would be the hardest part of the job.

* * *

"What about this here Mel Gibson?" Huck said. We was sittin on Lady's chair for the second night runnin, lookin at the screen and pressin buttons on the keyboard.

"I was kinda partial to Brad Pitt," I said.

"They's always Matt Damon."

"I think he's too young for Lady. Lady's 'most thirty-five, and he ain't more 'n twenty-eight or so. Besides Huck, he killed a man in *The Talented Mr. Ripley*. Think a murderer's gonna make Peter get all worked up? It ain't *hardly* likely." I shook my head.

"It sure would help if we knew which one was most likely to make Peter sweat." He paused. "Let's do that Brad fellow—or Tom Cruise."

"Huck, these here is all too well-known. What's Brad Pitt gonna be doin in Rhinebeck *and* moanin over Lady? No this kind of celebrity won't do at all."

"Not even Ben Affleck?"

"Nope. We need us a good lookin second tier celebrity—"

"What's that."

"Like a writer or a sports figure or a talk show host or even a contestant from a game show. Famous—but not so famous as a movie star."

"Stephen King," Huck said.

"Too old."

"Derek Jeter."

"Too bulky."

"David Letterman."

"Too many teeth, not enough hair—"

"Well, if he can't be too famous *or* too good lookin, how's he gonna fetch Peter?"

"We'll just have to make him up ourselves and *let on* he's famous," I said.

"Ya mean like Mel Gibson's eyes, and Brad Pitt's smile and Tom Cruise's nose? How we gonna do that?"

"Cut and paste. And we'll let on he's as rich as Bill Gates and as witty as Mel Brooks. That oughta fetch Peter."

Huck thumped his tail twice, and we started pressin buttons and when we finished we had us a grand likeness—of somebody. All we needed to do was slap it on over the pillow case, and not even that—cause Lady had a printer where a body could put anything he could think of right on a T-shirt. Me and Huck didn't think dumb innanimate machinery would know the difference if it ran over a pillow case instead.

And all that was left was to bring him to life and let on to Peter there was another high bidder in the auction. That would fetch 'im sure.

* * *

We called Lady in cause we needed her to help us get the effigy into the regular house—and it was times like that when I wished we was boys already.

"What's this?" she said comin into the Tree House.

"It's Bradley Bill Brooks—"

"The handsomest, richest, wittiest man in Rhinebeck," says Huck. "He's Brad Pitt and Bill Gates and Mel Brooks all rolled into one."

"He looks a little limp," she laughed.

'Course, bein stuffed with fur combings, he was sort of in the same family as a rag doll. But he warn't no life-sized poppet—and we warn't gonna stick pins in him.

"We're gonna nanimate him," Huck said. "He'll walk and talk and be as suave as silk."

"And when we do, Peter's gonna fall in a pile at your feet like leaves in autumn."

"Just so he isn't like dead leaves—all dried up and crackly," Lady laughed.

But I was certain come the night of the full moon ritual, our plan would work.

CHAPTER EIGHT

FULL MOON–EMPTY ARMS–
NEARLY VETTED

"How we goin to bring him to life?" I asked Huck the day before the ritual.

Huck said, "My idea is since it's 'most always dark in the altar room, we prop 'im up in the corner—in the deep shadows. Then we get us a tape recorder and cut in some bits of dialogue from a film so's he can talk some; then we hide ourselves right behind him and shift him around a little—like they do with marionettes, so his arms'll work and all. It's as straightforward as can be."

"Yes, it's straightforward, but there hain't a bit of style to it, Huck. Not a bit. Think one of those Merlin-y magicians'd do it that way? Or the sorceror's apprentice or Harry Potter? Why, they'd chuck old Harry right out of his school for a plan like that one."

"What's your idea, Tom?"

"We got to have incantations and spells and all kinds of things that's a heap of trouble to go through. You take Dr. Frankenstein, did he just lay down a man on his operatin table and then work him like a puppet and call him alive? No, he had to creep into cemeteries of a night and dig up bodies and cut 'em up, then sew them back and then

43

rig up lightnin and masses of electronics to make his *man* do the tango. You bet."

"We already got our'n put together, and we cain't make scissors work nohow."

"Well we can *let on* like we dug him up and stitched him out of parts from sundry corpses, cain't we?"

"Yes. And lettin on don't cost no trouble, and it's *heaps* better than goin to a graveyard, 'cause a shovel is bigger than a cat and there ain't no way we could dig a body in no coffin up out of the dirt."

"We'll let on like we did though—or better yet: like we witched our corpses out of the ground. Like 'Lazarus, Come Forth.'"

"Who's Lazarus Comeforth?"

"He was dead three whole days when Jesus brung him out of the tomb."

"My, I bet he was ripe. I'm glad Brad Brooks don't smell hardly at all. 'Cept maybe a little mildew where his clothes got damp when they was down in the basement before we smouched 'em."

I was pacin around the ritual room a little. "Now we just need us the spell to nanimate him." I jumped on the altar and nudged open the big heavy book, but it was powerful hard to turn the thin leaves of the pages. "I don't see a thing in here bout bringin a effigy to life," I said a few minutes later.

"Well, what are we gonna do?"

"Wait. Here's one that'll answer: 'Pulling the Wool over a Mortal's Eyes.'"

"How's that?"

"We're gonna make Peter *think* Bradley Bill Brooks is alive; only we'll let on like we performed all kinds of mystifyin rites. And if one single thing is done wrong or said wrong, the spell backfires on the sayers and all kinds of terrible things happen to em. We'll let on how dangerous it was to us—but we done it—and brought our creation to human form."

"How we gonna pull the wool over Peter's eyes? What's it say?"

I jumped down. "We're gonna give him three big glasses of whiskey and keep the room dark and run us a audiotape of *What Women Want*."

"Is Brad gonna move some?"

"With all that whiskey, Peter'll be seeing double, and that'll be movement a plenty."

* * *

But that ain't the way it played at all. Lady, she got him there all right. Trouble was, he took one look at me and decided I needed to be neutered.

Well that was all right for a cat—but I had aspirations of bein a boy again.

* * *

It was gettin on for 6 p.m. that night, and the Harvest Moon rose just noble goodish over a stand of trees on a knoll back of Lady's house. It was that autumn-yellow color and round and big as a circus tent. Me and Huck seen it and headed from the Tree House and loped off pronto for the second-floor altar room.

It smelled good in there. Lady had batches of candles lit, and there was incense smokin up the place, and now besides that massive leather-bound book on her desk, there was a silver goblet and a ruby-colored vase with some flowers and some crystal stones and other witchy regalia.

She had on a flowered satin robe that was my favorite from Victoria's Secret with little tiny blossoms strewn here and there. She was barefoot, but had on a thin golden ankle bracelet. She wore a few silver rings, too; and her hair was loose and flowin down her back. She looked 'most as pretty as the moon itself.

Brad was stuffed into one corner, and me and Huck was there, so all we needed now was Peter Bennett to round out the party.

"Well, boys," Lady said, "shall we get started?"

Huck gave out a little *prrrp!* that was yes for both of us. I could hardly wait to see the whole thing in action, and I hunkered down close as I could get to her, and Huck was right beside me.

Lady took a sip from the goblet. I smelled it was full of the clearest, most crystalline water; it smelt almost as good as a mountain stream, and I reckoned if she left any, after the ceremony me and Huck would be buttin heads over whose snoot got into the glass first to take a sip. But she passed it on, lowerin it, and I had a drink—it was liquid moonlight. Then Huck, he did, too. She wiped the rim with a white handkercher and set it back on the table.

She dipped down—half kneelin, half in a stoop—and bowed her head.

And I thought, *Here it comes, the spell that's gonna send Dr. Peter Bennett into a tailspin and have him near foamin at the mouth over Lady B.*

But all she did was say, "By all that is good in the universe, let my true love come to me. And so it harm none, so mote it be."

Then she stood up and pressed out the candlewicks, shifted a few things around and smiled.

"That's it? That's all you're gonna do?"

"Yes," she said.

"Well, wait a minute; here, me and Huck's gone to all the bother of makin Brad and memorizin incantations galore and focusin and concentratin and I don't know what else the last seven days, and in two minutes the show's over, the light's 're out, and the ushers are sweepin up the empty popcorn boxes? And that's it?"

"That's it."

We were disappointed a plenty. "We never even got to turn on the tape recordin," Huck said to me in private. "If that was all it took, seemed to me she could have just picked up the phone after all. Humans," he said, "beat all. I cain't hardly believe they burnt women just for layin out a few flowers and sayin half a prayer."

"Looky-here. If this was a revival and that was the long and short of it, the preacher'd starve. Why, do you think a body would drive miles and miles over rutted country roads gettin sweated up and tired and come to a tent and pay over their money and then be shooed out the flaps in less than ten minutes? No sir. They'd tar the man who called himself a preacher and did that. Call this a religion—" I swatted a fake fur mouse down the hallway and was satisfied to see him careen off the wall. Then I gave a pounce, pretended to fasten on the back of his neck and gave him a little shake.

Huck trotted over and gave the gray mouse a little thwack. "Well, maybe it's like hoodoo, Tom. That's a religion. And they don't do nothin but give a sign and make a mumble and then watch their victims drop down dead in the dust."

"Hoodoo," I said. "Anybody can do it. Seems to me this here wiccan religion needs a lot more flash and style. Why it's just nothin a body couldn't do while he was shinin his shoes or combin his hair or taking a squat in the litter box."

"Maybe it's all the preparation ahead of time," Huck said.

"Does the pastor clean the whole church—every blasted window and pew and scrub up the bells before a Sunday? No sir. And yet a body goes and sits bein punished for hours listenin to him drone on and then has Sunday school and more church and singin—there warn't even any *singin*!"

"Maybe they kinda toned it down over the years so's to hide themselves and keep from bein burned up and prosecuted, Tom."

"But there ain't a *bit* of sparkle to it. There warn't even a dead baby smeared with blood or screamin victims tied to the altar or Satan signs or none of the grand things that gaud it up and is in all the books."

"But maybe it'll work," Huck said.

I didn't answer. Huck was just a saphead about certain things. What if it did work? I'd still have to go to all the trouble of lettin on how hard it was to conjure and how dangerous. And it warn't anything more to it than a schoolchild's ABCs.

* * *

Five minutes later, the telephone rung. All three of us knew it was Peter Bennett.

CHAPTER NINE

PETER–LILY–
LILY'S DATE WITH DESTINY

"Well, Barbara, I was just wondering how Tom and Huck are doing."

"They're fine, Peter."

Me and Huck were hangin around the conversation, and because we understood Lady so well, we could catch flickers of what Peter was sayin to her—even if we couldn't hear his voice directly.

"The thing is—and I'm not trying to drum up business—but it's getting on for the time when they should be neutered."

"I don't know what to say to that," Lady said.

I knew—the answer had to be a unqualified *no*—if me and Huck was goin to be boys and not eunuchs when we learnt to switch over from bein familiars to humans again.

"Male cats—well, they spray," Peter said. "It can get ugly fast inside a house."

"Tom and Huck do go outdoors," Lady said.

You bet, I thought.

"They can have a tendency to wander if they go out and they're not neutered. Also to get into scrapes and fights—"

49

"Peter, I'm going to let you in on a little secret," she said and I thought, *Here it comes, our cover is blown to smithereens and flinders and what chance is there a vet'nary doctor's gonna take on a woman as unscientific as a witch what believes in spells and mystery and a bunch of notions that have been around since the Middle Ages and longer?*

"These aren't typical cats."

"They're not typical," Peter repeated.

"No. In fact, I think it would be a good idea if you came over to see exactly what I mean."

Here's where I thought Peter was gonna bang down his end of the phone and tell her to call him if she discovered—as he was certain she would—what kind of ordeal she was in for with cats doin what come naturally and makin more trouble and heartache for her than any twelve juvenile delinquents with overactive minds and glands.

"How about tomorrow night? I could stop by when the clinic closes—say around five?"

"That would be fine."

You coulda knocked me over with the tip of a mouse tail—but Lady went one better still:

"And Peter, we might have a glass of wine together, and if you're free for the rest of the evening, you're welcome to stay for dinner."

Shut the door on that one—you can guess what he said next.

And, the scrubbin *this* time, I thought, was gonna be in Lady's bedroom. I'd have bet my lucky cat's-eye marble there was gonna be lavender scentin up the room and waftin off the sheets and linens like fog driftin over a pond at sunrise.

* * *

It was all goin accordin to Lady B's plan. Peter showed up on time to the dot. And he brought a bottle of wine, so there was considerable celebratin planned from his point of view, too. Lady B had shined up her best silver and set the dinin room table with it and laid down some yellow antique plates and enough glassware and crystal to stun a diamond merchant. They was masses of white candles—pillars and tapers and votives. All of 'em twinklin away like anything and makin the crystal and windows and mirror throw off a million rainbow stars. Peter was a goner—that was sure.

Me and Huck watched from the hallway where there was a pair a old-fashioned sliding doors, which Lady B had closed to make the atmosphere more intimate, and which we opened a crack so we could hear and see.

They were laughin and tellin stories and all that boy-meets-girl stuff and Peter was a gent—not like me. He never once kissed her or told her they oughta get engaged, which was the mistake I made straight off with Becky Thatcher. But it didn't take a Shakespeare to see he was smitten from the start gun and just bidin his time, like was right and proper. Not to mention, for all he said he was comin over to give me and Huck the once-over, he never even brought us up into the conversation. Not that we all didn't know his own cover was blown to hell and back. It didn't matter though. He and Lady B was havin as good a time as two fleas settin smack in the middle of a great big sheepdog.

* * *

I judged Peter was just about to cover Lady B's hand with his when there was a rattlin at the back door, and two seconds later a hurricane blown in. The natural disaster known as Lily Blum barrelled inside bellowin like a ruttin moose.

"B, hey B! How are you! Where you hiding out?"

She had a nose like a bloodhound, so it warn't even a second before she'd skipped through the swingin door from the kitchen to the dining room table. Where the dimples had suddenly disappeared from Peter's and Lady's cheeks and their mouths was hangin open with the expression you see when somebody has just found half a cock-a-roach in their bologna sandwich.

And anybody else would have blushed the color of claret and felt like an ass in a parade and beat a retreat fast enough to baffle a strafer in an airplane—anybody that is, but Lily.

She set right down across from Lady B and looked like you'd need a crowbar to pry her out of the chair.

There warn't nothin for Lady B to do but meet it with the natural good grace she had and fetch another place settin and a glass for wine and paste a welcome smile on her face. And poor Peter—he had to tag along and act happy to see Lily, too.

About a minute later, we heard a noise like in one of them Japanese horror movies where insects the size of heavy machinery are chewin up oak trees, houses and humans. Then there was a sound like a plunger being rammed down inside a stuck toilet, which was Lily swallerin, and we heard her say, "This filet mignon is superb, what's in the marinade?"

We didn't wait to hear no answer—but I hoped Lady B'd tell her the sauce was loaded with saffron—just to put Lily on edge so to speak since she'd been smearin herself with the stuff night and day tryna transport. But, like I said, we didn't wait.

Instead, we took off when I hissed soft into Huck's ear, "This is our chance to put Bradley Bill Brooks to real good use." Huck thumped twice and his eyes got the most delicious light in 'em—like they was tastin the time we froze Lily and contemplatin havin seconds.

"After you, Tom" he said, smilin wide.

And we both scatted up the stairs.

There was two of us, and if we couldn't drag a dumb effigy with our teeth down the hall and on to the landin and nudge the thing down the steps, why, I 'llowed we'd witch it down.

* * *

I once heard of a man who lived near 'Orleans and was known as the Duke—because he said he could trace his line back before the Dolphin that was supposed to rule in France, and he warn't exactly rollin in dough anymore, but he did retain his sense of humor. His idea of a capital joke was invitin his friends over to dinner along with one person who was new in town or a stranger. All his friends had been hoodwinked by the Duke over time—so everybody always said yes and could hardly wait to see how the guest reacted—because each and every time the Duke had a skeleton sittin at the head of the long wooden table. Sometimes he dressed it in a tuxedo and called it Uncle Henri and stuck a cigar betwixt its bony fingers; sometimes he put it in a blue satin dress and stuck a child's party hat on its head and called it Granny Renee and said it was *her* birthday; sometimes he let it just sit there naked and chapfallen and 'most giving everybody who sat down with it the screaming meemies. Sometimes all the guests pretended to talk to it like it was real and human; or they might a ignored it completely like the chair was empty—either way the unnitiated newcomer 'most always kept lookin at his glass—to make sure he warn't neither poisoned nor taken with an acute case of the D.T.'s.

It warn't exactly the same with me and Huck when we hauled in Bradley Bill Brooks—but, if the Duke—who was a real Duke and not like those frauds Huck and Jim had to put up with on the raft—had been there and in on the joke, he'd a loved it.

* * *

Luck is a good thing—and it was lucky that old Lily had to retreat to empty her bladder—which me and Huck knowed would give us plenty of time. We hissed Lady out into the hall and she caught on to the gambit right away. So, she carried Bill into the dining room, laughin, and told Peter, "Ho ho ho—look what the cat dragged in." Then she sat Bill at the other end of the table and said he's a decoration for her upcoming Halloween gala—which surely he'd like to come to, and she's gonna conduct a little experiment and would he mind playing along? Sure he's going to come to the party, and sure he'll play along. Without saying so, he'd got old Lily's number. And Lady was privy to even more about 'er—but let that go for the moment.

She filled Lily's wineglass right up to the brim—and I don't know but she didn't slip something into it.

In came Lily, and Lady said to 'er, "Lily, I'd like you to meet Brad Brooks. Brad, this is is Lily Blum." With special emphasis on the short U—of course.

It worked noble. Lily sat down and started chattin with him—just like Lady'd gone to the trouble of arrangin her a double date. Me and Huck near about died on the other side of the doors.

"What line are you in, Brad?"

* * *

I don't know what she was hearin for answers, but she talked near two hours with the dummy. Told him all kinds of things about herself—includin the details of her divorce, her witchy ways and her

penchant for doin housework in the nude. And Peter and Lady B got
on splendid. Take it all around, the evening was a smashin success.

CHAPTER TEN

TREE HOUSE–LILY UNBUTTONED–
UP, UP, AND AWAY

Lady B was too smart to let Peter hang around all night—they said their good-byes and made their plans to meet up again, and all three of us lit out for the Tree House. Lily sat at the table with her legs sprawled out and her head cocked back and snorin 'most loud enough to make Brad get up and run. Lady and us judged when she waked up, she'd just go on home, so we left her there while we strolled out under a star-studded sky.

Inside the skin of the tree, we made ourselves cozy and we got to gigglin about this and that and got so giddy, Lady decided to tell us a thing or two about Lily Blum.

"Did you boys ever hear that witches believe what goes around comes around? And that whatever you send out comes back at you threefold?" Lady said. She was sittin cross-legged in front of the fireplace eatin Peanut M&M'S and every now and then I'd stick a paw in the bag and pull one out to bat around some. They made dandy cat toys.

"No," Huck told her. "Seems like all the witches in St. Petersburg doted on makin trouble and never give a thought to curses boomerangin back."

Lady's hand stole out and she gave Huck a little pat. "Well, it's true. Though Lily likes to pretend it isn't so. She had a boyfriend that left her flat way back in 1978—said he got an itch for another girl. So Lily gave him another kind of itch. Gave him hives—great big red splotchy ones. And everytime they'd start to get better and the ex-boyfriend thought *this time the doctor cured me*, she'd start 'em up again. She'd just think 'hives' at him and he broke out." Lady paused. "And most of these hives were in all the wrong places—if you take my meaning. This went on for years—I mean years," she laughed. "But do you know what happened in the end? That vengeance came and just sat on Lily like an incubus."

"So, does Lily have hives all up and down her privates?" I said.

"No, she has nice big red scrofulous patches all over her entire body. And whenever she manages to get a man into her bed, she has to spend so much concentration making him think he's seeing alabaster skin instead of something that looks its been three weeks getting to the coroner's office, she just lays there like a stone lizard."

"Sounds like she and Brad are suited fine," Huck said.

We all laughed at that. Then Lady, she laid back and took a good long look up through the branches overhead and into the night sky and said, "How'd you boys like to take in a little scenery in this evening?"

We'd like it; oh yes, indeed.

"All right, then—the three of us are going to take a little jaunt," she said.

Lady thought for our first venture we'd be best off flyin as a trio and using the Flokati rug as our base of operations so to speak. We hunkered down, she put an arm around each of us, and the fluffy white carpet began to slowly lift into the air.

"Scared?"

"No," we said at the same time.

Lady moved us in a few lazy circles around the room and the carpet began to spiral up higher and higher inside the Tree House, and the next me and Huck knowed, it was all as gaudy down below as a ferris wheel. We skirted the top of the tree, the stars and moon wheelin overhead; then we banked west and Lady floated us easy and gentle as dandelion fluff along the flank of the river.

We drifted down as far as the Newburgh-Beacon bridge, watchin boats move up and down the river, their runnin lights flashin. Saw the trees linin the banks, the lights of the towns twinklin up at us. Cars moved on roads, and trains coursed north and south on either side of the water snakin along banks cut into the run of the terrain.

"Oh, Tom, don't this beat even a raft," Huck said.

"There ain't a body back in St. Petersburg would even believe it— even if they could see it with their own two eyes."

Lady guided us slow and easy, so that the wind rufflin our fur warn't more than the littlest breeze and neither one of us felt afraid— not with her by our side.

She turned to when we passed the bridge and headed north again and, a little while later, there was tiny Rhinebeck and the topmast of the Tree House, and we was droppin into her lower and lower and the Flokati rug hovered a moment over the floor then thumped down and the fire was warmin us—but truth to tell, nothin could heat us up the way flyin with Lady did. It was so big—it was beyond words.

She knowed it, too.

We sat awhile, all three together. Then she got up easy and headed to the main house, and me and Huck went with her to go up to our bed.

We fell straight asleep on the big soft coverlet, and I reckon all three of us had happy dreams that night. Dreams such as those that come to mortals whose entwined lives make a mountain of contentment.

I slept with my arms around Huck and his around me. Toward first light his whiskers tickled me to wakin and I lifted my head. In his sleep, I heard him say, "Lady—she is peace."

There ain't anyone who could say it better. Not even a regular Stephen Charles Mark William Shakespeare—all rolled into one.

CHAPTER ELEVEN

PLANS FOR OUR FIRST HALLOWEEN—
LILY AGAIN

Ghosts are okay cause they don't do nothin.

Werewolfs are mainly borin to be around. When the moon is in the off stage, they mostly just look like people with really bad taste in clothin. Never seem to get style right, so to speak. As the moon gets closer to the full, they get a sharpish look in their eye, but with everything so sivilized nowadays, they cain't do much more than take down a deer and leave it on the highway—as if some drunken hillbilly in a rusty truck hit the thing. And if they dare run a ways downstate, the pickins are even slimmer. Many's the time me and Huck have heard Lady talk about drivin down Route 9-D toward the Newburgh-Beacon bridge and seein three dead raccoons right in a row lyin on the yellow line. And how that was a sign that the poor werewolfs was just bein starved out of their natural habitats and forced to go after no-account animals like raccoons and smelly possums and skunks and even the occasional domestic cat.

She said it was a shame, 'cause in their own native lands they ran wild and free for centuries till the war messed 'em up, and then people like that horrible Lon Chaney and Maria Ouspenskya let on there was

59

such things as werewolfs and they was hunted right out of Romania or wherever and now there was only a few gen-u-ine ones left.

F'rinstance, the ones here in New York had to try and mingle in as best they could. One wolfman she knew was the owner of an antique shop—it comforted him, she said, to be around old things.

Bein so agile and strong and all, another wolfy guy that Lady knew had took up bein a gymnastics expert for a while, and he was supposed to be in the Olympics and all, but warn't it his terrible bad luck—here the games was bein held in his native Hungary—but the problem was they was scheduled plumb in the middle of a full moon, so he had to withdraw, and Lady told how he got so sad and hangdog about it, he was always broodin and thinkin about how he coulda been famous and changed the whole face of how people all over the world saw werewolfs, and he coulda stood up right and proud for them as a race and a species and all. Well, he got so droopy-tailed, he ended up doin no more than runnin a bowlin alley across the river—and everyone *knows* how they've declined in status over the years. Lady, she tried to get him to become a undertaker, that bein a right smart line of business, but he was afraid he'd eat into the profits.

Well, like I said, she had these ghosts comin to this here annual party of hers, and me and Huck warn't too worried about *them*, and the werewolfs—long as they're fed—they don't bother a body, and a few of her witchy friends. Nope, it was the vampires that was scheduled to come that had me and Huck up a tree. You don't even want to be a cat around folks who drink blood. And you can take that to the bank.

* * *

So, the Witches' Ball was comin up and Lady, she had me and Huck fairly run ragged gettin ready for the thing. The first big problem came when Luna Raven or Raven Loon or whatever Lily Blum's witchy name was came over one afternoon for Tea and Gunpowder or whatever she drunk and decided me and Huck oughta be decorated, too.

* * *

"Say, B.D., aren't you going to have the boys 'en masque?'" she said while I'm just a layin nicety-nice on Lady's lap and gettin all kinds of strokin.

"Mask? You mean costume?"

My ears pricked up when Lady said that, you can be sure, cause Huck never held with clothes when he was a boy, and he liked it even less now. This was soundin dangerous.

"You know, something to convey the spirit of the season? Something black?"

Well, she talked it up all around, but what her idea was came down to how Lady oughta get some kind of temporary dye and color us in.

I skedaddled and ran to find Huck before another word could pass between 'em. If they was goin to paint us up like a bunch of stereotype familiars and go dippin us in wet, dark stuff, it might be time for me and Huck to head out for the Territories.

* * *

"I never did like that Ravin Lunatic, or whatever she's called," Huck said. "For all that she wears all that black gunk around her eyes and looks like somethin you'd hire to ha'nt houses, she always stares at me like a starvin man turned loose at a free buffet table."

"She tried last week to throw a glamour at me," I said. A glamour is a kind of spell witches use on folks to convince 'em what is *ain't* or what ain't *is*. It ain't a bit like Huck who tried to fool his Pap and all the townfolk that he was killed and drug off to the river, or us showin up to hear our funeral orgies—them was plots and pranks. A witch who throws a glamour has a lot more on her mind.

"What glammer did she try on you?" Huck asked.

"Tried to steal the eyes right outta my head. Wanted blue cats' eyes to throw around and dazzle folks when she went out on the town for a night. Had to be cats' eyes on account of the pupil."

"Guess she thought that'd look really witchy," Huck said.

"Yeah, and good thing Lady caught her, or I'd a been blind as a mole and even after I was healed, it'd be like starin through a fog for a week—maybe more."

"What'd she do?"

"Told Luna Lily go get herself some contact lenses if she wanted blue cats' eyes that bad—and leave witchery to *real* witches."

We was whisperin all this while, but now me and Huck decided to listen up sharp and see what Luna had in mind. I was startin to wonder was she mad at Lady and pretendin not to be—or mad at me and Huck. She didn't let on to know about the scurvy trick we played over her with Bradley Bill, but she coulda been keeping mum about it. And then, too, things was going nice and easy between Peter and Lady—lots of phone chat and twice out to dinner and a film ... so I figured it was possible Lily might be feelin jealous some—enough to put a wrench into somebody's cog. Huck, he thought the same as me.

"Tom, I'm agreed. But, we oughta listen in first and see what she's plannin," he said. So Huck crept forward; and we both hunkered down just around the corner of the room where we was in earshot, but out of eyesight.

CHAPTER TWELVE

LILY'S HAMMER—WHAT HAPPENED ON THE EVE OF THE BALL

"Well, no, Lily I don't think the boys would sit still for being dyed black or any other color." Lady held up her hand before Lily could jump in. "And I don't think spray paint—not even the kind that washes out or wears off that all the punk and Goth kids use—would suit them any better."

"But think of the atmosphere they could lend to your gala," Lily said. "People pay all kinds of money for Halloween decorations and to have a couple of live black cats perched around—"

"Huck and Tom can do just as they please that night," Lady said again. "And if a hundred pairs of feet tromping around make them want to stay up in my bedroom, that's fine."

"Sure—certainly," Lily said droppin her eyes to the table.

"That woman's lyin through her teeth, Tom," Huck said. "What's she thinkin?"

"I don't know." I couldn't get a fix on Lily's mind. But I hoped Lady could.

We asked her straight off—soon as Lily was gone.

"Oh, I think she wanted to dress herself up as Cleopatra, Queen of the Nile—and if I'd been willing to go along with dyeing you poor boys, she'd have wanted to collar you up and leash you to have a coupla black cats to spiff up her costume." Lady said, turnin over the pages of her guest list.

On the face of things, it seemed all right as an answer, but I warn't convinced. Lady was just that tiny bit distracted, and Queen of Sheba or no, I didn't think that was all Lily Blum had in mind. And I was right—she started to try and boost her stock before the ball was even begun.

"Seems like more people would have R.S.V.P'd by now," Lady said tickin off names. "We haven't heard from more than half. Oh well—there's still a few days left and with any luck, I won't have to start making calls to track folks down."

"Lady? If they's any vampires left on that list, me and Tom won't mind a bit if you don't check and see are they comin."

Lady chuckled at that, and she leaned over and gave Huck's head a quick scratch that turned into a pat; then smiled to hear him purr.

* * *

We cleaned, dusted, and strung near 'bout a hundred mile of fake white spider silk. Even Peter pitched in and put a huge black cauldron in the front yard and built a fire under 'er and lots of dry ice bubblin inside like it was potion enough to transform a whole university worth a mad scientists. We hung rubber bats and washed glassware. Well, we watched Peter and Lady when it come to any folderol with water. But me and Huck was right there givin Lady suggestions about how to orient the buffet tables and aim the black lights and rig up the coffin for Bradley Bill, since as Huck pointed out there warn't no sense in wastin a perfectly good effigy when he'd make such a gaudy looking corpse. And we made sure Lady remembered to buy film (she said the vampires wouldn't show up on nuther Kodak or Fuji nor no other film, but she aimed to get some good shots of the witches and werewolfs and such). The preparations was comin along splendid. And me and Huck laid out the spots we planned to watch the party from: the top of the landing; under the dinin room sideboard to avoid gettin stepped on; and, if the vampires got too splashy, or the rest of the crowd got a little wild and wooly, inside the Tree House. Couldn't nobody come and fasten on us in there.

Before we knowed it, it was October 30th and the night before the big event and things was goin haywire fast.

* * *

Mr. Twain always used to tell a story about this rich old lady who knows her time is nigh and decides to give this big splash of a party. Oh, she's goin all out—hires an orchestra; and a florist to set out big green potted palms. Hires all kinds of high-falutin caterers, and liveried butlers to serve up the iced champagne. But the main thing the old lady wants to do is get even—to spite a pair a newcomers to her neighborhood which has treated her like she was a bug on top of a birthday cake. She invites every person in town for miles around— 'cept the newcomers; and a course she's just chortlin and as happy as bubblin mud, picturin how they for sure have heard tell of the party and are just about eaten up with envy. The big day arrives, and she has hairdressers to comb her up, and dressmakers to fit her out in pewter gray satin.

Comes 10 o'clock and the lanterns are lit, but no cars turn into her drive way. It's 11 p.m. and the orchestra plays on and on and no one comes. She sits, dressed to the nines, in her wheelchair, waitin for the townfolks to pour in the big oak front door. But no one has rung the bell. Long about midnight, she tells the orchestra to tune up on the Blue Danube Waltz; she asks the butler to wheel her over to the gleamin table in the dinin room and to serve her some pheasant and a nice cool glass of champagne. She's just about to tuck in, when she hears the doorbell chime and some chatter in the hall. She's all a-flutter and looks up over the candlelight and flowers; then she sees the newcomers sashaying into her dinin room.

Well, it makes her so mad, she plunges her hands against the arms of the wheelchair and actually hoists herself up proud and tall.

"I'm sorry," she says, "but this is a private party."

Off they go, in a huff, tuxedo tails and mink wraps flyin. She hears the front door slam.

Still standin, the old lady downs her champagne; then she collapses in the chair. The butlers and maids carry her off to bed and she's tossin her head and mutterin. "No one else came. They were the only two who came here—after all my hard work—they were the only two who showed up and *they* weren't even invited!"

Well, it was all too much, and they found the old lady dead and dry as cold toast the next morning ... but when they cleaned up her effects, what do you think they found? Every one of those invitations was still in her desk: She hadn't mailed so much as a single sheet of ivory vellum.

It warn't exactly the same with Lady and her big blow-out. But it was close. Lady had written out all her handmade invitations in two batches and stuffed the insides of the envelopes with black cat and orange pumpkin confetti. They was stamped and addressed and ready to go. Lily had dropped by that day.

She said she was fixin to go to the post office and she'd be glad to mail out the rest of the invitations.

Course, bein Lily, she cain't leave without a stack of somethin or other, so she asks Lady can she borrow this catalogue? And this magazine? And this brochure? And this flyer?

And that's where Huck found 'em—the bulk of 'em, anyhow, cause Lady had wrote 'em up in two sittins and the first batch was mailed. But in her haste to scoop up those catalogues so she could devour bargains, close-outs, and sale items, and drool over the magazine spreads with the latest doins of the great and near great, Lily had let slip about sixty of the pretty little envelopes—and they was still buried near the bottom of the basket by Lady's back door where she kept her overflow of junk mail.

"She done it a purpose, I bet," Huck said, shakin his head with disgust.

"She's passive-aggressive—but here's one time we can't prove she did it out of spite," Lady said, headin for the phone.

"You gonna ream her out?" I asked. "She can pretend she dropped 'em with the junk mail by accident, but she can't be that addled ... not all the time ... not permanently ... even if she ain't got no more brains than a fiddlehead fern or a Boston ivy."

Lady flapped her hand at me. "She'll just deny it anyhow. No, I'm gonna call these people up and see if some of them can still make it."

* * *

Natur'ly a lot of people had plans; but even some of those said they'd stop by later on if they could.

"Mostly the vampires; wouldn't ya know it," Huck said. "'Course they'll go *anywhere* for a drink."

But even with the mix-up, after Lady got on the phone, we had at least half the original hundred folks booked solid for the big night and another fifteen or so plannin on tryin to come by. So take it all around, Lady's party was gonna be a rattlin good time. I was glad—she'd gone to a lot of trouble and there was tons of food—some of it still on the hoof. And it woulda been a shame to waste it—especially with starvin werewolfs and all.

CHAPTER THIRTEEN

THE WITCHES BALL–LILY, QUEEN OF THE NILE– CALVIN AND ALEXANDER, CONSORTS TO THE QUEEN

The party invitation said 10 p.m.—which was to give the vampires plenty a time to dust themselves off before arrivin, and for the ghosts to appear at their best advantage—'cause you cain't hardly see a ghost by twilight, and to allow the werewolves a coupla hours a pre-prandial snackin and deer huntin. The humans just figured it was a late-night type party and, the witches—well they 'most never meet too long before the witchin hour. So, countin the stragglers and the show-offs who like to make grand entrances, by 11:30, the gala was in full swing.

"Who'd have thought in chi-chi Rhinebeck, fully three-fourths of the guests would show up as werewolves, ghosts, vampires and witches?" Peter said to a man standin in front of the sideboard. "I thought more people would have really unusual costumes," he said. "Like yours."

The man—a ghost for sure—was cradlin a drink in his right hand; he'd dressed in the big fancy wig, the long curling mustache, waistcoat, breeches and buckled shoes that transformed him into Captain Hook—me and Huck thought he was just the gaudiest pirate.

"Well, I think some of these guests *are* vampires, werewolves and witches," the man said, rockin on his heels a little. His drink was empty.

Peter just laughed and slapped the man's shoulder, because of course, naturally, he thought the man was sayin it for a joke. The man moved on, staggerin a little toward the bar set up in the kitchen. Then he tripped, started to fall, and whipped out his hook sending it point first thuddin into the corner of the sideboard. "Saved," he muttered; and I guessed there'd be some foo-far-raw about that gouge in Lady's antique sideboard post-party. He straightened up mentally as well as physically, then lost it again and went reelin towards the kitchen.

Peter, dressed like a surgeon in operatin greens, watched him go while a young blond witch sidled over to him; he rubbed the gored spot with a licked finger and shook his head, sighing. "That man needs a sign saying, 'Don't let me drive, I'm three sheets past bedtime,'" he said to the tall blond witch.

"Ghosts simply cannot hold their liquor," she agreed.

Peter laughed—'cause he thought she meant the man's historical dress; Huck rolled his eyes at me, and the witch lingered, chatting with Peter.

It warn't long before Lily's radar flared—since Peter was nearby—and me and Huck saw Lily swishin up to the buffet in an Egyptian get-up that would have shamed Cleopatra. The younger yellow-haired witch moved off.

"Nerfertiri, I presume?" Peter said, polite as robins' eggs. "Or is it Nefertiti—"

"No, I am Queen Nuff-titty," Lily said with a smirk. She had on a headdress; that was all right. She had on some kind of belly squeezin skirt thing that went down to the floor and shaved the tips of her sandals. That was all right. But the rest of her was some kind of linen wrap open to reveal a pair of plastic breastworks that must have been 48 double D's. The nipples on those things was the size around a red wooden checkers and popped two inches from the fake flesh.

I could hardly wait to see her fix a plate and eat. It'd be like tryna feed yourself if somebody suddenly clapped a microwave oven acrost your chest.

"If she can bend her elbows around those water wings, I'll eat white rice and dog food for a week," Huck said. "She's gonna have to hunker down and stick her head in a bowl like a pig feedin in a trough."

Meanwhile, Peter was laughin with his mouth, but his eyes was pleadin *get me away from here,* and he was dartin little glances toward the swingin door to the kitchen where Lady was dishin stuff up and helpin guests at the bar.

A coupla more witches went by shriekin hello and wavin to Lily, then a vampire come up and leered at her right breast and pretended to bite it, but Lily had her sights on brighter stars—and after she gave the vampire a look that said, *Go away before I turn you into an asp,* he milled off. She kept right on gossipin at Peter and he was more or less pinned to the spot he stood on. Peter was just too damn polite for his own good, if you ask me.

Lily thought she was enjoying a smashin social success. Me and Huck watched postively amazed when she took a big swig from her wineglass—those fake mounds was pliable and squshed right up when Lily curved her arm like a longbow to get her hand to her mouth. And Peter's eyes near dropped out of his head, too.

"Unlike implants, mine move just like the real thing," she giggled and poked her own plastic rightie, lettin a finger tip linger near the chocolate-covered-cherry-sized outcropping that was her false nipple.

"Let me refill that for you, Lily," Peter said, beatin a hasty retreat. No question in our minds, he warn't coming back.

Lily didn't care. Just then two humans—a coupla guys from over to Kingsport College that Lady more or less knew second hand—came along and not fifteen seconds later Lily swept them, spider-like—into her web. I 'most felt sorry for them. Or, would have—if the pair of em warn't so perfectly awful.

"Fuckin' A," the first one said, "Al, I don't know what the fuck we're drinking, but it's fuckin outrageous."

"Fuck me, Cal—I am so fucked up. Dude. This is fucking righteous."

They had come dressed as each other, and gave each other high fives. Al usually wore a tan fishin hat, so Cal had it on, and Cal had shoulder-length hair, so Al had on a long brown wig. They thought they was the height of wittiness.

"What's your other name, Cleopatra?" Al said to Lily as she slinked over to 'im.

"Depends on the time of day. Lily before sunset; and Luna Raven at night. Just now I am Queen Nuff-titty," she guffawed.

"Dude. How much real stuff you got under that friggin latex?" Cal said.

"But this *is* real," she said tweakin herself, and throwin a glammer at them. The two morons high-fived again. "What's your name?" she asked the one standin closest to her.

"I'm Al, he's Cal."

"He don't know shit. I'm Al, he's Cal," and they snorted, laughin again. "He's just wearin my friggin fly hat and my friggin green rubber boots."

These two guys by name of Calvin and Alexander was each other's best friends and taught over to the college. Lily wanted to believe that made 'em okay, but me and Huck could see right through 'em and we knew better. Cal taught somethin called Media Images that was one of the most popular courses in the history of the school—bein as it involved just sittin around watching old reruns of MTV, *Ren and Stimpy*, and *Xena the Warrior Princess*; and studyin 'em up like they was first folio editions of William Shakespeare. Students at Kingsport signed up for it years in advance. You couldn't find an empty seat in that classroom unless you come in with a Mauser submachine gun. His big qualification for teachin that course was that he once drew cartoons for Disney—about a million years ago—and all the teachers at Kingsport thought his comic book speech was quaint and natural, because they was afraid to be politically incorrect and snobbish and come right out and say he talked like the no-class community college drop-out he was. Instead, they touted his life experience and talked up how important it was for students to learn from someone *in* the business. You'd a thought he was Alan Dershowitz teachin law at Harvard or Rudolf Najinksi instructin ballet and the History of Russian dance—instead of an acid head with a TV set he bought on time from Sears. His students wrote senior theses on things like "Revisiting the 60's: Social Commentary in *Dharma and Greg*."

Old Alex—the other genius—taught fingerpaintin and papier-mache, but bein a lifetime cartoon and TV fan, he was eminently qualified to run Cal's course; so Cal had got him a berth teachin an extra section of the TV Rerun course—but with hands-on experience. So his students made collages and installations. *Their* senior theses was

3D slush like "Homer Simpson Deconstructed," which showed a plastic doll with its head blown off and peeled apart in itsy-bitsy careful layers—like Greek pastry or when like some guys in bars shred up matches to show you the joke about how two paper matches can have sex. In *his* class, they didn't even need to know English.

When they warn't teachin "arts and letters" at the college, they worked construction for serious drinkin money or went fishin. When they wanted to relax, they watched wrestlin. When they felt like bein intellectual, they watched *Junk Yard Wars* or *Survivor*. The college called them "artists in residence" and gave them a little two room place that used to be a gatehouse. Just like they was Truman Capote at Yaddo. Except of course, the only thing they produced was a seven-foot circle of Budweiser beer cans that went clear up to the ceilin, and a pile of laundry, girly magazines and pizza boxes that would shame the Collier Brothers. They called the beer cans "Summer Monument"—although during the actual month of August, while they was drinkin it into construction, they called it "Summer Project" because it was still in *process*.

I don't know if it was common sense, being leery of Lily, or our witchin powers, but we saw through them two rapscallions in seconds flat.

"Hey, dude—Lily, Cleopatra, whatever—you wanna dance?" Cal jerked his thumb toward the music-swelled parlor on the right.

Me and Huck thought this would be worth seein, so we followed the trio into the livin room, divin under the sofa where we could keep an eye for drunken stompin feet.

"Shake your booty," Al screamed, his own Frankenstein-style boots crash landin hard enough to undermine the mortised floorboards.

"Hey, Cleo, Lily, whatever—you like a threesome?" Cal leered at the same time he pumped his hips against her bottom and Al turned around to put his behind against her front and they made a swayin, layered conga line. They was pressed together just like laminated plywood. It was enough to shame the toughest talkin fancy gal in a Nevada saloon.

"Oh, baby," Lily sang, scoochin Al's back and shoulders with her frontage. "Baby. Baby. Baby! Baby love. My baby love ... my heart is churnin! Yearnin!"

"Yeah, honey, churn that butt for your backdoor man!" Cal said, twitchin his own skinny rear, then breakin away to take a few steps. He tilted his head back and poured the rest of his drink down his throat.

He and Al were gettin drunker by the minute, and I doubted if by the end of the evenin either one of them would be able to find the keys to their truck—much less take turns boffin ol' Lily. Cal had lurched off toward the sunporch; it took him a while to navigate. No beeline for Cal—he stumblebummed past the dancers like a zombie in *Night of the Livin Dead*.

"Hey, what's the matter with Cal?" Lily said, now shimmyin face-to-face with Al.

"He's frigged up," Al said spinnin around, then coming to a stop. He drank a hefty gulp from his glass and wiped his mouth with his sleeve. "Lucky me, I friggin get you all to myself," he said.

"Ho ho ho," Lily chortled. "You're cuter, anyhow." She stuck her hands in the floppin wig—in a sort of runnin-her-fingers-through-his-hair gesture. The music loop segued into "Heard it Through the Grapevine," and Lily and Al kept dancin like a pair of crazed puppets worked by some psycho mannin a *Punch and Judy* show.

"Hey Lily, you like oral sex?"

"Getting or giving?" she asked giving a bump and grind.

"Givin it; I ain't no friggin muff diver."

"Ho ho, you're joking with me, Al." She flapped a hand.

"Ha ha. The frig I am, givin it's like lickin raw fish."

"Don't you like sushi?"

"Friggin Japanese are taking over the whole friggin country. First the cars, then the computers, now our friggin food."

"You crack me up, Al."

"Friggin A, Lilybell."

"Merinda over there says you teach at Kingsport." She nodded toward a white-haired witch from her coven who was a regular champion of folk art at the College. Merinda thought Al and Cal were the pastoral form of underprivileged urban types that get to paint murals and all. Course, the difference was, the disadvantaged city crowd had actual talent.

"Who?"

"Merinda Klauser—she's in your department," Lily shouted through the small cupped megaphone of her hand. Then she pointed. "Mer-in-da. Your de-partment."

"She ain't never been to my apartment." Al shook his head. "'Sides, now the school has given me and Cal a gatehouse. It's friggin awesome."

"Really. What's it like?" Lily was snappin her fingers like a gypsy and bent over slightly to ripple her enormously outsized cupcakes.

"We're friggin artists in residence, man. Me and the man. Friggin Cal." Somebody came round with a pitcher of the witches brew—which was a dull pinkish red like plasma—and Al held up his glass to be refilled. He drank it off and stuck out his arm for more.

"Have you done anything interesting lately?"

"Just fishing and shit. And teaching. Whatever."

"No, I meant art-wise."

"We got this project, it's like commentary on how screwed up American society is. Crass consumerism. It's, like, you know, beer cans," he said, drawin an outsized circle and pointing his finger down at the floor first, then lifting his arm upwards. "It's like ten feet around and goes right to the friggin ceiling."

"A pyramid of beer cans?"

"Christ, no, that's high school shit. We got a regular straight up circle—like a column."

"And it's—"

"It's in the living room. But now with that friggin 9/11 mother, we're gonna take her down and rebuild her squared off and then we're frigging gonna make another one, and fly like radio planes into 'em, one at a time and film the whole fucker. S'cuse me. I meant to say frigger, your Highness." He smiled. "Anyway, then Cal's gonna draw like flames comin out of the towers and smoke and shit. He knows how to do that shit, because he had a internship one summer at Disney."

"Really?"

"Yep—back when we was at D.C—"

"Dutchess Community?" she interrupted.

"No, Dutchess Correctional—it was just kid shit in high school, you know a little drugs, a little dealing, breaking into some old geezer's house; but the warden like wanted us to learn a friggin skill, ya know?

So Cal did like a course of drawing by mail. I coulda done the Iowa Writers School, but I was too busy."

"So it's going to be a film—" Lily said, changing the subject fast.

"Well, after it's towers, it'll be a film, yeah."

"And it's not towers yet?"

"Frig *no*—we gotta drink the other tower."

"Oh, I see."

"Cal thinks we oughta spray paint the friggin Bud cans a kind of blue color, but lettin the Budwiser logo sort of still shimmer through so we don't like lose the friggin social commentary shit, but I dunno. Paintin all those cans would be, like, a lotta work."

"It's a good idea, though ... and all art *is* hard."

"Don't I frigg*ing* know it! Makes my balls ache just thinking about drinkin that much beer," he laughed.

Lily laughed, too. Under the couch, Huck and I were tryin not ta choke.

Al leaned over and gave Lily's left party favor a little flick on the nipple part. "So's it gonna be your place or mine, Cleo?"

"Well, I guess that remains to be seen," she said, still dancin around Al.

"Yeah," he said, drainin the glass. "This crap looks like watered down blood, but it tastes great. What is it, anyhow?"

"Vodka and tomato juice and grain alcohol They're called—"

"Bloody Hangovers," he said. "I know."

He started to take a step, then abruptly wheeled around and more or less fell over or collapsed—as opposed to sittin down—into the couch. "You're aces, Lilybell," he said, then keeled over sideways. "Friggin aces, man," he murmured; then his eyes sank shut.

The cartoon kings and creators of rural kitchsh were both down for the count.

Skirts rustlin, breasts riotin, Lily exited through the French doors and hightailed it for the sunporch.

She looked mad enough to curdle milk.

CHAPTER FOURTEEN

TRICKS AND TREATS—
PETER AND LADY B

Meanwhile, me and Huck was starin at Al's big lumberjack he-man boots; he was still draped over the couch like damp laundry spread out to dry in a double wide trailer house. We was underneath the sofa, considerin.

"These here perfessors is bigger frauds than the duke and the king," Huck said.

"I'm agreed; they make the duke and the king look like Damon and Pythias."

"Tom, I got to ask you somethin," Huck paused. "Do we sound like Al and Cal? 'Cause if we do, I hain't never gonna say 'ain't' again." His eyes got rounder in the dim light.

"Nope. 'Cause we make sense when we talk—and we cain't help it if we was born with Southern drawls—'sides they don't drawl, they talk white trash talk."

"Tom, is we white trash?"

"You think Lady would adopt us if we was?"

He nodded. "She's quality, all right. That settles it."

"But my, Huck, ain't them two just fool jackasses? I wish we could play 'em a trick or two, but they're so dern drunken, it'd probly be a waste of our good time."

"Maybe. Maybe not." He grinned. "I got an idea—"

"Let's hear it."

We put our heads close together, whiskers touchin, and Huck he laid out a grand scheme. It was noble good, and it would pay back Lily Blum for her scurvy trick of forgetin on purpose to mail out the invites to Lady's party. It was a smasher. And I couldna done no better myself.

* * *

"What are you boys up to?"

It was Lady. The party was windin down some, and she come across us explainin our scheme to Earle and Teodor, known here in the U.S. as Ted. These two was the werewolfs that was her friends who owned the antique shop and the bowlin alley that she had told us about the first time she took us flyin and we had met them right after Lady took us in.

"Is nice costume, nice party, Bar-bar-a," Ted said to her. He meant Lady's get-up. Me and Hucky had convinced her to dress as the Wicked Witch of the West from that there *Wizard of Oz* movie. Mainly witches hated Margaret Hamilton—but me and Huck had watched that video a dozen times and we thought she was a heap more interestin than that sparkly Glinda, the good witch. Billie Burke doin that awful warble thing with her voice and that pasted-on perpetual smile gave me the fidgets. Old Margaret was so nice and green. Pointy, too. Maybe Lady's face was younger and rounder, but she had put on the rusty black hat and dress, plus a set of long curvy yellow nails, and her make-up was so good even her hands curled around the broom was the perfect sour green.

"Thank you, Ted."

"I have this honor." He gave a little heel-click and bowed his neck some. That was Ted for you—he didn't always make exact sense, but me and Huck reckoned that as long as Earle did most of the talkin when they was around Lily, that might even run in Ted's favor. Earle was from south of the Mason-Dixon line originally, but he didn't talk exactly like me and Huck. I guess it was on account of his wolf-y nature.

"Your boys here, want us to change clothes with those hooligans," Earle said, noddin at the still-passed-out Al. "They want us to take Lily for a little spin."

"A *friggin* spin," Ted said grinning. Huck and me had rehearsed him on the perfessors' speech patterns, and except for his Hungarian accent, Ted was doin prime.

"This Al and Cal good friends of yours, Barb?" Earl asked.

"Not especially," she said.

"They was invited here second-hand by someone else," I said. "A friend of Lily Blum's."

"It'd be a shame to disappoint Lily when she went to so much trouble to appear at her best," Huck said.

"And she was so taken with Al and Cal," I added, givin Lady a wicked smile.

"Harm, boys. Remember the wiccan credo, 'An it harm *none*.'"

"Cross our hearts and hope to die," Huck said; he spit on his paw to show her he was serious. It warn't no real oath, though, I knew. Not without blood writin like the times me and Huck done before.

"Even emotional harm is out of the question—"

"Shucks," I said. "You couldn't hurt Lily Blum's feelins with a steel bear trap and a Remington rifle to go in for the kill. This here's just a prank, Lady. An old-fashion' Halloween prank." I gave her my most innocent wide-eyed look.

"All right," she was hesitant; but she was gonna let it go, I could see.

"I'll get you, my pretty," Huck and I said simultaneously; then we laughed and slapped each other's paws.

* * *

"You think it's gonna work, Tom?"

"Lily was mighty anxious."

"Yeah, and mighty pie-eyed herself."

Anyway, it was a cloudy night and dark as pitch. So we just nipped off for the Tree House to retrieve the white Flokati rug while Earle and Ted loaded Al and Cal—just like you'd load up cordwood—into the back of their truck. Me and Huck was just floatin into viewin range when Earle opened the truck door and helped Lily climb aboard. Then we lit down gently between Al and Cal who was mostly hid under paint cloths and the rest of their junk; and Ted, now wearin Cal's—which was really Al's—fly fishin hat, winked at us and slid open the back window of the truck. Who'd a thought werewolfs would ever come in so handy?

* * *

Lily was sittin in between 'em and Earle was drivin and doin most of the talkin.

"Really," she said, "we could have walked. I practially live around the corner."

"But then we could not have had the pleasure of your frigging practial magic. Miss Dude," Ted said. For a werewolf and native Hungarian with naturally courtly ways, he was tryin. I'll give him that. His hand was on her knee.

"Ha, ha, Cal."

I caught a whiff of Lily's thoughts—she was good and liquored up herself, and she thought Earl and Ted was tryna speak careful—the way drunks'll do sometime.

"Whoops," Earl said, shiftin the gear knob on the floor and first sendin his elbow into Lily's breastworks and then his hand slidin up between her thighs.

"Ho, ho, Al," Lily giggled.

Huck rolled his eyes at me, but I whispered to 'im I thought it'd be all right since Earle doted on antiques, anyhow.

"I gave you boys up for dead," Lily said.

"The sight of you could resurrect a week-old corpse," Earl told her.

"A frigging corpse," Ted put in.

"Emm," she purred, while me and Huck hunkered down some under the canvas drop cloths, and Earl parked the truck under a huge old maple tree in front of her house.

* * *

I don't know precisely what Lily done to 'em—I'm not sure I want to know—and maybe you don't, nuther. It's plain gruesome just to contemplate.

* * *

First there was a smell that rose around us, you may say, like a swarm of mosquitos in a bog at sunset. I thought the stink was comin from under the canvas and emanatin from Cal and Al and the litter of sandwich bags, Big Mac boxes and beer bottles surroundin 'em—but it got riper than just a mere garbage stench, and after a couple more minutes had passed and I heard stealthy slurpin sounds from inside the truck, I knowed that scent for what it was. My olfactories let on it was gettin more potent by the second and pretty soon it was as strong as what comes off a wet hound in a Mississippi bayou; then it got hotter and more hellish and transformed into somethin like skunk musk.

Huck, he twitched his whiskers and looked up at me.

Meanwhile, we heard heavy breathin, then a rustlin sound—but it warn't the wind rushin through the leaves like Huck and me thought at first. It got louder; then we knew what it was: It was the sound of cotton cloth that is bein ripped to shreds and tatters.

The truck warn't even rockin—yet.

* * *

"Oh, my god!" Lily shrieked. "Werewolves!"

It warn't the full moon, but Lily's sexual antics had bulged em up and tipped Ted and Earle right over into the hairy beasts they was an 'most exploded the clothes off 'em.

The doors of the truck flew open.

Ted lammed out the right side, bristlin and foamin. He was still wearin the fishin hat, but the rest of his outfit was just gone—'cept a patch here and a ragged flap there. He threw his shaggy head back, howled, and scampered into the darknesss, and I heard him half-bark, half-talk through the daggers of his teeth. "Yes, oh yes, fifty yards are rabbits." He was just a streak, you might say, after that.

81

Earle was further along in his transformation and it was like a regular circus when a creature that was a wolf but as big as a man snarled and raced out the driver seat. I judged there'd be a deer or two less in Rhinebeck come dawn.

Lily was sittin inside with her hands over her ears.

We heard her sniffle twice. Sounded like she was rearrangin her clothes, too. And most likely, I guessed, that chunk of real estate she'd been sportin as a pair of bosoms.

"Fucking werewolves," she said.

She gathered herself up and walked slowly and daintily up the path to her front door.

"*Fucking* werewolves!" she said again.

When she got inside, she slammed that wooden door hard enough to rattle the windows of her house *and* the windows in the truck.

I hated to think what the percussion of that blast done to her cleavage.

Al and Cal slept on.

Their clothes'd been slashed to ribbons; when they waked they'd be drivin the truck back to the gatehouse wearin their skivvies. Which was none too clean. But Huck figured they might come sniffin round Old Lily again—seein as they'd think she was such a tigress she had ripped the shirts and pants right off 'em. His pap was a sure enough drunk and plenty's the time Huck told me Pap'd make up stories to explain what he couldn't remember. Huck always liked that part, 'cause when his pap got his tall tale factory goin he was a regular Arthur Conan Doyle for plots and machinations.

We was satisfied; we couldn't do no more, and it had gone as noble good as we planned and even better. There ain't no more serene feelin than that.

Me and Huck floated home on our white rug—contentment on a cloud.

* * *

We slept in the Tree House, so it was something of a surprise when we waltzed into the main house around noon and found Peter still hangin around. He and Lady B were in the dinin room. They'd cleared out most of the wreckage from the party, and they was havin a leisurely brunch—just the two of 'em. They had big glasses of orange juice, a pot of coffee, heaps of eggs and bacon, mountains of toast and muffins piled on plates, and what looked like every kind of jam Lady owned opened up in the middle of the table.

Me and Huck went straight up to Lady, one to a side, and put our paws on her legs—not to jump on to her lap—but just to say hello. She petted us both and said our names—and it was when she was ticklin behind my ear I noticed she was wearin a ring with a big light yellow jewel and purple amethysts circlin under the main stone. I didn't remember seein it before. I'd have tapped it with my paw and given Lady a questionin look—but I didn't have to—the back door squeaked open, then closed; we all recognized the footsteps ploddin through the kitchen. Lily was awake and back in action.

It warn't even ten seconds before she was through the swingin door and helpin herself from the platters on the table. She'd even hooked a dish and silverware from the kitchen on her way in.

"Some party," she began, scoopin sausage and scrambled egg onto her plate.

"How'd you make out with Al and Cal?" Peter asked. There was a big grin on his face and his voice sounded so innocent and his eyes looked so mirthful, I coulda kissed him.

"Hmmph," Lily sniffed. "Those two. What a pair of werewo—I mean, they were a couple of wolves." Her interest in breakfast suddenly tripled.

"Meaning they lacked a certain refinement?" Lady B said.

"They were *lacking* in every way. Including hygiene," Lily said.

Huck winked, then rubbed his nose with his paw, which was our signal to meet under the table when Lily was around. We gave each other high fives.

"I said to them," Lily went on in a Blanche Dubois voice, "you boys simply must not expect a lady such as myself to consider you as serious boyfriend material. Perhaps you do indeed teach at that institute of higher learning, Kingsport College, but I'm afraid we are hopelessly mismatched in terms of interest and intellect."

"What'd they say to that?" Peter put in around cuttin up a particularly plump sausage.

The real answer from those two scoundrels, Al and Cal, would have been something like, 'Go frig yourself, friggin Lily.' But she was on a roll.

"They were disappointed, naturally, seeing as they were both so taken with my charms—"

"And your dancing," Lady B interrupted quietly.

"And your costume—" Peter said. Butter wouldna melted in his mouth, but he forked in mouthful of sausage and chewed on it slowly.

"Yes, they were disappointed when I didn't invite them in, but I told them I believed it would be better if they returned to their own residence and sought female companionship of a type more fitting to their class and interests—perhaps some jolly *joie de vivre* girl—"

"You mean a bar whore?" Peter said, and I thought Lady was goin to spit coffee clear across the table, but she managed to keep it inside her mouth and swaller.

Lily warn't listenin to him though. "They sent roses—a dozen yellow roses—first thing this morning, exquisitely arranged by Hyde Park's most exclusive and creative florist, and I thought it would be a shame to refuse—"

Lily suddenly stopped yammerin, and her eyes near about ping-ponged out of her head. "What is *that*," she said pointing at Lady's ring.

"This?" Lady turned her hand around the fork she was holdin and tilted the ring toward Lily.

"That!"

"It's a champagne colored diamond surmounting three rows of amethysts. An estate piece, I believe. Four carats." Lady said at the same time Peter jumped in with, "It's Barbara's engagement ring, of course."

"Engagement ring!" Lily was postively apoplectic.

"Well, it's a rather nice way to celebrate a birthday, don't you think?" Peter smiled.

"But it isn't Barbara's birthday—"

"No. It's mine." Peter said. "I think it's a lovely custom—giving presents on your birthday. More fun, too." He grinned. "Like you said, Lily, 'some party.'"

You could have swept her off the floor with a whisk broom after that. She didn't hang around long after the big news, you bet. Her stock was flat and Lady B's was sky high. Take it all around, Peter had sprung his surprise noble good.

CHAPTER FIFTEEN

ENTRAILS AND OTHER MATTERS–THE DEVIL MAKES YOU DO IT–LADY'S BETE NOIR

It was a coupla weeks later and Thanksgiving was hovin into view; Huck warn't much on people food in general, but we both liked chicken livers and the entrail *things* that most folks throw away, so I figured we'd prob'ly dote on turkey innards, too. Not to mention that gizzards and hearts and such like is just perfect for prophesyin. You toss 'em up in the air, see where they land, and make your statement about what you see comin down the road in the future—'less of course your bloody organs and guts makes a shape that puts you in mind of the present. Or the past.

Sometimes you c'n make out a letter of the alphabet, and that'll be a clue. Or the strewn guts form a circle like a lady's ring or somethin that might be a house, a castle—or a chicken coop with a sprung door. It don't matter cause you got to go on *feelin* and *intuition* and you cain't never be wrong—not with the whole history of a man or a woman's life hangin right in front of you, so's the odds are all on your side. Most everybody—'less they lived inside a specimen bottle in a freak show tent their whole life—has had some experience with rings, houses and just about anythin else your prophecy machine can spin up. If they never saw no castle, you tell 'em "Well, you can dream, can'tcha?" And if they say they h'aint never seen no tiger which is what *you* see in those chicken guts, you look 'em square in the eye and ask, "Well, was you raised without no imagination or just born that way? Ain't you never seen a book with a *picture* of a tiger? Hain't you never gone to a *zoo*? Don't you get the Discovery Channel on cable or satellite out there in the boondocks and yet you say you *never* seen no tiger?"

Most of your subjects will back down right there, you bet.

Especially if you keep fixin 'em with your eyes.

And if they do hem and haw and actually admit ignorance— "Nope, never saw no zoo—Paw always said, there was no sense payin to go see animals what screeched when we had our own by the herdful what mooed all over the place."

Why, that's just pie. That's when you look em square again and say loudly, "This here is prophecy and didn't I just say you'll be *goin* to a zoo? In the future? This is the 21st century, and they have travelin zoos. And when you go, you can just bet your *last* dollar you're gonna see a tiger."

Then you just go on an collect the money from that squeamish huckleberry and tell 'em the signs is unclear as to what may or may not happen when they see that tiger. But one thing's sure—when they do, they won't forget what you said. It builds clientele better than the brazenest highwire act.

* * *

And there's more: Entrails is a whole sight better readin than tea leaves—me and Huck'll take 'em everytime. First off, gizzards are a heap bigger. Why, tea leaves is just *microscopic* alongside a nice fat chicken heart. And tea leavins and dregs are dirty brown; they're wet and they smell funny. And you want to remember, when you give entrails a wind-up and let them fall where they may, well, your bird guts spread around so a body can see 'em and little drips and splashes falls off 'em nice and gory-like. It's like decoratin your kitchen with chinese ideograms—and everybody knows just how popular Feng Shui is these days, 'cordin to what Lady told us.

Best of all, when you're done declaimin and lettin on what you see, you can eat entrails. It's the most profitable kind of prophecy there is.

And once they're down inside you, you can just bet there won't be any disagreements about whether that chicken neck or goose liver looked more like a angel or your subject's grandmother's alley cat.

Huck said it himself: If Jim had known about how grand entrails was, he'd a throwed his hairball clean away. Besides, who ever heard of making gravy or pate out of a hairball? There ain't no foie de gras cooked up from hairballs—not in your better restaurants where the quality go for fine dinin—and you know it.

* * *

Anyhow, meanwhile Lady had reserved a Thansgivin turkey from a nearby game farm and told us it was fattin up just prime, and she had a crowd comin to celebrate the day with her and Peter. And bein Lady, that meant natur'lly there'd be a lot of cleanin and bustlin ahead a time—but Peter was there to pitch in, and that took a lot of the burden off me and Huck. Not that we actually went around with dust rags and silver polish and spray wax and window cleaner—you understand; but before Peter was on the premises as a more or less permanent fixture, we had to act all interested whenever Lady went on a cleanin streak. And that cut seriously into our nappin time. It uses up a lot of energy watching somebody do that much work, and it's hell on the nerves and ears—especially vacuum cleaners.

And, bein a human, you may not know this, but all vacuum cleaners—yes, each and every one—is possessed by strings of demons. Even their names is fraught with the worst kind of evil: Eureka, Hoover, Electrolux, Oreck—if them ain't devil names, I don't know what would be. One company tried to slip one by the unsuspecting human public and actually called their spawn Dirt Devil—and you can go buy it right off any shelf in Home Depot or Walmart or wherever, but you're lettin Satan into your house sure as if you hung crosses upside down or adopted Rosemary's Baby or had a black mass said in your basement.

You've been overlookin this vileness for years—human frailty! And that is just the evil imp's ways to disguise itself all the better to fool you. You believe a vacuum is a convenience when it's a cloven-foot creature right straight out of hell.

What else in your house shrieks and groans and moves itself around on wheels? Hanh? What other infernal machine drops pieces of itself clatterin every time you pick up its vile carryin case? Vomitin brushes and poles and coilin hoses like unto a serpent?

All that dirt you collect in those little bags is actually not dirt. And it is not dust. And it is not dog nor cat fur nor little threads nor golden earrings nor dimes nor lint, nuther. No sir. It is pure and simple and plain for anyone to see that what you call *dirt* is Satan-sperm. And you save it in a bag, and it multiplies! In the night! Secretly! And every single time you take out Satan's tool, you are condemnin yourself further and sinkin deeper into the fiery pit. Never ever, *ever* to be released. Never.

In fact, if you have one lick of sense, you will go right now to the sacred shrine room where your vacuum cleaner is entombed, and you will douse its plastic body with holy water and take that vacuum straight out to the trash. I would advise burnin it, but I don't want you to break laws. But you'll see, when you pull it out and it starts shriekin in its high metallic voice and groanin as it caroms down the stairs and begins droppin pieces of itself all over the floor—then you will see that I am right.

Save yourself. Throw the vacuum away. And if you have more than one—or if you own one of its wicked hideous minions known as dust busters, quick brooms, or fast vacs—they are also in league with the evil one and must be exorcised as well. Minor demons can do just as much harm as the big mojo himself.

Trust me on this. You'll be glad you did.

* * *

Anyway, prophesyin, cleanin and consortin with the devil aside, Thanksgivin was comin closer, and one p'ticular Friday night when Peter was over to his vet'nary clinic, Lady decided to spiff up the altar room and have a little meditation and ritual. And me and Huck went upstairs to keep her company and help out as best we could—not with tidyin the room, of course, but in case she needed our assistance in any spells she might be hatchin up. And we hadn't forgotten our interest in transformin back into boys, nuther.

She had lots of candles lit and placed all around the room, and she was just sittin quietly, cross-legged, on the Oriental rug in front of the altar. Me and Huck snuggled close to her, but she didn't reach out like usual to pat us. Just kept her hands clasped and stared off in the distance. A little while later, she blinked twice and heaved up a sigh. Then she cleared her throat.

"Boys, I'm worried."

"What about?" Huck asked.

"Remember that prayer we said for my true love? And now here I am engaged to Peter," Lady paused.

"Seems to me like that would make you glad. What's there to worry about? Peter's crazy about you—and me and Huck like him just fine—except when he starts talkin up neuterin," I said.

"But that's just it," Lady said. "Not the neutering"—she smiled, givin me a quick fingernail scratch under my chin—"but what if that prayer was a spell and that's why Peter took to me?"

"Well, it worked—"

"Yeah," Huck said. "Ol' Lily Blum would kill to have a spell that worked anywhere near as good as that one."

"But if it was a spell," she said, "it won't last." Her voice rose up a little higher and her speech got faster. "If it was a spell, it'll turn and—well, I don't know what—but something bad will happen. Because it's dead wrong to *make* someone love you."

"Maybe Peter just came of his own accord," Huck said.

"I don't know," she shook her head. "I don't know if it was him or it was me and I've been meditating about it, but I can't seem to look into it clearly. If he's my true love, it's all right. But—"

"You said his name beforehand," I said, noddin.

"Yes, Tom, I did." She bit her lip. "The night we prayed, I cleared my mind and got my intentions right—but I could have been calling him without meaning to."

"Guess we'll just have to wait and see," Huck said.

"Maybe if it was a spell and it turns and somethin bad happens, it'll only be a little bad," I said.

"Maybe."

She put out the candles with her brass snuffer one by one. None of us left the altar room with a light heart. I didn't think Lady—or Peter—deserved any bad thing. Lady once told me and Huck the secret

91

to bein happy was to enjoy your pleasures the way children do. Adults, she said, forget that happiness doesn't lie in getting what you want or bein unhappy and miserable because you don't. Lily was like that—she was a hollow place that was filled with discontentment. She covered it up and pretended otherwise, but you couldn't come near her and not know it.

Anyhow, Lady said children are by and large happy because they get glad over things like the way the wind feels blowin your hair back, or the way the lawn smells after it rains or when they see the first snowfall of the season. And mostly, that's the way Lady was happy, and how I wanted her to *stay* happy. But it warn't up to me—if it was, I'd a given her a lifetime of May baskets and the taste of ice cream the first day hot weather comes. I'd have given her the smell of the river washed clean in spring; and the sight of the moon and the evenin star sparklin together—low on the horizon just before twilight. If it were up to me, I'd *know* Lady deserved all of that and more—and I'd have given it to her just to look at the light in her eyes, which was only a byproduct, you might say, of the warmth that lived inside her heart.

CHAPTER SIXTEEN

TRUE LOVE PUT TO THE TEST–
PART ONE: THE INTERNET

"Lady's mighty worried that she captivated old Peter usin a spell," Huck said. We were out in the backyard, enjoyin a little late autmn sunshine and keepin a sharp eye out for errant blue jays. Blue jays is tough eatin, but they are a world of fun to bring down on the wing, so to speak. Lady had a silver gazin ball out there on a two-foot pedestal, and it was prime for crouchin in the grass and using its angles and reflective powers to catch unsuspectin birds of all kinds.

"Don't I know it," I said, givin a little sideways glance toward the gazin ball, which was empty of bird reflection at the moment.

"Seems to me we could help her out," Huck said. He always was tenderhearted—and if he didn't have me around to keep him in line he'd a wore himself out doin too much for other folks. Not to mention how he protected Baby Theandromula from night terrors. Or, take the simple fact of moth patrol. All right, I was in agreement with Lady B on that one. The damn things would flit around half the night and drive a body crazy when they got inside the house. It was even more irritatin when they'd get me and Huck worked into a lather; and if we broke somethin tryin to bring one into line, Lady would hear that crystal crashin and come to wherever we were on the run. It was much better when they flew low at what the foolish creatures thought was some kind of stealth level. One swipe and you had your moth pinned, and it warn't nothin to get your mouth on it and eat it up. Then you got a pat and a treat (to take the nasty moth taste off your tongue) from Lady B, cause when you sqush a moth against the wall, they make a hell of a mess. But Huck went after the wasps that got in the house, too. Then he'd get stung on the rear and be sick from their poison ... well, he was tenderhearted, like I say. I told him time and again there was no call for yellow jacket police work, but Huck was a protector and a true gallant at heart.

"Seems to me, it wouldn't be all that hard to prove whether or not Peter is Lady's true love," Huck said. "And if it turns out he's not, well, we can still make sure she's not a bit lonely."

"What do you mean?" I raised an eyebrow and thumped my tail twice.

"See we can advertise on the Internet—and if her real true love shows, why so be it ... and if he doesn't, well, then it's likely it *is* Peter and that'll set her mind at rest."

"Advertise?"

"I heard Lily talkin about it ..." he said and gave me the inside track on an outfit called DateLuckDotCom and how we'd manage the whole scheme. It was a gem, all right.

Hucky was slyer than he looked—no two ways about it.

* * *

"First off, we got to create a name and a profile for her," Hucky said loggin into the site. "And we're gonna need a picture."

"There's a big box on top of the closet. We can knock it down easy. Let's cull through her collection and—"

"We just have to look at the ones she's already saved right here on the computer," Huck said. Well, I don't *say* it warn't easier than havin to act the part of a feline pogo stick, but there warn't no style nor a bit of danger to it. I fetched up a sigh, but Huck was already pressing buttons and lookin over pictures of Lady in the yard, Lady by the Christmas tree, Lady on beaches, on mountaintops and everywhere else on the planet.

"This here one's real nice," he said. "Look at that smile."

It was a photo of Lady sittin in her living room, legs stretched out some, and she was holdin Huck.

"It's supposed to be a photo of *her*," I started.

"It is," he said. "But this here shows her off as warm and lovin. Proves she is a animal lover." Huck gave me a wink. He's got a dry wit, I'll give him that.

"And it won't hurt none," I told 'im "that a bunch of randy bucks will be seeing cat and thinkin ... kitty."

He smirked, pressed the button, and we had the first step of Lady's bran-new life in creation.

* * *

"Says here now we need us a headline," Huck said, movin on with step two.

We couldn't see what the ladies had come up with, so we looked over what men had written as grabbers. There was lots of "Lookin for Ms. Right." "Tall, Dark, Handsome ... at Last!" "Nice Guy, Lots of Fun and Smart, too!" and the like. "Artist in search of Muse and Soulmate" seemed pretty bouncy. But, the best of the bunch said: "Attention, I have found Osama Bid Laden." That guy had a sense of humor, for sure. But it *was* yesterday's news.

"We can be funnier than that," I said. "Men like a gal with a sense a humor" I paced a step or two. "Take this down: 'Smart. Cute. Sweet. Filthy Rich ... and, uh, Highly Creative.'"

We plugged it in right alongside the photo of Lady. Then we answered their borin questions about height and weight (we knew our pic said it all) and religion (Other) and even though Lady warn't a smoker, we said she'd tolerate one if she had to.

Next we made up a terrific personality essay for her.

Here's what Hucky wrote with the help of spell check and an online thesaurus:

> I'm a former heiress who was born into what some would deem a fairy tale existence. Growing up, I spent time shuttling between our penthouse apartments and country estates. In summer, the yacht cruised to exotic

ports. Winters found us in Gstaad, Bern, and the French Alps. It's true I speak five languages, but it was a callow existence. My parents were more interested in what they could buy for me than in providing me with the true nurturance that comes with genuine, honest love and affection.

One day, while having my bare foot traced on a sheet of pale gray paper, I was debating whether the sandler in Portofino actually did better custom work than the one in Positano on the Amalfi coast. But did it matter, I was in Portofino, I mused—Then suddenly, and all at once, a vision that was a veritable lightning bolt struck me. Sandals were not important! It didn't matter! Like Paul on the road to Damascus, I realized my life was shallow. Filled with activities money could by, but otherwise, empty. A hollow vessel.

Thus, I gave away my fortune to Universities, Hospitals, Charities, Art Museums, vagabonds, wanderers, and the occasional gypsy.

As a result, I now live in somewhat more modest circumstances. And, although, like the rest of the middle class in America, I am forced to contemplate the mundane and concern myself with utility bills, car payments, and coupons for $1.50 off Tidy Cat Scoop Away, I have also found the deeper, more spiritual side to my soul.

Love and the simple joys of existence are always and forever more infinitely precious than diamonds and gold. Or furs.

Humor. Creativity. Kindness. Intelligence. Passion. A sense of fun—these are the jewels and riches I hold in highest esteem.

So.

Wow me with a walk in the woods, woo me with a wild flower, win me with the sincerity of your heart and the depth of your feelings.

You can guess how Huck's profile worked: We had 127 responses in the first thirty-six hours from eleven different countries and most of the continental USA. They were wild over Lady—she was an international hit.

* * *

It snowed that year before Thanksgivin even had a chance to come around. If Jim had been with us, he'd of said it was a bad sign for sure—and he woulda been dead on right, too. Even in Rhinebeck you hardly ever see the white stuff stickin to the ground that early, and we had what was practically a blizzard. Folks got tetchy and crabbed. It warn't so bad for me and Huck, because we had all of Lady's international correspondence to tend to. We was uploadin and downloadin photos by the dozens. Everytime we logged on, someone new had sent her a letter or expressed interest, and me and Huck had to make on-the-spot decisions about the worth of that man and whether we ought to write back or delete him the hell out of Lady's cyber life.

You could block a sender, express interest in the man or wipe him off your list faster than you can say, "Would you like to look at my etchins?"

It all happened—or didn't—with the push of a single button. Sittin at that computer was like bein a country leader durin the Cold War years—you had the power to press the red button anytime day or night and blast hell outta the opposition.

And on the flip side, Lady needed to check and see who was out there, cause it wouldn't do no good for her to passively sit back and just see who showed up on her screen. What kind of true love search would that be? So we had to look through more photo and personality files of men than a assistant editor at a major publishing house sloggin through the slush pile of bad manuscripts that come in over-the-transom—and it was just the same. Most of it was junk and hardly worth the time of openin it up for a look.

The trouble was gonna come when it came to the place when the man or Lady should be askin for a phone number for a chat and possible hook-up kind of meetin. We knew that, but weren't sure how we'd fix it.

"This here ain't just a nineteenth letter writing contest," was how Huck put it. "She's gonna have to talk to 'em an go out on dates. What should we do?"

"Lemme think on it, Huck," I said.

"Think away, just don't get too gaudy when you come up with a scheme."

But I just couldn't figure my way around it. How was Lady gonna talk on the phone—or harder still, meet someone for lunch, dinner or drinks?

"She can keep writin to the guy in Auckland and the other international folderol," Huck said. "They won't show up in Dutchess on a whim. But you got guys in Danbury, Connecticut and Raritan, New Jersey and just across the river in Newburgh champin at the bit to drive over here."

"We can delete the guy from Iraq—I think he's just a terrorist looking for a way to sneak into the country."

"Right," Huck said, pressin down on delete so that Aboud27 "Looking for Nice Friend, Girl" was just so much ancient history, you may say.

"Deletin and winnowin out the flock is a good start—lets us go through and get rid of as many as we can." We gave 114 of them the boot. We were down to twenty-five men or so that looked prime.

"This is good, Tom. We have eliminated a power of work, here." Huck said.

But there was two problems we didn't reckon on.

First off, every day more people lighted on to Lady and wanted to sweep her up—which meant you could almost never catch up. But secondly, Al and Cal had discovered the Internet; and they couldn't wait to spread the word on who was right out in the open for the takin. They didn't give a damn about Lily—but they were flabbergasted to see Lady floatin around cyberspace. I never would have guessed either of them two could run a computer, but it's always the little things a body don't count on what trips 'im up. Anyhow, they got on to Lily with the big newsflash about Lady ... and Lily ... well, Thanksgivin was comin. A day when gratitude is supposed to be everyone's watchword. Lily, as you may surmise, was grateful she found out ahead of time that Lady was seekin out men for "a serious relationship that might lead to marriage."

As for me and Huck prophesyin on it—twenty sets of turkey guts wouldn've done it—a familiar woulda needed a crystal ball the size of the globe Atlas sports at Rockefeller Center in New York City to see this one comin.

CHAPTER SEVENTEEN

TRUE LOVE PUT TO THE TEST, PART TWO–
THANKSGIVING–LILY–THE BENNETT CLAN

The table in the dinin room was set with Lady's best linen. China and crystal glasses spangled alongside her good silver. Every place had a little decoration of paper leaves and pumpkins and a homemade chocolate turkey sittin in the center. Bein Lady there was scads of candles; take it all around, it was a festive sight.

The guests was scheduled to start arrivin around 2 p.m. And the pies had been set out on the sideboard, and the turkey—in the oven slow-cookin since the crack of dawn—was sending out the most larrupin good smells a body can imagine. Me and Huck don't even like cooked meat and we was salivatin.

Lady was in the kitchen doin last minute things to vegetables— summer squash, and corn and cranberries and potatoes and asparagus and mushrooms. She'd put out a big platter of cheese and crackers and such in the livin room so's folks could work up an appetite before they plunked down at the groanin board; and she'd set up a little wheeled bar with soda and wines and sherry and such if they wanted a drink before they dined, too.

Not includin me and Huck, we was gonna be thirteen at the table. And I didn't like that number. I couldn't say why, but it was puttin me in mind of the Last Supper. I told Lady, too, that mornin when she was layin out all the places.

"Now who's superstitious? she laughed, tickin her fingers to add up the crowd. "Let's see," she said. "Peter and myself. His aunts, his mother. His sister, Delores, and her boys. Lily—oh, and Peter's cousin, Wade."

"You mean to say," Huck thumped in with, "Peter scared up a escort for Lily."

She flapped a hand. "Just someone for Lily to talk to—"

"You mean talk the ears off of," Huck said.

"—Or hornswaggle into thinkin she's the *big* stuffed elephant prize on the top shelf at the shootin gallery, instead of the plastic spider *booby* prize under the counter—"

"Thirteen's bad," Huck said. "Cain't Peter invite another guest or two."

"It would be so last minute—it'd be rude," Lady said. That was like her. Me and Huck was getting the jimjams just lookin at the table with its thirteen glasses and thirteen plates and thirteen napkins and thirteen chairs, and she was worryin about etiquette and social graces.

"It wouldn't be considered rude to Earle and Ted. Why doncha call up Earle and Ted and see if they'd like dinner that sets still for a change—"

Huck took me right up on it. "I bet theys never even had no traditional Thanksgivin dinner. Seems to me they'd just dote on it."

"I bet Huck's right. I bet nobody hain't ever invited Earle and Ted to Thanksgivin, cause they're afraid their table manners won't be up to snuff. And I bet they feel real bad about it, too. I would if I was a werewolf—"

Lady fixed me with a good, hard look. "Seems to me as I recall, Huck couldn't stand being 'sivilized' over to the Widow's—and was just pining to break loose and get away from collars and clothes and rules about sitting still—"

I gave 'er one last shot. "Yes, but that was back in the 19th century and now that the milennium's come, ain't it important to make someone feel welcome and equal regardless of their background?"

"Hmmph," was all she'd say. You cain't put nothin over on Lady—she knows when she's hearin twaddle and poppycock and specious arguments. "Anyhow," she wound up, "there's a stack of plates and tons of silverware wrapped in yellow napkins, right here," she said, tappin the sideboard. "So *anyone* who drops by can just draw up a chair and tuck in if they want to." She tightened up the strings on her apron, retyin it tighter around her waist. "So much for *thirteen*," she said, disappearin back into the kitchen.

We was just cats—there warn't a thing we could do about it.

* * *

The doorbell was bongin at 1:45 and the first of the Bennetts was wipin their feet on the mat and hurryin into the hall out of the cold.

Me and Huck started off at the landin at the top of the stairs peerin through the spindles to check out the crowd. Lady came through the kitchen door, dryin her hands on a dish towel, and Peter did the introductions. There was his Aunt Bess, his Aunt Caroline—and they looked as much alike as me and Huck did—they had gray hair cut short, and they both wore dangly earrings and wool trousers with silk blouses. Their husbands, Peter's Uncle Bob and Uncle Chuck, flickered in behind them. Peter's mother—Jane Bennett—gave Lady a hug and said she was proud to have her in the family. Delores had her three kids in tow: a set of ten-year-old twin girls with smooth blonde hair, and a little wretch disguised as a human boy child—and that was where the first trouble sprouted. I shoulda known—havin been a boy, myself; but I'd been focusin on that number thirteen and wonderin which one of the inviteees was gonna play Judas Iscariot.

The young one, Drew—a six-year-old brown-eyed devil in a bowl haircut—saw me and Huck at the top of the stairs and our day of woe began.

"Kitty-kitty-kitty!" Drew screamed and took his hard-shoe shod self runnin up the stairs and soundin like a fast break thunderin over a basketball court.

"Kitty-kitty-kitty," he shouted in time with his feet.

"Cain't he count," I said as me and Huck scattered fast.

"Hain't his mother never heard of sneakers?" Huck said flyin alongside me. We lit out for the altar room. Delores was shoutin

103

something down below to the effect that Drew musn't run. She might as well have been tellin a storm cloud not to shed lightnin.

We hid out under the desk listenin to Drew clackin around in the hall lookin for us. "Tommy, Hucky," he crooned. He was openin doors and linen closets and slammin into bookcases and tappin the heels and toes of those damn Sunday best shoes so loud it was like a ruler bein smacked on a wooden table. I already had a headache that made my ears squinch flat and Lily warn't even here yet. I judged me and her 'arranged date,' cousin Wade, was gonna get along fine.

Hucky said not only was his ears hurtin, but Drew was makin his eyes cross. "And I ain't even Siamese, Tom." I gave him a lick alongside his ear to comfort him, but I was powerful glad we had a vet in the family—even if some of the time I didn't trust Peter around the knives.

Drew's eye lit onto Lady's computer; he wouldn't be a six-year-old boy if he didn't want to investigate. We was under the desk and Drew's fingers was a hailstorm, you may say, on the keyboard. "'Puter games," he was singin. "'Puter games!" when Peter entered the room to retrieve him and, simultaneously, rescue us. The doorbell rang again. We heard Lady call from downstairs, "Let him watch TV on the computer, if he wants, till dinner's ready," and then her voice was lost in another rush in the hall, and I judged it was Peter's cousin arrivin at the front door nearly in synch with Lily's landin-invasion on the back porch.

But up here in the altar room, Peter was hesitatin. Drew sat at the desk chair and his feet were wavin around and undulatin like a vicicous underwater plant growth what can drown a swimmer; and we was avoidin his calves, ankles and hard shoes like mad. Huck eased out alongside the chair, and I followed him. And we both saw the problem at once.

In his haste to get Drew settled into a TV show or video, Peter had pressed Run and what came up was the last Internet address—for the datin service. And perhaps, unable to help himself, he looked at the site. 'Course to find out anything, he'd have to log in with Lady's Date Id and her password, but he was puzzled.

There were people countin on him to play host downstairs, so he found Drew a cartoon and headed back down the hallway.

Huck and I exchanged looks, and then before Drew could snag us or yank our tails or pat our heads the way boys do—as if they are poundin bugs into oblivion one hefty tap at a time—we scatted.

* * *

Dinner was in progress. We waited till Drew flew past us, and then we hung out in the hallway, eyein the party through the crack in the double slidin doors. Everyone was more or less fallin to, and there were a lot of raves about Lady's cookin. It was our first chance to really get a close up on the Bennett family—which we surmised would be around a lot in the future. Peter's aunts was cheerful; their husbands Chuck and Bob seemed nice enough. Bob told a joke about a preacher and an old maid, and everybody laughed politely. Delores looked a little harried—as many a single mother might. She was older than Peter and thin in an unhealthy lookin way.

Lily chatted some with the group but most of her stinky conversational debris wound up flung at Wade—her talk was just so much silt cloggin' up a riverbed. She was gettin his vital statistics about where he worked and what he did and what his hobbies were, and when it came out he was divorced, Lily toted out her own war stories—plus her usual declaration 'bout how she liked doin housework in the nude. She sort of choked down the last word, since there was minors at the table—I'll give her that, anyhow.

And then it happened. Long about the time the gravy was just startin to congeal inside its silver boat and everybody was sighin and wavin their napkins and pushin back a tad from the table, Lily wanted to know how Wade generally sought out female companionship.

"Do you meet women at church, or your job, or do you go to clubs?"

Wade, who was somewhere in the midrange of his forties, 'llowed as how occasionally he did go to bars, and that while occasionally he met a nice woman, it wasn't his favorite happy huntin ground.

Lily decided to play the first pair of cards in her hand, so to speak. "Have you tried one of those Internet dating services?" she asked, and oh boy, you bet, me and Huck just perked our ears straight up. Takin another sip of white wine, Lily went on. "It's not a bit like the old personal ads—there was a long article in the New York Times," she said, implyin not that it was a newspaper but the voice of God, "about how twenty-somethings use the services all the time, and how they don't see it as an act of desperation, but just another avenue to meet singles."

"Did you know I read somewhere, thirty-five percent of people who use dating services are actually married?" Delores hove in with.

"Well, it pays to keep your options open, I guess," Lily laughed. I was about to lay off that remark to her own remote past, but Lily was like a riverboat gambler with poker fever, an quick as blazes, she threw down her full house while every one of 'em was settin there looked stunned and skint. "I've advertised on a couple of those networks, and of course, *Barbara* has, too."

Huck put his head down and gave a little mewl. We knew Lily, and she warn't about to stop—not before she scooped up all the cash and left the losers flabbergasted.

"What's your ad on DateLuckDotCom say, Barb, 'Cute, Smart, Rich'?"

Lady looked blank. Peter looked horrified. I couldn't stand to look at his aunts and his mother and sister.

"What are you talking about, Lily?"

"Your current ad. Al and Cal told me all about it. In fact, as a kind of joke, they marked your interest box."

"But what makes them think it's me—"

"Why, your photograph of course—right here in your living room with the cat, with Huck."

Lady turned a sort of reddish shade then went paler. She started gatherin up plates, and she bustled into the kitchen.

Lily flapped a hand. "Oh, Peter, half these things are just to while away the time. I got twenty-seven responses in one week—and half of them were from bongo players in the Netherlands. It's a game. Doesn't mean a thing." She snatched her party favor chocolate and bit off the turkey's head, chewin daintily.

Peter looked miserable and embarrassed at the same time. Lily, now that she'd set everyone's teeth on edge, was urgin Delores to send in a profile and chirpin at Wade about some thirty-five-year old construction worker with tattoos on his back moonin over her and floodin her email box with about ten misspelled messages a day. The construction worker had hair down to his rear end and wrote music no one was interested in. He was, like Lily, a regular artiste. Or, more likely, another Ravin Lunatic.

I wished he'd gone just that little bit further and written to ol Lily thirteen times; maybe she woulda gotten a big dose of bad luck and she wouldn't be sittin here right now spoilin Lady's holiday.

CHAPTER EIGHTEEN

MOMENT OF TRUTH–
LOVE AMONG THE RUINS–MAGIC

The farewells from the Bennett clan were subdued. Peter's mother held his forearm when she kissed him goodbye, sayin, "We'll be in touch." After his aunts left and Delores rounded up her crew, the tension and silence between Peter and Lady rose higher. They cleaned up the kitchen together, but there was no laughter and no banter and little talk; just the dull clang of the silverware and the sound of water runnin in the sink. The refrigerator door seemed awfully loud everytime Lady opened it or closed it to stuff in the leftovers. But as terrible as these noises were, they were nothing to the sound of Peter's feet movin up the stairs to the altar room—and the computer—after everything had been tidied down below. "'Puter games," he whispered. "Games."

Me and Huck told Lady we was the ones behind the DateLuckDotCom scheme; but how was she to let on to him that her cats done it? Peter didn't even half-suspect Lady was a witch and we was her familiars.

We coulda hypnotized 'im into forgettin the Internet datin business—not that it wouldn't a been a power of work with his mother, sister, aunts, uncles and cousin harrangin him everytime they had him on the phone. And not that you can't guess how those conversations would go: "Far be it from me, Peter, to tell you not to run around with a slut who is two-timing you already." I mean there warn't any question Huck and me coulda held our own—clear up to the "Weddin March" down the aisle—and we woulda done it for Lady, but—there it was. The reason it all started in the first place was starin at us like the glazed eyeball in a dead fish: she wanted Peter on true love's terms—not witched into a lovesick calf with no more brains than wallpaper paste.

* * *

And before I move on with the story proper, so to speak, I have to put in a few of Mr. Twain's idears about cat lovin versus the human kind.

Cats are pretty much catch as catch can when it comes to spoonin. Humans, though, has got to add all kinds of gimcrack and gingerbread—like true love. But you take swans, say, what mate for life. Why do they stick together? Because swans know that raisin issues just wrecks the hell outa marriage; so swans never worry about which way the toilet paper is put back on the holder. Swans don't never correct each other's grammar mistakes—most 'specially in front of comp'ny. Swans don't go out of an evenin with the boys—or the girls—and come home breathin hundred-proof fumes that would pickle an oak armoire; nor at four in the mornin with their brassieres or jockey shorts on backwards. Swans do not even use toilet paper. And cats don't nuther.

Cats know how to save up their emotions for when it counts. Me and Huck love each other tops, you bet. And your ordinary cat's gonna most positively adore the human that's feedin it, cooin at it, and letting it sleep anywheres it wants in the house. Cats is smart that way. As smart as swans—or maybe smarter—since cats can come inside a house and curl up right alongside a hearth fire, and swans is forced by their very natures to sleep in ponds and live their entire lives with wet feet and cold backsides. Which is prob'ly one more reason they mate for life because swans is already so miserable by always being draggled and wet, they have no energy to argue about somethin as stupid as whether the ring is up or down on the toilet seat, or whether or not their swan-mate is sayin somethin with a undertone what sounds downright patronizin. Or hostile.

Take it all around, swans is like Russians or Eskimos. They're so grateful to find a body in a big cold country what can plant his warm bottom next to her cold bottom and to have an actual critter of the same species anywheres within a hundred thousand square miles what can fend off the damp a little, that they shut up when it comes to issues. You can take it from me and Huck and Mr. Mark Twain—and if he didn't write this down nowheres, he thought it plenty a times— humans can learn all they need ta know about lovin from the animal kingdom—most 'specially cats.

* * *

Peter sat in front of the computer lookin at the screen, his mouth scrinched in a frown. Me and Huck knew he couldn't access Lady's account what we created without her password. But he could, as a trial member, browse around the profiles. And he done that and naturally, Lady's photo come up pretty quick.

I don't think he cared all that much about who she was attractin. For my money, it was the principle of the thing that was gallin him. Here he loved 'er and there she was trollin the cyberspace ocean for some other catch.

I watched him from the hallway. He folded his hands and gave a little sigh. A few minutes later, I heard Lady comin up the stairs—and so did he.

"Well, you can't deny it," Peter said, as she crossed the threshold. His voice warn't angry; it had the sadder sound of someone who was resigned to a cripplin fate. My heart was sinkin. I'd almost ruther he was shoutin—much as cats cannot stand the sound of raised voices.

Lady came and stood next to him. She even put one hand on his shoulder and stared at her own image and the profile me and Huck come up with.

Huck crept close to me, and we waited to hear what she was gonna say. If she denied settin up her date-packagin, she'd have to explain the whole witch thing. Whether he *was* her true love or not, I was sorry we got her into this mess. That's not to say she and Peter

111

would have gotten on all right in the long run, but in the short term, I liked Peter a hell of a lot. Peter had heart. Sure he was smart and did all right financially, but that day at dinner—before Lily sent everythin to hell in a handcart—I watched how he acted—not just with Lady, but with the rest of his relatives. He was terrific with his ten-year-old nieces. He even got along with the never-to-be-tamed-wild-boy-of-Larchmont, Drew.

* * *

Drew had got bored pretty fast at dinner. His mother had him clamped down enough so he warn't about to start throwin the Pillsbury biscuits at his sisters, but he was makin everybody nervous.

First he tipped over a glass of water; then when he reached for it, he sent two wineglasses tumblin into pick-up-stick status. The people nearest him—his grandma and his mother and his sisters—got busy moppin up the tablecloth, the plates, and what have you, and generally wieldin big fistfuls a paper towelin everywhere. Meanwhile Drew sat kickin the mahogany table leg with his foot.

"Eat your dinner, Drew," Delores told him. "The boy eats like a bird," she said to no one in particular, and for the moment she was so flustered, I guess she was forgettin that birds eat twenty seven times their own weight every day.

"Dinner," he repeated. Drew tipped his head back a little and opened his mouth good an' wide. I thought he was doin a jumped-up version of the old airplane routine. You know, that game where the nearest adult makes buzzin and zoomin sounds and feeds the child gobbets of food flown on the fork and straight on in to the hangar.

But no, he picked up on what his mother said and started in on flappin his hands and draggin his good shirt cuffs 'cross his gravy-laden plate. He was singin, "Baby bird, baby bird, baby bird."

A nanosecond later, he sprung up from his chair wavin his arms and took off runnin around the table, zig-zaggin into the walls, the furniture and the other guests—like a panicky sparrow what comes down the chimbly and into the house by mistake.

"Sit down!" his mother screeched, sounding pretty bird-like herself.

He flitted over to his plate, ate one forkful of mash' potato and took off again. He was too smart to stay cornered in the dinin room. Arms spread, he flew through the swingin door into the kitchen, pounded across the tiles—and by then I guess he swallered down his food cause he was chantin "Baby Bird" again.

He caromed through the door that led to the hall and zoomed past me and Huck into the dinin room. He'd grab a forkful a turkey, or say, carrots from his plate while he was on the wing, so to speak. He did the circuit three more times around before they got 'im to sit in his chair again.

Me and Huck watched from across the hall. And if it had been up to us, we'd have used any means—fair or foul—to keep that kid permanently attached to his chair.

"Krazy glue," Huck said. "Lasso him up like you do with a runaway steer, grab a holt of 'im then stick 'im to the seat. What's trousers and expensive wood compared to peace of mind?"

"Chains would work, too," I put in. "And you could padlock him ever so easy—seein as Lady has those openwork chair backs."

Huck nodded in agreement. "Tape. Lots a duck tape. He couldn't lift a foot nor squirm a inch; and with the extra on the roll, you could keep his mouth sealed in the bargain."

Everybody in the room looked uncomfortable—this was before Lily's hot newsflash—but it was Peter who got Drew to calm down and behave. He did it in a way that every boy would love and was guaranteed to work; to work so well, you could start to feel there was hope for the human race after all.

It was simple. It was genius. He showed Drew magic.

"How many fingers do you have, Drew?" Drew looked at Peter like it was a school-quiz question. That didn't faze Peter none.

"How 'bout you, Delores? How many do you have? Mom?" He looked his mother square in the eye, and she caught on.

"Ten."

Delores chimed in with her ten, and he turned to Drew again. "How many fingers?"

"Ten."

"Well, it's the oddest thing," Peter said. "But I have eleven."

"No—"

"Yep. I do." He held his hands up and began wagglin his fingers, countin right to left. "One, two, three, four, five." He began to fold down the fingers on the left. "Six, seven, eight, nine, ten. Hmm." He paused. "I was sure I had eleven. Let me count again." Now he spreads his hands wide and starts from the left side. "Ten, nine, eight, seven, six—and five!" he said, throwing in the right. "That makes eleven! Six and five is eleven! I knew it all along."

Drew looked astonished enough to stuff the remainders of the turkey carcass into the big O of his mouth. Everybody else began to laugh. He wanted to see it again, but Peter plunged straight ahead.

"My hands are so magical, in fact, that I can make silverware float in the air." Peter went round the table peerin down at the utensils and spielin his patter. Nope, that knife didn't look right, nor that table spoon. After a minute or so, he lighted on Drew's unused silver knife. "Ah, this looks likely." He picked it up. "Nice balance to it, too."

He set it down on the tablecloth crosswise; then his palms hovered above it, his right hand grippin his left wrist. He gave a grunt and raised up his arms; but the knife sat there.

"Darn," Peter said. "You know, I think I need everybody to concentrate. Everybody keep your eyes on that knife, and when I say three, shout 'Lift!'"

Well, he went into his antic, counted, and when they shouted "Lift," up came the knife seemin to cling like a magnet against his skin. A quarter of a minute later, he said, "I can't hold it any longer,"and let it fall with a clatter back onto the table.

"Wow." Drew was awestruck.

Next, Peter did a coin trick with a quarter he borrowed from his Uncle Chuck and made it disappear through the table, then reappear; then move from under his "magic elbow" into "hyperspace." It reappeared in Drew's hand.

As a finale, he borrowed his mother's yellow dinner napkin and made it mysteriously knot, then unknot.

Everyone clapped. The conversation got lively again. And Drew— well, you just knew that boy had found a hero. When they was leavin, he threw his arms out huggin tight and said, "I love you, Uncle Peter." You could see he meant it, too.

* * *

Magic routines aside, me and Huck was feeling mighty bad; Peter had shown how worthwhile he was. Not too many people could have turned Drew's fussin into the whole family gettin along and havin a good time and enjoyin theirselves. And Drew, he was positively in a froth of happiness. Nope, not everybody coulda done it—not by a long shot.

Lady had the measure of Peter, but I guess she warn't ready to come clean with her witchery. So she kept mum. "I don't know what to say, Peter," was all she came out with.

"My feelings haven't changed, Barb," he said softly. "But it looks to me like we need to step back from this relationship. I'll see you and we can talk—but I guess I have to give you time to find out if it's what you want. I guess—and this might be hardest—I have to give myself time to find out if it's the one for me, too."

"Oh, Peter, I'm so sorry. I wouldn't hurt you for the world."

"Time will tell, I suppose." His voice was lead.

She slid the yellow diamond ring off and put it in his palm. "I can't ask you to let me keep this while we sort this out."

"But if we do, if we do, Barb—the day I put this back on your finger I'll be the happiest man in the world."

She nodded. There were tears glimmerin in his eyes, and I guess he didn't want to cry right there in front of her. So he went; but before he did, he put the ring deep in his pocket and held her shoulders lightly and kissed her forehead.

The house went deadly quiet, then. Sorrow has a way of suckin vibrancy from everythin around it; and the house drew into itself on that account.

PART 2:
THE CHANCERY
HOUSE

CHAPTER NINETEEN

GRAND FUNK–YULETIDE–
INNKEEPER'S SECRETS

For the next little while, me and Huck and Lady was more or less at odds with one another as you might imagine. We'd lost Peter for her and, even if it was Lily who really tipped the candle, she wouldna had no news to spread if we'd stayed the hell away from the damn Internet datin' service.

"We was only tryna help," Huck told Lady sadly.

"Well, thanks, but now I think you've helped enough," Lady said.

"But it ain't fair for you to be madder at us than you are at Lily Monster," I said.

That stopped her for a moment. We was all three in the kitchen. She was at the stove makin herself a scrambled egg supper and me and Huck was at our accustomed places sittin on the table and grabbin a mouthful now and then of crunchies from our kitty bowls. She swirled the eggs with a wooden spoon slowly twice more and said, "Well, I guess that's so—"

That's all the openin Huck needed. "Say, listen," he said swallerin fast to make his point, "at least me and Tom had our hearts in the right place—cause we was tryna help you determine if Peter fell in love on

119

his own account or not. And, we figured if he didn't, we'd make sure you warn't alone afterwards—"

"Lily, on the other hand," I hove in with, "knew damn well she'd cause embarrassment—at the very least." I gave a little hmmph and added two thumps and a tail swish for emphasis.

Lady drifted over to the table carryin the scrambled eggs turned out onto a plate. She sat down across from us and forked a mouthful.

"Yes, but I still want you to erase all that stuff off the Internet. I'm not really interested in meeting anyone—not that way." Her chest hitched a little, and I knew she was missin Peter. He'd called once or twice, an while they weren't warrin, they weren't cozyin, nuther. She took another bite, then sipped orange juice.

"We'll delete your datin' profile ... we promise."

"Okay," she said, then gave us a little smile. It was partly a sad smile, though, I thought; I didn't like to see Lady drawin apart from us.

And it turned out it warn't just us—Lady drew a circle around herself like you'd draw a cloak over your shoulders to keep out the cold. Most of the time she sat readin' in the library or under the cashmere throw in her office. I sure felt bad, and I judged me and Huck owed it to Lady to make it up to her 'cause these days the only one comin to visit was Lily—and she had no more sense than a brass straight pin and would just natter along and not even pay any mind to how she was pricklin and scratchin Lady's sensibilities. Lady needed company. Company that could cheer her up an make her eyes light and her cheeks sparkle. Aunt Polly's heart was broke when she thought I was drownded; and Lady's was near about broke. It was the third week in December, and there ain't nothin' lonelier than the thought of Christmas without the person you love most.

Lady had taken up readin and re-readin in Mr. Tennessee Williams; he was her favorite playwright, and you recall she named her former familiar after 'im; but when I sneaked in the library one night and looked in on that play of his, *Summer and Smoke,* I liked to die and was just plain heartsick thinkin about those doomed, star-crossed lovers. Lady, I judged, was headin for the worst kind of Christmas heartbreak there is—all on account of that meddlin Lily Blum.

"C'mon, Huck, we're goin on the Internet again," I said just before dawn and pullin at his collar with my teeth to get him to wake up. I gave him a light swat.

"We ain't supposed to; 'sides, we already deleted the profile," he said, then yawned. He rolled on his back and covered his eyes with one paw.

I bapped him again. "Get up, we gotta write some of that e-mail—or Lady's gonna slip into a blue funk and no tellin what'll happen to her or us—" I didn't think she'd start takin up with sorry men like that poor Miss Alma in Mr. Williams' play, but I warn't takin no chances.

"Okay, okay," he said. "Who we gonna write to?" He yawned again, then trotted after me toward the office. "We cain't write to Peter—she'll kill us."

"Hush up, now Huck. She needs a diversion. We're gonna write to—" I was thinking fast, 'cause of course I hadn't no plan formed, just a sort of vibration, as you may say. "To Earle and Ted. Yes, we'll write to Earle and Ted and invite 'em over."

"Earle and Ted," he said. "Werewolfs. Yeah, that'll make a nice diversion."

He gave a little sigh, but he slid onto the chair and got Lady's computer up and hummin.

* * *

The next night about 7 p.m., Earle and Ted showed up just like they had dropped in to spread a little impromptu holiday cheer—and just like we planned over the course of about thirteen emails in the previous twenty-four hours. We'd told 'em we wanted Lady cheered. We'd told 'em we didn't want her to know we invited them. We told them about how Lady had taken up readin in Mr. Tennessee Williams. We told him about Miss Alma—and Ted, bein tenderhearted naturally, even got a little sprig of holly to pin to Lady's collar—just like in the play. Earle bought a bottle of wine and a poinsettia.

"Bar-ba-ra, darling, we have not seen you in so long, we wanted to stop and bring you Christmas joy and glad tidings," Ted said.

"Hi Barb," Earle kissed her cheek and leaned in towards the hall from the porch.

"This is merely our good wishes; we come to visit on a whim," Ted said.

"C'mon in," Lady said and stood aside.

"Thank you Bar-ba-ra, and here is some charming plastic holly to pin on your coat and a lace-trimmed handkerchief," he said giving a little heel click and his patented formal head dip. When Ted gets on the investigating side of things, he does it up, I'll say that. 'Course, he was givin Lady the presents what was handed over to Miss Alma by the girl who ends up stealin her boyfriend—but I guess he didn't get to the part with that ugly little twist in his readin.

Anyhow, Lady fetched a deep sigh. That cotton handkercher was beginning to seem like he'd brought it as a cryin towel.

They hung their coats on the rack in the hall, then all three of em trooped into the livin room, and me and Huck listened in. Lady got some wineglasses off the bar.

"No tree, Barb?" Earle sounded a little shocked.

"Well, I thought, well ... I mean there's still time," she said. But we were all aware she was avoidin the subject.

"You must allow us to help," Ted said.

"No—"

"No, I insist. Bar-ba-ra, this is not right that you should be here alone without a Christmas tree. I would not let a dog in a manger suffer so."

Pretty high praise—comin from a werewolf, too, wouldn't ya say? And Lady was perkin up some. I reckoned she didn't have the heart to giggle outright at Ted, but smiles was leakin around the edges of her mouth.

"All right," she said, noddin.

"And Bar-ba-ra—" Ted said, puttin his hand across her wrist, and soundin very serious—even for Ted, "this will cost you nothing, because I know just the place in the forest to get a tree for you. A gorgeous balsalm—unless you prefer Scotch Pine?"

But that did it. Naturally, Ted would know where in his huntin grounds he could lay hands on a tree; and I'm sure there was a time or two he lifted a leg to use the trees for other purposes besides Christmas decorations. Lady couldn't help but laugh. "The woods," she whooped. "A balsalm will be fine."

All three of 'em snorted, and Ted said, "Come Earle. We go now, in the truck."

Ted bent over and kissed Lady's hand.

"One hour, dear lady. We are back with the tree and all of us shall make merry and put it up."

"B.D., get your decorations down from the attic. We're having a spur-of-the-moment tree-trimming party. And if you have any eggnog, get it in the punch bowl pronto!" He gave her a quick kiss. We heard them grab their coats, and shut the front door. Less than a minute later, they roared past the front windows in Earle's truck.

Lady stood there a minute. "Dear Earle and Ted," she shook her head. "The dearest friends." Then she stopped. "But what am I thinking; I've got to get the decorations, and the lights—"

Ted and Earle had galvanized her into action.

"Told ya it would work," I said to Huck.

"Yeah, and Tom, they's bringin a tree right inside the house, here!" His eyes went about as big as a pair of sleigh bells. "A living tree!"

"Hmm."

I warn't about to admit that in my delight that the scheme was already payin off, I clean forgot to get excited about our first Christmas tree.

* * *

Four hours and six pails a eggnog later, me and Huck was just baskin in Yuletide glow. There hain't nothin like sittin under an actual tree in a livin room. Unless of course you count climbin up in it after everyone has gone to bed for the evenin, or out shoppin for the day. But meanwhile, Ted and Earle had come up with a bran-new plan to get Lady back into circulation, and that's what they was talkin about while they sat lookin back and admirin their handywork.

"Bar-ba-ra," Ted began, his accent even heavier on account of the drink, "it is not good that you live here in this big house all alone." He held up his hand. "Yes, I know that it is not lost cause with Peter, but still, you need something to occupy you."

"What Ted means," Earle said, blushin a little, "is that you should open a Bed and Breakfast—"

"I don't want a lot of strangers trooping—" she stopped. "Listen, I *hate* getting up early in the morning—"

Earle put out his hand. "But we would manage it for you."

He let that one sink in a moment.

"Ted wants to sell his business."

"It is too ultimately degrading to run a bowling alley—"

"And, as far as my antique shop, well, we could convert the garage and use that as a shop. The Internet and e-Bay make it ridiculous to pay rent on a regular place, anyhow."

She was startin to listen I could tell. Leanin forward and she warn't interruptin none.

"Lots of B & B's have shops—you could put in specialty items, stationery, baked goods, knickknacks, art work—just about anything along with the antiques. It's just another added attraction and natural selling point," Earle said. "Me and Ted could convert the loft above the garage to our living quarters—"

"And Bar-ba-ra," Ted added, "we will pay for the conversion and all the labor, so you will not be feeling you have spongers or interlopers descending on you, eh?" He tipped his wineglass.

"It's a natural, Barb. Plenty of Bed and Breakfast inns advertise 'cats on the premises, literary leanings'—you must have a zillion books around the joint—'and hauntings'—should a guest want a night in a haunted room. Hauntings are big."

"Sounds like you two did quite a bit of research," she said.

Earle blushed. "It's just a plan that makes sense, that's all. And we'd all be helping out each other."

"And whose idea was this? Why do I have a feeling the furry princes of the Internet," she looked at me and Huck, "had a paw in this?"

"It was kinda mutual," Huck said. He wrinkled his nose in a way Lady was particularly fond of and licked her wrist. "And with Earle and Ted runnin things ..."

"We would only need a little less than a week off every twenty eight days," Ted said solemnly.

She clapped her hands over her mouth, tryin not to giggle at the thought of the two of them transformin.

"But we could still do breakfast," Ted said. He smiled and then stopped, a little anxious—I suppose—that he was literally lookin long in the tooth. "What do regular hu—what would guests prefer, do you think?"

"Mostly eggs," I said fast, thinkin Ted was on the verge of suggestin a nice presentation of racoon tartarre or some other ghashly thing.

"And speaking of haunted inns, why they are real popular. There are tours that specialize in doins like that all over New Orleans. All over the country, really. People even pay to stay at Lizzie Borden's old house," Earle said.

Huck has a cry that sounds like "Noo—awh," and he let it out now. We all turned to look at him.

"No! Uh-uh. You couldn pay me to stay in no house where no crazy woman murdered her natural pa and ma with no bloody axe. No sir," Huck shivered. "It hain't natural and would give a body the shakes 'n sweats just lookin at the place from the outside. It was bad enough when I pretended like someone kilt me with a axe to escape Pap—"

Earle cut in. "And the haunted places are smart—lots of em list under the 'Haunted Inns,' section," he said. "But there's not a word on their own website about rubbing elbows with the disembodied. So those who know about it and want a ghost can ask; and some guests visit and don't even know the house's repuation."

"Me and Huck could help design the website," I put in—which I suppose gave us away for the Internet snoops we were. Because of course, we'd been all over the damn thing lookin at sites, checkin how the Inns looked, how they advertised, where they advertised. The whole shebang. But we figured Lady could make some money—heck, the house was just sittin there; and it was a big place. Lizzie Borden's old stompin grounds was about the size of a French subway car—and that ain't a lot of house. Hard to believe you could swing a cat in there, much less a axe.

But if you have ever seen one of them horror movies where some uptight knife-wielding coed gets mad at her roommates what generlly taunt the life out of her, and has to wreak havoc and revenge just to get a little ordinary peace of mind, you'll understand why Lizzie decided to do away with fifty percent of the population that was clutterin up her little home on Second Street. Generally speakin, slashin and stabbin with knives and axes is a real motivator for most folks to stand back and give you all the space you need.

See, I read in this here book called, *A Private Disgrace*, that her father was a regular tightwad—and even though he could have afforded the stateliest mansion, he made his wife and two girls live in a place that was so narrow it squeezed em near about breathless. His cramped house, you might say, was just an exact match for his limited mind-set and miserly leanins. Meanwhile his wife, Lizzie's stepmother, was a fat, whiny recluse. You get a tightwad and a shrieking tub of lard what you have to obey and what furthermore *never* leaves the premises in a house *that* small, and it ain't gonna be long before you start thinking how lucky the hound dog across the street is, because at least he has his own *goddamn* house.

And you know teenagers is really the same the world over: Lizzie liked hijinks and antics—and space to cut a rug. And, even if she *was* upwards of thirty, she'd been suppressed and held down for all those years so she was like a young girl. It was Victorian times to boot—and it don't take no Sigmund Freud to know that gal's natural love of freedom and desire to make her own mark in the world was just *bound* to erupt. She didn't want to be plain old Lizzie Borden livin on the wrong side of the tracks—she wanted style. Who wouldn't? She even changed her name to Lisbeth after she was finally out on her own.

Yep. Bein true to her dreams and movin up in the world was important to her; so you could say Lizzie B. was practically a regular feminist who understood sometimes you gotta leave convention behind. And you cain't make no omelette without breakin a coupla eggs. So, it's no wonder she bought herself a great big Xanadu after her parents died of unnatural causes. The girl needed breathin room— that's my guess. In fact, Lizzie's method of finding room to grow and a means to express her feelings worked so well, that her older sister stopped living with her, too. Which was fine with Lizzie since Emma was a regular party pooper, and Lizzie liked the high life and cuttin loose every now and then.

And if the itty-bitty Borden house could have a museum and a gift shop and tours and people clamorin to sleep and eat in rooms where murder was done, I thought payin customers'd positively *flock* to our place where the supernatural was our byword. But we can leave that argument for now; more importantly, I figured if things still continued to be at a standstill with Peter, maybe one of Lady's guests would take an interest in *her*.

"Movin on to those who request a cat or two to keep 'em company, me and Tom's reservin the right not to sleep with certain guests," Huck said. "I'm not gonna lay down with kickers or sneeezers nor anybody who smells funny."

I nudged him to shut up. We was goin good again now and didn't want to create any headaches this early in the scheme.

"No snorers, nuther," Huck said and I bapped him again. You just cain't get him off a subject sometimes.

"Books, cats," Lady ticked her fingers. "What about the hauntings?" Her eyes were bright, she was intrigued, but her mind warn't made up—not yet, anyhow. "Old as this place is, I don't think any famous axe murderers ever lived here."

"Oh, we can half-glimmer if we need to," Earle said, takin a sip of eggnog. "And if you throw a sheet over me or Ted, when we fade in and out, we'll look ghost-y enough, I guess."

"Let me sleep on it a night or two," Lady said.

But I already knowed it was a smasher of a plan—especially with Earle and Ted—who was *gen-u-ine* werewolves—livin on the premises and helpin out—and that she was gonna say yes.

As for the hauntin aspect, I thought we could import a coupla Lady's vampire friends on the nights Earle and Ted was off. Or, if that made Huck too nervous, we could borrow Lily now and again—she'd scare the pants off anybody who spent the night and thought they wanted to see an apparition in the flesh. So to speak.

With the right lightin and sound effects rigged, we might even catch us a bran- new suicide or human who'd die of a broken heart. All the prime inns with the best and liveliest ghosts had pucks of em—and they raked in customers almost as often as the vampire or the voodoo tours in New Orleans, and the supernatural is a lot more interestin and a much bigger draw than your everyday axe murder scene—leastaways, that's what *my* research showed.

CHAPTER TWENTY

THE INN–NAME GAMES–
CHRISTMAS EVE

The truly excellent part of this plan was the way it naturally faded Christmas into the background for Lady. Instead of mopin about how she'd sent Peter and herself into a tailspin, she got caught up in the details of the new arrangements.

Ted got the bowlin alley sold right off the bat; the new owners was gonna turn it into a animal shelter, and Earle give his notice on the monstrous rent he was payin on the antique shop. His lease was up, anyhow. They set to work with a will, first transformin the garage—what had at one time been a great big carriage house—into a first-rate lookin shop. You can't beat werewolves for action.

In the meantime, Earle transferred his stock into Lady's basement and attic, and we all started makin suggestions for the website, for decoratin the rooms at the inn, and plannin what other kinds of goodies we wanted to sell in the shop.

But the first order was what to call our business. 'Most everynight after we ate supper (we, bein me and Huck and Lady, since Ted and Earle preferred to snack on fast food somewhat later in the night), we had us a big powwow in the dinin room.

129

"I like The Hideaway," Earle said.

"Gott in Himmel!" Ted gave a little shudder. "Earle, what are you thinking? We don't want *gangsters* here," he said, crossin himself.

"I wouldn't mind a robber or two," I said—but Lady and Huck flapped at me.

"Clover Farm," Huck said.

"There's no clover. And no farm." We all said at once.

"Maple Moor," I said. At least we had a big maple out front.

"Sounds like a ice cream flavor," Huck countered.

"Retreat," Lady said, "how about something with the word, 'retreat.'"

"Sounds like a convent," Earle told her.

"Castle Haven?" Ted was near about desperate to get the word castle into the thing, him bein from the old country and all.

Then Lady got the name in a flash: "Chancery House."

We all looked at her. It was good. I liked it; you could tell we all did.

"Chancery House. It will look nice on a sign," Ted said, nodding.

"I know a sign painter," Earle added, which was helpful, since Ted's ideas on signs was still mainly influenced by Bowl-a-Rama-type neon. "He'll do a great job."

"And by the way," she added, "chancery also means hopeless predicament."

She covered her mouth with her hands and began giggling like mad in that pretty way she has. And that got all of us laughing. But The Chancery House it was.

* * *

Lady had five bedrooms in the house—not includin her own and the little altar room-cum-office. Huck showed her on the Internet how people named the various rooms in their inns. Sometimes they used colors as in "The Green Room"; sometimes they named em for people what owned the house long ago or lived in the area. We was goin literary, and we was goin for ha'nts—should a guest want to give theirselves a little *frisson* and a coupla goosebumps—and that stirred up a big debate on what to call the rooms.

"God, I thought we were done with this naming business," Lady said.

"No ma'am," Huck told her. "And, what's more, what we call these here rooms will determine how we decorate 'em up and all."

"I knew this was going to be more trouble than it was worth."

"Steady now," I told her.

It was Christmas Eve, and the three of us were in the livin room— me and Huck were hangin out near the packages. An unsurprisin number of 'em contained lumpy things that smelled distinctly of cat nip. Every now and then I'd lean over and sniff one, and when Lady warn't lookin, take a surreptitious bite of wrapping paper. I had one gift 'most chomped through before too long, and I was closin in on another that felt to be a cookie-cutter shape like a big dopy puppy, but smelled like heaven. I couldn't wait to sink my teeth into it and then bat it all over to blazes and back. There's nothin like abusin your natural enemy and winnin the battle each and every time. I was gonna pounce that catnip-stuffed dog till he popped and split like a Victorian party cracker.

Meanwhile the lights was blazin on the tree, and Lady had some beeswax candles lit around the room and stuck up ever so pretty in wall sconces. Earle and Ted had gone to Midnight Mass; well, that's what they called it, but I think then they was gonna try for another kind of mass—a deer, or mayhap some other festive flesh to celebrate, if you take my meanin.

We wouldn't see 'em till it got near dawn.

"Literary. Ghosts. Hauntins." Huck said. "What about callin one of the rooms after Washington Irving?" He hopped up next to Lady on the sofa.

"Oh, God," Lady said, "If I hear one more reference to Rip Van Winkle or Sleepy Hollow in this area, I will cry." She covered her eyes briefly, but I think the paper-rustlin noise got to her. She glanced over at me. "Leave that package alone, Tom."

It was hard, but I scuttled away from the dog that was a catnip treasure—inwardly, I was wishin it was Christmas mornin, but I turned to the immediate matter. "You have about a million books," I said. All right, it warn't a million, but she had pretty close to four thousand ... she could catalogue those things and use 'em to decorate and have enough for a little library in the sunporch to boot.

"What about names like these here?" I asked, "Playwright's Corner, British Mystery, Humoresque. ..." Avoidin catnip dreams and temptations, I was countin literary sheep, so to speak: Tennessee Williams, Arthur Miller ... Agatha Christie ...

"And 'Things that go Bump in the Night' for the attic," she finished. "I like it, Tom Sawyer. I like it," she nodded.

"And it just leaves one more category," I said.

"What should it be?"

"American Genius," I grinned.

"Long as you stick Henry James in with the Brits," Huck said. "The man is postively thorny. And borin. And Mr. Mark Twain would have about seventeen conniptions bein alongside of him."

"If we made two rooms out of the space in the attic, we'd have enough rooms in the Inn to create a brand new genre, Lady said. "Truly Soporific Bedtime Reading." She laughed, "With—say— Boetheius—*The Consolation of Philosophy.*"

"I ain't never heard of Botheratious, but for all of me, you can lump in that ol Pap Hemin'way and F. Scotch Fitzgerald," Huck said.

"No, you better put them in with the rest of the Americans, or you'll just tick people off," Lady giggled. "But I truly hated Steinbeck's *The Pearl.*"

"Faulkner."

"Hey," Lady said, "I like Faulkner. But what about Lucius Apuleius' *The Golden Ass*, or John Locke's *The Second Treatise of Government?*"

"Sold." I didn't know them books, but I knew what she meant. "We can give 'em their own shelf an call it 'The Be Glad They're Dead Writers Society.'" I snickered; we was just horsin around a course, an we all knew it.

"We'd only have to put about fifty of each kind in the room ... too many books in a bedroom is gloomy, anyway," Huck said. 'Course, Huck warn't what you'd call a famous reader. The bright visceral splash of the Internet was much more his speed. If we ever became boys, he'd be a hell of a programmer—or a hacker, I judged.

"It's Christmas Eve," Huck said. "Let's us go on over to the Tree House and the three of us take a little spin on the Flokati rug ... I'd sure like to see all the lights and decorations."

Lady stood up at once. "C'mon boys, we're off."

* * *

It was just a beautiful night for flyin. Crisp and clear and a little wisp of a moon. Down below you could see the lights shimmerin in the towns and here and there spangin off the river. There was a newish snow cover on the ground, so the white set the lights off even prettier. The wind was maybe a little cold, but we hunkered up close next to Lady, and she kept us warm.

Some of the churches was ringin their bells 'long of midnight and twice I heard carrollers singin away in those sweet voices. It was a wonderful night.

"Looky there, Tom!" Huck said. "Ain't it glorious?" It was one of the little towns all done up with lights strung across the main street, shop windows lit with yellowish, welcomin glow, and a huge tower of a tree in the square with great big gaudy soap bubbles of lights.

Huck was enchanted. We circled around it three times and at the last, a train went snaking by and tootin at a distance and making the snow crisped scene more perfect still. "It's like a fairyland," Huck whispered. "A fairyland come true."

"I love you, boys," Lady said, givin us both a little squeeze where we was nestled under her arms. The moon had lit up her face, and her hair was blowin around and her eyes were bright and alive. Most alive I'd seen 'em for a month or more.

"Merry Christmas," I told her.

"Merry Christmas," Huck said.

She scooched us again. We snuggled closer, and we three rode on into the night.

It was prime, you bet.

* * *

It was perhaps an hour and a half later when we parked the rug and sped laughin back into the house. "Let's poke up the fire and open presents," Lady said.

We skittered into the livin room.

But the fire was already blazin. In addition, there was a small table set up with a bucket of champagne, some fishy smellin snacks—which

133

back then we was too young and stupid to know was real Beluga caviar—and a new pile of presents under the tree. A man stood with his back to us, warmin his fingers. He turned.

"Merry Christmas, Barbara."

It was Peter.

Me and Huck scattered quick as mice and left 'em to it.

But I sure wished I'd snatched that catnip-stuffed dog before we fled. They was havin Champagne and caviar and all; and what's fair is fair. Me and Huck coulda used our presents and a little Christmas Cheer ourselves. But that's humans for you—always makin out like their handwringin emotions and heartwarmin celebrations and teary-eyed reunions is more important than what happens to cats. I'd bet anything old Lizzie Borden thought all the mayhem and folderol she stirred up was more important than a cat's feelings. And any cat livin in that house woulda been downright appalled by the screams and bloodstains and the ruckus of police troopin in and out afterwards. Cats is naturally sensitive to loud noises. Take it all round, blood's messy and cats 're neat.

Humans can act so completely obsessed and consumed with theirselves and their enterprises and activities, it almost made me wish that me and Huck'd never be boys again. Well, sometimes, anyhow.

CHAPTER TWENTY-ONE

LADY'S SECRET–
COAL IN OUR STOCKINGS AND UNDER OUR SKIN–
WHAT CHRISTMAS WROUGHT

Me and Huck had been lurkin in the upper hallway for pretty near an hour. We was powerful sleepy, and it was a little chilly up there, but we was waitin for Lady to come up to bed.

"She musta told Peter by now," Huck yawned. "If they's spoonin down there, no tellin what time they's gonna come up." He paused; his eyes went brighter. "Let's each witch just *one* itty bitty present up here. I want my Christmas."

I thumped twice. I'd never realized what a tail can do to get your mind around a subject. There ain't nothin that can hardly beat it for gettin the idea mill goin. "Well, I want mine, too," I told Huck. "But if she hain't told Peter yet about the witchery, what's he gonna say when he sees a pile of gifts floatin across the livin room?"

"What if we mentally tugged 'em real slow-like, like they was on a string?"

"This here ain't no stunt on *Candied Camera*, Huck." I turned my head and looked at him. "Anyway, I *know* you're thinkin about that big

135

mammoth in red candy cane paper that's in front of the tree—you ain't focusin on no teensy-weensy catnip mouse toy—"

"Do you think it's a TV set or a Cat Condo?" Huck's eyes were very wide now.

"I *knew* that's the one you had in your mind and the one what'll be glidin up here like some possessed an whirligiggin U-Haul box out of *Poltergeist*—"

I would have given Huck another piece of my mind, but just then we heard Lady and Peter in the hall by the front door. I peeped around the corner, just in time to see him give Lady a quick kiss and then head out onto the porch.

"Now what," Huck sighed, and I nudged him some to be quiet.

But Lady knowed we was there, and she called up to us to come down and join her in the livin room for a bit.

"Oh boy, we gonna have us our Christmas!" Huck made his *chirr-uppp* noise—which was a happy sound; but somehow I had the feelin things was not gonna be festive and convivial. Huck fairly bounced down the stairs; but I took a slower pace.

Huck practically dove under the tree, and I saw Lady was gonna let him have his Christmas and enjoy himself and that she was waitin to say whatever she was gonna say. But I couldn't get no pleasure out of gifts when she was so tense-lookin; and openin presents like that—well, the atmosphere just weighs on a body and as long as I warn't gonna get any fun out of it, I'd ruther have the bad news first and get it out of the way.

"Hold up, Huck," I said. Then I looked Lady in the eye. "You got somethin to tell us, and I'd a heap rather hear it now—when it's like this, hangin in the air, I cain't tell how bad it's gonna be, and that just shakes all the glory right out of all those star-covered packages and surprises."

"Oh," she said in a small voice, "but this isn't something you can change or do anything about." She lifted one shoulder in a shrug. "I thought you might as well have a bit of fun before we talked about it."

"No ma'am," Huck said. He had a small green squarish lookin gift between his paws, and I knew he was just dyin to play with its gold ribbon as much as what was inside, but he let it go and turned right around to face her on the sofa. "No. I'm agreed with Tom. It's not even daylight yet. You go on and tell us, we'll have our Christmas in the mornin."

"Do you know a play called *Bell, Book and Candle*?" she asked. She said it like that, but I knew she meant me, and it didn't take no John Van Druten expert to guess what came next. It was a witch play, and I dipped into it aplenty and read it out to Huck, too.

"What? You mean that old wives' tale is true—I don't believe it," I said; but I was just tryin to buck her up.

"It is, indeed. When a witch falls in love with an ordinary human, she loses her powers."

Huck rubbed his nose. "You goin to give up witchery?"

"I don't know what to do. I don't think I can help being in love with Peter."

"Maybe it's only true 'cause you think it's true," Huck said. "Maybe if you didn't know that story, it wouldn't happen that your powers has fled."

"Well how's she gonna un-know somthin she already knows?"

"I saw a hypnotist once," Huck said, "what made a townie-boy act just like a chicken. If that there ponce could forget he was human and decked out in blue silks and white satins to boot and go struttin and peckin and scratchin 'round a stage, a story oughta be easy. We could hire us a hypnotist and get him to make Lady forget that old wives' tale."

She shook her head. "I don't think it would work."

"Anyhow, maybe you're just overtired or have a touch of flu or somethin," I said. "Are you sure they're really gone?"

She fetched up a sigh. "I can't even do the simplest things." She focused on the tree, and I guessed she was gonna make the lights blink or turn into candles or turn the whole magilla into a two-story birthday cake—but nothin happened.

"But you flew with us," Huck said.

"Exactly right." A tear glimmered on the edge of her lower lid. "You boys did it, and I was along for the ride."

That give me an idea—and an idea, well you know an idea is just another kind of hope, and where there's hope, there's life. "Well if a bunch of stupid dogs can minister to blind people, I guess me and Huck can take over till this here gets straightened out." I puffed my chest out a little. "We can do *your* witchery—"

"Instead of bein 'seein eye dogs,' are we gonna be 'doin tricks cats?'"

"Yep, and it'll be just as easy as johnnycakes and flapjacks," I said.

"With m'lasses," Huck said, and we slapped high fives and gave Lady a pair of grins.

"And no chance of me and Huck decampin like that sheep in cat's clothin, Pyewacket, who up and left poor Gillian flat in the play." I meant the witch what lost her powers in *Bell, Book and Candle* and had her a sorry Siamese excuse of a familiar—he just lit out when she couldn't witch no more.

"And the movie," she added. But I could see we'd cheered her up some. It was like when Aunt Polly was so touched because I *really* did kiss her when I come back that night whilst we was still hidin out on Jackson's island.

"You can count on us," I told her, and I meant it. "We're gonna stay and we're gonna help."

"You boys are true hearts. Yes, that's just what you are."

"Yes'm." It was pretty much what Aunt Polly said.

"I think I've just gotten the best Christmas gift yet," Lady said, stoopin over to pat us and then nuzzle us and get all girly-lovie. Well, the hugs were nice—I loved it when Lady touched us any way at all—but, I wanted my catnip and my Christmas, too.

I licked her cheek, then I pounced on a knobbly-lookin package bound up in silver tissue. It crackled ever so satisfyin under my paws, so I lowered my head and got it between my teeth and gave it a shake. Heaven. And I hadn't even started chewin on the ribbon yet.

* * *

Well, by and by, a lot more came out regardin this here witch business what Lady was now not only inclined, but postively on the ropes—so to speak—to share with us, since me and Huck had to perform her duties. First off, the reason she decided to go ahead with the Bed and Breakfast was because her powers were gone. Witches are funny creatures. And, like most humans, they do things in a way what cats do not understand. You take a cat who wants to cross a room or jump on a table. Your cat will go about this task in the most straightforward fashion and usin the least amount of energy—and never mind the broken crockery in his path.

But humans are forever goin after things in a roundabout manner. And witches is the worst at this. Say they want money—do they just send out a spell to the universe 'bout "Bring me here a great big pile of spondulicks and to hell with the IRS?" No, they have to tote in all kinds of useless notions about whether they're harmin someone, or whether if what they want that money for is to buy a house and whether they should just wish for the house *itself*, and then some miracle will happen like someone who knows their cousin Clara's aunt's best friend's daughter will suddenly take it in *her* mind to move to the English countryside, so she is lookin for someone to house-sit in Barnegat for three years so their livin expenses will be free—or some equally bothersome nonsense, and they call this labyrinthe "asking for what you really want."

I say, get the money—then your options are wide open, and it might be *you* living in splendor in a foreign country with nothin more to do than daydream in the hammock while pucks of gardeners are stakin your dahlias and servants are tiptoein toward you with trays of mint-sprigged ice tea, and you can ponder the munificence of the four secret numbers that open the gates to the untold millions in your Swiss bank account—what cannot be traced. Or you might want to go on a cruise, buy a wardrobe or start a newspaper. See, the point is—once you have that *money*—a two-room summerhouse on Cape Cod might seem like a three-week vacation in hell. But you cain't tell witches nothin—they're as stubborn as mules.

Anyhow, before I give account 'bout all the new chores me and Huck had to take on and how much work it was to start gettin the house ready to become an Inn and keepin Ted and Earle's huntin proclivities in line, I suppose you will want to know about Christmas and Lady and Peter and all, cause most likely if you are readin this you are a human and humans are always curious about each other's doins—which is just the opposite of cats, which are curious about more important things: Like the best nappin spot in the house at ten in the mornin, why a bra strap is danglin out of a dresser drawer just beggin to be swatted or chewed, and which mouse hole still has live mice.

* * *

Lady told us that Peter was strugglin with his feelings. He was willin to go so far as to bring over Champagne and caviar, and he still cared, but he was still in a wait-and-see mode. Near as I can recall, their conversation went somethin like this:

"This is a surprise."

"You didn't think I'd forget Christmas?" Peter was itchin to take her hand or kiss her hello but Lady saw she would have to make the first move to reassure him. He'd already gone out of his way to ease tensions with the visit and all.

"And champagne," her green eyes glimmered. She went to the bucket and ran a finger over the label. He'd brought Piper Heidsieck, which he knew was her favorite.

He opened the bottle and it popped; then poured the froth into two champagne glasses he'd already set out.

"To the end of this year and the beginning of the next," Peter said.

"Merry Christmas," Lady looked deeply into his eyes. They kissed, lightly, then each sipped, and that seemed to seal the friendship—at least—that was between them.

"I have a couple of presents for the boys," Peter began, still hedgin a little, you see.

"Nothing too vettish, I hope," Lady giggled.

Peter picked right up on it. "Well, I thought they'd just dote on rabies shots! Not to mention there's an anal thermometer and vaseline, plus a really swell metal examining table and a digital scale you can just step on like a welcome mat—"

"Oh boy, I can just guess what you must have brought me," Lady said.

He pinched her cheek. "Ah. A speed dialing component and a microphone for your computer and one of those cameras so you can see who you're talking to on the Internet ... and they can see you. So, streetwear is advisable."

He was beginnin to get his sense of humor about the thing, anyhow.

She put a hand on his knee. "It's all erased, Peter. I know that doesn't change the fact that it was done ... and, well, there are some things I could explain that would make you feel better right now, but we'll let it go for the moment."

He nodded, but truth to tell, I don't think he really listened to or understood the last part of her comment. He was human and humans don't like unpleasantness. He just wanted to slide past this hard part and be easy with her again.

"Let's have some of the caviar while we open gifts."

He'd laid it all out on little red plates with toast triangles and chopped egg and onion—even if Beluga is just fine all by itself. Now he spread a canapé and handed it to her and they sipped a bit more Champagne and chatted.

"Open that one, Peter," she said. He smiled broadly, and Lady could tell he was genuinely pleased that she'd bought him presents.

* * *

Well, they'd gotten each other four or five gifts apiece—things like sweaters and books—nothin you'd call overtly romantic, though they'd both taken care with their choices, and Lady was pretty het up about a Aeolian Harp he'd gotten her. Peter, he still held on to her ring; so it was just one of those things where the trust was goin to have to be rebuilt—if it could be at all—and that would take some time. And you already know about their kiss at the door and how they left it that no matter what, they'd be good friends to one another, and they'd try spendin more time together, but they was back to square one. It was gonna have to be a new beginnin or no beginnin at all.

* * *

Me and Huck made out like bandits that Christmas. We had more stuff than any ten children spoiled by their parents and grandparents put together. There was catnip toys galore, a kitty condo with about a million yards of tunnels and snuggle spaces so you could wriggle up inside it and pop out of a hole that was miles off the ground and perch and look down with menace at enemies and dust mites. There was a real glass fishbowl with scads a flashin neon an' angelfish swimmin in it—an' another 'quarium program that Hucky said it'd shuffle itself till kingdom come on the computer screen and this here cyber-sea had all kinds a cartoon porgies, and hot pink wall-eyed pike, and 'lectric blue saugers dartin back and forth; and I reckoned Lady give it to us in case the live ones died on us—or got ate up in the excitement of a game or two. There was sardine snacks and wind-up mice and all manner of things—and not a single flea collar or examination table in the lot—Peter's jokes nothwithstandin.

The day itself was quiet ... we had a big breakfast, and then Earle and Ted hove in lookin like they'd been sleepin in the woods, and Lady commenced to fixin a big spiral ham and we was all havin a pretty good day. Right up till Lily Blum decided it was time to drop in with a plate of stale cookies so's she could drink wine for free and spread some yuletide gossip and misery.

* * *

Earle and Ted had decided to do a little more sheetrockin downstairs in the former carriage house that was about to become their shop. They had a radio goin out there, and every now and then one of them would come into the kitchen for a drink of water or somethin else they needed. Meanwhile, Lily was perched on the sofa by the Christmas tree in the living room, and Lady was entertainin her. In the way of witches, not only had Lily and Lady exchanged Christmas gifts (a crystal ball and a embroidered pillow that said "The Witch is In" ... so, Lily got the better of that deal since the crystal ball–a real beauty—weighed in at about $70, and the homemade pillow Lady received had a big wad of dog fur stuck to its purple velveteen back and defintely had that "recycled gift" look), but their familiars exchanged gifts, too.

Lily's familiar was a black Labrador named Coal Porter ... and he pretty much lived up to both those names since Lily had him trottin back and forth to fetch mail, newspapers and anything else she had a mind to ferry around her house. It was pretty much a toss up who hated him more—me or Huck—and we was defintely not thrilled with the idea of havin to get him a present when Lady mentioned it was a witch rule.

"He has that hot stinky breath he's always breathin on you," Huck said the day Lady told us about this ugly gift tradition.

"And he's always pantin," I said. "So it's like he uses up all the good air around you and puts out this fog of doggy body heat, dirty fur and Alpo."

"You just don't like dogs," Lady said to both of us.

"What's to like?" Huck said to me under his breath and snickerin.

"He thinks playin consists of droolin on a rubber toy and practically goes into 'poplectic fits when the damn thing squeaks. As if every rubber dog toy in the *history of the world* didn't make that ugly noise when you bite on it," I whispered to Huck. "He's not the brightest animal in the world," I said out loud to Lady.

"Well, he's just a puppy, sort of—"

"He's the size of a sheep," Huck said. "You call that a puppy?"

"And if his brains have been juiced up by bein a familiar, I cain't imagine what he'd be like as a ordinary dog," I said. "Probably somethin with all the personality of a cement birdbath—"

"Or a squashed cigarette butt."

"Okay, okay." Lady shushed us. "But you still have to buy him a gift."

"What would he like?" I said. "A package of organic dog poop to sniff? Dogs love nosin other dog's leavins—"

"How about a pair of old smelly chewed-up sneakers? We could give him one now and save the other for his birthday present." Huck giggled and hid his nose against my ear.

"Boys, you are not being nice," Lady said.

But Huck's ticklin was making me giddy on top of the thought of us sneakin into the Salvation Army some moonlit night and smouching a pair of dirty Reboks. "There's always a gen-u-ine, freshly-fallen-from-the-tree stick. Dogs just *dote* on sticks. Should we try and find him a maple twig or a oak branch ?" I snorted.

"No, one of those drinkin bowls with sticky feet," Huck said. "Dogs are so stupid they're like' to overturn their own water dishes."

"How about one of them feedin stands what stands a foot off the ground to save his poor back?"

"But he's just a puppy, he cain't have back problems yet!"

"Tom Sawyer and Huck Finn!" Lady said. "Where is your Christmas spirit?"

She probably warn't seriously mad at us, but she was layin down the law about when enough was enough; so we was forced to come up with a real gift for Coal Porter ... which in the end we used our 'llowance and chose a very handsome dark green pouf for him to sleep on with some kind of buckwheat stuff inside so it would be comfortable and conform to the shape of his big ol' miserable dog body. And we got him a bag of those crunchy bone-shaped dog biscuits so his teeth wouldn't rot out of his head, and what Huck said was the best chance we had of improvin his bad breath considerable.

The only good news was that Lily didn't drag 'im over when she came like she done before. She accepted his gifts sayin, "I'm sure Coal will just love the bed and the treats." Her voice was as solemn as a preacher's on account, I guess, she knew her gifts warn't much. That dog bed we bought 'im cost $50. She gave us—to share—a cotton Christmas tree ornament shaped like a mouse, and Lady hung it up. Then as an encore, she handed over a a yellow diamond-shaped plastic refrigerator magnet that said, "Cat Crossing."

Then she give us our "personal gifts" from that mangy Coal Porter.

Huck unwrapped his first. It was a pink plastic rod what you attached to a wall with a suction cup. An elastic cord hung down and from it dangled a sort of free-form bluebird with a bell and a green feather. "This is swell," Huck said—meanin it looked like it probably wouldn't stay attached to the wall for five seconds, and if it did, the cord would break after you tugged it more than twice, and you'd be left with the freeform bird, the bell, the feather and the little piece of attached elastic still hooked up to the bird's innards, and the instant you gave it a swat or a bite, the feather would come off, and you'd be lucky if you didn't accidentally swallow the goddamn bell. At which point what was left of the tiny free form bird would only be good for givin a kick that would send it into the nearest wall—and that would surely be the end of the worthless junk toy.

"Thanks," Huck said. "It's a dandy," he said, catchin Lady's eye. "Almost as lively as a real bird," he said in the driest voice I'd heard him use to date. "I'm sure I'll enjoy killi—I mean, *playin* with it."

My only hope was that since we were twins, a second evil feathered friend—but in a *different* color—was not gonna be foisted off on me.

I unwrapped mine, wishin I could take the money we spent on the dog bed and the biscuits and buy Coal a nice "shock" mat instead. I would've loved to see him try and sleep on one of those. I got the paper off a my gift, but there was a box inside. I tipped it over and yanked the lid. My present from Coal was a ceramic figurine of a cat that was also an angel, I guess, since it had wings. It had green glittery eyes and some kind of out-a-proportion and useless medallion on its chest and a little sign around its feet in gold letters that said, "I'm Watchin Out for You."

It was the most revoltin gift I ever received and I figured Coal was just that dumb—that damn dog was warnin me and Huck—and especially me—he was just bidin his time till he got us. Maybe he'd been watchin too many old movies about the Mafia on TV or somethin, but Lily wouldn't let him give me and Huck a dead fish wrapped in newspaper. Anyhow, I judged me and Huck would make ol Coal's fleas jump before he got the best of us—that was sure. And if it came to a battle of wills and witch tricks and a war of the familiars, me and Huck was gonna bust his stock down to dog meat.

"Tell Coal thanks," I said. "I know just where I'm gonna put this." I gave her a big old Chesire tomcat of a grin. I could hardly wait till the next time we went to visit over to their place to get a holt of him—and maybe the dresser drawer that held Lily's best nightgowns.

* * *

Meantime, Earle and Ted finished up for the day and came in with their tool kits and all and to say hello and *bang*! out come the secret we was startin the inn, and all of it with Ted's first words. "My dear, Bar-ba-ra, we shall be open sooner than we hoped, and I think it would be a good idea to have the advertisements geared towards some kind of special for the Valentine's Day, yes?"

"Open for what?" Lily says.

"For the inn."

"In what?"

"I'm turning the house into a Bed and Breakfast," Lady said.

"What on Earth for?"

"Oh, just a change of scenery, I suppose," Lady said, and I saw her look off into the distance at the same time Lily squinted her eyes and stared at her hard, and Lady was no way able to block the truth of the matter.

"You've lost your powers," she said, her voice awestruck; and for once she sounded genuinely sincere. "How can that be? Peter's in love with you."

145

"You mean was," I jumped in. "*Was* till you opened up on Thanksgiving and let out that Lady's picture was splashed all over DateLuckDotCom what was me and Huck put it out there, anyhow, because in case Peter decamped, we didn't want Lady to be lonely and all, and now he ain't sure 'bout how he feels."

"Well, I didn't think—"

"She never does," Huck said to me, but we both sneaked a glance at Lady and saw she was real unhappy with the tenor and pitch of this conversation so we reckoned we ought to lay off a Lily—a little, anyhow.

"But doesn't Peter know you're a witch?" Lily said.

"No, he don't," I answered.

"Ohhhhh," she said; and she nodded so hard some chinkle chankle pendant thing she had on started dancin on her chest. "*That* explains it—"

"Explains what?" I said. I could feel my face flushin. It was near about killin me to think I'd have to have my plateful of facts from Lily Blum aka Luna Raven. I got lucky though, and Lady jumped in to give me the lowdown.

"It's not *exactly* the way it's described in *Bell, Book, and Candle* ... it's not falling in love with a human, it's falling in love with anyone or anything that doesn't love you back. If the witch is committed to that person or path, she can't turn back. But if the love isn't reciprocal ... well, her energies and powers are drained by that loss."

"Cain't you just tell him you're a witch?" Huck said.

Lady shook her head at him. Then she stood up briefly. "Lily, I don't mean to be at all rude—not in the least, but ... I think I need to talk to the boys on our own for a bit."

"Sure, B.D.," she said. And for once, I think even Lily was too stunned to think of just retreatin into the kitchen or somewhere nearby. Anyway, she gathered up her gifts and Coal's and started for the door. At the same time, Earle and Ted glanced at Lady and beat an even hastier retreat. I heard the back door swing open with a whoosh, then crunch shut. A few seconds later, I could hear them hammerin out in the carriage house.

* * *

Lisa Mannetti

"It's not the telling, Huck," Lady said gently. "It's the loving ... and I think if Peter knew, he'd draw away even more—and that would be dangerous to me." We were settled now, the three of us, but I had a knot in my stomach.

"But you was afraid from practically the start he warn't in love with you," Huck said. But I saw what she meant: she'd fallen for him, and *that* was why she was afraid she'd called him unintentionally with her spell-prayer. Now she was in it up to her neck and hadn't nary a clue whether he was her true love or not, or whether what was happenin to her was the result of the bad karma she sent around—by mistake or no.

"Well, you're in love with me and Tom," Huck said. "Don't that count?"

"Sssh, Huck," I told him. But when Huck gets his heart up in his mouth, there's no stoppin 'im.

"You ain't a gonna die, are you, Lady?" he wailed. And I looked at her and saw—well, she didn't look exactly older, but she looked tired. Huck, I reckoned, had noticed that. And when you put it with Lady needin us to help with her witchin, it was truly worrisome. I was worried plenty. Huck was beside himself.

"Make us *boys,* and we'll love you, Lady," he cried. "And Peter won't matter a bit!" Tears was comin down his face. "Please! Please. We'll marry you. Me and Tom will marry you!" He ran to her and buried his face in her thighs, and I saw his shoulders was heavin some, and he was making little pained *ow-ow-oaws*.

She stroked his back. "There, there, Huck. There, there." She motioned to me and I scuttled alongside her, too, and felt her hands on my fur. "I love you, boys," she said; but that warn't answerin the question. I didn't know how we could truly help her—not then—there was just too much about this witchy stuff I was plainly ignorant about, but I warn't gonna let that stop me, and I knowed it wouldn't stop Huck, nuther. We'd do whatever we had to if it meant savin Lady.

CHAPTER TWENTY-TWO

CHRISTMAS UNTO NEW YEAR'S—THE BREATH
OF ZEPHYR—THE TREE HOUSE REVEALED

A day or so later, me and Huck was hangin out under the Christmas tree—just takin a rest, you might say, from all our newfound duties. 'Course we was lookin at what was still left under there, and I had found a itty-bitty sweater box; and when I got the top knocked off it to scrunch myself inside, I found there was the added bonus of a real cashmere sweater—which made that box a kind of Christmas gift in itself. There ain't nothin like cashmere for linin a box to lay up in. It was prime. Huck, he'd found a piece of ribbon what got overlooked in the wreckage, and he commenced to chewin and swallerin on it— which I have told him time and again only means lots of trouble in the litter box. But never mind—he was havin fun.

I was done entertainin myself by chewin through the lowest strand of lights on the tree, so we warn't bothered no more with those hot little bulbs diggin into our eyes and ears and all. But by and by, I thought I'd take a nip from the other end of Huck's ribbon.

"Leave off, Tom—this here's *my* ribbon."

"I only want to chomp it a little," I said.

149

"What about the tissue paper that's around that there sweater, then?"

"It's all to flinders. C'mon, Huck, let me have just a little of it."

"Well—"

"I tell you what," I said, thinkin back to that time in the schoolroom me and Joe Harper worried and drove a beetle with pins on my writin slate. "You chaw from that end, an I'll chaw from this one, and we can have us a tug-of-war game."

"All right,"

It was at least a yard long and Huck trotted off with the end securely in his teeth whilst I got a hold of my end, and we both started in chewin and pullin with a will. It was as good as one of those college fraternity games where everybody starts yankin, and the losers get jerked into a creek. In fact, I thought about witchin an itty-bitty creek between me and Huck, which would have given the contest some real flavor, but Lady had already lit into me about water and electricity. I didn't want to fry my own twin brother.

Huck let go of his end suddenly and I fell back, naturally; then he sprang from where he was, feet out front, and landed on me and we was exchangin rights and lefts and I got in a good one and he yelped. Then he tussled some more and I was underneath him and *he* got in a good one and I *yewwweed!* And we was gener'lly havin a grand old roughhousin match, but Lady came in just then, and even though she knowed our fightin was play-fightin, it made her nervous, so we had to quit. "You was gonna lose anyhow in about three seconds, Tom Sawyer," Huck said and gave me a sideways swat into my right ear. "Huh!" I countered—

"What have you boys been up to?" Lady said.

"Nothin,"

"Well *'nothin'* looks like *something* if you ask me." She was stoopin right over the box with the sweater in it, and even I could see there was a drift of white fur pilin up in there. Peter *would* buy black ... I sighed inwardly.

"This is no place to play," she said. But I saw her mind was fixed on somethin else; she was rummagin through the stack of boxes till she dug out the big one with the Aeolian Harp in it. "This is very expensive and not only could you damage it, you could get hurt."

"What is that thing, anyhow?" Huck put his nose out and sniffed an edge. The harp—a big rectangle—was about three feet long, and there was a cover you slid aside. Under that, it was lined with strings and there was a hole like on a 'coustic guitar in the middle.

"How do you play it?" I have to admit I was itchin to run a paw across the strings.

"You don't—"

"Then what do you do with it? Hang it up on the wall and dust it once a year?" Huck looked irritated.

"No. You lay it in a window and the breeze moves over it, and the wind plays it."

"Well, since it's the dead of winter, I guess this here is a gift what has to wait till springtime, and meanwhile, it will have to hang someplace, and me and Huck will have to dust it and maybe even polish it an' all," I said.

"We can keep it in the box," she said, pattin my head. "But right now, I have to admit, I want to hear it sing."

There was a little brass key for tunin; Lady plucked a few strings and adjusted a coupla pegs and got it ready for its debut performance and then went into the sunporch and opened the northwest window—which was the biggest one in there, anyhow—and laid the harp onto the sill. Then she lowered the window to just above the strings.

"That funnels the air across the harp and helps it 'play,'" Lady explained.

"Now what?" Huck said. It was pretty—a nice dark mahogany kinda wood. There was also a lighter color for the sounding board all decorated up and down the length of it with very pretty flowers that was painted on; Lady pointed out a line from a Samuel Taylor Coleridge poem what was inscribed around the hole. "We just sit in front of it, like it was a concert pianist about to perform an—"

"Sssh, Huck. You'll see."

Well, you have probably noticed that when you are waitin and wantin somethin to happen it never does; and this here instrument was a prime example of passive aggression—it was just a stone gargoyle, you may say, for all the noise that came out of its throat—which was none.

"Sounds like a angel," Huck said to me, laughin under his breath. And I knew he meant that angels—like this here wind harp—was silent as the tomb.

"What will it play next, I wonder?" I said.

Huck gave me a push in the chest with his paw and a big smirk. " 'Sonata for a Stone Post,' perhaps." He let out a yelp of laughter. "Or, 'Concerto for Clams in C Minor,'" he whooped.

"Oh I think I hear somethin," I said, placin one paw alongside my ear.

"You'll see," Lady said. She was less than enthralled with our impatience and sarcasm.

"Well, while we're waitin for the orchestra to tune up, I think I'll take a groomin-bath and a nap." Huck gave a long yawn and trotted back towards the cashmere sweater box under the tree. "Wake me when the musician's strike is over," he said sleepily. I stayed sittin on the rug in the playroom and keepin an eye on Lady, who was deep into the set of bookshelves tucked along the wall, and lookin, she explained, for a book of poems by good old Samuel T.

"Here it is," she said, and started thumbin through to find "The Eolian Harp."

A coupla seconds later, the wind gusted up outside. I saw the bare tree limbs shiverin, and they made that clickin sound they do when the branches and twigs are clotty with ice. It's an eerie sound—but it warn't *nothin* to the sound of the harp.

The wind seemed to find it and—like a spirit drawn to a weak soul it wants to possess—it just laced into the thing and out come a sound that was like the howlin of the damned.

Huck near about jumped out of his skin. "What the hell is that!" And I knowed if we warn't in the room with the harp, Huck never would have come in—he'd a headed for the cellar, the attic or any place else out of the sound of that thing. But he did sort of slink along till he was back hangin in the door to the sunporch, his face lookin tense.

ZzzzzzZzzzZZZZZzzzzz, the harp sang. Well, it was unearthly, I'll give you that. Not like a zither and not like the wind screamin around a chimbly of a freezin night, but some weird atonal song—it was pretty much the way I imagined the wind sounded in the polar regions when the monster is chasin Dr. Frankenstein in Mary Shelley's book. I figured Mary had heard her share of Aeolian Harps, too.

"Listen," Lady said. "Isn't it something?" The look on her face was like Mary Shelley and Samuel Taylor Coleridge had both just descended from the aether and lit down here in her sunporch in Rhinebeck, New York.

It started up again with a sound that was like to make a corpse's flesh melt faster. MmmmmmmMMMMMMMmmmmmmm MMMMMMMzzzzzzzzzahhhhhhhmmmmmmm.

"'And that simplest Lute, Placed length-ways in the clasping casement, hark! How by the desultory breeze caress'd, Like some coy maid half yielding to her lover,'" Lady read from the poem.

Well I was astonished. "Coy maid!"

"Sounds like that old emergency broadcast test they used to do on cheap TV stations," Huck said. "It'll keep dogs off the lawn—I'll say that in its favor."

"Hah, you boys don't know what good is," Lady said. Her face was rapt, and now and again she shut her eyes to hear the harp shriek, then fell back to readin on the poem.

* * *

Don't humans beat all?

Here was somethin in my day, people woulda hove shoes out the window at to shut it up from screamin all night like like ruttin alley cats—and Peter Bennett had paid good money for it, and Lady looked like she just won the New Jersey state lottery and a Speed Queen Automatic Washer to boot.

Take my word for it, Samuel Taylor Coleridge was addicted to laudanum, and that poem he wrote proves it. He musta been high as a kite on the stuff if he thought that yowlin and razor sharp shriek was a sound like "twilight elfins make."

"Yeah, a flock of elves'd make *that* noise if they was run through with hot knittin needles," Huck said. "Or if you dropped 'em like human dumplins into a vat of boilin water."

"It's pitiful," I agreed.

"I tell you what, " Huck said, "when I see that thing come out, I'm headin for the Tree House. I'll never make it through the whole of

153

springtime with that thing pitchin fits. I'm gonna conjure me some *central air conditionin*; and with the windows closed, that'll shut it up."

I had a brain wave. "We might get some laughs out of it though, Huck," I said. I gestured toward it. "Meet Harpo—our first resident ghost."

Huck gave a broad grin. "I can hardly wait till the first guest hears it—especially if we play it down here and they cain't tell *where* the ha'nt is a caterwaulin. But I want to call our ghost Sara—after the gal in that guy's poem."

"Sure. Sara's fine." I could picture the guests havin fan-tods galore.

"We might even get on TV with this, " Huck said. "I'd like that—long as I don't have to meet that demon child in high heels, Linda Blair. I never could stand vomiters, Tom," he said solemnly. "They's so haphazard and downright contagious."

* * *

By and by we heard Lady shut the window in the sunporch, and a minute or so after she laid the harp in its box, she came into the livin room again. Out back, Earle and Ted was slappin a very pretty coat of dark green paint onto the walls of the carriage-house-turned-shop.

"Well, boys," Lady said, "do you think you're about ready for your first transforming lessons?"

I was about to give the kitty equivalent of clickin my heels—which is a spring, a *prrrruPPPP!* and two tail swishes—but something in her voice made me stop. She sounded wistful; so I put the glad part of me that wanted to be a boy again and was dead set on learnin the art of transformation on hold, so to speak, and stared at her. "Why do I have the feeling somethin's wrong?" I said.

"Cats," she began with an attempt at humor and shakin her head, "the most botheratious of familiars—always think they're psychic, never think they're wrong!" She sat down on the sofa and patted the cushion next to her. But her light words and teasin voice struck me as an imitation of drollery; she was upset and she was tryna cover it up. I jumped up next to her and Huck did the same, but I knew she warn't easy in her mind or heart. She reminded me of an old woman what knows she's dyin and is resigned to it and is thinkin about what silver

154

teapot oughta go to her granddaughter Susie and whether her piano should be sold or given to the old folks home.

"Say on," I prompted. I warn't about to come right out with my feelins, I wanted to draw her out, then reel her in.

"We should probably be doing this up in the altar room, but somehow I don't feel like climbing all those stairs." The winter light was grayish that day and it seemed to wash the color out of her face, too; but my ears pricked up when she said she didn't feel like climbin stairs.

Lady could have easy witched all her housework done, but she'd already told us that over the years she got a little bored with that particular set of spells, so she often did her own chores. Oh, she'd use the witchin to keep up with mowin and paintin and big jobs, but she had lots of energy to take on smaller tasks herself. And now, she was feelin too tired to climb stairs? Well, I know when it's time to give the heave-ho to a plan, and drawin her out slow and careful was the plan to go.

"You ain't tellin us everythin," I said. "There's somethin wrong—I mean, really wrong—and you ain't lettin us in on it."

"Well, haven't you been saying from day one you wanted to be boys again?" It came out all right, but she was lookin straight ahead, and I saw one hand clench at the hem of her skirt, and I knew she was avoidin the issue.

"Yeah, but there's somethin behind this you ain't sayin. Out with it, Lady. Me and Huck love you, and you know better than to keep somethin back from whoever loves you for real and true."

I saw a tear glitter briefly at the corner of one eye, and she said, "I thought I could just let you be boys again, then get on with what I have to do."

"And what is that?" I asked.

"Oh, move on to the next level, I guess you'd call it—"

"Don't guess—and don't make me guess—explain." My voice was a little on the curt side, and I would't look at Huck. I knew he was pretty much struck silent, and I was afraid—like Lady, herself—if I looked at him, he'd dissolve into a puddle of tears.

She looked uncertain; she bit her lip. "Where to begin ..."

"At the beginnin," Huck and me said together.

* * *

"You boys know that I agreed to starting the inn because for years I witched whatever money I needed—and with those powers fading—I thought the inn would make up for it, and help all of us out—"

"That don't sound like the beginnin," I said. But for once, Huck hushed me.

"Quiet, Tom. Let her tell it how she wants."

"It would help you boys, too, because if anything happened to me and your own powers weren't fully developed, well, you'd get on all right till they were." She passed a hand over her forehead as if all of this was not only emotionally hard for her to say, but costin her some physically, too.

"I'm old boys. Very old." Lady smiled, and for just a second, I saw the bones rise through her flesh, and the flesh I saw was lined and wasted. I shook my head, and she was Lady again. A little thinner-lookin, but Lady years and years before even middle age crept up on her. "I don't know how old, exactly—"

Now, Huck burst in. "You knew Mr. Twain, didn't you?"

She gave a little laugh. "I did, yes."

"All of 'em," I said, breathless. I swiveled my head. "All these books. You knew Coleridge and Dickens and Mary Shelley and Byron."

She nodded. "Even Lucius Apuleius, yes," she paused. "I can remember some of it, some of those times, not all of the memories of course; anymore than a person can account for and remember every incident in her life. You know what I mean—someone says, 'Remember the time we went to dinner at such and such a restaurant,' and you realize you'd forgotten it till you're reminded. The books are like that for me ... they jog my memory sometimes." She paused. "I liked the idea of a literary connection as one of the selling points for Chancery House."

I suddenly recalled one of the meanins of that word, chancery: hopeless predicament. I wanted to let myself swoon, but I didn't. "What's the hopeless predicament?"

"I think it's time for me to move on—"

"But you told us the tree ... the Tree House—that we'd never be sick, nothin could ever hurt us, we'd never grow old or die inside there," I said.

156

"And that is true; unless a witch makes up her mind to move on."

"You cain't," Huck cried out.

I sat straight up now. "And what has this got to do with transformations—there's somethin else, and it ain't about showin us a new trick."

She swallowed. She turned those huge green eyes on the Christmas tree and up toward the ceiling, but she warn't answering. It didn't matter, though, cause I had plucked it from her mind.

"If we're boys, we cain't be your familiars," I said. "As boys, we ain't gonna have no power—not for years and years, anyhow. And, well, you could move on to the next plane, and me and Huck—we couldn't stop you or save you."

"Yes," she said. But her voice was only a whisper.

"Right now," I said, "all three of us is goin out to the Tree House, and we're gonna ponder on this. All three of us is gonna look it over. 'Cause I never will be a boy—if it means I have to lose you."

I said it—and I knew I was speakin as much and maybe even more for Huck as myself, but I had a hunch there was more to the tree and its powers than Lady was willin to let on. Well, me and Huck had been explorers and adventurers a hundred times before—in our dreams, in our fantasies, and in *fact*—accordin to what Mr. Twain wrote. And I knew whatever secret was inside that healin tree, we'd have it laid open like the roto section in Sunday's newspaper, because knowin what the secret was meant savin Lady, and that was everything to both of us.

* * *

Lady and Huck and me went inside the Tree House, and she laid out on the couch, and while Huck jumped alongside her, I lay on the Flokati rug and I started thinkin about how the Tree House really looked. For one thing, if a person saw it at all from the yard, it would just be an ordinary smooth-faced tree; nothin to mark it as unusual or different from a hundred million other big old maples. It warn't even any different from the regular maple that was on the front lawn. Yet, when me and Huck approached it, we had a sense of the tree's beckonin to us. Its skin would seem to ripple—the way a person shivers when somebody they love is gonna touch 'em. It warn't exactly a siren song or a mermaid's summonin, but it was close—and it made you want to go inside the tree or die tryin. Once you were in there, a kind of double reality existed. It warn't the same as a dream—but I don't have no other words to explain it right. First off, like I told you, you could look around and see the cunnin little fireplace with its Dutch tiles, and the kitchen and sofa and furnishins and all. You could see the whitewashed walls and the old-fashion wooden joists. You could also look up inside that circular shape and see the bedroom above. But, when you took the time to concentrate, you could look past the walls, and first you'd see the inner palish yellow of the bark, and beyond that—it was as if it was a glass wall—you'd see outside. If your house was glass from the ground to the ceilin—with nothin else—you'd see the very blades of grass that leaned against the window wall at the bottom and the tips of the branches that swagged along the roof. That might not seem like a lot—till you remember how odd it would seem—not if you was outside lookin at scenery—but *inside* a place feelin like you was livin it.

Then, too, in Lady's Tree House, like I said, when you looked up beyond the little round cubby of a bedroom, you'd see the branches and leaves and the sky. If it was daytime, the sun hung overhead. At night, clouds and stars and planets drifted on their paths. At the moment, it was snowin softly so it was like layin at the bottom of one of those fairyland globes watchin the speckles drift down on you and swirl around ever so pretty.

I knew that if you wanted to drift up and outside the tree, you could light anywhere you wanted. Lady had shown us Venice and Portofino and the Pyramids. Now I knew she'd grown up an Egyptian girl once or twice in the shadow of those monoliths. Just like if it seemed she didn't need a map to navigate the crooked alleys in Venice, it was because she'd walked those streets a thousand times when she lived there alongside of Casanova a coupla hundred years before. That was the magic that happened when you went up, anyhow, I thought. And then another thought skittered inside my head, and I gave a little jump and said, "What's below?"

"What?" Huck asked me.

"As above, so below ... Lady, what's under the Tree House?" I said.

She looked at me and she gave a little sigh, and she didn't say anything, but I had a hunch I was on target.

"C'mon, Huck," I said, and he jumped off the couch. "We're gonna do us some explorin." 'Course, even then, I didn't dream of what I'd find when we plummeted through the roots of the thing. It made Alice's tumble down the rabbit hole as ordinary as drinkin lemonade on half the porches in America.

CHAPTER TWENTY-THREE

GO ASK ALICE–THE ARTIST'S WAY–
THE HEALING TREE

Me and Huck never noticed it before, but there was a little irregular-shaped trapdoor—about the size of a sewer grate—between the stove and the table in the kitchen area. And I don't think we'd have seen it then—unless Lady put it in our minds to run across it. It was dovetailed in with the rest of the boards, and to look at it, you'd not only miss seein it, you'd never think there was a way to wedge so much as the thinnest shim inside the grooves to lift its lid. Huck didn't think we ought to even bother tryin. So, he just blinked his eyes twice—and maybe it warn't the most original spell in the world for him to tell the door to *open sesame*—but intent counts, so it worked just fine. We heard a creak and then watched it ratchet itself till it was upright, a little spill of earth fallin down inside the dark space that was its throat.

"Tom, is we gonna be all right crawlin down there?" Huck whispered.

I sure didn't know, and a part of me was wonderin somethin fierce if we'd do better in the underground labyrinth as cats with powers or boys who could carry flashlights.

You may have heard that a tree's root system is pretty near a match for the leafy stuff you see throwin its arms up to the sky. The roots alone had to be the size of a small city, I thought. She was old, and the tree was old, and I guessed there'd be tunnels inside it, some of 'em maybe even bricked—and who knew what else.

"People have gotten lost in the catacombs," I said to Huck.

"You and Becky come out all right in the cave—but that was luck," he said. I saw him lick his lip—he was nervous.

"And maybe the world owes me some more luck," I said, and then I jumped down inside the hole. It warn't two seconds before I heard Huck right alongside me.

* * *

We was like Alice fallin—but there warn't no rabbit leadin the way, and there sure as hell warn't no cupboards with pots of marmalade—empty or otherwise. First of all, it was dank inside there. The smell of raw earth that has never been warmed by sunlight just goes through you. It smells wet and cold and it eats up your insides till you feel like you're all alone inside some terrible grave. There was roots, and wigglin things givin off a kind of slimy sheen, and rocks and more and more of that ugly brown dirt.

The further we fell inside this hollow, the more awful I felt. Pretty soon, my heart was as sick and sore as a miner's trapped in a cave-in: No light, air goin, hurt some maybe—and you don't know whether to hope you'll be found or to give up.

The descent was slower at times—and with so little to see—that seemed to make my own thoughts jump out at me harder. I started to think—scare myself mostly—about what it really would be like to be trapped inside a true cave-in. The memory I had as a boy warn't the same. For one thing, it was too much tied up with my ideas on tryna save Becky and tryna use my wits to get us out of there and savin bits of candle and sharin up that tiny slice of cake. For another, inside the cave, dangerous as it was, me and Becky could move about—stand and walk or lie full out. That's not always the case when the ground comes down on you. Bein able to move gave us an outlet for our nervous energies ... and that was a good thing. But if you was lyin pinned under tons of dirt, all that hope for a rescue would be so terribly drainin. Hopin would be as big an agony as the accident itself.

"Tom, look below there," Huck said.

His voice sounded so small and far away. "See that light—it's an openin maybe. Try and catch on when we go past," he said.

In the dim light, I saw his white paw flash out, but I warn't quick enough and I sailed past. Then I was brought up short and hanging with my face down and my feet flailin and it hurt like hell. Roowwww!

"Huh! Caught you." Huck had me by the tail, and he hauled me upside down onto the ledge of the horizontal tunnel he sat on.

I licked a paw and rubbed it alongside my face to gather myself, so to speak. Behind Huck there was a very pale pinkish glow. Don't take it wrong ... it warn't no pretty garden pink ... it was more like the ugly glare of those cheap energy savin lights boomin off the dirty white tiles in the Lincoln Tunnel. It gave me the creepin willies just as much as all that damp raw earth—and the thought of lyin underneath it.

"It don't make sense, Huck," I said. We was still perched on the edge of the openin, more or less huddled together.

"Why're you whisperin?"

I warn't whisperin, but his voice was thin, too. I guess that dead air was just suckin out the carryin power of all sound. I just shrugged, because he'd catch on in a second anyhow, and I needed to say my thoughts out loud. "I don't rightly know why up there in the Tree House is so beautiful and down here it's ... it's ..." I stopped.

"Like nothin could ever be alive or happy," he said. "It's terrible in here, Tom." He pushed his nose into my face, and I put my paw over his shoulder. I knew what he meant. It was more than the mottlin of the dirt on his white fur, more than the hollow feelin that was around us and inside us both.

"Huck, do you think what I said is right—*As above, so below?*"

"I did, I do—but ... then I don't know what to make of this horrible dark."

"It seems to me if I could just puzzle it out, it would make sense," I said.

"Sleep on it," Huck said.

We curled up—as we'd been used to doin—since we was in our Mama's womb. And our arms around each other, our faces close, we lay exhausted and soothed by each other's smell and warmth and breathin, til we slept.

* * *

Whilst I was sleepin so hard, it seems to me Mr. Twain stepped up to say a how ya do in my dreams. "You know Tom," he tells me, "there was a space of about two years there when I just laid Huck's book aside."

"You did?" In the way of dreams, we was sittin in a book-lined study and as comfortable together as two old war heroes about to uncork our first tot from a hip flask. It felt strange to be a boy—yet not strange at all, since I was *his* boy, if you take my meanin. It was summertime and the windows was open, and the breeze was warm and just right to put a body in mind of a nap or some drowsy talk. A couple of fat bumblebees was hummin in the flowers in the window box.

"Why'd you put down the book?"

"I came to an impasse," he said. His eyes were bright—you just looked at him and you knowed seriousness was always gonna take a back seat to his mirth, but just the same, you could see that he knew all about sadness—every kind there is. "You know what that is—when the rock has fallen, and the way is blocked, and you can't see your way around or through a thing."

"Yes, sir." I watched him, and I could see him shapin his thoughts and figurin on how he wanted to say what he wanted to tell me. So I sat still, kept quiet, my hands folded in my lap.

"There's cave-ins in life and inside a person's head that happen without all the mess and bother of mud and twisted metal and earth shifting faster than you can say Bridgeport," he said, lightin a cigar. He was in a rocker now, and every now and then he'd tilt it forward. He was handsome to look at, and it was a pleasure to see him, 'specially when he was hittin his stride.

"Lots of critics—smart ones, too—they pounce on that fact that I let *Huckleberry Finn* go all that time. Much as they like the book, they say it changed when I picked it up again. But a critic, you know isn't necessarily an artist. In fact, there's lots that have more in common with a jackass than with a man or woman who's got a hand on a pen or a brush or a wood chisel," he said and smiled.

164

He lit a cigar; and then he did pour two glasses of whiskey out and handed me one and we clinked.

"You know, Tom, lots of people—critics and teachers and such." He snapped his knees to make the rocker creak a little. "They like to believe that all writing is conscious writing, that there's a meaning to ferret out." He drew some cigar smoke into his mouth. "And maybe there is ... same as if somebody sees somethin in you you never saw ... or outside you," he said. "Say I splashed whiskey on my shirtfront and didn't know it; you might see it or smell it, right?"

"Sure."

"And what do you suppose, Tom Sawyer, would be the meaning of that?"

"Well, that you'd been drinkin—"

He leaned over now and looked at me. "Right. Whiskey drinking would be the issue, not who saw the stain first, me who spilled it, or you who noticed it; those things matter—but only a little, they are incidental to—"

"The drinkin," I said.

He gave me a wide grin. "Right ... and even whether or not I had a good time getting lickered up, a rotten time of it, or whether I got careless and spilled or someone bumped into me and spilt my glass. That's all besides the drinking."

"The storytellin, you mean," I said.

"Exactly. Look here, Tom. Did you think the book fell off after that impasse?"

"I thought it needed a little livenin." I smiled. "And I was glad to provide it."

"Things aren't always the same after an impasse or a cave-in or anything else that changes the landscape all around you—or inside you."

"But the story stays, it goes on—"

"And it never goes away. Bein a storyteller—famous or forgotten, rich or poor—has its burdens, Tom." He looked right in my eyes. "Do you know what I mean?"

* * *

The dream broke off then, but I thought I did know. Lady had come to a place in her own story where she wanted to put it aside. All right, I reckoned I'd let her leave off it a while—but I warn't about to let her come to a halt and write Yours Truly The End—like Huck did to sign off on his *Adventures*. I thought about this half-glimsped dream with its promise of truth that was still only a hint. It was the story that mattered. She's weary, perhaps; tired of tryin. She can rest by and by, I thought, and maybe heal inside that gap ... and she might come out changed on the other side of it, but I warn't gonna let her off the hook. She'd made all this beauty in the top part of her mind—that tree was a stunner to gaze at; and she needed to recreate beauty deep inside herself now. As above, so below.

* * *

It was Huck who found the little hollowed-out crypt of a room. It was a smallish space, and the air inside it felt a little thick, a little stale. There was a kind of raised platform, more like somethin you'd sink a coffin inside of, then lay on top of to gather your strength, but we witched Lady down and laid her out like a sleeping beauty in a fairy tale to let her dream ... to heal. Me and Huck lay alongside her a while. I drowsed.

I waked up first. And I nudged Huck.

"Look," I said. It was hard to keep the hush out of my voice.

The room was already spinnin itself into existence around her.

When we left, I saw the rock walls had covered themselves with silk. Soft as flutterin curtains, holy as the green of ivy twinin over stone walls and ancient tree stumps. A little while later there were shinin jewels set into the cloth, and then livin garlands of roses and clematis and moonflower begun to spin themselves along the ceiling and the floor and climb upon the silk, and it smelled most beautiful and was the peacefullest place you ever saw.

I didn't know how long it would take; I only knew she would come to herself again. Inside the tree, in its deepest core, stillness created peace and healin.

So I thought—til time taught me different.

CHAPTER TWENTY-FOUR

LILY'S PECULIAR VISIT—
THE BOOK OF SHADOWS

We left Lady asleep—or whatever she was—inside the crypt of the Tree House, and me and Huck went topside, witchin ourselves out the trapdoor and into the kitchen. I was just lowerin it back into place with a little closure spell of my own invention (which, alas, I must keep a secret even from *you*, dear Reader) when I saw Lily Blum comin 'round the side of the big house.

That warn't nothin unusal—what was out of joint was that although she looked like she was headin for the back porch steps, she was starin at the Tree House. Huck saw it, too.

"Tom, do ya think old Lily can see *us*? Appears to me like she's lookin right at us!"

"Hunker down a minute, and let's see what she does." The trapdoor lid, luckily, dropped by inches, which meant it shut quietly, so she wouldn't hear it at least.

Sure enough, she *stopped*—right at the foot of the stairs. She had one gloved hand resting on the white of the newel post. You almost could have tossed it off to Lily hesitatin a little and thinkin there was a chance we were all over in the carriage house gettin set up for the inn

167

or helpin Ted and Earle put some finishin touches upstairs in their loft apartment. *Almost.*

"Is she listenin to hear where we're all at, Tom?" Huck whispered.

She did look as though she was tryna catch a sound, maybe even a random whiff—the way a predatory creature like a lion scents dinner on the hoof.

But the picture warn't as clear as that. "Somethin else, Huck, but I don't know for certain sure—" I looked at Lily through the skin of the tree, studyin her. She had on black wool gloves. She was wearin a long crinkly skirt that stuck out past the hem of her toggle coat. She had on a big scarf that was yards long and twirled over the shoulders of the coat, and she was wearin a pair of heavy boots. It was cold out all right, so why was she just standin there? Then I looked at her face and I saw that her eyes had that slightly glazed look that comes over a witch when she's scryin—tryna make shapes and sense of what she sees in a crystal ball or the tea leaves.

"I think the Tree House is comin into focus for her, Huck," I said. I was tryin to keep the panic out of my voice. I was still whisperin, but my fear was scrapin at the roots of my voice box, and at the last second I couldn't control it completely, so a little mewler came out.

Huck shook his head as if to clear his thoughts. The bells on his collar tinkled softly. "No, Tom—she already knows about the Tree House," he said.

"Are you sure? I don't think she sees us." It was like she was lookin past us or through us and we warn't no more important than beads of rainwater on a windowpane.

A second later, we saw Lily smile, and then she did walk up the stairs and open the back door.

Huck made a move to melt through the skin of the tree, but I put a paw out to stop him. "Stay here—she'll come back out in a minute when she finds nobody's to home."

It was more than a minute—and when she left, she only gave a haphazard glance toward the carriage house.

"You'd think she'd want to go check on how the shop's comin along—or maybe ask for the hundredth time if she can sell her stinky old love potions—" At the very least, I figured she'd wanna grill Lady over how our big powwow had gone yesterday after she left. Askin those phony butter-wouldn't-melt-in-my-mouth questions—as if she was only urgin a body to say what they wanted and no more—when in reality it was like someone holdin a meat cleaver over your wrist and threatenin to cut off your hand if you didn't confess confess confess.

She hunched her shoulders a little against the wind, but she kept walkin down the drive that skirted alongside the big house.

"Look, Tom," Huck said.

I gave a soft whistle.

Lily was walkin over fresh snow in heavy boots—and she warn't leavin any tracks.

* * *

"What do you think she's up to?" Huck said. By now we had left the Tree House and we was trottin up the back steps ourselves.

"Maybe she don't want us to know she was here." I couldn't think of any other reason she woulda witched herself over the snow and down the drive. There warn't no prints on the steps nuther. That told me it had all been a big act when she went inside the house—else why bother to witch herself up the stairs?

"She's up to somethin," I told Huck.

"It scares me, Tom, 'cause I think she's countin on being more powerful than you and me—"

"Yeah," I said. "And Lady, too."

* * *

A coupla days later, me and Huck had witched all the Christmas decorations down and got the ornaments stored in their boxes. We still had the lights to pull off the tree, and the two strands we'd gotten off so far was lyin on the floor and writhin in a big tangled heap like vipers in a snake pit.

"It's hopeless, Tom, these lights is the most ornery ever. Can't get 'em to unravel nohow."

"Just tell 'em to go straight—"

"I did and they strung theirselves like crepe paper acrost the whole damn room and started blinkin like slot machines."

"Did you tell them to unplug—" I was busy tellin the silver eggnog set to polish itself before it wrapped up good and tight in tissue and went back into its box.

"Course—but it didn't do no good ... plugged in or not, they's movin like snakes and flashin fast enough to bring on seizures—"

Well, I'd meant did he unplug 'em to get them unsnarled; but what if—

The other strands—three or four—suddenly lifted from the tree and joined the others on the floor, windin themselves into the movin mass and flickerin.

"Huh!" Huck was about to blast the whole batch of 'em into oblivion.

"Wait!" I shouted.

"They's only lights," Huck said.

"Hang on—ain't there somethin in one of Lady's spell books bout naninate objects communicatin—"

He hove a frustrated puff. "Pah—what's lights gonna say: 'On, off ... On, off ...'"

"Huck maybe there's somethin to this."

He sat in the outer trail of the light strings, wavin his tail like one those kit-kat clocks, "On. Off ... On, off ..."

"Hush a minute and let me think—" Lady was still inside the Tree House—way down deep under the bulgiest roots. We'd gone back down and checked on her every few hours. It warn't none of our doin, so it must've been the Tree House itself healin things up. Maybe it was Lady, I warn't sure. The room she was in seemed to be comin back—now there was spots of color on the walls shinin as bright as gems—but she was still lyin there silent as ... well, silent.

"On ... off," I whispered. Sudden-like, another thought that was terrible to think on came to me: Was she recyclin her power like electrical current—or was someone shuttin her down?

"Huck, I think Lady's in trouble, and I don't know to fix it."

* * *

You can name this here phenomenon of the blinkin lights anything you want. A sign. A clue. An omen. Call it what you will, but what it amounts to is, there was information I needed to know, so the world around me called my attention to it and kept it up till I got it. That's how what *you* call witchcraft works a lot of the time ... your unconscious—bein a sight more powerful than the top million layers of your mind—knows more than you do. It keeps at you till you wake up and hear what it's shouting. It's almost as bothersome as a conscience. What will also work at you till you hollar uncle and do what it wants—mostly your conscience, as Mr. Twain has pointed out, is proddin you to give up something you can enjoy and take up something downright inconvenient. You know—like tradin a savory bad habit or a delicious vice for somethin that's good for you or healthy. And in the end, you have to convince yourself that you really *do* like carrot sticks better than potato chips and Ring Dings, and that you're havin a much better time runnin till your legs feel like they've been mashed between pressin boards than you ever had when you was smokin. If you don't believe me about the convenience part, you just remember you probably only have to drive a block or so to the nearest 7-11 if you want Slim Jims—'stead of way the hell over to the supermarket for carrot sticks. And you can light up your cigarette or your cigar on the coldest night of the year at 3 a.m. during a blizzard—but runnin on snow-covered roads is only askin for trouble.

* * *

The Christmas tree lights was still slitherin around and blinkin away like mad. They was weavin in and out of one another in a mass until they resembled some sentient robot version of the hideous snake-hair that made up a Medusa's head. The way they was bobbin and liftin themselves up—as if they wanted to look at me and Huck—was a pure terror.

"On, off," I whispered, trying to puzzle it out. "Off and On ..." I broke off. "Oh damn, I think it's some kind of code."

"But Tom we don't know no Morse code—all them crazy dits and dots." There was worry in his voice and now he sat with his body tensed, too, and starin at the lights.

The strands went on weavin and interlacin, twinin, and windin—

"What if it's some kind of bindin spell," I said.

"But those are the very worst," Huck said.

171

The Christmas tree lights went on beatin their silent tattoo: bright and dark and bright and dark; all the while slow-movin in and out amongst each other.

"We got to look this here up in Lady's book," I said. "Right away."

We went up to the altar room, and whilst there was a big book of spell craft, I wanted to find Lady's own writins on the subject.

Every witch keeps what they call a Book of Shadows—it's a kind of witch's journal of her life on the wiccan path. Lots of 'em write down spells and incantations, or they might just record a ritual that seemed powerful or that made them feel connected to reams of angels and other worlds. Sometimes they just wrote about things they had strong opinions about—and I guessed Lady would have *plenty* to say on the subject of bindin spells. Any bindin spell is strickly black magic—and while it might work for a time, eventually the dark art would come around and work its mischief and evil on you three times as hard as whatever you sent out.

I sniffed around—mentally, you might say—to try and ferret out where Lady's book might be while Huck went through the spell craft volume, turnin its Bible-thin leaves one at a time, till I thought the raspy shiver of those tissue pages would make me run screamin.

* * *

"Tom," Huck swallowed. His voice was strained. "This here about bindin spells is mighty scary stuff." He tapped with his paw on a page and I seen that Lady had drawed blue ink pentacles right around all the margins. Each of them five point stars was inside a circle inside a square—to keep the bad out and the good in, I reckon.

There was tons of bindin spells. Takin little papers or nubs of parchment and windin 'em up with bits of colored threads—black or red or white—like a spider wrappin up an insect till it was crippled and foul. Makin tiny poppets and usin a person's hair, then tyin ribbons round and round and round till your victim was a miniature mummy. You cannot imagine how hideous these minute bundles looked—it was enough to give you the icy sweats.

Always the witch doin the spell buried the object or hid it to make certain sure another witch couldn't find it and change the spell. Meanwhile, these ugly little charms—what was hid away—grew in power. And from what I read—and later saw—as their power increased, the talismans became ranker and ranker—like a festerin sore. By and by, these witched bits and pieces went runny and black, but worst of all they was *alive*, too. And touchin one was like puttin your hand into an ant nest—the shiny scurryin insectile bodies like a million bitin, hungry eyes.

It scared me so bad, I had to make a coupla jokes—it was just whistlin while you walk past a graveyard or makin fun of the monster in a movie.

"Think it would count against us if we bound Lily's hound of hell, Coal Porter, to a set of railroad tracks—"

"Hush, Tom—don't even talk that way."

I moved a paw down over the page and was surprised to learn even separatin two people by a spell was *still* a kind of bindin—and it didn't make no difference if you was separatin some other couple or tryna get yourself the witch's equivalent of a Reno divorce. It was still usin the other person's will and bindin him or her to yours.

There was all kinds of strange drawins and pictures done by age-old witches; and whenever you turned a page, you saw somebody bound to a wheel—like some medieval torture device—but it all came to the same thing—you was changin destiny, and sooner or later you'd be the one strapped onto the blood-soaked wood of the wheel. Spinnin away till the flesh fell from your bones.

"A Book of Shadows is a mighty personal thing," I said to Huck.

"Do you think if we look into it that's black magic, too?"

"It might be," I said, thinkin on Lady's inked-in pentagrams. Well, I'd done my laughin out of one side of my mouth, and lookin at those pictures—especially the poppets with their strange lopsided eyes and crudely drawn mouths—was givin me the cold shivers.

"If we's tryn to save Lady, does that good intent cancel out a bad action?"

"I don't know ... and somethin else, Huck—I don't know how to find the answer or who we can even ask."

"There must be somebody, somewhere—"

"Lady's the only one I know whose answer I'd even trust." I sighed. "We don't really know any other witches—'cept Lily—and I think she's a lot more wicked than we thought—or even Lady reckoned."

"Tom," Huck's voice cracked. "I just thought of somethin even worse: if it is a bindin spell, we don't know if it's the result of Lady's spell on Peter—"

"Or if someone else has cast a spell against Lady—"

"Or both," he finished miserably.

Take it all around, this business of biddin and bindin was lookin very bad for us and Lady; and I began to see why this kind of spell—which might seem harmless on the face of things—was so bad. It was a lot more complex than some teenager with spots on her face wishin the high school heartthrob would ask her to a movie. Or Amy Lawrence wishin we was still engaged like we was before I took up with Becky Thatcher. Here was Lady—out of commission one way or another. That would affect Peter. And maybe his practice—both the animals and humans. And his family—from his mother and sister and aunts and uncles to his nephew, Drew. S'pose Peter got downhearted and didn't feel like makin up magic tricks and Drew didn't have a cheerful uncle to buoy up his spirits? Maybe without that good influence, old Drew would keep on bein a hellion and keep at it clear through adulthood. And we was openin the inn, so Ted and Earle would be struck by Lady's absence—and maybe all the guests who came to stay. It was the ripple effect with a vengeance and way too much for me. When I tried to think of all those guests and their families and their family's families and friends and so on and so on, it gave me a headache that was almost a nightmare. I couldn't cipher it out—no how. 'Specially since I didn't even know if Lady had mistakenly started the whole speed train herself. Witchcraft can get away from you—and that's a fact.

I was ponderin all this when Lady herself was suddenly standing at the door of the altar room—and I believe I was never so happy to see a person in all my born days as a human *or* a cat.

"Here I am, boys—back to business and twice as large as life!" she said.

I thought Huck was gonna cry with relief—bein the tenderhearted chap he always was. "Oh, oh, oh Lady," was all he could say before I caught his eyes wellin up around the edges.

"We was so worried," I said. "Leastaways, Huck was mostly. We started thinkin some kind of black magic put you in a trance—"

"And not even Tom could figure it out," Huck said. "And he's always been just a regular wiz at comin up with schemes and solutions and such."

"Well, there's nothing to fret over now," she said. "The healing alcove inside the tree kept spinning and spinning until it sucked away all that was clotted up inside me and, then—like magic," she giggled, "it filled me with wholeness and light. Jewels as brilliant as stars, and ... well," she gave a little twirl, "here I am."

"We was afraid you was inside the web of a bindin spell an' wouldn't never get clear of it," Huck said.

"There isn't a spell in the world that can hold me."

"Tom was sure of it—'specially 'cause the Christmas tree lights was actin like possessed neon."

Now I blushed inwards, ashamed I'd made too much drama out of the incident. It warn't often I felt my imagination carried me wrong, but maybe this time—

"Well, I was just recycling my energy, testing my charge—and I guess the lights caught that signal." Lady shrugged. "The Tree was doing its job—but slowly."

It was embarrassing bein as off-base as the townfolk who thought we was all drowned when we was just over to Jackson's Island—I wanted a trump—just like when we came back and hid in the choir and got to hear our own funerals orgies preached that time in Missouri. I told Lady about Lily's sneakin around.

"And I still say that Lily—she's got something wicked hidden up her sleeves—"

"Oh," she laughed. "She's harmless, harmless."

I was so knocked down by my misjudgment of the situation and so glad to see Lady, I didn't pay no mind to how her voice sounded a little off—softer maybe, or flatter. Or somethin. She looked a little paler than usual, but even Mr. Twain had pointed out you don't always come out on the other side exactly the same. So I just let it go—and by the time I remembered that sketchy little feelin, it was too late. Way too late.

CHAPTER TWENTY-FIVE

WEB SITE–THE VALENTINE SPECIAL–
THE GUEST FROM HELL

Well, The Chancery House rooms had turned out just splendid, and we had lots of little touches like mini-fridges and herb shampoos and flowers splashed around on the nightstands and mantels. A guest could hardly take a step without bumpin into another one of our flytraps—I mean, complimentary services.

On the website, the inn looked grand and welcomin, and you could tour around it lookin at the rooms, the carriage house and even nearby points of interest. For regular folk with no interest in the doin's of the disembodied, that probly translated into places like the Vanderbilt mansion, and Franklin Roosevelt's house. In the winter, we could hook *them* up with horse-drawn sleigh rides and skatin rinks and such. Summertime, there was plenty of swimmin and fishin holes and tennis and all that truck; and in the fall, they could go apple pickin or horseback ridin. We had all the amenities—and plenty of kickbacks from everybody—includin local restaurants, so there warn't a chance they wouldn't be linin' our coffers just as much as the thrill-seekers what stayed with us.

We had a trick or two on the website for *them* chumps what scoured the Internet lookin for haunted attractions. We labeled one room off the attic: "The Secret Passage."

Once you was inside, if you clicked around a certain way, a skeleton would pop out of a closet; and then if you clicked on Mr. Bones, he disappeared and a old-fashion scroll unrolled and let you know even though we had our own slew of spirits right on hand, if you wanted more, and if you was brave enough, why The Chancery House would be happy to arrange your participation on a haunted tour—that would show all the goriest local sites, tumbledown graveyards, ghost-infested houses, and the like.

'Course, we didn't have a clue where we'd actually take people or what we'd show 'em—but like Huck said, "We'll just make it up as we go along—and that'll be a prime sellin factor. It'll be unique every time. Lizzie Borden's old house don't change their ghosts nor shift their spirits and gore around. How many times can a body look at the spot where Andrew got cleaved? Less they liven it up some come Halloween with fake blood or a dummy corpse or somethin. But our tour'll be like them Web games—different each and every single time you enter."

"It's prime," I agreed; and it had just the kind of style I doted on. "Not to mention, since it's all a big secret, we don't even have to describe it—and then we ain't committin no kind of fraud, nuther," I said.

And, in case I forgot to mention it, we decided to throw a kind of glammer on the house—and what's more, we could change that glammer whenever we wanted—kind of like a back up system on your computer, you might say. Or that old chestnut about a genie who gives three wishes, and your last wish is for unlimited wishes. Anyhow, Huck reasoned it might be more fun if the house always appeared different, so we used a spell we invented that we called The Randomizer Glammer. And we had every intention of patentin it, too, so other witches what owned Bed and Breakfasts couldn't get the drop on us. It was was a noble good spell.

Some days the house looked sort of like Victorian gingerbread. Sometimes it was the great big old ramblin pseudo Federal Style it actually *was*—as you recall—and sometimes it kind a looked like that oddly invitin house what Charles Addams used to draw up. People kep on seein it different—depending on what they wanted to see or find in a night's lodgin, but mostly it just changed of its own will—just like a program does with your cursor or your mail notifier that changes every time you boot up.

Mr. Twain—lovin inventions and cats as much as he did—would have agreed it was a smasher. It was the handiest thing around—Huck built right into the spell that no matter what, the whole house would always look tidy and clean. I can't tell you how much housework that saved us—not to mention laundry and consortin with demonic vacuums.

* * *

"How much you think we should charge for the haunted ghost tour? What are they gettin per head for that voodoo thing down to N'Orleans?" I said.

"Shoot. New Orleans—that's just humdrum compared to what we can cook up. And it seems to me, the more secret it is, the more a body'll be willin to pay for it."

Well, I knew he was a thinkin of the duke and the king again and them two rapscallions playin the Royal Nonesuch—which warn't nothin but a shellackin of a whole village—for which they charged 'bout ten times as much as when the old bald and beardy duke played Juliet and the rest of them high-toned Shakespeare folk along with the king—who pretended he was a reg'lar on the London stage. "Well, if farms around here can get forty-five dollars a head for two hours of settin on a sweaty old plug they call a horse, we should easy be able to get a clear hundred for the chance to see 'beyond this human veil.'"

"Less us make it for ninety-eight dollars—you know how suspicious humans get when they hear round numbers—"

"But the tax, Huck, don't forget the tax and the handlin charge."

"Less see, that comes to $107.50. Will that be Visa, MasterCard, American Express or Discover, ma'am?"

"Give 'em a group discount rate, Huck, that'll draw 'em even more."

"Less us say a group is two people. Fifty dollars apiece then, for two tickets—not includin the tax and extras, and groups of three or more can pile on the Mystery Train for the knock down bargain price of thirty-five bucks a throw."

If a group was two or more people, we was punishin the singles since they'd have to pay twicet as much for their ticket—on the other hand, what else would a person on a tour all alone have to spend money on? If they couldn't even find one other person to travel around with, that warn't our fault and there warn't no sense in us not gettin money as if they *was* two people.

Take it all around, that tour was gonna be clear profit, anyhow. Which is always a good thing. We could advertise it in the Haunted Inn listin and tell the trick of how to find the Secret Passage on the website, but chances are a body wouldn't stumble across it just browsin our page; so it wouldn't be off puttin at all to folk who just wanted to come on over to Rhinebeck and get skinned the regular way by visitin antique shops, West Point or that run down pea pod of a house where Eleanor Roosevelt served everybody—from royalty to visitin dignitaries—cheap hot dogs and bad lemonade.

Is it any wonder why Europeans hated us all those years after the war?

* * *

Well, around the first of February, which is a lucky day for witches, anyhow, Lady took out a big ad in the *New York Times*—which you may have seen—for our grand openin Valentine's Weekend. You already know we had five rooms; but quicker than you can say 'love potion number nine,' they was all booked solid—and when folks let on they was disappointed to miss out on the openin, we extended the bargain rate right through the month of February.

The night before we was gonna welcome our guests, we had a prep session and a sort of rehearsal at our usual station in the dinin room. The main purpose was who was gonna do what and all that kind of thing.

* * *

"And all the decorations, yes, Miss Barb-ar-a," Ted nodded at her, "which you honored me to have entrusted to my discretion ... all the lovely, frilly red hearts are in place. Here is a sample," he said, holdin up a doily. "I have hung these precious red, red hearts in the guest bathrooms, the guest bedrooms and in various other most be-yoot-ti-ful locations throughout, this, our charming inn," Ted began. "I have placed the small red, heart-shaped box of fresh Belgian chocolates on each pillow. Each guest bathroom features a very special Valentine's addition of Theme No. 1 Fancy Red Disposable guest hand towels made of the highest quality paper—such as would please even Miss Leona Helms-ley, herself—and whom I understood was a very important human hotelier."

Lady was about to snicker, but she bit it back because she knew that Ted thought it was the height of generosity that she trusted him to help with the inn—him bein beyond the pale, you might say. Ted never noticed; he just kep readin from his stack of notes.

"And so, on Saturday I will prepare the heart-shaped waffles with strawberry sauce `a la Ted and garnished with a puff of whipped cream, which I will serve wearing my red apron. And—"

"Sounds like you've got it all covered, Ted—"

Ted, bein so chivalrous, was thinkin of all those human hearts a flutter with love—he couldn't have a regular girlfriend, of course, and mostly to your average werewolf, red meant one thing: dinner. But not Ted; he was a real romantic, all right.

"But I have not yet made my report on the small red novelty pillows or the red carnations which will fill the vases in the guestrooms or the roses here in our most gracious dining room where gourmet breakfast is served year-round, often with a seasonal theme—"

"You spoke to the florist. Got the candles—" Lady was tickin her fingers.

"I did not mention the candles—"

"Ted, old boy," Earle hove in, "I can see from that there list of yours, just about every box is checked, so I vote we move on to our next item—"

"No, no," Ted said, in a panicky voice. "Look. This is terrible! I have forgotten to order the strawberries. How could I be so foolish, now all will be ruined!" His elbows was down on the table and he was pullin at his hair, and makin this sort of *OwwOww* cry.

He was gonna start leakin—and maybe worse I thought, since his ears got a little pointy—so, I gave Huck the high sign and Huck, he told Ted not to worry, we'd either witch 'em up or smouch 'em from the *Stop and Shop* and by God, when he opened the refrigerator come Saturday mornin, the strawberries would be right there.

"Thank you little one, Huck." He blew his nose loudly. "I do not know what I should have done—"

"Right, all set." Earle said. "Moving on, now has any of these here guests signed up for being booked over to the sleigh riding jaunt?"

"Nope. Far as me and Huck can tell, the whole ten of 'em's gonna lay around in front of the fireplace all weekend, waitin for a shot at the Scrabble board. We didn't even sell a single haunted tour, and you said none of 'em's asked about the ghost."

"Well, if they do decide they're bored enough to put love on the back burner in favor of havin the whim-whams, what have you all got planned?" Earle folded his arms and tipped his chair back a little.

"Nothin—" Huck started to say, but I gave him a backhanded swat I pretended was just me stretchin and jumped in.

"Don't you worry, Earle. Me and Huck ain't gonna do *nothin* that won't be a heap of fun for our lovely guests."

Huck started to hiss at me—well, all right, I knew he was gonna ask, what *was* we gonna do—but I hadn't studied on it yet, and besides, we didn't have no takers at the moment, anyhow. I couldn't see no sense in gettin up some big gaudy plan and then never even get to try it out and have to remember it all for some other occasion.

By and by, Lady said it looked like us "managers" had it all under control and she was gettin tired, so she was goin off to her room to read a while. We all said our goodnights.

We four sat a while longer at the table, not sayin a word for a moment or two after we heard her climbin up the stairs. Then Ted said it bang out.

"I am worried. Barb-ar-a is not herself lately."

"Maybe the guests will liven things up." Huck put in.

And he was right. He could have set himself up as a psychic and sold tickets to the Prophets. From the minute the first guests showed, the Chancery House was as lively as New Year's Eve in Times Square—and it felt just about as crowded and twice as chaotic.

* * *

The first guests to arrive on Friday was a Reverend and Mrs. Dudley Entwiler, what was goin to have a kind of second honeymoon. They was somewhere in their late fifties, and both of 'em was kind of dried-up lookin, but they was nice enough and tipped Earle a dollar for carryin their bags up to the British Mystery Room. They came in their own car from Delhi, New York—and looked independent enough to find their way to restaurants and such—so we all figured the next we'd see 'em would be at breakfast on Saturday.

Right on their heels was a young man with enormous gray eyes and thick black hair what put me instantly in mind of Heathcliff—the one what gave that poor girl in Emily Bronte's book so much damn trouble. And sure enough, he said he had a big fight with his girlfriend; and he was askin straight off if he could have a rebate on the room since now he was here by hisself.

"You're booked into Playwright's Corner," Earle said, "In any case, all our rooms are taken and we have no accomodations that are specifically for singles."

"But the attic room is less—"

"Yes, and it's already reserved."

"Well couldn't some kind of allowance be made?"

"I'm afraid not," Earle said. He said it nice enough, but his voice was firm. Me and Huck thought that was right—I mean we was in business—but Heathcliff didn't take it that way.

"You're sure?" he fumed.

We had set up a kind of check-in station business desk kind of thing in the front hall—it even had a little lamp over it so guests wouldn't break their necks on the stairs—and it was one of Earle's finest English Pine antiques we used for the desk, and it looked very official and welcomin at the same time. Earle tapped the register. "We're completely full as you can see."

"Ohohhhhh, nothing goes right for me, nothing!" Heathcliff cried, squeezin his thin hands into fists at his side. Then he dropped straight to the floor in front of Earle and starting rolling on Lady's good Axminster rug like you do when your shirt has burst into flames. A half minute later he began to babble. "First my darling Jane refuses to come away with me, and now the curse of my perpetual bad luck is upon me again." His eyes rolled back, then he gave a kind of bay that warn't very loud but put me in mind of the kind of yelp what is the harbinger of death when a stray dog tunes up—me and Huck knew about that, you bet. A long thread of spittle dripped out of Heathcliff's mouth—and then his eyes was snappin open and shut and flutterin like a drag queen's in a camp revue.

"No wonder he booked Playwright's Corner," Huck hissed at me. "This guy is doin Hamlet—at least that line that says all the world's a stage—cause he sure is doin one hell of a job actin right here on the rug."

"If Lawrence Olivier was still alive, I don't think he'd have to worry none about the competition—" I meant because he'd played both Heathcliff *and* Hamlet, of course.

Our Heathcliff, meanwhile, got to his hands and knees and shook his head a time or two—his great shock of hair swingin. He cleared this throat and then looked up at Earle and said, "It's passed now, I'm all right again."

Then he levered himself upright usin the newel post—which creaked considerable considerin how skinny the guy was. He had on a huge, dark gray sweater I reckoned weighed more than he did.

"All right," Earle repeated in a voice that was so flat it sounded computer-generated. He warn't happy a bit. And I could tell he was thinkin about givin old Heathcliff his money back just to get rid of him. You just knew he was thinkin about what the hell would the Reverend and Missus make of him at breakfast—if he started in on his *Lost Weekend* routine.

"Perhaps—some compensation could be made—" But that was as far as Earle got.

Heathcliff stuck out a hand and closed it over Earle's wrist. "Please let me stay. Oh please. I'll be good. There won't be any more instances. None. Really."

Well, he might have called it a fight with his girlfriend, but if you ask me the girlfriend warn't nothin but a legend in his own mind. Probably somebody who talked to him once and woulda thought twice 'bout spittin on him to put him out if he was on fire, but it looked like we was stuck with 'im for the weekend.

"Please!" his eyes snapped shut again, and I do believe if Earle had said no, he woulda started in rollin on the floor again.

Earle nodded. "Oh Ted," he called, when as we all knew Ted was just inside the door to the kitchen—probably with his ear against it. "Oh, Ted-ddddd!"

Ted popped out a second later, and he looked terrified behind his fake smile.

"Would you take Mr. Linton's bags to Playwright's—"

"No luggage," Heathcliff whispered.

"Will you show him up—"

"I'll find it," Heathcliff said through gritted teeth. And then he bit his lip, and leanin as heavily as a drunk who lives in a five-floor walk-up, began clompin up the stairs.

"If his real name is Edgar Linton," Earle said, "then I'm Mark Antony."

"He is haunted," Ted said, watchin him totter up the stairs and then turn left.

"Crazy," Huck said.

"No, *haunted*," Ted corrected. He gave a little shiver and went back to the kitchen. I figured Ted would have more to say about Heathcliff by and by.

* * *

By 8:00, we'd checked in all but two of the guests. We'd stashed a forty-somethin blonde couple named Stephen and Myra Burnes in the *Great American Novelists* room and another very young couple who was all in black and wearing trench coats into *European Masters*. We figured the young couple—Catharine and Lazlo—who warn't married probably wouldn't even show up for breakfast. They looked mighty cozy around one another. They probably wouldn't do no readin, nuther.

We was sittin at the dining room table takin our ease when Hucky said, "Well, I guess that's everyone."

"No," I reminded him, "whoever has booked the attic ain't showed yet."

"They are not coming until very late," Ted said.

"Well, I hope they don't disturb Lady," I said. She was in her altar room, but she was restin—said she had a kind of headache. I figured she was just used to goin in there of a Friday night, and even with the

185

door shut and no ritual goin on, she could take some comfort in the memories of her old routine. I didn't think she'd get all the incense goin and candles burnin with guests around—mostly because they'd probably just be a distraction—and if there's one thing witchcraft and rituals demand it's concentration. And I was pretty sure, come along midnight when things quieted down she'd want to light up and have a little chat with the goddess.

"No. Earle and I will let them in very quietly. It will be fine."

"What time they hovin in?"

"Three of the clock," Ted said.

"Who comes at three in the mornin—" And I thought I saw a signal cross between Earle and Ted, but Ted was already givin me the lowdown.

"It is all be right—they are friends of mine and Earle's."

"Friends—"

"We have wanted to make sure Miss Bar-bara's first weekend was success with all rooms taken, so we have asked our friends to please call and make reservation, which they have oh so kindly done, and they will be here—somewhat late, of course, but—"

"You booked a coupla werewolfs?"

"The attic is problem," Ted began. "We wanted someone who could withstand supernatural interference—"

Well, I thought Huck was gonna explode.

"But it ain't ha'nted—!"

"Oh, yes," Ted started to say.

"Werewolfs," I said cuttin him off. But how much further could I go? I mean him and Earle was werewolfs, and I didn't wanna start sayin stuff that sounded mean or low-down, but if this didn't beat all ... we didn't even have a single guest who gave a *damn* about ha'nts, and fifty percent of the adults in the house warn't even *human*.

"But you know it ees haunted," Ted said. And he looked at Earle.

"We made that up—"

"Oh but do you not know, sweet little Huck, that to write a thing down is to make it true?"

"More old-world hogwash!" Huck threw out a paw. "You tell him, Earle!"

"Well I would, Huck, 'cept what he says is true." Earle stopped. "It might not a been true before, but it is now ... there's at least one ghost and maybe more hanging out in the attic."

"Yes, and perhaps elsewhere in the house."

You could have knocked me over with a pillow case—never mind flummoxin me with the bedsheet we was gonna 'riginally use to gussy up our resident werewolfs.

"Oh Lord. And not one guest with even the slightest interest in spooks."

Earle and Ted just stared at me, and the more they looked, the deeper the feelin I had was sinkin way down inside me.

"You mean they asked about whether we was ha'nted? You shoulda told me," I said, "'stead of askin me whether me and Huck had a little scare-fest planned." I thought he'd just been keepin something back, and I warn't a bit happy about it, nuther.

"No, they do not ask when they book the rooms," Ted said.

"But—"

"Nope, none of 'em's come out and said a word," Earle added.

"They do not need to ask," Ted said, foldin his hands neatly on the table. "They are merely ... drawn."

"Drawn!"

"Attracted to this place ... to the emanations," Ted said.

"Emanations—that's the same as spooks and sperits, ain't it?" Huck cried out. Ted nodded. "Oh, my Lord, Tom! We's ha'nted for real!"

We might a started out thinkin about the big bucks and foolin with the slithery sound that Aeolian harp made and cuttin up the bed linens to throw over Ted and Earle and treatin the whole thing as a lark and a joke, but we was in a tighter spot now. We warn't just an inn, we was home to a whole troop of folk we could not even *see*. Not yet, anyhow.

CHAPTER TWENTY-SIX

GHOST WALK—
WAFFLING WITH TED

Well, with four werewolfs, a nutty guest, and ghosts roamin about, things was bound to get lively. 'Most livelier and gaudier than even I was sure I wanted in on. In the meantime, I figured we better go let Lady in on the latest developments. I also thought—Ted's quaint Old World notion aside—she might have a line on how this phantom folderol got started. I mean, did we now have a secret passage—what was somethin else we concocted out of thin air and nothin more substantial than HTML? No, it didn't make no sense. Maybe I was just bein natur'lly cynical as a direct result of bein hatched out of Mr. Clemens' fertile brain—but that was another tack, and I warn't ready to look into that yet or start to wonderin if he'd been real that day under the Tree House or just part of my dream.

But when I tapped at her door with my paw, there warn't no answer. I didn't want to disturb her if she was meditatin, so I just went on into the bedroom and hopped up onto the white coverlet. She'd come in soon, and the three of us would snuggle like we always did, I thought—and fell asleep under the spell of that happy fallacy.

* * *

By and by it was comin on for nearly four in the mornin—and still dark as six-feet under—when I heard a god-awful snappin and snarlin like wolves or wild dogs tangled in a terrible fight. You know that sound; it's enough to make your blood freeze clean through. I didn't know what to do—my cat nature was cowerin, though I hate to admit it. Huck's voice from under the covers where we'd crept in to sleep was a whisper muffled in fear.

"Oh, Tom, what is *that*?"

That being a low, throaty *grrring* that suddenly erupted into an angry bark, and it seemed to run louder when it passed across the soundin board of the big canine's teeth. A fast furious boiling tension was in the air. I could almost hear the bony sound of tooth gratin against tooth when the bitin starts between fightin dogs. That dangerous noise is as powerful and menacing as a fast movin storm sheddin thunder and lightnin and rippin out trees. And it's just as scary to humans as it is to cats.

"It's the werewolfs," Huck said.

"No." I meant it, too. I might not have been able to put it into words then, but some part of me caught on to the fact there warn't a trace of humanity in this sound. These warn't men who spent some of their time as animals—they was animals who'd never been anything *but* animals. Predators—lean and angry and starved.

There was more that was gnawin at my innards.

"Huck, I don't think anyone 'cept us hears it."

"No—"

"I do mean it. Wouldn't that old Reverend's wife be shriekin by now if she thought a pack of rabid carnivores was mixin it up practically outside her bedroom door?"

"Where's Lady?" Huck said, dippin his head into my shoulder.

"She didn't come to bed last night at all, I reckon." Well I got it out, but that scared me, too.

The dog warrior noise dropped off a few seconds later, and though we breathed in the intervenin silence, we both sensed somethin else knifin unseen through the dark air. I heard shatterin glass. Huck heard the whooshin sound the guillotine makes on its evil descent. The other guests was roused now, too.

190

"What's that child crying?" I head the Reverend Missus ask in a stricken voice.

"Stop pounding, stop your pounding!"

"That was Heathcliff." I swallered uneasy-like. "I heard *glass* breakin, not poundin nor no child whimperin—"

A scream came from what sounded like the cellar, and a second later, the young foreign couple was in a commotion out in the hallway sayin *they* heard what sounded like a waterfall pourin through the roof.

"I didn't hear none of that," Huck said. Not the baby, nor the pounding. Just the dogs and the metal blade like they done in France, but not the rest of them devil works." In the dark of Lady's bedroom, I felt his paw pull at my mine. "Oh, Tom we're just stuffed with ghosts. Right up to the rafters."

* * *

Doors were openin and now everybody was out in the hall, so me and Huck thought we'd better go take a look. It was just what you'd expect. Everybody barefoot and half undressed—in nightgowns and bathrobes and pajama bottoms—and talkin all at once in each other's faces and turnin faster than revolvin doors to tell the next neighbor whose ear they could catch what *they'd* heard.

"Sounded like goddamn Niagara Falls—"

"It was a child and someone was hurting it—"

"Like a battering ram—boom! Boom!"

Suddenly there was Lady standin at the other end of the upper hall.

"Sorry," she was sayin. "An accident."

Everyone stopped and heads swiveled to look at her.

"I'm sorry ... I fell asleep ... downstairs watching a movie. An old movie." She gave a wan smile. "*The Haunting of Hill House*—the one with Claire Bloom and Julie Harris—not that recent monstrosity," she said. "When I woke up, instead of turning it off, I hit the volume button accidentally ... and ..." She gave a thin shrug. "Boom-boom."

"Oh," the Reverend Missus said, and you could see relief just shutter down over her face like a shade bein lowered. "Is that all? I thought it was—well, I don't know what I thought it was—" She tried

191

a tiny laugh on—but you could see her mind workin and rememberin that part of the film and insistin on makin the connection.

There was the usual mutterin and what you'd expect as everybody more or less wound down and started headin towards their bedrooms, a coupla "goodnights" and sarcastic-soundin "sweet dreams" floated around the hall.

I looked toward Lady and saw Myra Burnes standin outside the threshold of the *Great American Novelists* room, her arms crossed and her face set. She didn't bother to lower her voice. "Your story about the movie is just that," she said; her body was very still, her long blonde hair never ruffled.

Lady didn't say anything. Myra went on. "It won't get better, you know. Only worse." Myra paused. "But of course, I see that you do know that," she gave a little nod to Lady. Lady only stared.

"I've as much experience in these matters as you—even if I'm not a w—" she caught Lady's signal—a finger held to her lips—and Myra, she changed course. "Still, I mean to communicate with"—and now she did speak very softly—"with *whatever* roams here."

"Goodnight," Lady said.

Myra Burnes went into her room, closin the door so gently the latch made just the tiniest snick.

* * *

The first disaster of the day was breakfast—and us bein a Bed and Breakfast—some folks might say fifty percent of who we were was entirely out of commission. We got Ted the strawberries all right, so's he could make his special sauce for the waffles; the problem was Ted's sauce was a little too special.

Maybe it was runnin a bowlin alley all those years; maybe it was because he fancied himself a little deprived by the lack of imagination that came with the territory of ownin that particular kind of business—anyhow, Ted decided that his sauce was gonna be unique on the planet. He got the unique part in just fine. Any ordinary chef woulda felt like he'd just played the trump card if his strawberry sauce had a little extra zing that took it to a new level. You know just the sort of thing I mean—some lemon zest or a sprig of mint or a dash of somethin—but not Ted.

I don't know what he did to that simple valentine-heart-shaped fruit, or what he put into the pot to make 'em turn traitor—but the strawberries at the first-ever breakfast served up at The Chancery House looked exactly like chicken hearts—and they was floatin in a liquid that was the runny darklin red of fresh blood.

The kitchen looked like a hundred kindergarten kids had invaded all hell-bent on earnin their cookin badges on the same day. Pots and pans were strewn like mines in a paranoid farmer's pumpkin patch come Halloween. But, 'stead of blowin your legs off with blastin powder, what got exploded around Ted was a conglomeration of flour, eggshell, milk, strawberries, and melted butter. Even the walls and refrigerator doors was so smeary with fingerprints the F.B.I. coulda used 'em to train new agents. Every time Ted got somethin on one of his hands, he'd wipe it off—but after he ran out of paper towels, dish towels and napkins, he started in on his red apron. By the time the first batch of waffles was heatin on the griddle, he was down to his last clean apron. That was about the time me and Huck wandered in to eat our own breakfast, which we couldn't—since earlier that mornin Ted had turned on the blender to whisk up his homemade waffle batter, but since he heard some butter on the fry plate suddenly sizzle up so high and fast he was afraid it was gonna burn, he flipped the switch and the blender spewed waffle mix like Vesuvius. A lot of it landed right in our kitty bowls—floodin the food that was in there, and natur'ly Ted didn't have no time to put out more kitty crunchies. I knew just how Jane Eyre felt with every meal ruint; my stomach was rumblin.

"What's up, Ted? You sure you got a handle on this?" I said.

"Yes, yes. At last, all is in order." He didn't mean the kitchen walls, of course. "And the first batch of waffles are ready to serve."

He had a stack of plates laid out, and now he was countin to himself and pullin waffles off the iron. I should say pieces of waffles, because they was stickin to that black iron griddle like two-year-old postage stamps.

"No, oh no." Ted mourned over the shredded waffles; then, a course he was distracted, so he wiped his hand on his last clean apron without thinkin.

"You need some help?" Huck asked.

"It's under control!" Ted said. He warn't really angry, just frustrated.

193

By and by, he had six plates all ready (the werewolfs, along with Catherine and Lazlo, was skippin breakfast), each of 'em piled with a little hump of broken waffle parts.

"This is not attractive at all!"

He was right. You couldn't tell the waffles ever started out in the shape of a heart.

"Maybe you could sorta arrange the pieces like a heart and then when you coat 'em up with sauce, it'd be all right," Huck said, tryin to help. We hadn't seen the sauce yet.

"Oh Huck, little one, this is brilliant idea!" Ted danced over and, I swear, he picked Huck up and gave him a kiss on the nose. Then he set Huck down again and pirouetted back to his stack of plates.

He commenced to sort of moldin the waffle leavins, then flattenin 'em down like a paper heart—just like a preschool child workin with clay.

Each plate now contained a golden heart—well, it was a heart if you squinched your eyes up and opened 'em real fast and someone had already told you you was lookin for a heart shape.

Ted sprinkled some powdered sugar 'round the edges of the pink plates.

Then he hove in with the pot with the sauce and a big wooden spoon. He started ladlin sauce on the waffles on plate number one.

"What is that?" Huck asked.

"Strawberries en sauce 'a la Ted," Ted said.

"Where's the strawberries?"

"Right here," Ted said holdin one up, then layin it down and wipin his fingers on his apron.

"It looks just like a chicken heart." I said. "How'd you turn the strawberries so slick and brownish lookin—"

"It is special and secret," Ted said. "Secret recipe from Hungary. Guests will love," he said and went right on layin those chicken gutty-lookin things all over the breakfast.

"The sauce looks like somebody cut an artery," I said.

"It is special, I tell you," Ted yelled, slammin the pot down. "I have thought and considered and worked and experimented and this sauce—even if we do not have same Alpine strawberries like is in old country—is perfect. *Perfect*. Guests will love!" he finished; then he went back to drownin the plates.

A minute later, he stoked up a fancy multitiered tray so's he could layer the servings and carry all the plates at once; he hefted it up, bumped his rear against the swingin door and went into the dining room—where the shuffle of feet and desult'ry conversation told us everybody was done with butterin rolls and sugarin coffee and sippin juice and just perishin for the main event.

"Maybe he's right and they will love it," Huck said.

* * *

The screams said different.

"Oh my God!"

"What is this? What is this?"

The Reverend was shoutin, "It's an abomination," and then Missus Entweiler started prayin at the food, just like it was real black witchcraft and she was wardin off the evil one. "Lord Jesus, save us! You have the power. Save us! You have the power!"

"I think I failed to mention I am a vegetarian," Heathcliff said above the din. "I demand a credit on the price of my room, I paid for breakfast—I can't eat this meat."

"No meat, strawberries," Ted said. "*Strawberries!*"

"This is the most disgusting thing I've ever seen ..."

* * *

But I will close the door on the rest. The dinin room cleared out faster than a college cafeteria under a bomb threat. Me and Huck could hear the guests railin and throwin napkins down and mutterin about *Egg McMuffin* and *The Silver Dollar Diner* over in Red Hook and stompin away. Nobody stayed long enough to even ask if we had any Wheaties on hand. The front stairs creaked again and again with the passage of feet goin up and comin down. The front door slammed.

We heard Ted give a groan; then slump his tall body down against the wall.

"Miss Bar-bar-a will never forgive me," he said very softly, and without a word passin between us, me and Huck we took what Ted was sayin as our cue to go in there and give him a little boost. Now the dinin room was wrecked, too; and at least one plate of the goo had been overturned on to the table and was drippin on the floor. Ted was sittin spread-legged on the floor and cryin into his apron; he kept flippin the hem of it against his face to wipe his chin and cheeks, so spatters of waffle makins and blood sauce was gettin unceremoniously flung against the wall.

"Don't cry, Ted," Huck told 'im. He laid his length alongside Ted's right thigh.

"Anybody can make a mistake," I said, flankin Ted on the left.

"I do not understand what is the problem," Ted said, tears clottin his voice. "Yes, the *waffles* were ... a shade." He grimaced. "Unappealing ... all scattered and not at all nice and crisp and be-yoot-i-fully formed as I had hoped." He paused. "But the sauce was *perfect*." He threw off the red apron onto the chairback that was nearest; me and Huck scooched away some. Then Ted stood up all at once; he took a long step forward. "I defy anyone to tell the difference between my strawberry sauce and a puree with genuine avian organs. I defy them!" His usual brown eyes was goin towards caution-light yellow.

"But, Ted, see—"

"All the pretty hearts—perfect, it was perfection!" He grabbed a waffle bit drippin that bloody gravy from a plate on the table and held it up. "What is the matter with these *people?*"

We didn't have time to tell him. Just then his two werewolf buddies popped in from the hallway. A red-headed He-Wolf and a great big She-Wolf what looked like she topped six feet tall. They sniffed the gen'ral air and atmosphere delicately, then sat right down in front of the untouched plates, never mindin the discarded napery or half-filled glasses.

"Ted this is gorgeous," the She-Wolf said, then tucked right in.

"Genius, Ted. Sheer genius," the red-headed He-Wolf said. "I love the presentation." He-Wolf admired his plate—what had been the Reverend's—for a second; then, sneakin a glance to see no humans was lookin, he lowered his head and, with his hands spread on either side of the dish, started gobblin and lickin at Ted's waffles. He snarfled up a big bite and chewed fast. "Nobody would know to look at it, that this wasn't the prime delicacy inside the most sublime chicken ever raised," the red-headed He-Wolf finished up.

"It's wonderful," the She-Wolf said. "Pickings were slim last night and I was almost starved! Starved. This is almost as good as the real thing—and so pretty, too!" she said, spoonin up another mushy gobbet. "Hearts for Valentine's Day; what could be better?"

Ted gave a big grin and sat down and pulled a plate toward him and lit into it as happy as an ingénue on Broadway. His debut was a smasher after all.

* * *

Well, after the fiasco at breakfast, I thought everybody woulda checked out, but no, they stayed on since we wouldn't give them their money back, and they'd already paid for Saturday night. I warn't surprised to see a number of 'em come in around four o'clock totin grocery bags with the usual array of peanut butter and jelly, whole wheat bread and boxes of Kellogg's Cornflakes. They warn't takin no chances on Sunday's brunch, that was sure.

Meantime, me and Huck had a hell of a time cleanin up the kitchen and the dinin area. Ted was so overwrought, when he tried to clean up in the usual way, he dropped two glasses for ever' one that made it into the dishwasher, so we shooed 'im out the back door to the carriage house for a nap, and we started in tryna witch it all tidy again. And by and by we got it all to rights. Not that we should have bothered—not with Myra Burnes conducting a séance that night and invitin the sloppiest ghosts in the universe what had no class whatsoever and flung things ever' which way and 'most smashed the place to smithereens and flinders.

Huck, he says he always did hate a messy ghost.

Me, I just wanted to make sure flyin crockery and crashin mirrors warn't gonna use up a coupla my extra lives. When the furnishins and appointments in your very own house start cyclonin around, you want to find the eye of the storm, so to speak. And duck and cover's your watchword every time, you bet.

CHAPTER TWENTY-SEVEN

RAISIN THE STAKES–SATURDAY SÉANCE–
SPIRIT IN THE SKY

Good old Myra Burnes had gone around knockin on doors and recruitin the guests to see who was interested in contacting the spirits. Catharine and Lazlo—what was practically next door to Gothic—said yes, of course. Heathcliff was a shoo-in since he didn't have nothin else to do. That made five of 'em, and accordin to Myra, five was a highly unstable number. It was change—but not the sort that brings new things in a good way. "Six would be all right," me and Huck heard her say while we lurked in the hall outside her door. "Even seven would work—seven represents choice at least."

She was gonna keep lobbyin, and we figured next on her hit-up list was gonna be the Reverend and the Mrs., but no—she clomped straight up the attic stairs and asked He- and She-Wolfs if they wanted in on the action. It warn't nothin but old pie for me and Huck to steal along in the shadows so's we could listen in.

"I don't believe we've met," Myra began, holding out her hand to She-Wolf and tellin her name.

"Nice to meet you." She-Wolf gave a bit of a slurp, but we didn't think Myra caught it—havin nothin but human hearin. "I'm Pilar Fortinbras—"

"Shoot," I elbowed Huck. "She's callin herself Hairy Strong Arm." I hung my head and let a small groan roll out of me.

"My companion," She-Wolf grinned, gesturing back toward the bed, "Georges Lapins."

Huck rolled his eyes. *His* name was compounded from a play on sound and meaning: *Gorges Rabbits.* Swell, I groaned softly again, but it sailed right over Myra's head—not because she warn't bright or intuitive or *couldn't* be—she was just so hellbent on her mission. "Hi George." She twittered her fingers at him, and he nodded.

Now, Myra spoke more quietly. "There's something peculiar in this house—and I'd like to find out what. I'm a psychic and want to hold a séance this evening downstairs in the living room." She paused, waiting for their reply.

"Have you spoken to Earle and Ted?" She-Wolf asked cautiously.

"No. It's been my experience that those who are resistant to the idea of the supernatural just get in the way of things like this."

I thought I heard She-Wolf—I mean Pilar—snicker, but she covered it in a kind of coughin sound, which Myra took for a sneeze.

"Bless you," Myra said, pattin the tall wolf woman's arm.

No two doubts about it, Myra the psychic was now battin zero. I'd thought she'd been pretty astute when she talked to Lady in the hallway the night before, but then I reckoned it didn't take no seer to pick up on any of that noisy truck and screamin' nonsense. She was lookin pretty punk at the moment with her ego stickin out a mile in the air.

"I think Georges and I would feel better if Ted and Earle were present."

"Well, I'll think about it," Myra said.

"All right," She-Wolf said.

And I figured Myra was gonna get stuck now with followin up on a contingency plan and talkin over the spirit meetin with the Reverend and the Missus.

I could hardly wait.

* * *

"Well whatya wanna bet?" Huck said whilst we dashed after Myra Burnes, her fall of blonde hair twitchin like a gypsy curtain as she trotted down the stairs and into the second floor hallway.

"That depends. Which way you bettin?" I asked. See, I knowed there were only two ways the Reverend could go: Either he'd get up on his soapbox and start rantin over raisin demons or he'd pitch right in and do his part in case the folks at Chancery House needed some help quellin the undead. If it was me, I'd have gone in for it like Merlin wadin onto King Arthur's parade ground and come up on the other side with the gaudiest fight with the evil one since that priest wrestled with the high and mighty demon Pazuzzu in Georgetown. I'd a thrown in my best effects and weapons till *my* exorcism made Linda Blair peein on carpets, spittin pea soup, and beatin off with a crucifix in *The Exorcist* look like a camp initiation at Lake Winnipasaukee. A little nerve wrackin, maybe, but as innocent as milk and bluebirds. You bet I'd have done it up right—even if I had to witch the thing myself—or pay Satan to come up out of hell and lend me a hoof.

"Which way am I bettin?" Huck said. "There ain't a bit a fairness in that, Tom Sawyer. You oughta say what you're gonna use as coll—collaberation—"

"Collateral—yes. But you know odds makes a difference, Huck. When you go to the race track, when you bet on the favorite, why then your payback ain't the same. Long shot pays much higher."

Huck nodded. "Well what d'ya figger is the long shot here?"

I hate to say I almost choked with pride, but I did. Had 'im right where I wanted 'im, and now I could call the horse race winner—as well as decidin on the size of the silver cup. It was just one of those things where I couldn't help myself. Like when I was white washin the fence back in St. Petersburg. "The Reverend could say yes or he might say no," I said slowly while we hung back a little. Myra was down the hall tappin at the door, but there warn't no response. Maybe they was takin a nap or something.

If I was still a boy, this is the point where I'd lace my hands behind my back and take a step or two—as if I had to think on it, then maybe bite out a chunk of apple for good measure—when actually I already knew exactly what I planned on. Barrin apples and hands, I rubbed a paw across my nose instead. "Less see, you got to figure in the Missus, too, to calculate these here odds."

"You do?"

"Sure. The Reverend don't live in a vacuum." I winced at the suggestion, but covered it up quick. "We got to figger how much store he sets by his wife. And you saw how she was takin on at breakfast. He might say yes, and she could throw a faint or pitch a fit, and he'd wind up quittin on the spot. Then where's your yes or no? See what I mean?"

Huck agreed. "I think he's gonna say no," he said. "And I'm willin to bet you a solid month of runnin the vacuum cleaner on it."

That was pretty good. Huck had picked right up on the undertow meanin and gone for it. Even when when we used witchery to run the Oreck, it was pure-d hell listening to that damn thing clatterin and wheelin around and screamin.

"I think he's gonna say yes. And I'm willin to counter your little offer with an interestin prop'sition of my own. I'll bet the two weeks of havin to see to Coal Porter when Lily Blum takes her vacation." Figuratively speakin, I just stuck my cocked thumbs inside the straps to my denim overalls and gave the straw in my mouth a quick little chomp, then rolled it from one corner of my lips to t'other. Right before I grinned. For now though, I was stuck with the cat's *Aw shucks*, which is sittin on my haunches and lickin the side of a paw and glancin sideways at Huck when I finished puttin spit on my nose.

"You don't say," Huck marveled. Takin care of Coal was big guns all right, and we was dreadin it—especially with Lady more or less out of sorts and the inn to run and all. "Is this gonna be winner take all, Tom?" Huck squinted at me, his blue eyes tryna look shrewd.

He meant who ever lost was gonna have to vacuum *and* take care of that slaverin demon hound.

"Sure," I said. Then I threw in my sucker punch. "What's gonna be the next level of the bet—if he says yes, but then the *Missus* makes him quit on it?"

"Well, I don't rightly know, but—"

"Or say, it ain't the Missus, but when the demons and ha'nts come bilin out a the chimney, the kitchen sink and every other orifice in the house and it's all too much for the Revrund, and he throws in the towel on account of that."

Huck's blue eyes was wide now.

"Oh, my. You think of everything, Tom. You can see right around the corners of human puzzles." His pink tongue showed against his lips, and I knew he was a little nervous. "My."

"See," I said, loadin my shovel for Huck to dig himself deeper, "if he says *yes*, but then gives up the job, why, it'll be a dead draw. We'll just end up exchangin our currency and that ain't the *same* as winner take all."

"Right. I'd have to take care of Coal and you'd have to do the vacuumin."

"So that's a contingency we got to bet on," I said, and stopped, just waitin. When I go in for a skinnin I don't stop with no pound of flesh like Shylock. I want the whole pelt.

"It's like we're bettin on whether Myra's gonna raise sperrits," Huck said.

Well I knowed he'd take *that* tack—it was the first step and the most logical. But tackin a sail is one thing and playin poker on a riverboat's another: you don't stack the deck with logic. No, you want to make sure you got five aces with a couple more extras up your sleeves and everybody's so distracted nobody counts how many have been thrown. Even if it's *twelve*—along with pucks of your Kings, Queens and Jacks doin their own bit with the smoke and mirrors. Which in this case, I determined was gonna be the easy part—not to mention the most fun.

I pretended to take a bead on Myra. "How psychic is she, I wonder ..."

Huck looked like he'd just gone home to heaven on an angel's wing. Which was just where I wanted 'im. "If the sperrits come and he throws it over, that's a no and I win. If his missus makes him quit on the job, that counts as a no, and I still win."

"But if the spirits come, and he's *forced to quit* because the devils an' demons proves too much for him—then, it's a yes and I win," I said.

Huck gave me a questionin look, then his eyes brightened. "Yais, I see what you mean. If he was to fall down in a swoon or wind up plastered against the ceilin or flung out the attic window, that wouldn't be quittin—the sperrits would have ejected him offa the payroll."

"Exactly," I said pattin his head like he was the smartest student in the class. When in fact, I had 'im right where I wanted him—fragile as an orchid under a bell jar in the hothouse. I 'llowed as how I was certain I could conjure whatever effects I needed to get the Reverund squashed by the goriest demons that ever came smokin out of the pit. Not that it mattered, really. I smiled to myself. Huck was afraid of ha'nts, and the minute the hullabaloo and terror started, he'd run screamin. If he waited *that* long. It would be just like all those scaredy cat crowds when Hank Morgan worked his eclipses and purple fire and gushing water and nonesuch in Mr. Twain's *Connecticut Yankee* book. And just like Hank, I prob'bly wouldn't even have to pull out all my tricks, though I like to keep in practice. It's better to save hellfire for times when you absolutely need it. This was the surest bet a cat or a boy ever made—cause without even realizin it, Huck had just bet against his own self. He was gonna be another Merlin—whose stock had gone just as flat as the day-old bubbles in uncorked root beer when Hank Morgan got the best of him.

* * *

Things was quiet for a while and though we knowed it was the ominous kind a quiet before a storm comes rippin out of the west and flattens, pummels and hurls everything in its path, there warn't much me for me and Huck to do but take a nap and sleep on it. As for the effects and festivities I planned for that night, well, I 'llow as how old Hank Morgan had to lay in his supplies and get his minions to do the spadework, but there ain't nothin grander than bein a familiar. All your tools are right to hand, so to speak.

I lit out for the altar room and paged through Lady B's Book of Shadows and her spell book and what not, and while it all circled madly in my head, lay right down on that swansdown chase lounger and got swaddled up in the afghan and took one of the most delicious siestas ever in a life of delightful respites.

Repose is good for the soul, you know, and it's been *proven* that naps improve mood, creativity and nearly every other thing you can think up. And I expected the call for my creative abilities and manifest powers was gonna be one hell of a challenge. It was gonna be a drain on my resources that would rival the mightiest power surge in Brooklyn during the worst heat wave in a hot summer. But I was up to it.

I'd been hatched up by Mr. Twain, same as Hank Morgan; and now I was a familiar with witchy powers to boot.

* * *

It was around 10 of the clock when I woke up. Huck had just jumped on to the chase lounger and stuck his nose in my ear.

"I think they's getting ready to conduct the séance down below," he said.

"Shoot," I told 'im. "It's hours yet till midnight. Who's old Myra gonna summon this time of night?" I was thinkin about that old newscaster's tag line about "It's 10 p.m. do you know where your children are?" Huh! As if it warn't a time-honored American tradition for kids to sneak out at night and get up to hijinks and didoes. Me and Huck done it a plenty.

"I just heard 'em moving furnishins and such—"

I could hear her directin down there, too. "Drat the woman—she ain't got a bit of style." I shook my head. If Myra had any smarts, she'd a waited till the séance got bouncin along and then got the spirits to move her tables and lamps and whatnot. 'Course she wanted to prove they was present and manifestin—since thanks to Houdini, hardly anybody believes in séances—so she had to go and make it look as if everything was just as ordinary as a copy of the *Hartford Courant*.

Them ghost-cams work on the same principle—you know the ones I mean—what is fixed on what is a very plain room that like as not is decorated by somebody with taste that's been cultivated by a lifetime spent under the Golden Arches.

Taste so bad, as a rule, it makes you wonder why a ghost would *want* to haunt the spot. The livin don't often get a choice, but you bet if I was dead I'd be hauntin chateaus in Heidelberg and villas in Monaco—you couldn't pay me to hang around a dirty basement or a bunch of grubby plastic toys in a children's playroom.

I tell you, there's places in England I never want to visit. Some of them ghost cams took all the romance right out of my head. 'Stead of stately castles and whispery women in white moanin on the moors, haunted England has all the charm of a hospital waiting room. Sometimes it don't pay to scrap a cliché. I'd a heap rather look at a drafty old hall in a manor with worm-eaten wood or a ruined gazebo than some kitchenette with a fiberboard ceiling with little holes in the tiles that hails from the 1960s and three ugly yellow vinyl-topped stools at the breakfast bar what look like they come from a garage sale.

"Put it there," we heard Myra say. Me and Huck looked at each other.

We have a sort of room in the inn what was always just a insignificant type parlor, but now that we was The Chancery House, we had to refer to it as The Library. And that's where it sounded like old Myra was settin up her base of operations. It was just one of those extra rooms the Victorians were so fond of sticking all over a place so's the members of a family who warn't speakin to one another on a particular day—or month or decade—had a retreat, so to speak.

Humans beat all for grudge matches, don't ya know it?

Talk about cat fights! I don't necessarily hold with canine groveling, but cats are peaceable creatures. Me and Huck are nearly always in the same room—and if it's at all possible, that room has Lady inside it, too. And if we go to sleep in different parts of the house it ain't never on account of a hiss-fit, but the kind of pure exhaustion that comes from battin around a ball of yarn or layin waste to troops of mice—real or imagined.

People, on the other hand, generally love their relations and spouses much better from a distance. Which is why telephones and the Internet is so popular and maybe—come to think of it—why they's so fond of séances, prayers and generally drummin up the dead from the Great Beyond. It don't get much more distant than *that*.

Me and Huck more or less eeled down the stairs and ribboned and wound our way through the first floor till we got to the library and we could hunker down on the fringe of things and size up Myra and her prep work. Mostly she'd just shifted things here and there and thrown in a great big old tape recorder for the effect of the thing, and she was layin down the candles and the incense and she covered up the table with a big white bedsheet and she was lookin busy as much as she was bein busy—but that was all right with me.

I knew she was gonna have more to deal with than she ever imagined—so it was just as well if she rested up a tad before the curtain went up on the main event.

* * *

It was closin in on midnight and Myra had dragged in a big table from the dinin room for everybody to sit around. There was the Reverend and Mrs. Entwiler, the Wolf Crew, Catherine and Lazlo, and him we called "Heathcliff" all linked up and holding hands in the flickerin candlelight. It warn't but old berry pie for me and Huck to conceal ourselves in the heavy shadows in the corners of the room.

"I have prepared the way for the spirits," Myra said. We must be open and inviting. One thing you must know is that spirits are highly sensitive. For example, the proper term nowadays is to refer to them—lovingly—as DPs—"

"DTs?" I said to Huck

"DPs," he said, givin me a little smirk. "Dead Persons. I seen it on a website, it's what they call that there 'politically correct.'"

"Why the hell would the dead care?" I said.

"Beats me," Huck shrugged. "Why's it matter if you call lepers lepers? Ain't none of 'em around to hear ya since they's all locked up. And if they was around, ain't nobody would get within a hundred yards anyhow—"

"They don't lock up the lepers," I said.

"You're kiddin me, Tom, go on. Not lock up a leper—"

"They have medicine now, Huck and—"

"You mean we might a been around lepers and not even knowed it?" He was rollin his eyes and switchin his tail.

"Stay on the subject, Huck. We're talkin 'bout how it don't matter about the folks formerly upright and breathin who are now rottin in the ground or settin up in jars on mantelpieces because they are ashes and what has parts of their essence still caromin around the universe and just about runnin a fever to come back and torment the livin or get their ease. We are talking about the dead. Period."

"DPs—dead persons," he hiss-whispered.

"I have prepared the way for the spirits," Myra said. "You'll notice the white sheet on the table and the planchette." She meant, I reckoned, a little triangle of light balsa wood settin on three tiny legs. At the top was a small hole fitted out with a pencil. Everyone at the table looked at it, and Myra pointed, sayin, "That is so any who may wish can communicate with us by automatic writing. Some of the shyer spirits only feel comfortable with that method." She nodded sagely. "There are three candles and incense, because—"

"Incense makes me sneeze," Heathcliff hove in with.

"This is just the sort of attitude that prevents spirits from presenting," Myra said. Her mouth was set in a hard line. They all looked uncomfortable; they didn't move none nor fidget, and no one said a word.

"I notice her husband ain't around," Huck whispered to me and gave me a pretty good nudge. "Reckon he knows somethin' about old Myra?"

"You bet. How many of her fraud shows can he watch?" I said. Too bad about tonight though; he'd of seen a doozie.

"The spirits need an inviting atmosphere," Myra told Heathcliff— at the same time she was eyeballin the rest of the group. She was like a admiral who ran a war-time fleet and warn't about to tolerate slackers, whiners, luffs nor old time salts what didn't like the food in the galley. Miss Myra was puttin em on notice the *only* policy was gonna be "All Hands on Deck." Pronto. Them that didn't like it was goin to the brig; or more likely, heaved overboard to dogpaddle the sea swells or flail amongst the sharks.

"We must be receptive: we must be open. In mind, spirit and soul. As the medium, I've even taken a cleansing bath—"

"Cleansin?" Huck hissed at me. "She smells like a sulphur pit."

No two ways about it, Myra stunk to high heaven. I almost felt sorry for Heathcliff settin next to 'er.

"With rosemary and myrrh and—"

"Is that what I smell?" Heathcliff said. "God, I thought it was just the incense—"

Myra jumped right in shoutin like Anthony Hopkins doin Captain Bligh. "WE WILL CLEAR OUR MINDS *NOW* AND FOCUS ON INVITING THE SPIRITS INTO THIS ROOM. WE WILL HAVE QUIET. WE WILL CONCENTRATE. IS THAT CLEAR?"

Nobody said a word—they didn't even murmur. Who would? Myra was shootin icicles for stares and looked steely enough to stuff the meanest spirit in the universe down the throat of anybody who even gave her a *hint* of mutiny. Walkin the plank would be paradise by comparison her eyes said.

She cleared her throat. "Good," she said softly, "now we can begin."

I guess her husband was in on it after all, and that was their pre-arranged signal. A CD started up somewhere and the noise of it like to made my skin crawl. It was one of those newfangled New Age things with tinklin bells for 'bout a half hour before the music starts—not that when you hear it you don't wish for the bells again. It was all waterfalls and angel-harp soundin things and waves washin on the beach. It was enough to give anybody who liked the hearing the sounds of nature in *actual* nature the screamin fan-tods.

* * *

Well, we all sat for nigh on to two hours with not a thing happenin. It warn't so bad for me and Huck, 'cause we could slip in and out of the room to visit our food bowls or the litter box. We could even squush up together and take naps. But the humans was gettin fidgety—and tryin' not to fidget, which made it a whole lot worse. Pretty soon, we was watchin bottoms waggle on the chairs, shoulders rolled and spines straightened. You know what came next: throat clearin, sighs fetched up from the depths of vacuity, and the very pit of boredom, like when a preacher gets t' ramblin too long on a warmish summer day. Long about the time the jaw springin and yawnin started in I figured it was time for me to gear up. Or the whole caboodle of 'em was gonna stand up en masse, shove their chairs back and leave the room for bed. It was time to make my audience sit up and take notice.

"Do you hear that?" It was Myra. For a second, everyone looked at her real suspicious-like—as if she was tryna keep up interest in somethin nonexistent long past the point of no return. But I warn't one to worry about some of my reputation stickin to her curricula vitae, so I wound 'er up again.

EeeeeeeePING PING PING eeeee ticktick PING PING PING!

It was a nice sound, somthin I conjured outta the Aeolian Harp, piano tunin regimens and that clickin noise a dishwasher makes when it moves to the next cycle. And of course, when I say nice, I don't mean it sounded pleasant, I mean it was a goodish effect—for starters. It warn't shucks for a spell, I just had to think "noise" and out it shrieked.

209

"They've come," Myra said in the same voice Mary Magdalene used when she found Jesus Christ's tomb was empty.

"Show yourselves, show yourselves," Myra trilled. "All are welcome here. Be free to *MANIFEST*!!!"

Well, I don't know about you, but I warn't about to come around the first time Myra called me; if I came at her command, she'd just start actin like she won first row balcony seats in heaven on Judgment day.

I stopped everything to let 'er stew a while.

You could barely see in the room, and the only sound now was human breathin and the tick of silence I like to think of as the deathwatch beetle. And the real clock, too, of course. Clocks, you will have noticed, sound loud as hell when it's quiet, and even louder when all hell is about to erupt. Which it was.

Right into the center pocket of that dead silence I dropped your average break-the-sound-barrier noise: BBBBOOOOOOOOOOMM!

"Hold hands!" Myra shouted. "Hold tight! Don't break the link!"

It was a stunner; they was cringin and duckin and I was pretty sure Heathcliff near about wet his own self, but I warn't about to let up now that the show was rippin through act one.

BBBBOOOOOOOOOOOOMMM! BBBOOOOMMMMMMMM!

"Just stay calm and hold onto your partner's hand!"

This was the equivalent of a schoolteacher tellin a pack of kindergarteners on a field trip not to run and scatter when Rodan descended out of the air, claws extended, and startin in on the peckin of all that tender flesh. And our guests warn't no different; they was ready to bolt, you bet.

"Stay calm," she shouted. "It's just confused; these noisy manifestations will cease shortly," she said fast. "We beg you to come quietly now."

They was waitin and terrified, but you never did see a group of faces in any tableau yet that was so drained and pasty with fright.

And there warn't no sense in not givin old Myra her way once in a while, so I switched gears—uh, manifestations. From the right ceilin corner, deep in the shadows, I let out a blast of purple fire that shot halfway across the room.

Catherine screamed.

It was fine, because the flames had been silent, just like Myra predicted, and now we'd have some real lively noise on the tape recorder with Catherine screamin and all.

Still, I gave them near on to another nanosecond to quiet their nerve endins.

Then I gushed green flames out of the right-hand ceilin corner. It was spectacular, it bein so dark in there.

"Jesus Christ!" Mrs Entweiler screamed.

"They're just confused!"

"Confused, my aching ass," Lazlo shouted. "They're aiming for us!"

"Stay still, be quiet, this spirit will calm itself in a moment. The transition is difficult for some to make—"

"Make this transition," Lazlo said, givin her the finger.

That was my cue. When I go in for a thing, I go all out.

I got the planchette spinnin like a dervish on the table and writin:

Die Lazlo Die

Die

LAZLO

Over and over in a ragged red bloody hand.

I sent oil paintings sailin around like paper airplanes that was goin for evasive action and dodgin the red flames comin from the western corner of the ceiling and the yellow fire blazin out of the southhand spot. It was bright enough now in there with all four of them gaudy colored fires just blazin like the finale at Fourth of July fireworks.

I got the rug undulatin like a python what has just swallered a malamute, and the lamps flickerin and spittin out that mad scientist lab noise: Gddge—Gddggge—Gddge!

Which put me in mind to change the rest of the sound effects whilst I was levitatin the table and creatin the illusion the ceiling was droppin, which meant they'd all get singed pretty soon from the goutin flamework, so I let out with a couple of banshee wails and the crescendo from the *Mephisto Waltz* played backwards for a cymbal crash or two and screechin up just dandy.

What with the folks screamin and scramblin and dashin hither and yon, I couldn't a been any prouder of my effects or any happier just watchin all the knee-tremblin terror I'd created in a bunch of rational humans and two werewolfs what might even tip over into wolfery if they got scared enough.

No, I couldn't a been any more chipper and gleesome—right up till the library doors slammed shut and locked with two tremendous BANGs followed by a gap of silence ... and then a little sneaky snick of a key turnin in the locks.

Then there was another deadly silence.

But I hadn't done any of *that*.

CHAPTER TWENTY-EIGHT

THE SÉANCE AFTERMATH–FOG–
DEATH RATTLE

Damnation, if it warn't like what Ted said—that if we wrote a thing down, it happened. Apparently the dead are so stupid that if you pretend to call them, they can't tell the difference between a joke and a real séance and just up and join the party.

The humans and the werewolfs was all frozen in place. Somewhere outside the house, I thought I could hear Ted and Earle racin around—as if they was tryna get inside to see what was happenin.

"Now you've done it, Tom Sawyer," Huck mewled at me. "You've gone and opened the very Gates of Perdition and let out the worst demons that ever was and they's in our *house*!"

"Maybe the Reverend can quell 'em," I said. But I warn't ready to admit I'd made a mistake—not yet, anyhow.

"These here sperrits is bout a million times peskier and more dangerous than the ones in the attic, and they's right on the first floor and can maybe follow us everywhere. We won't have no peace sleepin or eatin or nappin—"

"I'm thinkin on 'er Huck."

213

"Looky here, Tom ... s'pose one of them flame-throwin gremlins decides he oughta spit fire right when you's sittin in the litter box. What then, huh? You better think fast."

But there warn't time. The smoke and fog in the room was gettin thicker and heavier, and pretty soon we couldn't see none of the humans nor Ted and Earle's werewolf pals ... after a while we couldn't hear em, nuther.

Now it was gettin colder in the room, like November river mist before dawn that sinks right through the pores of your skin and settles deep in your bones. It was lonely in that swirlin dark and cold, as lonesome as three of the clock when you've lost a friend.

Huck, he edged up close to me. I sure didn't want to lose holt of him in the dark. On the other hand, we couldn't just lie there and set like ducks on a pond. "Huck, we got to creep around the room and find our way outta here, and once we get out, you can bet we'll figure out somethin to send these sperrits back from wherever they come."

"Where do you s'pose Myra and the rest of them guests has got to?"

"Don't know."

"It don't look good for the inn, Tom. Havin guests what come then disappear ... I mean less a person wanted to avoid prison or somethin this wouldn't be a good place to stay." He sounded desperately low. "What am I gonna write on the website! Do you want to vanish because yer up to your neck in debt? Do you need to avoid the FBI? Got cell fever? Afraid that pretty soon you're new jail neighbor's gonna be Michael Skaekel, the crazy Kennedy nephew what golf clubbed a little girl?"

I tried to cheer him up. "Don't you worry, Hucky. You jest set up one of them flash buttons under our Amenities banner what reads:

Mother-in-Law Referral Service

Available on Request

That'll fetch 'em." I gave him a little nudge, but I wasn't sure it helped much. It didn't help me much.

I knew the corner where we'd been hunkerin was our raft so to speak, and now we had to strike out. I told Huck to take hold of my tail and not let go no matter what.

Then I started slouchin forward—mindful to stay near the wall—toward what I thought was the door on the right. I didn't know what I'd do if I got there and it was still locked. I was more afraid I wouldn't find it at all.

* * *

It was just terrible creepin through that dark. Twenty times I lost heart and wanted to just lie down right where I was and give it all up. I cursed myself as twenty kinds of fool for gettin me and Huck in this mess. I almost understood how Lady must've felt when she decided things warn't ever gonna go right again and she'd seen enough and wanted to just be done with the business of livin. I 'most wished I was in the Tree House and dreamin I could stay there forever and never have to worry bout things ever again, but just be all peaceful-like. But I loved Huck too much for one thing—and what if while I was a dreamin through all time I never saw him again?

"Tom?" He edged up next to me—though truth to tell it made me nervous that he'd let go of my tail to do it.

"Where's they all gone to, if they's not in here with us?"

I shook my head. "Don't know, Huck."

There was a shadow on the wall—or maybe it was just projected against the fog like it was a kind of curtain you show movies on. I know how that sounds—a shadow there in the fog what you couldn't see your own hand inside of—but they was shadows there just the same. And they was movin.

I stopped dead still. Then Huck, he stopped and I knowed he was seein em too.

"Tom, is something movin over there?"

"Yais. A shadow—"

"But like a skeleton that's dancin or somethin."

I watched it whirl and hijink around some, like the veriest gypsy dancin drunk around a campfire and celebratin the best day in his life. It was terrifyin to see so much glee in something dead and ruined. What could it be gloryin in?

215

"I oncet saw a book over to the Widow's," Huck whispered "and it was picture of that there Rumpledskelton feller—"

"Rumpelstiltskin, yes—"

"His name don't matter a whit, Tom ... what does matter is that this here skelton of our'n is jest the same. In the book they was the meanest looking dwarf you ever saw, just pure meanness comin off him like a smell, like when Pap was so drunk even the fumes comin off him smelled mean. And that there dwarf had a big mouthful of dirty brown teeth what was supposed to be a grin, and he was hootin and stompin all about a campfire in the woods 'cause he knowed he was gonna win that child off the queen. And mebbe, you'd think, he was so happy 'cause he was gonna eat it or hurt it ... but that didn't matter, neither—he was positively shinin on all the misery and pain he was gonna cause to the queen, too." He stopped a second and licked his lip. "And that skelton yonder is just the very same as that dwarf, Rumpledskelton."

"Happy to be causin hurt—"

"And feedin on it, too."

Huck had the right of that one, I believe. The thing that was death was wallowin in whatever had happened to the others.

"I don't care for that Myra a bit, Tom, nor much for the others; but it ain't right and we got to shimmy up some and see if we can help 'em—if they *still* can be helped."

Huck was always a tenderhearted chap—ain't I been telling you so the whole time? And this here proved it. He didn't just leave off forgettin Jim in Mr. Twain's story, and he was always tryin to protect baby Theandromula way back when we was livin with Ellie. But this was even bigger, Huck bein 'most terrified to mortification of spirits and death and anything evil. I was plenty scared myself, but I was proud of Huck and I figured if he was gonna wade in, even if it was twenty battalions of demons, I was gonna wade in right alongside him.

"Yais, Huck, we have got to help or die tryin." I didn't want to sound like no scaredy-cat and if I'm gonna do somethin even if there ain't no style in it, I'm gonna talk it up as if there was.

I don't think neither of us had even half the heart Becky had back in the cave—and she'd given up. It looked here like we warn't gonna get no choice anyhow. Sooner or later that Death Rag was gonna light on us—maybe. Huck read the thought in my mind.

"Tom, sure enough, when it winds down from all that dervishin it's gonna get hungry and gear up again, and by and by, it'll cast that empty socket hither and yon till it spies *us* out. And then ..." He paused. "Then, Tom, where will Lady be without us?"

* * *

We was side-by-side now, creepin through the gray fog. We warn't mindin where we were no more in relation to the walls or the doorways, we was just marchin towards that jivin rack of bones. It was spinnin itself silly—and I'm not sure its white heel nubs ever touched the floor. There was still no sound, and that was eerie, too. The cold was down our throats and under our fur and comin up through the floors as if they was made of stone that never saw sun, and we was chasin a shadow inside shadows and the room seemed to have grown to the size of a cathedral.

It was as wearyin as founderin through deep snow and I was just about to tell Huck it warn't no use—we'd never reach the skeleton thing, never get close even—when I suddenly heard a sound so small, like one brief tap of a fingernail on a windowpane. You couldn't even be sure you heard anything. I knowed it warn't Huck, though.

"You smell that, Tom?" he whispered.

"I don't smell anything, I hear a sound—"

"Saffron," he hissed, wrinklin his nose.

At the same time, I heard a little voice singin way off, and the skeleton-thing was keepin time to its own tune. At first I couldn't make out but half the words, they was so screechy and dim—more like the sound of teeth grindin than real words, but then I heard clear enough: "Tonight I brew, tomorrow I bake! And then her life away I'll take. For little knows the lady dame, Luna Raven is my name!"

"It's her," we said together.

The death thing that had got into the house and was now a shadow flittin amongst shadows was Lily Blum.

217

CHAPTER TWENTY-NINE

REVELATIONS–HUMAN SPIDER FARE–
WITHIN AN INCH OF ESCAPE

I warn't so sure we was really smellin saffron or hearin that echo of that made-up Rumpelstiltskin; but what I was sure of was that we was each pickin up on the fact that this death shadow *was* Lily. Huck always had a prime set of olfactories, and with me lovin stories, when he mentioned old Rumpel S, it just naturally brought the tale into my head. So, if we was usin mental transference and E.S.P. and witchcraft and the like, we was just tunin in the way we was wired to get our information.

"You think that séance summoned up that ravin lunatic, Tom?"

"Well, maybe the crazy can pour in right alongside the dead when they's called on, but I think something else is operatin here."

"Where do you s'pose she sent the others?"

"I dunno. Cain't see 'em and cain't see one thing but her old shadow—self." I stopped. Somethin had nearly occurred to me, but then it started to flicker away.

"Shadow ... self," I said again. "Durn it, Huck, it's no use ... I had somethin important that we needed to know right on the tip of my tongue, and now it's gone."

219

"You mean to save Myra and them others?"

"Yais, but there was a whole lot more to it, too ... if this isn't the drattiest thing. I just hate when this happens."

"But if old Lily is a shadow, Tom, how can we fight her? Ain't no way to fight shadows."

"Say that again, Huck! Oh, say it, and I'll bless you till my dyin day!"

"Say what—that there ain't no way to fight shadows?"

"Bless the cat! He said it. Oh, I could listen to 'im all day!" I said. I warn't afraid no more, and I swished my tail and would've gotten off one a my own patented rabbit dances where I hop along on my hind legs come springtime—but there warn't no sense in lettin on to Lily where we was, since she was still caromin around that fog. "Huckleberry Finn, you've hit the very nail on the head!"

"What nail? What head?"

"Doncha see, Huck?" Lily thinks she's protectin herself by goin around here as a shadow self—what nobody can interfere with or do a thing to."

"I know *that*, Tom! But I'm blamed if I know how knowin it makes a bit a difference!"

"Looky here, Huck, has Lady seemed like herself to you?"

"'Course not!"

"And way back startin last fall, who was it ever' time was behind Lady droopin her tail and saggin her spirits more and more?"

"Why, Lily, course. First with all that foofaraw over the Internet and bustin up Lady and Peter and sashayin around here like she was Queen of the Nile."

"Yais! And don't forget that day we saw her slinkin around and sneakin into the house and floatin down the driveway like a dandelion puff—" I said, whisperin into his ear in the dank roiling air.

"Or one of them orbs what folks says is ghosts in a cemetery or a house—"

"And now we have ghosts and shadows and Lily; but what we *don't* have is the Lady we know and love."

"Lady!"

"Right. Huck, Lily has gone and put a hurt on Lady, and what's been comin and goin round here for a long long time is a shadow-self—it ain't Lady, it's just a projection of Lady that Lily is throwin at us."

"Lord, Tom. It's like the Randomizer Glammer gone to blackness and wickedry."

"The worst blackness and wickedry ever."

"How we gonna stop it?"

"Don't know yet. First, we gotta get outta this here fog and this here room and away from Lily—and then maybe we can scheme her out."

"How we gettin out?"

"Derned if I know ... when me and Becky was caught in the cave, I had string and then I wound 'er and unwound 'er and crept and stretched and peered till I saw that chink of light. But now we's cats and the botheratious thing about bein a cat is you don't have pockets! That's what we need most right now, Huck—pockets."

"But Tom, we don't need pockets, we need string. Hain't you always said, that's the problem with witches, always forgettin to go to the heart of the thing? Askin for a house when they need money and such? We need *string*. And we can conjure that, easy as old pie. Leastways we can, if that ravin lunatic hain't been suckin down our powers, too. Anyhow, if she has, I don't think she can steal 'em all. Not all of 'em."

When Huck had the right of a thing, he had the right of it.

We conjured us some string.

* * *

First, we needed a wall to grope along—but I didn't want to be ferryin hither and yon in the dark and cold and go over the same ground, so to speak, twenty times and not even know it. It was a resk, but I made Hucky hold on to the end of the string, and then I took the other end in my mouth and crept along straight towards what might fetch us up at a wall.

By the time I had slinked six or seven feet ahead, Huck and me couldn't even hear each other no more. I was worried plenty. If that shadow thing lit on 'im, I wouldn't even a knowed it. I knew I might end up trailin a long piece a twine in the dark and it anchored to nothin and me not even realizin it. Huck, he'd come up with a sort of signal—

he was gonna count to ten slow, and at every ten, he was gonna give the line a tug so's I'd know he was still on the other end. Well, I don't say it warn't like takin soundings on the river so's the pilot knows the depths and can bully his way through, makin straight or sneakin and tackin around to hit a landin, but I thought Huck ought to meow out, too. Like he done when we was boys and he wanted me to crawl out the window of a night.

"No. Callin don't do no good in the fog, Tom," he whispered. "Warn't I all tipsy-turvy plenty that night with Jim? First it seemed like he was behind me, then out to the front; then maybe behind again ... and pretty soon cain't nobody tell who is where or even where his own self is. Callin in the fog is whistlin up a chimney—just a waste of time, and dangerous, too. 'Cause you'll be listenin, and when you cain't tell if you heard me or not, you'll start losin track of your own bearins."

It was tough goin in that cold lightless place, and my heart was heavy with frets and burdens no boy or cat should have to carry. It warn't even just that Lily had come swoopin in and battenin down on the séance—I knew that might a been my fault and it make me feel pretty low to know my horseplay might a been like an engraved invitation from Buckingham Palace for a command performance to the evil that was Lily. That was bad enough, but then it was even worse for me to think about how all this time I'd been ignoring Lady and not payin mind to what was really goin on—even when I had my hunches, I'd just brushed 'em away like they was lint or dandruff on a dark suit. What if Lady—I mean the *real* Lady—couldn't come back no more? That'd weigh on me, too and there'd be no duckin it.

I'd been a boy back durin the nineteenth century and acted foolish plenty of times—what else was the point of comin back if I warn't goin to remember what I'd learned the first time through? I was a cat and a familiar, and I'd thrown over what I knew now, too. Lady loved me and Huck, and I'd let her love down badly.

There was a tug on the end of the twine.

I waded out into the dark river of fog that was that room.

* * *

The fog didn't exactly *lift*, but by and by, I realized I could see better; or maybe my senses was just adaptin the way blind people

222

compensate with extra sharp hearin, but anyhow, I was paddin forward when I had the sense they was a whole bunch of shadow shapes hoverin over my head. I stopped and glanced up, and then I see a thing that could make the bravest man in the world's blood freeze stone solid: All the guests what had been at Myra's séance was just danglin in midair.

Huck had inched along our string and stopped, too, and now his mouth was in my ear. "Lord, Tom, they's like moths in a spider web."

He was right about that. They was driftin and swayin the way insects do when the wind lifts the strands of a web, and the spider's supper starts swingin. It was terrible to see humans stung to unconsciousness and slowly turnin and bobbin like that. Myra's long hair trailed from her nape like a woman levitated on a magician's stage, but one leg was bent downards, and her ankle and high-heeled foot made tiny circles in the air. They was all there, Lazlo and Catherine and Heathcliff and the Reverend. Even the werewolfs were hangin from the rafters, saliva drippin from their slack jaws as if they was human stalactites. I picked out Mrs. Entweiler. She was perpendicular, her head and shoulders jammed up near the ceiling, her legs spiralin under her skirt like some terrible puppet queen. In the warm risin air, their clothes and hair lifted and fell like the floatin rags on drowned corpses. It was hard to look at and hard to look away. "What do you suppose she paralyzed 'em with, Huck?"

He shook his head. "Don't know. And what's she keepin 'em for?"

That was a more ominous thought, but there warn't nothin we could do for them—least not right now. We still had to get out, and the idea of one of them suddenly fallin on us like a human stone made me shiver. *We* have *to get out*, I thought again.

We have to find Lady—the real *Lady*, Huck whispered inside my head.

And when I heard him in *there*, I knowed that together we could set things right, and it give me courage to move on.

* * *

It was scent that was our light at the end of the tunnel. Huck, he suddenly pulled alongside me and stepped on my feet. "You smell that, Tom?"

"No," I said.

"Right over yonder is the house." He jerked his head to the right.

He meant that beyond the blanked-out, cold, no-scent of the fog, he could smell the warmth that was home: A mix of carpet wool and wood floors and flowers and perfume and polishin wax, and way beneath it, the little patches of spoor-scent from our fur and our feet. His nose was better than mine, so I let him take up the lead.

We hadn't gone more than a yard or two when I felt a sharp hand seize the nape of my neck diggin deep into my fur; and Huck, he felt the same.

CHAPTER THIRTY

DEATH LILY–LUCK DISCUSSED–
THE SEARCH FOR LADY

Once she had us fast in those hooked claws of hers, Lily Blum aka Luna Raven aka the Dancin Death Skeleton let out a shriek loud enough to concuss my eyeballs and make 'em vibrate and tuck inside my head. That's a bad feeling, and you know it if you've ever been around a sonic boom or anything else that'll rattle the windowpanes in your house. It's worse when it's your own eyes, though, and I let out a sharp yowl of my own.

Lily hauled me up in one hand and Huck in her other; she held us shoulder height and face-to-face, and I thought sure she was gonna dash our heads together like giants do in fairy tales. My heart near about fled up into my throat.

"Now don't you two look *familiar*," she brayed, turnin her head to look first at Huck, then at me. Her laughter at the stupid joke was as hideous—maybe more—than her grip.

Huck was squirmin, and I saw his paw swing back and his claws push out, but without knowin it, old Lily had struck a chord in me.

See, there was this unwritten rule Lady told us, that no witch could interfere with another witch's familiar. It went back to that *an so it harm*

225

none thing, which I always thought was pretty short-sighted, but to interfere with a witch's familiar was to—well, potentially cause all kinds of mischief and sorrow. First of all, you took away one of the things in this world she loved best. Lots of witches right on down through time had their very best and most important relationships with their familiars—especially if that familiar was a cat. People talk about dogs and loyalties and all manner of folderol and feathers—but they are mainly your insensitive types—as insensitive, say, as dogs. Cat lovers know better—much better. And you add in that bein a witch was often a secret thing and most men are just louts, well, it ain't hard to see why a smart woman would love her cat more than any old duff who came along just to ruffle her hair and leave his smelly shoes and socks under her bed. And not just because cats are tidy creatures, nuther.

And that relationship gets 'bout a million times stronger when you toss in that the cat familiar helps the witch accomplish her goals—and a spell, if you think about it, ain't anything more than a goal. A really important goal.

In fact, I bet you never knew this, but lots of them witches that was toasted, roasted, and pressed into newsprint from the middle ages on down wasn't just accused by folk who *wasn't* witches—no, heaps of 'em was turned in by other witches who got mad when *they* was interfered with.

"Huck and Tom," Lily said, "Lady's little boys."

I saw what she meant to do; she was gonna turn us into real boys and then, since we couldn't be familiars no more, she'd be able to take even *more* of Lady's powers. Lady's stock would fall flat, and she'd be as weak and used up as old Kleenex.

Well, I warn't havin *that*. No words Lily Blum could say was gonna keep *me* from Lady. Then, all at once, it seemed to me, Lady *was* there with us right in the room—but wasted down an dyin by inches. She was laid out on a cloth-covered pallet, her arms danglin limp as the white sheet flowing over her deathbed. Her eyes were closed and her face was the saddest I'd ever seen. I heard Huck's thoughts; I saw inside him, too; our minds were one, and I knowed he was seein Lady, too. And worse, seein Lily Blum conjure a witch's sacred dagger—the athame—right out of the air. She made it swirl and menace Lady; and then me and Huck watched her use her mind to raise that shinin knife straight up over Lady's helpless form.

226

"Hackelty-smackelty," she muttered.

The heavy blade began its evil descent.

She was holdin me with just enough tight in her hand so that I could kick backwards and dig my claws into her forearm ... and then, mouth open, teeth bared, ears laid back, and claws at the ready, I launched myself at her throat.

She was so startled—I guess she thought she had us under such a damn strong binding spell—that she let go of Huck, and the instant he hit the floor, he sprang back up and he leapt for the soft flesh of her neck, too. Huck was a movin white streak, a thunderbolt armed with teeth and claws.

Never a loyal woman, nor a lovin woman, old Lily Blum couldn't have seen that there warn't nothin me and Huck wouldn't do for Lady.

"Argh," she gurgled. She'd gone down when Huck's weight pummeled her. She was on her back, arms flailin and tryin to pull us off.

We had no time for talk, no time for spells. And neither did she.

It made me sick and it made Huck sick, but we didn't stop till we'd laid her throat bare to the bone and under her chin was nothin but a ragged dripping mess. She stopped movin long afore that, though—the blood all runnin down and puddlin under her head.

Lady wasn't there.

Lily was dead.

Me and Huck held each other and cried some. We had never killed nobody b'fore, and we didn't like that we had done it now. But we'd had to, else we would have lost ourselves and Lady for good. "I saw Lady right here," I said, "an' Lily fixin to do her with a knife."

Huck nodded; he was cryin harder. "We done it to save Lady."

But 'fore I could make an answer, we heard two thick, muffled clomps, like snow fallin from a roof. When we looked up, the fog was thinnin, and I saw that She-wolf and He-wolf had dropped to the floor. They was still unconscious, but I guessed some of Lily's power was leakin out now that she was dead. The humans was still spinnin around in midair like the world's slowest astronauts, but I judged we could leave 'em a while. "First thing we need to do is head out for the Tree House, Huck," I said. We was already trottin through the foyer and movin toward the back door so's we could get outside.

"I sure hope that Lily's dyin ain't killed Lady for real, too," he said.

I hadn't thought of *that*.

"What do you mean, Huck?"

"How do we know them werewolfs ain't *dead*?"

"I thought maybe Lily couldn't have near as much power over 'em as the humans and that they was on the way to wakin up," I said.

"Wakin up!" His eyes went wide, then he took a deep breath. "Why, bein beyond the pale, them wolfs might be even more vulnerable to Lily's dark work." He gave a glance toward the polished gleamin stairs, and I knew he was thinkin about Lady's Book of Shadows up in her altar room. "They's so much we don't know," he said. "But I been thinkin on it some, and, look here, Tom—what do you s'pose a curse amounts to? Plenty of them witches killed all through the dark times went to their deaths a cursin at their tormentors. It was practic'ly mandatory."

We glided into the dark kitchen, and then he paused by the back door briefly.

"I mean wouldn't you of done the very same and make sure yer accusers got paid back even after you was gone?" He looked up, rubbed a paw at his nose and the old-fashioned metal key began to turn in the lock; then it clicked and the heavy door edge popped away from the jamb.

"Doncha think some of them witches just wanted their killers to worry the rest of their natural born lives that they *was* cursed?" I said.

"I might a before," he said, "but now that I've seen real witches—and wicked ones to boot—I think some of 'em *did* curse the folks what done 'em in. Maybe not all of 'em, but some, some for sure. What else is bad luck?"

We'd snaked out the door and now we was burrowin our way across the snow-clad lawn toward the Tree House. There was enough light from the misty fingernail moon fall to see the gore streaked in Huck's fur. I knew I looked the same and I sure warn't happy about the prospect of washin—worse, lickin—Lily's blood from my whiskers.

"What's the veriest bad luck in the world, Tom Sawyer?"

I shrugged. There was heaps of it—way too much—you asked me. There was Huck's pap, who was a drunk. Pap both resented *and* liked livin the life of a hog and that was bad. Injun Joe died within site of the cave door and died hard collectin those tiny drips of moisture from the stalactite—because after me and Becky got free, the Judge had barred and steeled the door. Some mighta said he deserved that end, but I ain't so sure.

"But there's good luck, too, Huck. Lookit all the money we got."

All he said was, "Yes, and look at all Mr. Mark Twain accumulated by his wits—and then lost—all that money and his house he loved so much. An' he lost his wife and his daughters. Havin a little good luck, then havin it swept away is the worst luck of all."

"What's luck got to do with it?" I was agreed some people—good ones—was stuck with bearin all kinds of insult and injury and lots of times there was nothing inside 'em that you could pin your finger on to say why those bad things oughta happen to em.

"Well, Tom, when I puzzled her out, I saw that maybe some of those folks what had all that bad luck, I thought maybe a witch cursed one of their great old aunties way back when, and the curse just skipped around and lighted here and there like a stone skimmin over a pond, and that curse just landed smack on 'em and showed up as bad luck."

"Maybe so, Huck. Maybe so."

"Tom?"

"Yeah?"

"Ain't it nicer to think bad luck happens 'cause a witch laid out curses than to think God done it?" He nuzzled me. "I mean you take a lady as nice as the Widow Douglas ... an' it's awful sad to think she was prayin to a God that could do mean things to little children an' old people an' good people an' all."

There warn't nothin to say to that, so I nudged him so we could get movin again.

We foundered through the snow. We could a just floated over it easy enough I guess, but you know how it is sometimes: physical effort is necessary. Maybe we just wanted to shed all the adrenalin we'd been runnin so high on. As a rule, I hated snow—cold wet stuff, though it's pretty to look at—but it felt good leapin through it that night. Huck was right alongside me, and folks might a sworn we was yoked, the way we could move in tandem. The foggy moon gleamed along the white of his fur, and his breath was a mist in front of his face. He was most beautiful to look at.

We stopped just before the Tree House, me pantin a little.

"I ain't never seen yet when justice was served—outside a book that is," Huck said. "Heaps of times bad folks thrive and good folks suffer terrible. And I never did believe it was all made up in heaven or that—"

"When they come back, it'd be set right in the next life." I grinned. "But Huck, we're reincarnated."

We slid through the skin of the tree, and we were inside. The fire blazed up and we both made a beeline for the hearth. The snow pellets caught in our fur began to melt, and we was leavin drips on the floor, but we was gettin warm fast.

"Are we reincarnated, Tom?" Huck said. "Or are we just Lady's dream entwined inside of Mr. Twain's?"

"But Huck, we have our own thoughts—"

"Maybe it's like Ted said when you write a thing down ... maybe if you dream something up it can take a life of its own, too."

"But Lady said we could be boys again!"

"Maybe. Maybe she's guessin, and she don't know one way or the other either, or maybe if we was boys it'd just be a—a vaccination on what we are now.

"A variation?"

"Conjured is conjured," he shrugged.

We were dryin off, but we weren't up to lickin ourselves clean. I warn't about to put my tongue to work groomin out Lily Blum's blood. Neither was Huck.

Maybe vaccination warn't the wrong word after all.

* * *

Huck was lookin up through the hazy layers of the Tree House that always made the place seem like Brigadoon. You could see the bedchambers above and all the tidy coziness Lady had laid on to make the place a real retreat, and the branches—bare of leaves now—and beyond that, the night sky. Outside the tree, there was the little houses with their dark windows, or here and there some that showed yellow lamps.

"She's not up there," he said, then lowered his round blue eyes to meet mine, "but I don't have no sense of her in that cave of roots below, nuther."

We both looked down when he said that. It was the strangest thing that you couldn't see what lay under the Tree House, no matter how you tried to clear your mind or squint or concentrate or anything. You could only see those gloomy caverns by goin into them.

"Do you think she's still asleep an healin in that little bower we left her in way back when? Could Lily have set her spell on Lady and her sleepin all this while, and Lily throwin shadows at us?"

"Darn it, Huck, I just don't know!"

"If she was healin and all that lovely green was growin up 'round her, wouldn't she be healed by now? Wouldn't she have busted out and come up out a the earth and dusted Lily flat?"

"Maybe she couldn't hurt Lily," I said.

"What! And Lily just a trouncin over her and Lady cain't fight back. ..."

"*An it harm none*," I whispered. "Maybe Lady's take on it includes not even fightin back. Maybe she just bore up and took it. Maybe that's why we saw her so fragile and still back when Lily ..." I swallered. "Lily tried to terrorize us."

Huck pushed his face into my neck. "Oh, Tom, if that's true, Lady might be dead."

* * *

Well, we slid through all that rotten cold dirt, and clambered like fool monkeys over the roots and rocks and peered into near about every cave, niche and nook and cranny, always lookin, always searchin on the hunt for Lady. We even called out—but there was nothin but more brown earth, twistin roots as cold as icicles and miles of hollowed-out passages. We might as well as set out to dig our way to China the way small tots armed with plastic pails and shovels and bored with dippin their toes on a stretch of beach'll do. Now Lily's blood was covered underneath brown streaks of earth—if ever two cats or boys was a mess, that was me and Huck.

"Now what," Huck said.

We was nearin top side, disgusted and weary, and I finally saw the small raw space we'd laid Lady down to heal in. There was the bower—but what had become of the leaves and twinin ivy gave my heart a pang.

"Look, Tom, they's all gone brittle."

We went inside the niche.

The jewels was just milked over dead eyes caught here and there in the rotted silk. The spun leaves and greenery had gone brown and shriveled up, and the air we stirred with our footsteps made the curtains of bare stems that was like long-buried finger bones click and chitter. The leaves, curled in on themselves, was like tiny blackened hands of unborn children. The once-bright flowers was sickenin to smell. And everywhere was the stench of rottin earth that had gone bad down here in the dark.

"Where can she be?" I cried.

Huck sobbed against me, afraid that Lady was dead.

Overhead, I saw lightnin flash and heard the rumble of thunder.

The wind began to gust, and I could feel the heart of the tree swayin in the sudden storm. Another blast of lightnin struck close, and I saw its neon creepin along some of the roots beyond the niche.

"We got to go—we got to go now, Huck!" I screamed.

We leapt for the earth ledge and scrambled faster than I would have believed possible until we was just beneath the trapdoor. Huck nearly flew through the openin, and then we tore through the skin of the tree and didn't stop till we was on the backstairs and just in time. The lightnin was zigzaggin down from the sky and I saw it lunge for the tree. There was a noise louder than a thousand cannons, and the sound of tons of wood being torn in two; and then the quick crash as half the giant tree plummeted to the ground and sunk itself into the back lawn. Lady's tree lay riven while snow flew and lightnin ripped and Hucky and me cowered on the back steps.

"She's gone," he moaned. "Must be."

I didn't answer for I had no answer. Instead, I led Huck inside to what was for us an empty house.

PART 3:
YOURS TRULY,
TOM SAWYER AND
HUCK FINN

CHAPTER THIRTY-ONE

REMAINS OF THE DAY–
THE QUEEN OF HEARTS PLAN

It seemed like all my wittiness and high spirits was gone. Me and Huck ambled into the kitchen and our food bowls was there and it was still dark, but the room was warm—as if any minute somebody was going to put something tasty into an oven they'd been heatin to the proper temperature whilst they was thinkin about scones or muffins for breakfast and the good home smells those baked dainties would make. There is something very pure—almost holy—about the good clean smell of cookin done with love. Then suddenly I realized it warn't the smell that was missin out of the room—it was the love, and I couldn't find no hint of it in the house. I had no sense of Lady's presence and it made me so lonesome inside, I 'most started to cry again.

Huck, he went over to his dish and dropped his jaw over it and sniffed a time or two and then he walked away slowly. I didn't remember Huck ever turnin his back on food.

I'd been scared before and was used to makin jokes and talkin a thing up to hide my feelins, but this was different. It was the first time I was ever in Lady's house that I couldn't take no comfort. It might as well have been the moon—not the pretty moon you see hangin high

235

and hot and yellow as honey over the Mississippi, but the cold gray place them Life-magazine-type photographs show. Lady once told me that she liked to believe the astronauts never went there back in 1969. The moon was so beautiful, it spoiled it some to know people had walked around on it and took away its mystery.

"Where do you s'pose Ted and Earle have gone to, Tom?"

"Don't know—but we sure could use their help now. What are we s'posed to do with that crowd out in the library?"

"You'll think of something, Tom. You always do."

But I was so low, it was like my brain wouldn't hatch a thing. We was in charge of the inn, we had guests hangin like flies up on the ceiling, a coupla werewolves sprawled on the floor and one dead witch with her throat torn out muddyin up the carpet. The dead witch might mean the police. 'Course, they wouldn't arrest me and Huck—what was they gonna do? Put us in a kennel for the rest of our natural born lives with maybe a month off for good behavior? We couldn't make no license plates, so they'd just have us hangin around on their hands— 'sides, who ever heard of jailin cats?

"If they thought we done it and was rabid, they might kill us, Tom," Huck said in a low voice.

"Darn it, Huck, are you hearin me think again?"

"Cain't help it, Tom, it just happens."

"Well, Huck it 'most gives a body the fan-tods and gets me so mixed up I can't tell what you're thinkin and feelin and what's inside my own soul! Now look here, are you so blamed low that you don't even care if you live or die? 'Cause you're cloggin up my works, and I can't think for your thoughts cloudin up my whole head—"

"Sorry, Tom."

"Well, don't be sorry. It's like havin a cold in your brains. So you just stop it right now, Huck Finn, or we're gonna be in a lot worse trouble!" I paced a step or two. "Right this minute, you go eat somethin; that'll get your blood flowin and then I can think in peace."

"But Tom—"

"No buts—eat so I can think." Dratted cat is sendin me his miserable whinin notions. This ESP hain't all it's cracked up to be, and it sure has its downpoints. Ain't Mr. Twain told me about a thousand times how he was just so blue he didn't want to put one foot in front of the other, and yet there he sat and wrote some of his funniest work!

And the irony warn't lost on him, nuther. But I got to do like he done and puzzle us out of this. Else, Huck's right—the law'll fix on us and it'll be "off with their heads!" before you can box 'em up and write "Albany" on the carton. Fat lot of good it'll do to find out we ain't got rabies when we already ain't got heads!

I swished my tail good and hard and put it through a real lashin whilst I was thinkin on that one. Then I sat and gave my tail a couple hard thwacks and three thumps.

I was up and pacin good now—good as any panther you ever saw in a zoo who knew suppertime was only five or six hours a way, or possibly sooner, if a bystander got careless and fell in his pit—and I was talkin out loud: "First off, someone will miss that horrible Lily— she may not have friends, but her enemies will get to wonderin what she's up to—if only 'cause they're worrying about what curses she may have laid on 'em. Or, them other witches'll get curious and want to know if the counter-curses they hatched up have started to work and what the results are. I mean, wouldn't you want to check to see if Lily finally started growin a red hibiscus plant out of the middle of her forehead? Or if every time she spoke, instead of a normal speakin voice what come out was the blast of a referee's whistle? 'Course you would. Hain't I told you a thousand times, humans call us curious and it ain't nothin to how mortal curious *they* are."

"You have, Tom—"

"Take a road accident—" I was gearin up prime now, and if I was Mr. Twain troddin the square around the pool table in his office, I'd be puffin my cigar, hands behind my back, just contemplatin my next shot and which pocket I was gonna drop it in. But never mind pool, we was talkin about road accidents—

"Will a cat stop what it's doin to watch 'em cart the wounded out of the way and hose off the blood? Nope. Cats got better things to do. That's why humans hate crows, 'cause only crows are seriously interested in getting an up-close look—not to mention a healthy peck—at road kill. But humans hate crows, because they won't admit they're the very same when it comes to that partic'lar fascination.

"You take a species that's always screamin it don't have time—and says it has to drive twenty-five miles *over* the speed limit on highways, parkways, back roads, former cattle trails—and everywhere else just to feel like they's movin. But let there be an accident, and they crawl past

237

the wreckage like penitents on their knees stumpin their way up the steps to a European cathedral. Disappointed too, if they don't get a glimpse of somethin—the ambulance, the smashed car, the broken glass or a chunk of flesh."

"You're goin good, now, Tom—"

"So, somebody will be interested in the whereabouts of Ms. Lily Blum. And if it ain't a friend or a enemy, it will be the busybody post office—why? 'Cause they're worried about a citizen? No, on account of whoever delivers her mail will be annoyed if it starts stackin up in the box and they cain't cram no more inside. Then they will have to cart all the magazines and utility bills back to the post office and fill out paperwork and that will be a bother to *them*. So, a couple a days after this person's supervisor lands on 'em for not deliverin the mail *and* not fillin out the forms, *then* they will call the police. It's called passin the buck, 'cause then it will be the job of the police to find out what's what."

"And *that's* when they'll light on us and capture us and cut off our haids and send 'em straight up to Albany to see have we got rabies!"

"Don't you beat all, Huck. Why, if I was as ignorant as you, I'd never say more than 'Meow.'" I shook my head. "No, *then* there'll be a investigation. How's they gonna know Lily was here? No, they'll have to backtrack around and talk to her dry cleanin man and her tailor and the grocery store checkout girl, and the mail deliverer and look into her telephone records and bank statements and ATM transactions an' what have you to trace when she was last alive."

"That's some good news there, Tom—"

I looked at him. "'Cause it gives us time to figure out our plan?"

"No, 'cause by the time the police slow-poke around and do all that, Lily's familiar, that ugly no-account hound, Coal Porter, is sure to be starved down dead."

Well, I hadn't thought of that! I'd clean forgotten about that stupid beast. But it give me another idea. We could witch Lily's body over to her house, and with the least jot of luck, the police'd think the dog bit out her throat. Then they'd shoot *him* full of killer serum till he was good and dead, and the vet would saw *his* head off and box it up and send it off to the lab to see if *he* had rabies.

On the whole, I sure liked the idea of Coal Porter's head getting mailed up to the state capital at Albany 'stead of me and Huck's heads.

I thought our heads looked fine right where they was on our bodies. And since Lily was already dead, we wouldn't be interfering none with her familiar, so no bad karma would stick to us.

Hucky agreed it was prime as ideas went. "Won't they check the bite marks on her throat, Tom?" he said when I told him about the *Queen of Hearts Plan.* "Or look in his stomach for parts of Lily? And what if they find white fur on 'er when that hellhound, Coal, is as black as tar."

Huck was doin a little tail-lashin of his own. "And when they find that white fur and ask all around to Lily's friends and enemies and hear all about her visitin us over here, they'll come lookin for Lady, but she won't be here nuther, so *then* they will pounce on us and match up our fur and our teeth marks to the wounds right smack on Lily's old throat and then they will most likely 'lectrocute us or give us legal interjections and cut off our haids and send em to Albany to make sure we hain't got no rabies and we will be in every newspaper in the country as the killer cats and we'll be famous." He turned to look at me. "I seen about frensics on the Discovery Channel and on the Internet to boot." Huck paused, and his eyes went a little crossed, and his face got a little sickly-lookin. His voice sounded blank; he'd come to a conclusion that warn't a solution. "So. We'll be *famous*, but ... we'll be dead." He fetched up a sigh from inside his chest. "Famous and dead's not *so* bad, Tom—"

"Have you lost your mind?" I was in a perfect fury. The cat might go zoomin 'round the Internet, but he had no more brains than a potato masher. It was just the kind of thing, I knowed, would set Mr. Twain off, too. If I'd been human, my face would've been the unhealthy beet red of an incipient stroke victim. "We's *already* famous *and* dead!" I shouted at him.

"We are?"

"Huckleberry Finn was a boy that warn't never alive, and when he was a character in a book, it was 'bout a hundred years ago. Same for Thomas Sawyer!" I was getting so mad, I 'most wanted to kill Huck myself.

"But how can we be dead, Tom, if we's right here?"

"'Cause we're reincarnated—"

"Well, then it's all right, Tom, cause even if they kill us and cut off our heads 'cause we got rabies—which we don't have—we can get reincarnated again, anyhow."

"No more, Huck, please," I said. To tell the truth, he was giving me such a headache, I 'most wished somebody would come along and cut off my head—or his.

Anyhow, that was the first part of the *Queen of Hearts Plan* and that's what we—or, I—did—what was to witch Lily's body back to her own nondescript and too-small house right under the slaverin jaws of Coal Porter and it was just like I thought: the police, bein so busy with drug lords and trackin terrorists and teenage bombers, never did check on us. And maybe it didn't hurt none if old Coal took a nip or two out of his dead mistress's neck or maybe tried to lick her back to life a little. But then I considered 'bout how Lady'd say that I warn't bein very nice; and my conscience got to workin on me so I knowed she'd have the right of it, and then I felt a little sorry for 'im, too—gettin tethered to such a rotten witch. Anyhow, I didn't know till later what happened to Coal—but Lily was gone for good. And that was prime.

CHAPTER THIRTY-TWO

CORPUS DELICTI—TOM'S MASTER SPELL—
SUNDAY AT THE INN

Well, whether Coal Porter found Lily's corpse delicious or not, me
and Huck still had all those bodies crowdin the library from the rug to
the rafters. In the meantime, we'd witched old Lily to her own house,
like I told you, so this was still the first mornin after Miss Myra High-
Hat Burnes had conducted her failed séance, and the werewolfs was
still lyin on the floor, and the rest of 'em was air dancin on the ceiling.
It looked like the Macy's Thanksgivin Day parade gone haywire in
there. But it give me an idea for lassooin the Reverend and the rest of
'em down from the ceiling.

"How we gonna keep 'em down on the ground once we get 'em
there, Tom?" Huck was sittin on his haunches on the edge of the
carpet in there alongside a me and lookin at the guests up on the
ceiling. "'Pears to me you'll have to set a pile of anvils on 'em to keep
'em from floatin back up again."

"Have to think on that one a while, Huck," I sighed.

"And is they dead? 'Cause if they's dead, they's gonna stink up the
house pretty soon. And no tellin if they'll decide since they met their
untimely ends here whether they'll just take up residence as the

241

disembodied and then we'll have a whole new passel of ghosts to deal with," Huck said. "The whole kit and kaboodle of em's gonna be just as much trouble after they's dead as they'll be if they is dead, and you know how I feel about ha'nts—"

"Now hush a minute, Huck, and let me think. You never give me a moment to think—"

"Take as much time as you want, Tom; they's probably dead so they ain't goin nowhere real soon. They ain't missin no lunch dates or dentist appointments or what all—church maybe, it bein a Sunday, for the Revrund and the Missus. I don't think werewolfs go to church reg'lar."

I glared at him fit to hiss and he hushed.

What *was* we to do with the guests?

And then it come to me—a plan so bold it'd make Mr. Twain get right up out of his rocker and knock every ball on the pool table into the right corner pocket with one shot.

* * *

"We're gonna time travel 'em, Huck. So it's like they never been here. I pored over that Book of Shadows like it was the Bible and me studyin to be a Reverend, myself; and there is a heap of folderol in it about writin down calendar pages and sich like to make a person forget a secret, but if we time travel 'em back, they won't even have nothin to forget."

"But if we time travel them, Tom, won't we have Lily back on our hands—"

"How you talk, Huckleberry Finn—'course not. All the very best time travel storybooks says over and over how that ain't the way it happens. When Mr. Twain sent Hank Morgan back to the Age of Chivalry in his *Connecticut Yankee* book, did the whole gang over to the factory go along? They did not. Same as with ever other book—we're gonna send back this crew—and it'll be like they was *never* here."

"You gonna crush em alongside their heads with a crowbar like what was done to Hank Morgan, Tom?"

"Nope; gonna get me a spell for time travel and float 'em all nice as jug cream back to the day before yesterday—"

"Won't they just show up again?"

Well, drat the animal, he had me again! I hadn't reckoned on *that*.

For a brief second it was touch and go as I suddenly got the dizzyin image in my head like when you put two mirrors face to face and inside is a line of mirrors stretchin right over to infinity; only now every two days it was February 13th, and then Friday the 14th with the guests arrivin and the hellacious séance on Saturday—and the whole depressin weekend goin round and round and round like some bad, undergraduate imitation of *Waitin for Godot*, and all of 'em draggin in their luggage and getting thinner and thinner every time they lurched in the front door—and then out—and then in again. And I got all squinched up inside ... but then I hit on a way out of it.

"No. Cause we're gonna *cancel* their reservations!"

"What about the inn?"

"Leave it to me, Huck, I already got my scheme schemed."

* * *

Well, I told you before the whole thing with a spell is intention. It don't matter what you use—I mean if Mr. H.G. Wells wanted to use a fancy machine, that'd work. And if Mr. Twain wanted to have a crowbar swung, that'd work. So I witched some plumpy pillows down to the library and me and Huck lay on 'em. First we took a short snooze, though, 'cause a nap is one of the best things you can ever do to loosen up your mind to get your intentions clear. Stress just clutters the hell out of good intentions, but you take a nap and when you wake up, you might not even remember what was botherin the hell out of you before you conked out. So, just from a practical point of view, me and Huck napped hard. Then we had us a little snack, then another short nap to work off the food lyin in our stomachs, and by then we was pretty nigh ready to send the floaters and the immobile hunks of werewolf back to their own quiet lives.

After we laid out our pillows, me and Huck decided this here special ritual needed a whole night of concentratin and pleading with the head witch-goddess Lady told us about, Hecate, in order to make it work—and we needed it to work right away. Down the line a month or two wouldn't do us no good.

So, the cushions would come in handy so's we could be fresh for the work ahead and not take up no chill in our bones nor rheumatism

243

sittin out all night on the cold library floor. First we blessed 'em, which involved a dustin with secret ingredients that would cleanse those pillows of any negativity and infuse 'em with our own intentions. Oh, you can just scrawl your pentagram in the air over your ritual objects, but it's far better to anoint 'em with the proper herbs and the like. In this case, we chose catnip—for several reasons. Not least of which, it would keep us playful and open, which is critical to your creative spell. Plus, we liked it. Likin your scents is a big part of spell-makin. Lady oncet told me and Huck about a witchy friend of hers who liked to tip gin and included a big dollop of Gilbey's brand in every potion she made—or drank. And you might think it'd muddle her spells, but she was one of the top spellcasters around.

And you got to ready all your ritual objects in a like manner, so me and Huck had to rub up or chant over everything we planned on usin—candles and salt and crystals and water—and all kinds a mystical frippery.

Then, you got to account for the moon. They's ways around it, but the state of the moon can make or break your spell faster than you can say "which witch is which," if you ain't truly careful. Well, here was the difficulty—and you can judge just how much trouble this cost me and Huck. It bein Saturday the 15th and all, the moon was due for full on the 16th. Which is about the most powerful time a witch can conduct a spell; but when the moon is waxin, you want to perform a spell for growth—it's when it's wanin you want to send things out of your life. And we wanted to send the whole crew back to February 13th—and as far away from The Chancery House in Rhinebeck, New York as we could.

"How we goin to send 'em away when the moon is growin big 'round as a store-bought banjo?" Huck said. "This is a gatherin moon, not a banishin moon—and don't tell me we'll pretend like it's the fingernail moon, Tom Sawyer, cause the moon is as large as life and cain't no one pretend the moon *ain't* what the moon *is*."

"We can say they's going to avoid the pain of the séance when they return to the wholesome nest of their own homes—"

"*Avoid*. You said it—*avoid*."

"Well, hang it Huck, we just got to word it somehow! We'll make out that we's fillin our place with the peace of their absence—"

"*Absence*—won't do, Tom. You know it yourself: 'the difference between the right word and the almost right word,' like Mr. Twain said, 'is the difference between lightnin and the lightnin bug.' And what you got is one hell of a lightnin bug."

"We are fillin our home with peace and replenishin their god-blasted credit cards—unless they go home and decide to spend the money they paid here on a three-day toot, they're gainin, too."

Huck, he shook his head. "No, it don't answer, 'cause no matter how you look at it, we are takin away the last two days."

"Well Huck, that just shows how wrong you are, cause we are *givin* them two *extra* days they never would have had if we didn't re-start 'em on Thursday, February the 13th. Why, they get to celebrate Valentine's Day twice—and that's a gain. A pure profit, clear gain,"

And it was, too. There ain't a creature in the world that don't say one time or another, *I wish I could go back in time to such a place again.* And since they all wound up so miserable and was hexed to boot, I reckoned bein home and never seein the likes of The Chancery House and the hobgoblin crew hangin out here would suit all of 'em just fine.

Once I laid out all the spell talk, me and Huck next worked on how we was gonna manifest the thing. Huck, he was all for scarifyin up the calendar pages for Saturday and Friday and markin 'em up with big black X's and tearin 'em to flinders and settin the confetti on fire and scatterin the ashes to the east wind.

But you got to cast your circle with salt and do everything inside the blasted circle, and I never did like burnin candles so close to our fur—I thought tearin up the calendar pages and throwin the scraps out the window would answer just fine. And never mind the east wind, *any* wind that came along would help our cause.

There's a heap of trouble and plannin that goes into these spells and my eyes was so tired from readin and my head hurt from squinchin my eyes so long, I thought a short nap would get us geared up again.

When we woke for the third time, Huck gave a yawn and glanced up at the flyin guests overhead. "What's their part in all this? I mean when we freed Jim what was already free, Jim had to smouch the candlesticks from Auntie's pocket and scratch his name on the pie plate and tear up the sheets and all—"

"Well that was different because Jim, bein a prisoner, naturally had to help with his own escape. These here have been witched by Lily and bein immobile, they cain't do nothin but float around like human planets till we send 'em back to their right orbit."

"What do you suppose they's dreamin on, Tom?"

"If it was me, I'd be dreamin I was sleepin in a bed 'stead of bein hung out to dry like a load of wash."

"You think it hurts 'em some?" Huck's blue eyes rolled up.

"Well they won't remember it, so it will be like havin surgery and after the n'esia, you don't have no recall of the knife."

"And what about the werewolfs—"

"They oughta be the most grateful of all getting two free extra days in the month where they can wear shoes and act like regular folk—"

"But if they don't remember—"

"Well, it ain't like *not* rememberin a trip to Bermuda! What they won't remember is lyin all twisted up like rigor mortis victims on a hardwood floor for two days. Besides, Earle and Ted can tell 'em how they was saved from untimely death."

That said, we gathered up all the rigmarole and special papers and inks to write the words on—in blood ink, a course—and manifesting stones such as your rose quartz for love, and moonstone for mystery, and your herbs for pounding and burnin such as vetivert and mugwort and frankincense and myrrh, plus a couple thousand bottles of your cinnamon oil and your jasmine and your purest forms of patchouli and foxglove and what have you and we got the whole thing smokin and bilin and brewin and we witch-drew five pentagrams on the floor with salt and chalk and black ink—which particular ink we made from prisoners' tears and iron filings and the grave mud of executioners— and we gathered up scraps of personal items from each guest's suitcase and we chanted their names and we invoked the goddess for about two hours and we waved our special handcrafted wands what was wrapped in copper to contain the magic and were embedded with amethysts and carved with rune signs and we took special cleansin baths in more catnip and we hooked some of Lady's ceremonial and ritual ware and plunked down bowls of water for offerins for the goddess and even a silver bowl of Purina Right Bites that Huck, he didn't like so much, but thought the name was prime and the goddess would probably find the Right Bites to her liking, and another white jade bowl of Iams Original that Huck did like and said he would help the goddess eat if she left 'em alone and take it as a sign he could refresh himself if necessary, and hours and hours later, finally, just before the crack of dawn, those guests and werewolfs was gone.

Well, that's how we let on we done this spell, anyhow; but to be honest we more or less lay back on the pillows and imagined that whole airborne group what was like wannabe Wallendas and them dust-gatherin werewolfs what was lyin around like cordwood right back in their own houses on Thursday February 13th with nary a thought of comin over to the inn. It was a whole sight easier than gettin ourselves all involved with the mess of a ritual and just as good since we let on like we done it the hard way and with plenty of style. There warn't no mess to clean up and the house smelled better without all them burnin herbs. So, take it all around, we done just fine.

* * *

We had the Inn to ourselves, and it was Sunday morning. As far as me and Huck was concerned, not having to go to Church was already a blessin and was settin the day up fair as primroses. And even if we didn't use no fancy mumbo jumbo, sendin back the Reverend and Missus and Catherine and Lazlo and the werewolfs put me in mind that bein on our own, me and Huck ought to take advantage of the inn's amenities, so to speak. I don't mean the trumped up ones we wrote about on the Internet, but Lady's spell books and all. I thought maybe it was high time we was boys again—and there warn't no one around to interfere or catch on to our doins and me and Huck could work our magick in peace. And who knew but what heaps a good might come from it—it worked out just fine both when we was on the island an when we dug around in that old deserted house an struck it rich when we tracked the swag Injun Joe hid in McDougal's cave.

And Lily bein out of the way was much the same as when Injun Joe and Huck's pap was both finally out a the picture. 'Course, even if I felt sorry for Injun Joe dyin so hard, I warn't so sorry for Lily who was that ornery an low-down mean she made Huck's pap look like Mr. Rogers on a day he won the lottery.

"Look here, Huck," I said when we'd wakened an snarfled a little food and was just layin on the floor in a big flag of sunshine what come in through the front windows into the foyer. "Don't it seem like it's time for us to be boys again?"

The house was very quiet—naturally—since we was the only ones in it, and I heard two ticks of the mantel clock from way off in the living room before Huck spoke up.

"Well, how we gonna do it?"

"Oh, perform about fifty spells and send away for all kinds of arcanery—like Cleopatra's Eye and the testes of a unborn plattypuss and deadly nightshade and nettles from a virgin's grave, and then after we spend a fortune ferreting it all out an' collect even more rarities and oddments, and travel worldwide and steal what we cain't buy, well, then we probably have to turn ourselves inside out and maybe even go pull some fur from Ted and Earle or more likely, some *vicious* werewolfs when they's sleepin off the hunt and spend the next six months or so tryin to reverse all the mistakes we make—which could be dastardly and dangerous—'specially if we accident'lly become angel fish or tree toads or something."

"Sounds good. How do we do all that?"

"Well, first we got to find out the proper time to make this here spell, an' I'm guessin it must be worked by the light of the blue moon that is the third blue moon what falls in a single calendar year."

"We'll be daid by then."

"Well, we can *let* on like it's the third blue moon—an' long as we take precautions, we won't have to worry about the spell backfirin so bad we turn into girls—"

"Girls!" Huck's eyes were a blue blaze. "My, Tom—I hadn't thought a that. What would we do if we was *girls*?"

"Prob'ly have to spend another king's ransom to go over to Sweden or Cologne or Thailand or Philadelphia or Lord-knows-where-else and get that surgery to change us into men or die tryna effectuate 'bout 'nother thousand or so spells and maybe never even get to be cats again."

"I don't want to go to Philadelphia—"

"An' they's even worse could happen, Huck," I said, pitchin my voice low.

"No more, Tom—please—stop!"

"All right, we'll let 'er go for now, but it's up to us now to revere the memory of Lady and take over runnin the inn—which we cannot do as cats."

"But Tom—Lady didn't never want no inn—"

"That don't matter, Huck. In the end she started one up an' we have got to stand by that sacred cause. Why, do you think Louie the Sixteen give up when they was no more France? No, he didn't—and we cain't, neither."

"How you talk, Tom Sawyer! No France, why sure as you live there was a France then, and there's a France right this minute."

"Well, it warn't the *same* France—not with everything all smashed to flinders and heads rollin on the guillotine every minute of the day an' not a single baker able to make bread an' the whole country forced to eat cake. So anyways, whether we want to eat cake or not, we got to stick by Lady's wishes an' figure a way to run the inn, and the only way we can do *that* is if we's boys again."

"Won't we lose our powers?"

"Well, what if we do? We can shift right back to bein cats and familiars and witch up any old thing we need. It's in all the books—"

"That don't sound right to me—"

"If I was as ignorant as you, Huck Finn, I'd keep mum about it. Look here, it stands to reason: if you're cold, don't you put on a coat? And if you're hot, don't you take it off? Well, shape-shiftin is the same—you change back and forth accordin to the season, so to speak—"

"Confound it, Tom! You make it out it ain't no more trouble to shed *fur* and grow *flesh* than to trade wool earlaps for a summer straw! As if a *head* was a *hat!*"

"Well, if you don't want to go about it in the regular way, then I guess you don't have to. And you can sit there in white fur the rest of your life, and I'll come back of a night an' tell you about all the gaudy times I had fishin—"

"It's winter—"

"*Ice* fishin and goin to circuses and such and I guess I'll just have to run the inn on my own and keep all the money for myself." I gave him a long stare, but we both knew he was probably gonna cave in soon. But, I warn't about to let him slide into it; when I sink my claws into a thing, I go for blood. "Anyhow, now that you're such a whiz on the Internet, you can go read all about it yourself."

"I did," he said miserably. "And it's all about changin from a man to a moose and becomin a dolphin."

I'd known that, a course. There warn't enough information to fill a thimble on the topic out of the Internet. Not to mention the fact that no one in their right mind would want to be a moose. And as a cat, I didn't fancy no dolphin transmogrification. The idear of all that cold, wet water gave me the fan-tods.

"Nat'rally, you got to study up in a *real* Book of Shadows, and like I said, it'll be dangerous and terrifyin, but we'll keep at it till we can shift one way or t'other in the blink of an eye."

We was heading up the stairs by this time and just outside of Lady's altar room. I knowed there'd be a heap of information in her book, and I reckoned some of it would be in runes or hieroglyphics—but I don't let a little thing like that stop me. I'd puzzle 'em out if it took three blue moons and a month of Sundays. I figured there had to be some advantage to having nine lives, and I meant to capitalize on it.

We went into her room and I clambered up on the altar; but I'd done no more than open the cover of her enormous leather-covered book when, from the attic come a sound of misery and wailin that like to freeze me so I felt like I'd been dipped into an Alaskan blowhole and hauled out encased in solid ice. If somebody'd dropped me, I'd a shattered.

The long keenin wail rose again and Huck cowered against me, his nose buried in my neck. I heard the door to the attic open and heavy poundin movin down the hall toward us. "Lord, Tom, it's the ghosts again!"

CHAPTER THIRTY-THREE

GHOSTS–BURN, WITCH, BURN–
WHAT HAPPENED TO HUCK

I got that wood door locked in a trice, you bet; and me and Huck sat as still as mice on the other side of it. I was powerful glad it was such a heavy door—and I was considerin sheathin it with bolts and iron—if I could witch 'em up quick enough. A body cain't hardly have enough barricades against ghosts.

"Are these here the ghosts what Ted said come about 'cause they was wrote down?" Huck's voice was very thin, and I felt him tremblin against me.

"They could a got stirred up from all the remodelin and such we done. Lots of times, ghosts start pilin in after somebody makes changes in a house—and this is a real old house," I whispered back. "These sperrits might be folks who used to live here."

"Hey, Sperrit!" Huck shouted. "This is 2014! You're dead so go away, you don't live here no more. So go on right back!"

"What're you doin?" I growled at him at the same time I snagged his collar with my paw. "Have you gone crazy? They's liable to seize on us if you tell 'em where we're at."

"They *know* where we're at! Good as if they had radar, which is

251

why they are right outside *this* doorway in *this* hall in *this* house. I'm just tryin t' send em on—" Before I could hush him, Huck he cupped a paw around his mouth. "Go to the light, the beautiful light!" he screamed.

I put my face up to his. "Stop right now," I said.

"I seen it in a movie," Huck whimpered. "And it worked like smoke for this here little dwarf woman—"

"Well, this ain't a movie," I hissed at him.

"It worked for her," he muttered.

I could hear him thinkin: *Go to the Light. The* Light. *Not that light— the big* Light—*you morons. Drat 'em, they's aimin for the overhead chandelier in the hallway, the sapheads.*

Just then, a furious pounding what threatened to burst the door right off its hinges started in. You'd a sworn the door was bulgin in at us, and me and Huck stepped back lively, you bet.

"Now you've done it," I said. "They's gonna kill us, sure."

"At least if *we* was dead we'd have the brains to go towards the right goddamn light," he half-yelled to the door. "Damn-fool ha'nts with no more smart cells than moths. *Moths*, I say," he said louder.

"Huck!"

"I cain't help it, Tom. I cain't abide fools—ghosts or not—"

"And now they know our names, they know our names!" I moaned. It was just like in the Shirley Jackson book.

"That's all right then," Huck said, "they can tell theirs, and we'll all know who we're dealing with—"

It was like some kind of brain fever'd seized Huck. Here was a boy who counted the hours till bad luck hit if he so much as burned up a liver-colored house spider; a familiar who fled and quaked in terror if someone so much as mentioned ha'nts, and *now* he was suddenly goadin demons.

"What on Earth has gotten into the cat?" I said.

"Just this. I ain't a goin t' be scared of no ghost what we conjured by writin about it on the Internet, and I ain't gonna be terrorized by no ha'nt what lived here a century ago and maybe got curious enough to climb out a his coffin to see what the hammerin and sheetrockin was all about. And now just because his great Aunt Eleanor's picture ain't over the mantel no more, he's settin up a big fuss—"

"But Huck," I said, "we don't know for certain sure these ghosts is the ones we made up, or ones that they got called in when Ted and Earle started in on the remodeling—"

"We don't?"

"No."

"Well," and now his voice dropped very low, "who might they be, then?"

"They could be anybody—or anything."

"Lord, Tom, what have I done?" Then he turned and dived underneath the legs of the altar. He would a disappeared into the carpet pattern if he could a done it.

Outside, the poundin increased to a cannonade. Up and down the hallway, every door sang and groaned with the strain of the knockin that was a batterin ram; and the walls vibrated hard enough to make my teeth rattle. It was like being inside one of them snow globes and being shook ever' which way. I thought the ghosts wanted to shake the inn till it was all to flinders and no more than little bits of wood and plaster falling in a noisy, particulate rain. Even the ceilin overhead was alive with the sound of clumpin footsteps loud enough—and hard enough, I reckoned—to shatter joists and beams. In the bedrooms, the wall sconces with the crystal prisms were tinklin, then clangin in some weird atonal music. Then the lights—all over the house it seemed—began to flicker and buzz. Only an insane person would imagine they warn't gonna overload any second.

"Huck," I said. "We got to get out."

"Out?" He looked and sounded confused. His whiskers was all a-droop. His fur was rumpled and his eyes was cloudy.

"She's goin to go a smash," I said. "We need to be quick."

"Like the Tree House?"

"Not like the Tree House—the inn is gonna burn—and she'll catch like she's been doused in kerosene."

"How do you know—"

I could a told him it was in the books and how they all made out that when sperrits wanted to set a thing on fire, it might as well have been a duet between a lucifer match and a stick of dynamite for liveliness and lightnin quick results. And it would a been the truth, but I'd talked that way so many times I was afraid Huck would scoff and think I was pilin on the details to give the thing some flare—make out it was much worse than it was, I mean. But this just warn't book

253

knowin—this was the kind of knowin that sinks right down in a person's—or a familiar's—bones. And I knew something had been unleashed that warn't about to rest till Chancery House was n'more than smoke driftin over the hot pit of her ruined foundations.

"Now! Huck! Now! Run like the wind and don't never stop till we's on the banks of the river!"

There was a tremendous groan and a sound like live wires hissing on snow, and I saw the first tongues of blue fire lickin up from the electric outlet and racin over the walls. Fires move upwards in a building; but this would be a fire so hot eventually, I knew it would start to burn *down*—till it took the whole house and every floor.

There warn't time to make for the stairs.

"The window," I shrieked. "The window!"

I took the longest leap of my feline life and streaked through it, shattering glass and letting in a roar of wind that sent the flames ragin higher.

Jump, Huck! Jump now!

I thought with all my might.

I was sailin through a blood-red sunset—but no redder than the flames would be when they started eating the house and laughing evilly about it afterwards, roarin thirty feet or more into the night sky.

* * *

I landed in the snow with enough force that I sank in over my head. And there was a good deal of that nasty cold stuff up my nose and in my ears and even down my throat. Not to mention that my paws felt 'most brutalized by the jump and the snow. I floundered my way topside again, my head swivellin to look see where Huck had landed.

No Huck.

Where is he?

Then, above the roar of the flames, I heard mewlin.

He was in the window, a mere silhouette against the wall of firelight behind him.

"Jump," I yelled.

He was too scared, and he couldn't even call back to me. He was cryin with terror, and I knew I had to act fast. He gave a long scream, and I saw his fur was beginnin to smoke.

I didn't even think about it. Transvection. Well, plenty of times we'd flown with Lady and used the Flokati rug as our platform to sit upon, but this warn't the time to worry about niceties. I mighta witched him down, but I was afraid his panic might muddle the spell. So, instead, without even considerin, I rose up straight as an angel and when I was at the level of the window, I reached in and hauled him out.

I had him in my arms, and he was powerful heavy, but I warn't about to drop him. I nuzzled my nose against the back of his neck and whispered how much I loved him. Then I floated us down nice and easy, and I set Huck on the snow. He was so dazed and fear-struck, he couldn't move. So I scooped up some of the cold snow and packed it along his singed fur. He began to shiver.

"S'okay now, Huck. You're safe."

He was too stunned to do more than make a small sound.

"Won't never let you be hurt. Don't you worry."

"My eyes, Tom," he said. "I think the heat boiled my eyes. I can't see." He began to cry.

I understood now why he hadn't even tried to follow me out of the window, and I could imagine what it must've been like inside that inferno, with nothing but darkness and heat and fear. I put my tongue out to lick his lids, but he drew back.

"Hurts," he whimpered.

So I picked him up again in my arms, floating us both lightly along. He was 'most dead in my arms and he seemed weaker than he had as a kitten, and I guessed he was in shock. I didn't know what else to do—so I aimed us toward the riven Tree House and I hoped the part that was still livin would be enough to heal him and bring him back to himself and to me.

CHAPTER THIRTY-FOUR

THE TREE HOUSE AGAIN–
HUCK LAID LOW

The big white heart of the tree was exposed when it fell, but now the inner bark had weathered to the sickly gray of a hornet's nest. I rose up over the tangle of dead limbs still stabbin upwards from the lawn that were as high as a house. They were snarled and black and the horizontal surfaces—once upright—were snow-covered now. Lookin down on them was like looking at the worst destruction—like a bombed-out city or something ugly that is left in the aftermath of ruin and devastation.

With Huck in my arms, I melted through the skin of the tree and right away, of course, everything not only looked different, but it felt different, too.

Inside, all of Lady's cozy fittins and furnishins were all a jumble—what warn't broken or smashed, that is. Now standin inside, I felt like we was under glass and bein inspected. It didn't feel safe or give me a sense of peace of bein surrounded or protected—it was more like bein the X-ray a doctor holds up to the light. I had the feelin somebody was always lookin at my back, and it 'most gave me the heebie-jeebies.

257

I'd laid Huck down next to the wreck of the hearth and he was just lyin on his side and not movin. I licked him some, but he didn't do no more than squinch his eyes tighter.

"It's gonna be all right," I told him. I mean, what else was there to say? I warn't about to tell him I warn't sure at all the Tree House could heal him up—nor even the bower beneath it. And for all I knew, that niche where we laid Lady hadn't done her a speck of good. We didn't even know where she was—only that somehow, Lily had bound her up and used a shadow projection of her to walk around and act like it was Lady. To tell the truth, I still warn't sure Lady was even alive no more—or if she was—I didn't know where she was, or if she was hurt. And she was the only one I knew with power enough to heal Huck. His eyes, yes, but most especially, because his heart needed healing, too.

* * *

It was a terrible night. I snuggled next to Huck to keep us both warm, but he was so sluggish and dazed I worried the whole time. I kept laying my ear over his chest to make sure he was still breathin and his heart was still beatin. I never really slept and I think all my tossin and turnin would a kept him awake, except he was 'most passed out with the pain and the shock. His breath, when it came loud sometimes, sounded ragged and gaspy, and I was afeared he'd taken too much smoke inside his lungs—or worse—breathed down the flames and scorched them. When I nudged him with my head, it was just pushin a deadweight, and every time it happened, my heart stopped a moment inside my chest from fear and sorrow. Fifty times I thought I'd lost him. And the more still he grew, the more I was hurtin and there warn't no way to stop the tears that was bindin all inside my chest and sendin out sickly pains. And it warn't a bit better when they come up and flowed out my eyes or I threw my head back and cried.

I was in the one place I'd ever truly believed in ... the one place that always made me feel better, and there was more misery stuffed inside me than I'd known in any lifetime.

Outside, sirens wailed and firemen shouted and water gushed, and the hiss of the flames being quelled was loud enough to hurt your ears.

The fire roared on, and it was such a blot on all that I believed was good in life, such a desecration, I turned my mind away from it and just held Huck. Wood and shingles and plaster was for humans to cope with. Huck, he was mine, and the only living treasure I had, so I let the worry about the inn slip from my thoughts and cuddled him in my arms.

"I'm here, Hucky," I told him, "and I love you."

* * *

When I saw the first palin in the east, the color of the sky reminded me of ashes. I shuddered with the thought, but I wouldn't look at the house. I didn't think I could bear to see it gutted and tumbled into hideous black shapes with the smoke still risin around. I could smell it, anyhow, and that was more than enough. A burnt house is one of the most awful smells in the world—like everything dead and evil that can give off a bad scent has come to roost in it.

Huck was still with me, but now he kept sayin how thirsty he was—and that scared me more. I was terror struck he really *had* taken the flames down his throat; he was so small it wouldn't take much to burn him up inside and I kept tryin to think healin thoughts while I lay with him, but it warn't workin a bit. I was too cloudy with the heart pain and sorrow I felt. There'd been too much for too long with Lady gone. and I guess I was nearly worn down with sadness myself.

"So dry ... thirsty," he rasped again.

I went outside and took up some snow in my mouth, and when I came back I let the water it'd melted into dribble against Huck's lips. He licked 'em a little, but I judged it warn't enough—wouldn't let myself even think he was too sick, that he was past bein able to drink water.

"Hucky, maybe I should try and take you to that niche, that bower where we left Lady that time," I said. "Huck," I said again, tryin to wake him.

But it was like he'd gone into some strange dreamin state that was neither hallucination nor waking reality nor even the tellin of a dream itself, but more like I imagined the Oracle at Delphi must have sounded.

259

His voice was very low and I 'most had to put my ear next to his mouth to catch what he was sayin.

There's peace there and I kin just sleep and dream on all the good things. P'raps I'll even see Lady again ... there's mice, ooh such fat ones, and tricks to play and a great big cozy bed to sleep on ... the kind what poofs up all around you and you sink into her like sleepin on clouds—but better cuz goosey-down is warmer ... and there ain't no school, nor church sermons, nor smothery stuff what works a body up ... yais ...

I 'most thought I had the right of this and in another second, I'd have scooped Huck into my arms again and dragged us both down to that bower, but then—thank Providence—he said one more phrase.

Won't never have to anything, *never ever again.*

And that one was soul chillin in its implications. I could guess right enough what it meant—wherever Lady had disappeared to, Huck was goin to the same watering hole. I didn't like that one bit. Lady had said she was bone tired—well, all right, I didn't like it much, but it made a certain kind of sense with her havin lived all those centuries and lifetimes and whatnot. But Huck was new to life—and if you wanted to get right down to it, since he started his existence as a character what Mr. Twain fabricated, his life as a cat was his first time out as a creature what lived and breathed and walked in three dimensions. Huck he was scared sometimes, and so tender-hearted he was tender-headed, but he warn't wishin he was dead!

I petted him some, but he didn't say no more.

I thought about the fire, about Lily, about Lady disappearin, the tree crashin ... and here's what I come with: Lily had figgered her a way to bind Lady—and worse—take away her will to go on. And if all of that and what followed warn't awful enough, I knowed for sure she'd found a way to make her meddlesome spells live on even after she was gone—if she was really gone, I mean. And all those things she'd done, topplin the great tree and settin fire to the house and now makin Huck want to live some petrified nonexistence was black magic. And that damn bower was maybe its black heart.

She'd played us for fools—but no more.

I saw maybe that the tree was goin against Lady's original intentions; instead of bein a healin place, it'd become a hurtin place. I didn't know for certain how Lily had done that—but I warn't going to linger none to puzzle it out.

"Huck, they's only thing we can do—we got to lam it—"

He heard me this time, but he shook his head and gave out a little mewl.

"Hurts too bad, Tom," he said, and his eyes tried to open, but he couldn't manage it—he couldn't have seen me anyway, but we was used to lookin into each other's eyes when we talked. His head just kind of canted to the side then and that liked to nearly break my heart.

"Goin, yes indeed, we are, Huck."

"Where?" he wheezed.

"Rest easy in my arms, Huck, don't say another word. You just leave it to me."

* * *

I floated us outta there, and rose up high enough so that the smolderin wreck of the house warn't no more than a dot beneath us. I didn't fancy seein it, nor smellin it—and I sure didn't want Huck anywhere near that house. Who knew if the upset might be the stress that sent him beyond savin? When you're that far down, why any little thing can be the tippin point that sends you on the final spiral toward death.

He didn't move. He was limp in my arms, and in my heart I feared we was already too late. I aimed straight and true for my destination, and the whole time I was talkin to him, but secretly I thought he might already have gone.

"Jist a while longer, Huck, so you hang on here. Doncha know I won't never be happy—I mean really happy—'less you pull through. So you got to. You keep steady, Huck Finn. We was brothers under the skin a hundred years ago when Mr. Twain conceived us, and we're brothers for real, now. And twins, to boot. He would a liked that, Huck, and you know it. Loved twins—loved cats more. And I bet you'd a been his favorite cause you ain't so harum-scarum as I am. You're a lot more malleable and that would a sat with him prime."

Truth to tell, I almost overshot my mark. I kept swallerin so hard and tryin to keep the tears outta my voice that I kept shuttin my eyes.

But by and by, I looked down, and I saw I was 'most on top of it. It was seven in the mornin and the clinic wouldn't be open yet—but I warn't at the clinic. I'd flown straight to Peter Bennett's house.

* * *

I couldn't melt through the skin of his place—and naturally in the dead of winter there warn't no doors nor winders open, but I lit on his stoop which was brick, and I laid Huck down on the hemp Welcome mat; and then I commenced to spellin the doorbell till it rang like Big Marie in *The Hunchback of Notre Dame*.

"That'll fetch 'im, Huck."

He didn't answer me, nor move a muscle.

And inwardly I screamed "BELLS!"

While the doorchime gonged its lunatic song.

I could hear feet movin fast on the stairs, then poundin over the boards in the hallway—and a second later, the door was flung open and Peter stood on the other side of it, his hair twisted up into dream spikes. His jaw was covered with night-growth, and he looked puffy the way folks do when they wake up, but his eyes was alive, and I guessed vets had their share of midnight emergencies by the way he conveyed alertness underneath the last of his sleep fog.

I gave a sharp cry—

Before it was out of my mouth, Peter'd reached down and scooped Huck up and retreated back into the hallway. I trotted right at his heels.

* * *

It was all up with Lady, I judged, so there wouldn't be no harm now if I talked to Peter.

"There was a fire over to the inn," I said, "and Huck, he wouldn't jump out the winder, and the flames was all around him, and I reckon they got down inside his lungs and his eyes is all filmed over and he's blind and scairt and you *got* to save him!"

I was talkin so fast and furious myself, I didn't notice when he answered.

"I can only do my best, Tom."

"Is he dead? He ain't dead, is he?"

Peter didn't say. Only flung open the door to his cellar where he'd set up a home office with a vet's rig and galloped down the stairs.

He got Huck laid out on the metal-topped examining table, and I was practically blinding myself tryin to see if his chest was risin and fallin.

Quick as winks, Peter had his stethoscope out, and he was layin it here and there over Huck's chest. His fur—always like cotton—didn't look right to me. I mean it was singed up some, but fur on a live cat has a sort of animated look to it.

Peter kept movin the scope, his big gentle hand coverin Huck's midriff, his other hand sunk into the pulse at his neck. And he'd cock his head to listen harder, then ply the scope in another part, then listen at it again.

At last he hitched the plugs outta his ears and let the curved pipes rest against his own neck, and he fetched out a huge sigh—his face changed expression exactly the way a window shade covers glass when you lower it. And I knew.

"He's past it," Peter said. "I could give him a shot, but I don't think it will bring him back—kickstart his heart, I mean—and like you said, the fire's gone all down his lungs and ... all."

I screamed.

There warn't nothing else.

I opened my mouth and I screamed.

The tears, I knew, would be for later.

Peter reached a hand towards me; his other was still layin gently on Huck's head, and while part of me wanted to go to his fingers and feel his warmth, I was too upset. I was beyond thinkin and feelin. I just threw myself alongside Huck and wailed into his cheeks and whiskers and ears. It was a terrible sound, I knew. But not nearly as terrible as I felt inside.

* * *

Then I heard the clack of slippers on the stairs; and scant seconds later, Lady Bastet—also known as Barbara De Simone—came into the room, wearin a long, white silk robe.

263

I was 'most too astonished to breathe.

She didn't say a thing, she just put her hands on Huck—through him—it seemed like. And while I watched—near pop-eyed—with amazement, I seen a yellow light shimmerin around the tips of her fingers.

And I knowed it would be all right.

CHAPTER THIRTY-FIVE

BOYS WILL BE BOYS–THE KALEIDOSCOPE OF TIME–THE RETURN OF TED AND EARLE

"Save him, save him!" I cried. My waterworks was leakin in a way that would have shamed me under any other circumstance, but it didn't matter now. I knew how much I loved Huck—and I wanted him back with me, so's my life could make sense again.

Peter put his finger to his lips—not in any mean or scolding way, but just askin nice for me to quiet some. His eyes were very kind.

Lady's eyes were closed, and I judged she was concentratin, but I could hardly contain myself—I didn't have no more than a pin drop of patience in me. I was on fire for Huck to get healed and spring up and butt his head into my jaw and for the two of us to be scamperin around and gettin into the mischief we was so good at makin.

Both her hands moved over him—just skimmin the tips of his fur—and the light sometimes changed color from yellow to blue to mauve. When it went white, it was harder to see—it was more glow than light.

Still she hadn't said a word, nor had Huck so much as moved under her hands or twitched a paw. I knew he loved Lady, and I kept thinkin somewhere—wherever he was—he had to be wanting to open

265

his eyes and see her again and to feel all her love for him, too. Huck was in love with Lady—maybe even more than I was—that was sure.

After a while she says, "Some things can't be derailed from the natural order."

"What do you mean?" I said, growin alarmed. "Huck don't want to die—"

"I'm afraid the fire was too much for him—"

"Don't say it, Lady, don't—you got to save him!"

"Tom, it's time for you and Huck to become boys, now. Can you help Huck do it?"

"Boys—now? I don't understand!"

She stooped low, and she patted me and she stroked me till she saw I was calmed some, and I could follow what she was sayin.

"Huck's body is too small to heal those big wounds—but if he were a boy—they wouldn't be as invasive—and then, you see, maybe—*maybe*—my healing magic could work."

* * *

I hate to admit I was a little scared, but I was. I'd gotten used to bein a cat and a familiar, and I warn't sure how it would feel to be human again. Then I remembered that I warn't never really alive—and that silked my nerves some. I couldn't help askin about it though—I guess we never really lose that fear of changin from one state to another—whether it's just losin a habit or decidin to transform every cell in our bodies or somethin as simple as learnin to be sivilized—as Huck called it—or roamin wild and sleepin in hogshead casks.

"Is we gonna get to be cats again—and be your familiars and all?" I licked my lip—a sure sign of nervousness I'd never have let happened in front of anybody but Lady.

"Now we'll just have to see—won't we?" she said. But her voice was light. And well, you know I trusted Lady. Maybe even more than I loved her, I trusted her.

But was this Lady? I mean the real Lady—or was it another shadow from inside Lily Blum's stock of counterfeit souls?

"It's me, Tom." She spoke up nice and forthright—and that was like Lady—but for all I knew Lily Blum had caught on better to ways she could get around us. I was inclined to believe her, but I needed to be sure.

"Tell me somethin then, that only Lady could know." I warn't even sure that was the way to go about it—it was possible, I figured, that Lily Blum had sucked up all the soul and mind-knowin that had been Lady's. But it seemed a fair test—and I could watch her close for a reaction that gave her away, if it came to that. A liar's voice might not give him or her away—but you can watch for little signs: a dip of the head, or a tug on a earring, or something that contradicts what's said. I held my breath, and you bet I watched with keener vision than any hawk on the wing spyin out shrews or mice to light on.

"Since the first day you came here—even before—I could tell you apart. Not only that, I could tell—even with my eyes closed and the room as dark as pitch—which one of you jumped onto the bed even before you came to snuggle in my arms. And I didn't use witchery of any kind for the knowing: it was love."

Well, that was it for me. If I was makin a mistake, then I was suckered in of my own free will. But I judged it warn't a thing a character like Lily Blum could ever think of sayin—cause Lily had no more clue what love was than a toad had notions about pocket watches. And if Lily ever even hit close to feelin love, I reckoned she'd come at it through spells—there warn't enough human in her to love anything—or anyone—not for real and true.

I looked Lady square in the eye.

"Let's be quick then, before my heart squeezes down to a speck and disappears. I cain't do without Huck no more than a train can run without rails. He's body and soul to me, breath and life."

A little sigh came out of her throat—I think she was that relieved that I trusted her, and she held out her arms, and I leapt straight into them. Just the scent of her skin and the feel of her next to me was heaven. I didn't know what becomin a boy entailed, but if Lady said now was the time and it meant the savin of Huck, I'd of dived headlong into a volcano. If it was your twin, and it was Lady who'd done the asking, wouldn't you do the same?

She held me a second, and I licked the side of her cheek. Then she laid me down alongside Huck so's we was like a yin-yang sign, just spiraled up together. Layin there, I saw now that some of his fur was burnt away and, of course, the smell on him was the smell of fire. But I wouldn't let myself think too hard on that, 'cause it was too troublesome and too sad and now was a time for bravery and love. Things that really matter.

Lady made a pass over both of us with her hands, and then it was like I fell into a dream, but one of those dreams where everything is as real as wakin life, and wakin is as true as your dreams.

* * *

Time was a kaleidoscope in this dream, with the days and years like the pieces of pretty colored glass layin over each other and mixin up here and there so that every view was gladsome and new and filled with delicious light. I looked one way down the length of this dream, and there was me and Huck tryin to free Jim what was already freed; a tiny click-turn! and we was on Jackson's Island, everybody all heartsore and lonesome and then hidin in the loft to listen to our own funeral sermons; click-turn—and we was diggin for pirate's treasure under the shadder of the tree limb; click-turn—and Huck was meowin outside my window at Aunt Polly's, and I was shimmyin down; click-turn—and we was Coconut and Cream Puff and Hucky was snugglin for dear life with Baby Theandromula and snufflin up *her* warm vital smell; click-turn—and we was with Lady in the altar room; click-turn—and we was witchin the Christmas lights off the tree; click-turn—and we was floatin over the river, Lady's hair like a streamer behind her and Hucky's eyes wide as a child's when the circus comes to town. Click-turn!—there was Huck barefoot and in his raggedy clothes, the envy of every boy in St. Petersburg made to go to school; click-turn—there was Huck tuggin at his collar and chafin over Miss Watson's rules and regulations. Click-turn! there was Huck enjoyin the freedom of bein a familiar and his newfound powers. Click-turn—and I was with him even while it was just Huck and Jim on the river, and Huck with the king and the duke, because Mr. Twain had wrote about it, and anyhow, Huck carried me in his heart, too. Click. Turn. Cat. Boy. Cats. Boys ... Cats—

C'mon, Huck, I told him, *we got to light out for the Territories.*

* * *

Suddenly I sat up. I was a little dizzy. I felt a might constricted, and at first I thought it was because I was sharin a bed with somebody who'd not only smouched all the covers, but had scrounged up the whole space so I was 'most clingin to the mattress. I felt all tied up and uncomfortable—then I saw an unruly mop of dark hair over a dirty cheek, and I knowed I was seein Huckleberry Finn—and the tied up feelin was my own clothes—in fact, it was a shirt collar diggin into the side of my neck.

He had some red patches that was nasty lookin, and his eyes was still closed, but his chest was movin again.

Tears were in my own eyes, 'cause I knowed Huck had a chance now; but before I could even get my thoughts in order, Lady was there along with Peter, and they shooed me out of the way ... and whilst Peter cleaned the worst of Huck's burns, Lady, she commenced her healing.

Once again Lady placed her hands and palms parallel to Huckleberry's body, and she moved them ever so graceful and slow up and down, pausin at his shoulders, hoverin over his chest. It wasn't fast, but it still put me in mind of a virtuoso pianist—maybe it was her style and the smooth flow of her energy that made me think so. It was somethin to see, I can tell you that much. Every now and then, tiny wisps of light would flow from the tips of Lady's fingers, or from the centers of her palms and they would touch down like miniature bolts of lightning to the hurt places on Huck and then rebound back at Lady's hands. But it warn't like lookin at something destructive or harsh, the way lightning is—it was more like watchin a fairy or angel at work—and at times, I'd have sworn I heard the soft peal of bells, high and sweet and tinkly. I'm sure I smelt tuberoses or jasmine or lily-of-the-valley. All around Huck and Lady was this sense of peace and soft light and whatever there is in the universe that is essentially good.

By and by, Huck he waked up for sure. He let out a long sigh—just the same as when you wake up on Saturday and realize you can turn over for another forty winks. Nothin feels as delicious as *that* kind of sleep. His eyes opened very blue and wide and he smiled at Lady. Then he sat up and gave her a hug. And she held him and smoothed his hair, and kissed the top of his head.

"My boy," she murmured. "Huck," she said.

"You're real," he said. "It warn't a dream after all."

I thought Peter might be leakin a little 'round his own eyes. I know I was.

Even if Huck didn't realize it, we all did.

Lady gave him the first hug he'd ever had from a lovin mother.

* * *

Huckleberry Finn ate the largest breakfast I've ever seen man, boy, woman, or child consume in history. Truth to tell, I cain't say whether or not Lady had to witch some of it up because Peter's dinin room table was so weighed down with food and plates and cutlery and glassware, you might have been in a room where brunch was bein served at a buffet for twenty.

There was blueberry pancakes and bacon and eggs and heaps of muffins and bread. There was ham and sausage and pucks of bagels, scones, kippers, and sliced tomatoes. There was lox and scallions, and cream cheese in a big ceramic crock. There was butter and toast and orange juice and pineapple juice and home-fried potatoes. There was Danish pastry and crullers and doughnuts. There was maple syrup and strawberries and sweet watermelon. There was waffles and huckleberry pancakes and raspberries and honeydew. There was coffee and tea and huge pitchers of foaming milk and hot cocoa and pots of jam and jellies and preserves.

Whatever you reached for, it was always pipin hot or cool as if it just come in from th' icehouse—I mean, the refrigerator. That was the odd thing for me; I couldn't quite get around the fact that I was a *boy* now in the 21st century. I knowed things, but it was like I remembered 'em, too, from when I'd been tearin around St. Petersburg more than a hundred years ago. And when I heard a car pass by, part of my mind wondered why it warn't hearing the clip clop of horse hooves, and the whoosh of sled runners over snow, and harness bells jinglin. Bein a live boy was different from being a cat with Tom Sawyer's memories.

I ate though—cause there is no sense in wastin a prime spread whether it's in front of you in 2014 or 1886. Farm-fresh eggs is farm-fresh eggs every century.

"Have some more, Huck," Lady kept urgin, and she'd pass him another tray of dainties or heave up a platter 'most big as a wagon wheel and groanin with sliced ham and sausages. Or, "Tom," she'd say,

"I don't think you've tried the Belgian waffles," givin me a grin and layin on whipped cream like it was cotton candy.

She kept Peter's plate pretty well filled, too; but like Lady B, he was mostly tryin things here and there and samplin—he warn't tuckin in like us.

By and by, Huck he sat back and laced his hands over his stomach and gave a little sigh and I b'lieve he started to say, *My, oh my.*

Instead, it was "M-a-a-a-a-a-aaaaaahhhhhhh—"

What come out was a foghorn of a belch that could have passed for a steamship's *"Give Way!"* soundin blast on the river—it was that long and deep. Must have been thirty seconds or more—and if Huck had just eaten the largest meal I ever saw a human consume, his mouth-detonation was surely the largest and longest on record I ever heard about, too. I believe it shocked Huck just as much. He certainly looked surprised and I'd a sworn his eyes rolled right down and crossed to look at his pooched out lips.

"Had enough, I hope," Peter teased him.

But couldn't nobody ever get the drop on Huck Finn—he was a boy with style from his big toe to his cowlick.

"Just about, near about," Huck said, hidin his joviality behind his brazenness. "I believe just three more pancakes and another rasher or two'll set me up right as rainfall." And, if you can believe it, Huck he picked up his plate and held it out toward Lady.

Her eyes went near as big as an owl's.

And she started to reach for the platter, but she snatched her hand back and said, "Huckleberry Finn, you may have come back from the brink of death and deserve a hearty breakfast, but there's no cause to eat like it's your last meal on Earth."

"You ain't a cat no more, Huck," I told him. "And Lady ain't goin to let you eat till your belly's blown out and sleep it off in the sunshine or on top of the radiator."

"Meow," he said at me and put out his tongue.

With that, the front door banged open and in strode Ted and Earle. They was barefoot and had on jeans what was rucked up and muddy lookin, and I reckoned they'd been doin a little predawn huntin and feastin themselves. They sat right down alongside us and Ted said—as if he hadn't missed a beat, and had just watched the whole preceding hour and heard the whole conversation—"Hucky, leetle one, when you are now a boy, you must eat as a boy eats—when you will be a cat again, you can eat as cats do. This advice you can trust—Earle and I, we know, eh?" Then he reached over, and with the quickness of a magician, his big hand lighted on a huge slice of Canadian bacon, he popped it in his mouth and it was gone in a twinkle. "Some things, of course," Ted said, "carry over from one state to another—just as they should." He grinned.

And then we did all laugh—laughed till we was cryin.

It was the jolliest breakfast ever served in history.

CHAPTER THIRTY-SIX

LADY'S TALE–TED AND EARLE–
MAGIC MOVIE SCREEN

By and by, Earle gave a yawn and said, "We just stopped in to say hello to the boys, but with the moon going to the full, Ted and I are ready for seriously sleepin off—I mean *sleeping*—a while." He blushed, but I saw he was lookin a little long in the tooth—not in the sense of his age of course, but because I figured he and Ted had thrown off their werewolf hides for a time so they could see us and Lady and Peter that mornin.

"Bar-ba-ra, we would so like to stay and make everything oh-so-perfectly clear to our dear godchildren, but we will save our politesse for a few nights hence, eh?" He gave a courtly little bow of his head. "Until then, we must fly." He stood up and under normal circumstances he might have raised Lady's hand to his lips and grazed her knuckles with a kiss, but it warn't the time for niceties—him and Earle was strugglin not to bristle up with fur and all as it was. "We will see you after a bite—a *bit*—a *while*," he said; he and Earle loped out into the hallway, and we heard the front door crash open, and they was no more than brown streaks a second later flashin past the dining room windows, and then they was gone like smoke on a windy day.

"Never could train them to *shut* the door," Lady said. She gave a little glance in that direction and we all heard it swing on its hinges, then neatly close and latch itself.

But by now me and Huck was on fire to know everything.

And Lady, she didn't disappoint us none, either.

"Where have they been?" Huck began. "What did he mean, godchildren?"

"Where have you been?" I chimed in.

"How'd Peter come to know everything?"

"How'd you find each other again? And are you together—for certain, sure and true—and engaged and all?" I sneaked a glance at her hands to look for her ring, but they was under the table and in her lap.

We was rattlin off questions faster than we could get or hear answers, and Lady finally put her right hand up and said, "We'll just have to read one page at a time to let this tale unfold."

"Well then I guess, Lady, me and Tom are gonna let you begin at the beginnin—"

But I couldn't wait—beginning, middle or end, I reckoned it was gonna come out the same, so I just jumped in. "We never saw *you* at all after Christmas, that's my guess—and how on earth did Lily do that?"

"There's your *first* clue, Tom," Peter said. "Lily didn't do it on Earth."

"But—" I'd of raced ahead again, but now he and Lady began to talk; and for good measure, Huck swung his foot and gave me a little kick in the leg to make me shut up. I was outranked, and I knew it, so there warn't nothin to do but let them explain in their way; but my, it vexed me to yank it out of them like string unraveling an inch at a time.

"It was a binding spell—you were right about that, Tom," Lady said, "and it was the very worst kind there is—because Lily not only intended to keep me battened down, she meant for me and Peter to be put asunder."

"Then I guess she figured she'd step into everythin when Lady was out of the way," Huck said. "But was she goin to sidle round Peter as the imitation a Lady, or as Lily, the man-slayer?"

"I'm going to answer your question by asking you one, Huck," Peter said. "Are you going to be Huck Finn, the boy, or Huck Finn, the cat and Lady's familiar?"

"Don't know," he said. "But maybe a bit of both."

"Exactly. Well that's what Lily would have done. It's called 'expediency'; and if she needed to work her darkness by being Lady, she'd act the part of Lady. If she'd get further being Lily, she'd do that. And she could cause so much chaos and confusion, almost no one would ever be able to straighten it out—or even get it straight in their minds what had happened, or what was said, or *anything* at all about the situation—"

"Me and Huck had a dose of that," I said, noddin. "Couldn't really tell what was happenin or remember it all very well afterwards either." I started tickin my fingers. "First there was the Tree House—and me and Huck divin way down underneath it and fallin into sleep. We left Lady in a kind of bower ... seemed like it was her that come back to us and said she was all healed—and then not." I swallowed. "Then there was all those noises—"

"—And the ha'nts, and the worst demons and ghosts; and Tom's spells over to the séance went all scrambled and skittery like they was bowlin pins knocked four ways to Sund'ys by giants. And we saw you, Lady ... dyin," he said, his voice goin tight. "Lily she conjured a knife, and we—we thought—" His voice got choky-like and he lowered his head, to keep back tears.

Lady patted his arm to ease him up. "Lily had it in her head and her heart to destroy me drop by drop ... and she was trying to take every bit of my power and use it herself. That day you boys saw her sneaking around the house—"

"Floatin, she was floatin, and there warn't no tracks in the snow, not even up the kitchen steps."

"She'd buried a charm deep out there. And that charm was an upside-down cross made from broken sticks and tied with my hair and strips of Peter's shirt. And she doused the whole thing with her own—er—*female* blood—and who knows what else—and the idea was that if Peter or I stepped on it or even *near* it coming out the door, the act of trampling it symbolized crushing our relationship and it would crumble into dust."

"But even accidentally—"

"Tom, think on this: Have you ever heard of two people in love who accidentally let that love blow away? Maybe they don't mean it to happen, but it does. And one day they wake up and they know that what *was* love is only *ashes*, and all the wishing in the world can't make it change back."

She had the right of it. People call it fate or hard luck or stress or life circumstances—but whatever they call it, that ain't the point. Love sometimes just starts to dry up, and it gets brittle with age and gets all smashed to specks and flinders; and then after a while you can't find love in that relationship if you look with a microscope—it's just so many swirling atoms that never collide at all.

"But Barbara and I never used the back door at her house," Peter said.

"Then how—" But I stopped, because I suddenly knew. "Oh Lord, it was me and Huck! Lily was tarryin by the backstairs, and she seemed to look right over at us. We was in the Tree House!"

"She was calling you," Lady said.

"Lord, Huck, it was on account of us, that Lily was able to scheme her schemes." I never felt so awful in my life, and Huck looked like misery was suddenly his middle name.

"Yes, and it was a lucky thing she used you two—because in the end, it was her downfall."

There was more for her to tell and more for us to hear, but I couldn't help brightening at that. "Didn't I say so, Huck? All the books say the very same and love is the conquerin force that conquers all—"

"Well, in this case, Lily was also using your love for me to hone in on me, too," Lady said quietly.

"You mean to make you weaker?" Huck said. He looked shocked.

All right, my stock was flat again. I was crestfallen. Our love for Lady had put her in greater danger. Then I recalled we was all sittin there, and I felt vindicated some. It had come right in the end, so me and Huck warn't hopeless after all. I could listen after that.

"Go on and tell us the worst, Lady, we can take it." It warn't hard to urge her—not with all of us safe at the table in Peter Bennett's house. I thought Lady might have snickered a little inwardly—I felt the tug of her mind in mine, then it stole away again, but she let my bravado go without a comment and went on with her story.

"I'm not sure I have the right words to tell you what it was like inside that binding spell of Lily's," she said, giving a small gulp. "I just know it felt awful."

"She was loopy," Peter put in.

"What Peter means is that it was as if I'd taken a drug ... or maybe poison ... something that confused me and made me feel weak and always nauseated."

"Where were you?" I said.

"At first I was in the Tree House—I thought it would work its magic on me."

"Lily Blum infected it didn't she?" Huck said. "How'd she contrive that?"

"Once she got me dwindled down and took my power for her own, it was just a matter of reversing the energy."

"You mean as if *you* suddenly decided that the Tree House would be a terrible place and not a healin place?" I asked.

"Exactly. It was my magic, and she was using it—well, she just used it for her own ends."

"How'd me and Tom come into this here equation?"

"In the beginning, she thought she'd just fasten on you two the way she'd fastened on me—get you worn down and worn out; then do what she liked with you—"

"Expedience, again," Peter said. He gave a long look in Lady's direction as if he was still in shock over nearly losing her, then finding her again.

"Huh—!" Huck said. "Experience, my foot. More like Tom makin up his harum-scarum plans to fit the moment—like when we freed Jim what was already free ... I didn't think anybody had the beat of *that* boy. But I reckon I was wrong."

Nobody bothered to tell Huck that even if he had the word out of whack, he had the sense of it—havin the sense of it was more important, anyhow.

"I'd crawled out of the Tree House," Lady said. "Earle and Ted found me and they brought me here—"

"We couldn't let you know," Peter said.

He started to say more, but I guessed the nub of it: "If me an' Huck knew where you was, it would a been like a direct line to Lily— might's well put up neon signs sayin 'X marks the spot: kill off Lady Bastet here!'"

"Yes, boys, and I'm sorry—but I—well I just took it on *faith*—that it would come right and we'd all be together again."

It's a strange thing when witches start talkin about faith over powers, but we had to live with it same as mortals do who have no control over someone sick or maybe dyin' and all's they can do is pray; and a course, the whole time they's prayin, they don't know for sure their prayers are goin t' be answered. They may hope so, but they don't *know* so.

It was time to change the subject.

"How'd you let on all this stuff to Peter—that's what I want to know."

"That was Ted and Earle's doing of course; they brought her here and they said, 'Dr. Bennett, there are things it has come time for you to know. We want you to watch and listen.'" Peter folded his hands around the rim of his coffee cup, and looked down at them briefly. "And Ted and Earle, they put Barbara on the couch in my living room and then they turned around and said, 'Now we'll show you something that might make you say, *I cannot believe my eyes*, and with that ... they just stood there and transformed.

"I suppose you could say they took a risk—on the other hand they counted on my skills as a healer and a magician to see me through."

I thought back to his tricks and his winnin over his nephew Drew way back to Thanksgivin time, and I reckoned Ted and Earle had gone about showin Peter the right way.

"Then Ted said, 'And now, dear doctor, we will leave the lovely Bar-ba-ra to tell you the rest—our part is done—and you have seen some oddments and curiosities—things not shown in the pages of a medical textbook, eh?'"

Lady chuckled. "We can do better than this—this retelling, Peter," she said. "I'd like Tom and Huck to see it, because, well, Ted and Earle—it was so funny!"

She snapped her fingers and the room dimmed a bit, and then it was just like we was watchin the whole thing on some projection screen—as if it'd been caught on film and saved so we could view it. The only thing missin was the popcorn.

* * *

There was Lady lyin on the blue velvet couch, lookin very pale.

Peter was standin in his living room and Ted and Earle was in street clothes, and then a second later they was bulked up, fanged, an' hairy as brown bears ... then, they rippled a little and wavered. In the blink of an eye, they was men again.

"Good God!" Peter said.

But that didn't phase Earle none.

"Say doc, there's somethin I want to ask you—seeing as how me and Ted are more or less family—"

You couldn't tell from Peter's expression what he thought was comin next, but Earle hove in with a stunner:

"Every now and then I get an awful twinge in my back when I'm transformed—plays hell with trying to run down deer, and I was wondering if you could take a look at me some time and maybe see have I got arthritis when I'm a werewolf."

"Uh—"

"He would not hurt you, dear Doctor Peter," Ted said gravely, "I would certainly retain my human form to assist with the examination, and, of course, Earle and I are vegan werewolves—"

Peter gave a little snort at that. "Pardon my French, but what the hell exactly is a vegan werewolf?"

"We don't eat our friends," Earle said.

Peter looked shocked—or maybe he was just tryin to keep from either laughin or screamin—and Earle might not've wanted to eat him, but he most pos'tively wanted vettin.

"So what do you say, Doc, will you check me out while I'm under?"

"No problem, Earle," Peter said.

"And, there is one more thing," Ted said.

"You want to be checked, too? Maybe get a rabies shot?"

"No we want to know if you give a family discount."

"It's usually ten percent for the second—er—pet—" Peter said.

"Ten percent is pretty low," Earle said.

"But seeing as how you're Lady's family, I guess your vet bills can be on the house—"

"Oh, excellent," Ted said. "That is so gracious of you."

"And speaking of the house—" Earle said.

"We prefer house calls." Ted grinned.

279

"No problem guys—I don't think it would work out all that well if you came to the clinic."

Huck was laughin so hard he nearly tipped over. I mean you had to laugh, 'cause Ted and Earle was so serious, and you could just picture Peter's staff and clients—and all those dogs and cats—with their owners sittin nervously in the small plastic gray chairs around the waitin room and holding on to Fido and Fluffy for dear life, while two gigantic werewolfs was pacin around, their claws cuttin ruts in the linoleum while they was waitin their turn.

"Thanks, Doc," Earle said.

Then they left, and on the blue velvet couch Lady waked up some, stretchin ever so pretty and she said:

"It's time for me to tell you Peter, that I do love you ... and I'm a witch."

* * *

The little magically impromptu film ended there, and it warn't hard to figure out what transpired between Lady and Peter—and I reckon if he could agree to treat a couple of werewolfs which ten minutes prior he didn't even know *was* werewolfs, a thing like witchcraft must a seemed about as strange as a Johnson & Johnson's Band-Aid. Which is to say, not a bit out of the ordinary.

CHAPTER THIRTY-SEVEN

BIG SNOW—CRYSTAL VISIONS—
HUCK TELLS THE FUTURE

There ain't much left to tell in this here book. You'll just have to read the next one, I suppose—soon as me and Huck writes it; but some of the things—bein human—which you're prob'ly curious about, I'll set down.

Well, as you surely have guessed, Lady had come back to herself enough by the time me and Huck got to her, that she and Peter was engaged again. So everything was hunky-dory on that scene. But I had some questions for 'em, and familiar or boy, I warn't about to let 'em slide.

"But what was you waitin for?" I said the night after we arrived. It was one of the biggest snowstorms that winter, and we was all piled in 'round Peter's fireplace, listenin to that ghashly wind and the sound of the snow flickin at the winders and silently lay itself up around the foundations. "When did you reckon on comin back for me and Huck?"

"Well, I was waiting for Lily's—" she hesitated some—"end." Lady had her legs tucked up under a long, soft nightgown and a big, white robe, and her arms hugged her knees. The tips of her bare toes stuck out, though, and she wriggled them a little.

If I was a cat, I might a given the movin toes a little *bap!* with my paw, but for the moment, as a boy, I took the wigglin as a sign of her discomfort.

"Bein dead, you mean," I said. "But, looky here, s'pose she lived fifty years more, what would a become of me and Huck?"

"It wasn't like that, Tom," Lady said. She smiled. "Do you know what scrying is?"

"Sounds like a body weepin whilst they writes something down," Huck said.

Writin and cryin—that must've sounded like the very worst combination to Huck and made him nervous. I guessed he wanted his pipe—'specially as we was sittin by the firelight, but he warn't about to ask Lady to witch him one. We didn't think she held with boys smokin.

"It's looking into the future," Lady said.

"Really?"

"Yes, you can use a crystal ball or a basin with water and dark ink—anything that reflects—"

"Some people even use cloud shapes or smoke," Peter began, but I cut him off.

"So you looked into a crystal ball and saw Lily was gonna buy the farm, and you figgered *then* you'd step in and scoop up me and Huck." I was amazed. More. I could hardly wait to get hold of a crystal ball and take it for a test spin.

"Yes," Lady nodded.

"But didn't ya know about the fire, and how I 'most died?" Huck said.

"Well, you can look—and know some things, but not everything."

"Let's do it now," I said jumpin up. "Where's your crystal ball, Lady? What's gonna happen to me and Huck—are we gonna learn to be reg'lar shape-shifters?"

"I don't need a crystal ball for that one—you will, in time."

Hot damn! I thought. We was gonna get the best of both worlds, after all. We could have all kinds of adventures—bein robbers an' pirates an' spies an' warlocks—an' when things got a-boilin hot and John Q. Law was within singein distance, we could just witch ourselves into catdom, and let mortals cool their heels lookin for us.

"I'd like to try it anyhow," Huck said. "I mean the crystal ball."

So Lady disappeared upstairs for a moment or two, and when she returned, she had a goodish-sized sphere. Maybe four inches or so in diameter and as clear as the purest water you ever saw. She set the ball on a little silver stand and told us to look at it.

Me and Huck was sittin cross-legged and on opposite sides of the gazin globe. It was pickin up little itches and licks of firelight and tossin those bright speckles—like the tips of fairies' wings—onto the carpet an' hearth bricks.

"I'm concentratin, but I don't see nothin" I said.

"Just let your mind wander," Lady said.

My mind was wanderin all right. It was wanderin over to the Kenmore Cold Spot refrigerator in the kitchen and thinkin about some leftover roast chicken from yesterday's dinner. Then my stomach joined in for the ride—

"I see a weddin," Huck sang out.

"Where?"

"Right here," he said, pointin a finger at the glass.

I peered in. "Shucks, that ain't nothin but a white glob in the middle of yellow flame—and it don't take no crystal ball to know Lady and Peter's gettin married. They's engaged."

"But I see the dress and the guests and the whole thing, and it's back at Chancery House." Huck scratched his head. "Lady, are you going to build her again?"

"Why, Huck, you're a natural at this," Lady said.

"Huh," I put in. "What's the secret—I mean you're gettin hitched, ain't you?"

"Yes, but I am going to rebuild the house."

It were a lucky guess was my notion, but I kept still. Huck he could have his moment for all of me. Lady and Peter headed out for the kitchen, leavin me and Huck to our scryin session.

"And who's goin to live there?"

"I see Earle and Ted and Peter and Lady ... and you and me, Tom," Huck said, his eyes fixed on the crystal like a cat's on a mouse hole.

"Well, is we cats or boys?"

"Both."

"Uh-huh. And what else?"

"It's a few years from now—but it's the oddest thing—we don't look no older as boys; we're the same age we are now."

"Go on, Huck. You've got a whopper goin and I reckon it'll amuse us both to hear you out."

"It's just what I see, Tom."

"Well, scry away. Who's stoppin you?"

"Baby Theandromula's in our class at school."

"That'd be the only thing that'd make *you* go," I said.

"She smells just as good as ever, too."

"How can you know how she *smells*, this here is a *gazin* ball! If it was a smellin ball, that'd answer—but you can't smell no future in no lookin crystal!"

"Well, I do just the same," he said, soundin stung.

"School's borin anyhow," I told him. "What about adventures and fun?"

"Aw, now it's gone all dark," he said.

"Sure. Right about the time you have to spout somethin bran-new, the well dries up. Honor bright, tell the truth: there ain't nothin in there but firelight."

"I saw it all, Tom. ..."

Lady and Peter came back with a big tray of hefty sandwiches. I, for one, was glad. I always could think better when my stomach warn't grumblin.

"What about the inn—is they goin t' be an inn?" I asked Huck. I took a swig of milk and another gnaw out a my corn beef on rye.

He was still sittin on the floor—we all were—for the impromptu picnic by the fireplace—and he gave a glance at the ball, which Peter had set on the edge of the brick hearth.

"The Tree House is there!" Huck said. "And it's whole again—not smashed a bit."

"Wait a minute—" I gave a mighty swallow, but Lady got in ahead of me.

"Well, there isn't any reason I couldn't conjure it again, and of course, once I conjured it—I'd conjure it whole and healthy," she said.

"Ahh—he's just makin stuff up. Go on an' wish for a castle an' a genie to dance it around over all seven continents and fill it with gold an' diamonds."

"I see it, Tom, I do. And a man dyin during the storm. He's young, he has a boy he's real partial to, but he dies anyhow," Huck said. "And something else ..." he shivered. "It's a dark shape, and—" He stopped and looked at Lady. Their eyes met and somethin passed between them—but I couldn't make out what it was.

"That's enough for tonight," she said. "It's high time you boys went off to bed. Peter and I'll look in on you in a few minutes."

"Off you go boys—and brush your teeth," Peter said.

We left the room, and I heard Peter say "I guess we don't have to tell them no reading with flashlights under the covers." And they both laughed.

CHAPTER THE LAST

WHAT HUCK SAW–WHAT LADY KNOWS

A little while later, Lady came up and sat on the edge of Huck's bed in the room where we was sleepin at Peter's.

"How'd you boys like to be familiars again?" She said. "Start some of those lessons we talked about so you can switch back and forth between cats and boys?"

We told her we'd like it fine.

"Tomorrow, then," she nodded. "Tomorrow you can wake as cats and we'll take if from there."

"Will it be a long time before we get good at switchin back and forth?"

"Oh, I imagine by the end of the summer—by the time Peter and I get married and Chancery House is rebuilt, you'll have the hang of it just fine." She smiled, and she leaned across the space between the beds and rumpled my hair.

"Say, is Baby Theandromula really gonna be in our class at school? And do we have to go to school?"

"Well, some school is fun, you know," she said.

"Yeah, like learnin to be a boy *and* a familiar," Huck said.

"Transmogrify," I said.

"Well, transmortifyin's only the half of it." He paused. "Lady, about that dark shape—the one in the crystal—" He swallowed. "It's Lily, ain't it?"

"It's not time to worry about that, Huck. You leave *that* to me."

"Yeah, an' make sure when you're rebuildin the house, you leave out the ghosts this time," I said. "Huck's not least fond of them."

"No ghosts. We'll do a special ritual I know. Okay, Huck?" She kissed us goodnight, and then she shut the door gently.

"Tomorrow we'll be cats again, then we'll learn all bout how to be cats *and* boys. Won't it be a rip, Huck?"

"Sure," he said, but he sounded low.

"Did you really see old Lily in that gazin globe?"

"Yais."

"Shucks, that ain't nothin to worry about." I rolled over on my side and propped my head with my hand. "We're going to transmogrify and transmogrify and transmogrify; and then we'll get so good at it, we can beat hell out of old Lily and help Lady and have adventures and everything."

"Honest, Tom?"

"Sure, we done it once already. And where's Lily? Where are we?"

He nodded. "She's worm buffet and we're fine right here on cotton sheets with Lady and Peter. And anyhow, I reckon I can keep a look-out for 'er in the crystal ball."

"S'right. We're gonna be alchemists and wizards and the bulliest familiars and witches ever. Cain't no one get the drop on us—"

"Are we?—oh, Tom." His eyes was shinin.

"'Course. And even if it's never been done an' practic'lly impossible to learn every spell and counterspell, so's we have to witch up the very worst witches and powerfullest demons out of history and bind em with blood to do our biddin. That's what alchemists does.

"Really?"

"That, and change base metal into pure gold."

"What's base metal?"

"Oh, any old junk lyin around, lead pipes an' thrown-out radiators an' stuff you can find what folks don't want, or carts over to the dump—"

"Now, that's *like*. That makes sense. Why, there's collections of stuff—heaps of it—every spring just right on the street, an' we won't need but any old wagon to pick up washers an' fans and what have you." He stopped. "What are we gonna do with a solid gold washer, Tom?"

"We gotta melt it down, Huck. Get a vat and dissolve it in acid, then sieve it and strain it for the base metal, and then we got to perform 'bout a hundred powerful spells and set up all kinds of rituals and get hold of equipment for boilin it, and sieve it again, and then call up Hermes Trismagistus hisself to transmute our aluminum an' lead right smack into gold."

"Who is Herman Trismisstress?"

"Who is he—say, if I knew as little as you, I wouldn't let on, Huck," I said, gettin ready to prime him up again. "Who was he? Why, *Hermes Trismagistus* was only the greatest magician and alchemist of all time, he was. He knowed *everythin* there was to know about spells—and what he didn't know, he invented. And he had palaces galore, and he wrote 'bout a thousand books, an' when he wrote 'em down he put in all the nobbiest spells for summonin demons, and all he had to do was go to his bookshelf and pull out a big red leather book and say, 'Lemme see, here, Volume 941, Section 88z, Chapter 2041, page 4,' and then read out loud all his esoteric signs and scribbles what no one has yet ever deciphered—"

"If no one hain't ciphered 'em yet, how we goin to?"

"*How?* Why, we're witches and we can automatically read runes and glyphs and arcana, and just everythin. 'Course we have to read it by the light of the full moon in a month that ends with R, and we must do it on the stroke of 12 and not a minute sooner or a second later, and we gotta have a hand of glory—"

"Hand of Gory?"

"Glory. We go into a graveyard and we dig up the most recently buried criminal what has been executed and cut off his hand, and then we light the fingertips and when we hold the hand of glory over the alchemy symbols, there's masses a smoke and flashin blue lights, and lo and behold, them symbols ain't no more than readin your infant-schooliest ABCs, and then we recite the spell and summon ol Hermes hisself and his whole pack of demons straight out a hell to make our lead into gold and whatever else we want—and they gotta do it."

Huck was lyin on his back now, elbows out, hands cuppin his head. "Bein alchemists an' all an' holdin sway over demons, now that's somethin. An' even if its powerful hard and things to memorize and read and write down and just like a damn school, I'll stick to it till I rot. I really will."

"I know, Huck."

"And the first thing—dern, I wish we had that Herman Trismistress and his demons by the tails right now, Tom; there's a man—with a little boy—goin to die tomorrow in this snow, and I'd lay I'd make them demons save 'im or stop the weather—or somethin."

"Cain't save everybody, Huck."

"No, but—Tom?" He took a deep breath and rushed on before I could say anything. "Tom, there ain't *anythin* I wouldn't do—to help Lady or protect her—or just love her."

"I know—me, too."

"Or you."

I nodded. I knowed *that*, of course. And Huck already knowed I'd go through fire for him. We was just a pair—our minds and hearts was the same on the subject of each other and Lady. It was love all around.

I went to bed happy that night; so did Huck—except maybe for his worries about the man an' the black shape he'd seen; but he was still a boy—not a grown-up—so he could push those fears aside and sleep the sleep of innocence. When we waked up, we'd be cats, but we'd also be startin a bran-new adventure—and there ain't nothing like adventure to put a light in your eyes or make your heart glad. Huck was more than young enough to count on the bright things ahead—I was, too.

* * *

Lots happened in the seven years that have gone by, but Huck was right about heaps of it—includin Baby Theandromula smellin sweet and bein in our class, and us not ever lookin older as boys, and Lady and Peter marryin and the rebuildin of Chancery House. And he was right about that poor young policeman what died and left a widow and a boy, and that horrible Lily Blum showin her ugly face again, too—and creating more of her usual dark mayhem, madness and danger. Even Coal Porter was back. An' it chagrins me some to say it, 'specially after we treated him so scabbily, but we got to like 'im a lot more; I reckoned it was on account of our bein boys—and not cats—a good deal of the time.

But all of that will have to wait till I'm ready to set down again and write some more. This here book's done. And I'm glad of it—even with cut and paste and computers, writin a book is a rotten lot of work, and it ain't nearly as much fun as conjuring demons and warlocks or playin tricks on werewolfs or schemin schemes to catch old Lily—Luna Raven—the ravin lunatic.

Truth to tell ... sometimes writin ain't even as much fun as bein a cat—not a witch's cat, anyhow.

The end. Yours Truly, Tom Sawyer and Huck Finn.

AUTHOR'S NOTES & ACKNOWLEDGEMENTS

Some years ago, I was lucky enough to run across a pair of twin cats (like Twain, I've not only been a lifelong cat lover, but hopelessly drawn to the concept of twins) whom I promptly named Tom Sawyer and Huckleberry Finn.

Almost immediately, it seemed (in accordance with T.S. Eliot's postulates) I'd managed to discern—or perhaps they clairvoyantly divulged—their true, secret names. Tom, like Mark Twain's character, was the ringleader. He was a show-off and remains the only cat I've ever owned who would actually jump to the tops of doorways. (A sort of reversal of Tom's shinning down the lightning rod to sneak out of the house at night.) My Huck was scruffier than my Tom, and he also had freckles splotched across his nose. He wasn't as intelligent as his twin, (and surely in many ways, Twain's characters are brothers under the skin) but he was sweeter and less apt to get up didoes.

But, like the characters I'd been swept away by from childhood on, I was inordinately in love with the cats and the feeling—as only cats can demonstrate in their own interesting and unique way—was mutual.

They came to have voices because I started a series of telephone answering machine messages featuring brief playlets with the two of them describing their antics, hijinks, and the general mayhem they created in a very witty way. Believe it or not, I often found that even solicitors called back to listen to the outgoing Tom and Huck entertainment and would actually leave messages saying they thought they were hilarious and they were sorry to be a bother, but they had to call back and play them so their office mates could hear what the cats were up to. This went on for years and I routinely changed the greetings—right up to the point that I decided these voices were too

293

delectable to be confined to the 21st century version of clever radio commercials and the next thing we all knew, I was writing a book featuring the boys.

As I worked on the book and the plot evolved I decided it would be a lot of fun to start up a haunted website that echoed the Bed & Breakfast called The Chancery House. Since the site came into being around Halloween several years ago, over four million visitors have traipsed through, touring the house and enjoying some of its ancillary diversions like the free gothic e-cards or the inside scoop on the Lizzie Borden house.

Both writing the book and creating the website were enormous fun and involved tremendous work, and it goes without saying there are some people besides me who are directly responsible for the completion and success of both.

So, first I'd like to thank Gina FioRito who taught me how to create the site and for a long time did at least ninety-nine percent of the work, since I was clueless about HTML and everything else associated with web work. Even after I got better at handling graphics and creating pages, Gina fixed what I couldn't, improved what I did, and generally made it all hang together. I can't even begin to thank her enough, and I'm glad she's been such a constant encouragement and such a good friend over the years.

Along with Gina, Barbara McGill was an early fan of the novel and read along as I wrote and revised, and I noticed when I lurked in the kitchen (while she sat at my dining room table) she always laughed in the right places—something that keeps a writer going through rough spots when she returns to her desk and the whooshing sound of the computer fan that sometimes seems very loud in a silent room.

Also, although Mark Twain opens *Huckleberry Finn* with a note on the text, I'd like to close with my own observations. I worked with two editors before I submitted this and, as Twain would say, you add in the editors that read the manuscript and randomly put their stamps on it, and that means at least three sets of eyes perused it from word docs to galleys. Because the book was a mess? No, because every literate editor in America, it seems, has her own claim to stake when it comes to the national treasure we call Mark Twain. And all of us had differing views on how the language *I chose* would best reflect all of Mark Twain's works from *Tom Sawyer* to *Huck Finn* to *Puddn'head Wilson* to *A Connecticut Yankee in King Arthur's Court* and more.

Twain himself hired the esteemed William Dean Howells to edit *Huckleberry Finn* when he ran out of patience, and as the Riverside edition editor, Henry Nash Smith, points out, no one has ever quite managed to make the text completely consistent—not with so many different types of dialect included.

For example, (underlines mine) on page 21 of the Riverside edition the text reads:

"That law trial was a slow business; appeared like they *warn't* ever going to get started on it ..."

Well, *wasn't* he mad?"

Elsewhere in Twain's works, you'll also find "'most" for "almost" written with both the apostrophe to show the elision and without it; the use of sound for "becuz" in *Tom Sawyer* and the word "because" in *Huck Finn*—to point out (p'int) out but two of many ways in which Twain chose to lend color to his characters' speech and writing. You can also, for instance (f'rinstance) Google 'sivilize' and *Huckleberry Finn* will pop up almost immediately. This is just to let everyone know, editing this novel, as Twain discovered regarding his own, was a whole lot more difficult than actually writing it.

So, in this case there was a lively debate about whether in the *New Adventures*, for example, "Tree House" should be capitalized, the g's should be left off in a word like making—just to give the sense of the accents—and whether to add the apostrophe for words like and (an'), him ('im), them ('em), etc.

Mostly, we decided on going with the best case in that particular sentence, that particular place and that particular character. All this is by way of letting all three editors know how grateful I am for their patience and expertise, and cluing in my readers that any mistakes or inconsistencies are mine.

I'd also like to thank the amazing Glenn Chadbourne for his fabulous artwork—and yes, the cats you see pictured on the front cover are actual renditions of the wily (but eminently lovable) Tom and Huck.

And, finally, once again, I'd like to thank editor and publisher Weldon Burge for bringing Tom and Huck into the Smart Rhino family with this new edition. Weldon has published quite a lot of my work—including short stories—and he's not only a complete pro, he's smart as the dickens.

Lisa Mannetti

ABOUT THE AUTHOR

Lisa Mannetti's debut novel, *The Gentling Box*, garnered a Bram Stoker Award and she has since been thrice-nominated for the award in both the short and long fiction categories: ("1925: A Fall River Halloween," "The Hunger Artist," and *Dissolution*). Her story, "Everybody Wins," was made into a short film by director Paul Leyden starring Malin Ackerman and released under the title *Bye-Bye Sally*. Recent short stories include, "Corruption," in  *Nightscapes Volume 1* (August 2013); and "The Hunger Artist" in *Zippered Flesh II* (February 2013).

She has also authored two companion novellas in *Deathwatch*, (new edition Nightscape Press, December 2013); a macabre gag book, *51 Fiendish Ways to Leave Your Lover*, (Bad Moon Books, February 2010); as well as nonfiction books, and numerous articles and short stories in newspapers, magazines, and anthologies. Forthcoming works include additional short stories and a novella about Houdini, *The Box Jumper*. She is currently working on a paranormal novel, *Spy Glass Hill*.

Lisa lives in New York.

Visit Lisa's author website at www.lisamannetti.com

Visit the virtual version of the haunted Chancery House at www.thechanceryhouse.com

ABOUT THE ILLUSTRATOR

Glenn Chadbourne fell in love with the great old Warren mags published during his youth—*Famous Monster Of Filmland, Creepy, Eerie, Vampirella*—as well as the EC comics like *Tales from the Crypt.* His love for horror art eventually drove him to create his own art and send his work out to various outlets, selling a few things here and there.

Glenn said, "It wasn't until I met my great pal Rick Hautala that things began to blossom. I met Rick at a Borders book store and we began talking over books, the horror biz and so forth, and he asked to see some of my work. I drew a design for a short story collection of his called *Bedbugs*, which was to be published by Cemetery Dance Publications, and Rick loved it. From there, I formed a relationship with the fine folks at CD and I went on to draw/paint things for a variety of their books/comics/magazine.

"Along the way, other publishers noticed my art and tossed a few gigs in my direction and, as of today, my work has appeared in some fifty odd books, along with a bevy of comics and magazines. Most notable of course being the stuff I did for Stephen King's *Secretary of Dreams*, along with the really nice edition of *Colorado Kid*, published by PS Publishing. Lately, I've done some artwork for Doug Clegg for his book, *Isis*, and that's been morphed into a computer game. The game is very, very cool and it's another new direction I'd like to explore. And, of course, I've also caught up with the rest of the world with this online stuff now and I'm pretty excited about that."

Visit Glenn's website: www.glennchadbourne.com/

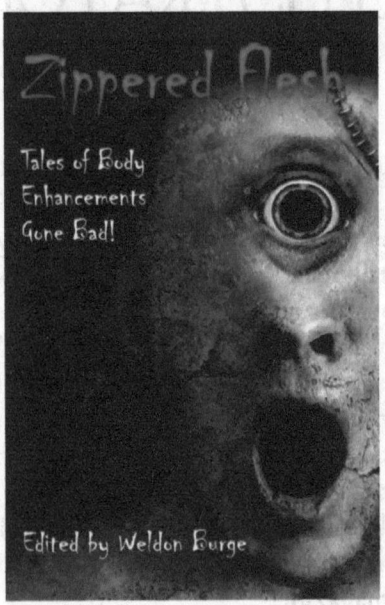

ZIPPERED FLESH 2:
More Tales of Body Enhancements Gone Bad!

So, you loved the first **ZIPPERED FLESH** anthology? Well, here are yet more tales of body enhancements that have gone horribly wrong! Chilling tales by some of the best horror writers today, determined to keep you fearful all night (and maybe even a little skittish during the day).

Bryan Hall * Shaun Meeks * Lisa Mannetti * Carson Buckingham * Christine Morgan * Kate Monroe * Daniel I. Russell * M.L. Roos * Rick Hudson * J.M. Reinbold * E.A. Black * L.L. Soares * Doug Blakeslee * Kealan Patrick Burke * A.P. Sessler * David Benton & W.D. Gagliani * Jonathan Templar * Christian A. Larsen * Shaun Jeffrey * Jezzy Wolfe * Charles Colyott * Michael Bailey

Available in paperback and Kindle eBook from Amazon.com.

Also visit smartrhino.com for the latest from Smart Rhino Publications.

SOMEONE WICKED:
A Written Remains Anthology

Avaricious, cruel, depraved, envious, mean-spirited, vengeful—the wicked have been with us since the beginnings of humankind. You might recognize them and you might not. But make no mistake. When the wicked cross your path, your life will never be the same. Do you know someone wicked? **You will.** The 21 stories in the Someone Wicked anthology were written by the members of the Written Remains Writers Guild and its friends, and was edited by JM Reinbold and Weldon Burge.

Gail Husch * Billie Sue Mosiman * Mike Dunne * Christine Morgan *
Ramona DeFelice Long * Russell Reece * Carson Buckingham * Chantal Noordeloos*
Patrick Derrickson * Barbara Ross * JM Reinbold * Shaun Meeks * Liz DeJesus *
Doug Blakeslee * Justynn Tyme *Ernestus Jiminy Chald * Weldon Burge *
Joseph Badal * Maria Masington * L.L. Soares * Shannon Connor Winward

Available in paperback and Kindle eBook from Amazon.com.

Also visit smartrhino.com for the latest from Smart Rhino Publications.